*For my beautiful, intelligent, and practically perfect daughters,
Hailey and Taylor. You put the light in the sky.*

Haunting Beauty

ERIN QUINN

BERKLEY SENSATION, NEW YORK

THE BERKLEY PUBLISHING GROUP
Published by the Penguin Group
Penguin Group (USA) Inc.
375 Hudson Street, New York, New York 10014, USA
Penguin Group (Canada), 90 Eglinton Avenue East, Suite 700, Toronto, Ontario M4P 2Y3, Canada
(a division of Pearson Penguin Canada Inc.)
Penguin Books Ltd., 80 Strand, London WC2R 0RL, England
Penguin Group Ireland, 25 St. Stephen's Green, Dublin 2, Ireland (a division of Penguin Books Ltd.)
Penguin Group (Australia), 250 Camberwell Road, Camberwell, Victoria 3124, Australia
(a division of Pearson Australia Group Pty. Ltd.)
Penguin Books India Pvt. Ltd., 11 Community Centre, Panchsheel Park, New Delhi—110 017, India
Penguin Group (NZ), 67 Apollo Drive, Rosedale, North Shore 0632, New Zealand
(a division of Pearson New Zealand Ltd.)
Penguin Books (South Africa) (Pty.) Ltd., 24 Sturdee Avenue, Rosebank, Johannesburg 2196,
South Africa

Penguin Books Ltd., Registered Offices: 80 Strand, London WC2R 0RL, England

This book is an original publication of The Berkley Publishing Group.

PRINTING HISTORY
Berkley Sensation trade paperback edition / August 2009

Library of Congress Cataloging-in-Publication Data

Quinn, Erin, 1963–
   Haunting beauty / Erin Quinn.—Berkley Sensation trade paperback ed.
      p,   cm.
   ISBN 978-0-425-22817-3
   1. Clairvoyants—Fiction. 2. Americans—Ireland—Fiction. 3. Domestic fiction.
I. Title.
   PS3617.U5635H38 2009
   813'.6—dc22   2009015903

PRINTED IN THE UNITED STATES OF AMERICA

10 9 8 7 6 5 4 3 2 1

Acknowledgments

A book never writes itself, and getting a novel into the hands of readers is a collaborative effort. I would like to thank my editor, Kate Seaver at Berkley, for falling in love with *Haunting Beauty* and helping to bring it to the bookshelves. It's been a pleasure working with you.

As always, I must thank fellow author, best critique partner in the world, and cherished friend, Lynn Coulter. I couldn't make this journey without you.

I should be drawn and quartered if I forget to mention my partners in crime (please don't ask which crimes because we'll never tell) who have supported me in my endeavors, listened when I cried, and cheered when I succeeded. Your support and friendship are priceless (alphabetically): Jennifer Ashley, Sylvia Day, Calista Fox, Wendy Hood, Kathryne Kennedy, Sherri Knauss, Mary Leo, Cathy McDavid, Mackenzie McKade, Cassie Ryan, and Susan Squires. And a very special thanks to Diana Gabaldon for taking time out of a breakneck schedule to read *Haunting Beauty* and give a wonderful endorsement quote. Howard Carron of the Maricopa Library District must be thanked as well for all of his support of local authors—especially me. He's been wonderful, and I feel fortunate to have met him.

Judi Barker, Rebecca Goude, Betty Grady, and Julie Mahler all read first drafts of *Haunting Beauty* and provided valuable feedback—mucho thanks. Ceaira Grady, niece and biggest fan, has my appreciation for all of her encouragement—it means more than you know. Much gratitude goes out to Kevin Graham of Intel for helping me harness the power of the universe and Caroline Curran for sharing all things Irish.

And last but never least, my wonderful, supportive husband, Rick. Twenty years and it only feels like a lifetime (*grin*). Seriously, I still love you as much as I did the day I said, "I do."

I am truly blessed to have such amazing people in my life.

Haunting Beauty

Chapter One

T HE man came to her just before dawn.

Danni had awoken with a start a few moments earlier, tangled in her bedding, unsure of what had pulled her from sleep. The inky blackness outside pressed against her windows, a dark entity that wanted to creep in and take over. Uneasy, she crawled from bed and shuffled to the kitchen for coffee.

That's when she felt the air turn.

It plunged in a silent, cold force that made her ears ring and her stomach sink. Like a latent memory, the sensation of it was suddenly there, filling her head—familiar and frightening, pressure and relief. She knew it; she feared it. She *remembered* it, though what the turning air heralded escaped her.

She spun to find the man waiting behind her. Tall, with broad shoulders and the layered muscles of a warrior, he leaned against her counter. As if it was perfectly natural for him to be there. As if he really *was* in her kitchen.

Dark brows and long black lashes emphasized the unusual color of his eyes—not quite green, not quite gray. Eyes like the sea, relentless and deep. A straight, blunt nose gave balance to his full lips and square jaw. There was a harsh and rugged edge to his features that flawed his beauty and made it something masculine, something more compelling than simple aesthetics. He wore a black leather coat over a crisp white shirt and jeans that tapered from lean hips to long legs. Not just tall. Not just broad. A big man.

He watched her, assessing and judging her with the same weighted concentration she gave him. She felt self-conscious in her faded *Save the Children* T-shirt and pink boxers, which was ridiculous—he wasn't really here.

Danni knew it, but the knowledge didn't stop her stomach from knotting with uncertainty and fear.

She sloshed coffee over the edge of her mug as she set it down. She would have dropped it if she held it any longer. The man interpreted this as acquiescence and began. Sometimes it was like that, she remembered. Sometimes they seemed to take Danni with them, like tour guides on a ghostly journey. Other times they were completely unaware they'd unraveled the fibers of reality and forced Danni to peer in at them.

When she'd been a child, the visits—the visions—had been frequent and exciting. The plunging turn of the air had felt like flying to her. But the visions had stopped so long ago she'd forgotten they'd ever happened at all. *No*, she corrected herself. She hadn't forgotten—she'd wiped the experiences from her memory with purposeful precision, because only the crazy saw people and things that weren't real.

But here it was happening again. Why? Why *now* after all these years?

The man took a step away, gesturing for her to follow as the familiar kitchen walls behind his broad shoulders vanished and, like a painting created before her very eyes, a stark landscape appeared in their place. The image had fuzzy edges and a grainy texture, but it breathed in a lifelike way, just as the man did.

It seemed so real. *Too real.*

A patchwork quilt of vivid greens, earthy browns, and heavy pewter spread out unendingly. Danni frowned, trying to put a name to the place. Did she know it? Had she seen it before? The man crossed from the pale kitchen tile to a spongy turf that should have left footprints but, of course, didn't. His steps were as unreal as his presence. Reluctantly, Danni went with him.

It felt like they walked for some time, but she knew they'd never left her kitchen. Still, the frosty cold of the earth against her feet, the wintry wind on her face, and the damp mist clinging to her hair and scant clothing chilled her to the bone. The sensations were crisp and visceral and frightening.

She followed the man across a valley to a destination she couldn't fathom. The sky above them grumbled and rolled in bleak shades of slate and steel. It seeped down to lush emerald pastures and saturated the air with freezing dampness. The brisk wind carried the spice of sea salt as it tormented the many-limbed alders and bandied with the stranger's long leather coat and short cropped hair. She could hear waves crashing somewhere close.

Where are you taking me?

He paused and looked back at her as if she'd spoken out loud. There was something in his eyes as he stared. A longing. A need. Her heart thumped painfully at the echo it dragged from inside her. Who was this man? Why did she feel as if she should know him?

They reached the edge of a precipice hanging out over the churning sea. A footpath cut a sharp trail down the side. Even as she prayed he'd turn away from it, the man started down the steep slope. His long legs covered the distance easily as he descended, but Danni had to scramble to keep up—certain a deadly plunge was in her future, not so clear on what that might mean. If she died in a vision, would it be for real?

The sounds of the tide thundering relentlessly were louder now, and she smelled the sharp scent of brine. She sensed something big looming high up to her left, but didn't know if it was real or imagined and couldn't turn to look back.

Enormous rocks poked from the hillside, forcing them to weave as they descended. The exertion warmed her and now she could hear sounds rising from down below. A woman's voice . . . Danni paused, listening to the agitated tone. *Frantic, pleading.* There were other voices, too. *A man, maybe two. And children. Frightened children.*

Danni's blood raced so fast she felt sick. The sound of their young, scared pleas propelled her back into her own history. To nights in the communal bedroom of the group home, where someone was always afraid, always crying.

Solemn and intent, the man continued down with effortless grace, dislodging pebbles that rappelled to the bottom. Danni remained frozen where she was, listening to the troubled but unintelligible words. Whatever was happening down there wasn't good, and every instinct Danni possessed urged her not to continue.

There was a loud bang—a shot followed by screams. Danni flinched, her palms slick with clammy fear. She didn't want to follow the man anymore. She wanted out of this vision. She wanted to be back in her kitchen where it was safe. She clenched her fists tight, wanting to escape it. To reject it.

The man paused and looked back. It seemed he knew what she was thinking. His eyes darkened with compassion, but also with disappointment he couldn't quite hide. She felt it as much as she saw it. He gave her a small nod. *Go ahead*, he was saying. The gesture came without condemnation. He was giving her permission to turn away. To run away.

For a moment the steep seawall, the glowering sky . . . the compelling man watching her . . . it all wavered and Danni could see her kitchen through the overlaid image. All she had to do was step through, step out.

Down below the children sobbed, and the woman beseeched with frantic, incoherent words. Danni felt her despair, her terror. Her desperate need . . .

The man started down again, now with urgency. Danni clenched her eyes tight and breathed deeply. Knowing she couldn't turn her back on such desperation, she mentally closed the passage to her kitchen, slamming the door on safety and sanity. She began to follow once more, hurrying to catch up as he disappeared into the deep gloom covering the bottom.

Broken shells and rocks crusted the shallow strip between massive boulders and angry surf. The path crunched painfully beneath her feet as she followed the man to a door cut into the base of the wall rising up to the cliffs. Danni peered through the gathering shadows and thick fog that hugged the ground, obscuring her feet.

She couldn't see anyone until she reached his side. And then, with the *pop* of her ears clearing and a surreal rush of color and texture, the source of the voices emerged from the blur into shocking focus.

Danni was suddenly inside a cavern of some sort that hunkered low over a tide pool. A stone floor circled it, and on the far side she saw people standing in the glow of a lantern. The muted lighting turned their faces into masks, distorting their features with ghoulish hollows and shiny plateaus. They stood in a cluster—a woman with two children. A man knelt on the ground just at the edge of the lantern's glow. He held something in his arms. Danni couldn't make out what.

She wanted to move closer. She wanted to see their faces. But she stayed where she was, motionless beside the green-eyed stranger as the scene played out.

The children she'd heard crying clung to the woman's legs, trying very hard to be a part of her. A boy and a girl. Danni guessed their ages at four or five, but she couldn't be sure. The woman was speaking again in a high-pitched, fearful tone. Someone cloaked in the concealing shadows responded. The voice was deep and masculine, but Danni couldn't see the speaker or understand what was said.

The man Danni had followed from her kitchen approached the woman. Pausing to look back at Danni, he lifted the hem of the woman's light jacket and blouse, revealing the bulge of an early pregnancy and . . . bruises. Huge discolorations that covered her ribs and abdomen in a mottled mixture of black, blue, neon yellow, and sickly green. Old and new, the marks layered one on top of the other.

The woman spun with a gasp, her eyes wide and frightened. She stared at the place where Danni stood for a long, breathless moment. Danni felt the contact of the woman's gaze as it settled on her face.

She can see me . . .

But that wasn't possible. Danni wasn't really there. None of them were. This was a vision . . . a hallucination . . . wasn't it?

As she searched for the cause of her discomfort, the woman continued to stare right at Danni. Danni saw a shiver work its way through her body, shuddering down to the hands that held on to her children. A feeling of déjà vu riveted Danni, the sense that she'd been here before as real as it was impossible. She didn't know this place, this woman, these children . . .

The silent denials collided with doubt. She looked at the boy standing so quietly beside his mother then at the little girl holding her other hand. The child's face was tear stained, her eyes big and gray, her hair golden brown. She blinked back at Danni with wide, knowing awareness.

It felt like a giant fist had punched through time and yanked Danni from her body. The little girl was no stranger, but neither was she an acquaintance or a friend. Like the vision itself, she was of the impossible. She was Danni . . . Danni as a child.

She was looking at herself . . . Herself as she'd been twenty years ago.

Danni felt hot with feelings she couldn't process, couldn't comprehend in this moment, that had no place, no substance in the world she knew. Slowly she shifted her attention back to the woman, now seeing the familiar features, remembering how it felt to put her arms around her, to be held by her.

The woman was her mother.

The mysterious male voice said something in a vicious, sharp tone, jerking her mother's attention abruptly away.

"No," Danni shouted. She rushed forward and tried to turn her mother back around. Tried to touch her, hold her, beg her to see Danni again. But whatever connection had been made for that brief instant was gone. The little girl began weeping inconsolably, and the man who knelt beside them rose, unsteady on his feet. Through the twilight, Danni saw his face was wet with tears, swollen and red, ravaged by grief. She felt his pain pulsing off him like the lapping waves in the pool at her feet.

From some forgotten alcove in the buried corner of her mind, a realization began to surface. It wasn't déjà vu—she *had* been here before. But even as she tried to bring the elusive memory into focus, it was gone.

There was terror in her mother's eyes now. In the way she flicked her gaze back and forth between the disembodied voice and the man at her side, who lifted his hands, holding them away from his body, palms out—the universal sign for compliance.

But the hostile words exchanged between the woman and her unseen antagonist grew louder until they echoed all around them. The tension in the air tightened like a noose of thin wire that would soon cut through the skin. Why couldn't Danni understand what was being said?

Suddenly another bang resounded in the cave, and Danni's screams joined those of her mother and the children. *A gun*, she thought. *That was a gun*. Even as her mind catalogued the sound, her body reacted to the bite of pain slicing through her. She felt it—*felt it*—as if a bullet had burrowed into her heart. She looked down, expecting to see blood. To see her life draining out of her. But there was nothing, nothing to explain the bewildering agony. She looked around her in shock, in panic, seeing again the crumpled shape on the ground beside the cluster of frightened people. Only then did she grasp what it was—what the man had been holding when they'd first come in. It was a body.

She managed to turn to the stranger who'd brought her here. He only watched her, his face impassive, his presence neither comforting nor threatening. As she stared at him, she felt trapped by his gaze. She couldn't look away, couldn't turn back to the unfolding drama. The voices of her mother and the children waned, taking with them the searing pain. They were fading—all of it, vanishing.

Danni wanted to cling to her mother like the child she'd once been. But she couldn't break the hold of his enigmatic green eyes, couldn't make her legs support the weight of her need.

Again a swirling mixture of grays and browns frosted the air, making Danni think of a giant God creating sand art on an unending pane of glass. The light changed from dark gloom to hazy murk, and they were outside again. The wind joined the sensation of biting fresh air and bitter cold. It was just the two of them now. The crushing pain of the gunshot was gone but Danni's heart filled with grief at the loss of her mother. *Again.* Again Danni had been abandoned by her.

The man moved, not giving her time to mourn. He had a mission. She'd forgotten that he was there for reasons of his own.

They were back in the valley. Danni followed him as he strode away, a tall dark figure in a world painted with shades of obscurity. Their time was nearly at an end. She could sense it, feel it in the crackling air. It would turn again and the vision would be over.

Towed in his wake, Danni trailed the man to a mound of dirt amidst the lush pasture. Silently she waited by his side, once again aware of something huge casting a shadow on them, but unable to turn and face whatever it was.

They'd stopped beside a shallow grave, freshly dug and unmarked. The bitter scent of tilled earth mingled with the damp fishiness wafting from the sea. She could hear waves crashing furiously against the rocks below.

Her stranger wore an expression of inconsolable remorse as he looked upon the open hole gaping in the oasis of green. Danni swallowed painfully, more afraid than she'd ever been. The grave was an ominous symbol in this vision. Or was it real? The muddied ground at her feet seemed to call out to her. It coaxed her closer. It promised sweet and seductive rewards.

Danni slowly leaned forward and looked into the hole. There were two bodies sprawled at the bottom as if they'd been carelessly tossed in. One was an adolescent boy, and some shadowy part of her mind said his was the body she'd seen in the cavern. He was gangly and hollow-chested. His legs were twisted beneath him in an unnatural position and his face turned away. Crumpled beside him was a woman wearing leggings and an oversized T-shirt—an outfit reminiscent of the eighties. Her long golden brown hair lay in a fall over her shoulders and against the boy's chest. Half of her face was concealed, but the other half . . .

Danni recoiled, her mind fighting what her eyes displayed as truth. Once again, she was face-to-face with herself, only this time not the child she'd been, but the woman she was now. The other body in the grave was Danni's.

Impossible, impossible, impossible . . .

The man beside her stared into the grave for another introspective moment. Then he looked to the distant, turbulent sea. Danni felt his grief and anger mix and grow until it burned like the whipping wind. She felt the power of it consume him, drive him to a point as perilous as the cliff's edge.

Then suddenly he turned those desperate eyes on Danni. He reached out, as if realizing for the first time that he might touch her. She waited for the contact with a biting combination of terror and anticipation.

Visions couldn't touch, couldn't feel . . .

He brushed her cheek with the back of his fingers, and his warmth was electric against her cold skin. She stared at him, stunned, seeing her own astonishment mirrored in the glittering silver and green of his eyes.

He touched her again, settling his palm against her jaw, cupping her face—both hands now. Both hands warm and rough and undeniably *real*. Transfixed, she stared at him, catching her breath when his gaze shifted to her mouth.

Her hands came up to the muscled wall of his chest, feeling it rise with his deep breath, grappling with the sense of his heart beating beneath her palms. Her fear knotted with the rush of sensation and became a ball of heat in her belly, a longing that smoldered and sparked. She waited as his head bent, his lips moving closer to hers. But the air was turning—she could feel it coming. Even as his mouth hovered over her lips, his breath a hot whisper, a seductive secret she couldn't quite hear, he began to fade.

She tried to stop him from going, tried to hold back the air even as it hissed away. In an instant, the man, the grave, the steel wool sky . . . all of it became a mist that floated just on the surface. Beneath it, Danni's kitchen waited for her to come home.

She felt a ripping sensation as she was sucked back to where she'd begun. She sagged against the counter, drawing in deep breaths of warm air. Her cup sat just where she'd left it, coffee not yet cooled, though it seemed hours should have passed. She couldn't stop the shaking in her legs or slow the pounding of her heart. She sank to the cold tile and curled in on herself.

She didn't understand what the vision meant, who the man was or why she'd seen him. Why he'd shown her the mother she barely remembered. She knew one thing, though. The green-eyed stranger was looking for Danni. And it was only a question of when he would find her.

Chapter Two

SEAN Ballagh paused on the sidewalk in front of the woman's house, trying to contain the uneasiness building inside him. It seemed to press in from everywhere. He looked over his shoulder, feeling the silent stalk of an invisible foe that could be imagined . . . or could be frighteningly real. He had no way to know.

Nothing moved but the whispering breeze and the long morning shadows. Low on the horizon, the first rays of sunlight trailed a golden haze across an endless azure, teasing shades of amethyst and ruby from a lacy layer of clouds. The sunrise was breathtaking, beautiful beyond description. But it didn't ease his tension or alleviate the cloying disquiet. For years he'd searched for the woman who called herself Danni Jones, and now that he'd found her, Sean feared it was too late.

It occurred to him that a surprise visit first thing in the morning might not be the best plan of action. He knew she was home, would be leaving for work within the hour. But he was a stranger and she might not open her door to him. Americans were funny about such things, he recalled, especially in a big city like Phoenix, Arizona. A part of him hoped she wouldn't let him in. Maybe she'd send him packing right back to Ireland without listening to a word of his tale. But that would require a kind of luck Sean Ballagh had never had.

He patted his pocket where he'd put the tiny jewelry box his grandmother had slipped in his hand before he'd left Ballyfionúir. She'd told him to give it to the girl when he found her. "This she'll not be able to deny," she'd said with a knowing look. The light object felt disproportionately heavy.

He took a deep breath, feeling his doubts fighting to surface. It wasn't wrong, what his grandmother wanted him to do. But it wasn't right either.

"You're a bloody tosser, is what you are," he muttered to himself, but like the morning shadows, a sense of inevitability surrounded him. He would play his part, a messenger bringing glad tidings—but in truth, his coming was nothing to rejoice over.

Danni Jones lived in a cozy cottage, which seemed somehow out of place in this arid desert location. A tiny patch of grass nestled up to an uneven brick walkway leading to her door. Lining the space beneath the front windows were halved kegs overflowing with wild splashes of orange, blue, pink, and yellow. Bright red hummingbird feeders dangled from the white awning, high up and out of reach of the enormous yellow cat watching him from the doorstep.

When he approached, the cat hissed and ran, disappearing in a hedge around the corner. A steel door with an intricate cutout of flowers and birds covered the entrance. Security doors, he'd heard them called, though such a thing was as alien as drought where he came from. The ornate pattern left wide and spacious openings through to the screen while creating a solid shield between doorstep and entry.

With reluctance he didn't want to feel, he rang the bell. As it echoed in the house, he heard a dog yapping furiously, and seconds later, a brown snout poked between the blinds and bared teeth at him. Several feet higher, another slat tilted up, letting him know someone else was looking, too. The slat closed again and a moment later, the dog's snout withdrew.

The door didn't open, but Sean sensed she was standing on the other side. After a moment, he tried calling out. "Miss Jones? My name is Sean Ballagh. I bring word from Cathán MacGrath of Ballyfionúir. Ireland."

The lie felt chalky on his tongue, but he followed it with what he hoped was a sincere smile, in case she could see him. From inside the house, he heard a faint shuffling and then silence. He waited uncomfortably, feeling like the Cheshire cat with his phony grin pasted on his face. He let it fade and then disappear altogether.

Just when he thought she would ignore him completely, he heard her say, "You must have the wrong person. I've never heard of Cathán whoever."

"That's a shame," he answered, lowering his voice so she'd have to strain to hear, hoping to coax the door open yet. "He's your father."

Long minutes seemed to crawl by, and then he heard the click of the dead bolt sliding back. In spite of himself, he felt triumphant. The door opened and he glimpsed a shadowy figure standing on the other side of the heavily meshed screening.

"What did you say?" she asked.

He stepped forward, trying to make out her features, but the dog launched itself against the door with a loud bang that made Sean jump back. He stared at the little beast in horror as it growled and snarled aggressively. She reached down and grabbed the monster by the collar and hauled it away. He glimpsed a pale face, long golden brown hair, and a baby blue sweater before she disappeared back in the shadowy entryway of her home.

It was enough. She was the woman he'd been looking for. As if there'd ever been a doubt.

"I said it was a shame you don't know the name of your own father."

An imperceptible pause and then, "I don't have a father. I don't have any family."

"Ah, but you're wrong."

He opened the manila envelope he'd brought with him and took out the snapshot. He stared at it for a moment before pressing it against the screening. The dog growled again, but the lure pulled the woman closer.

The sun shifted a little higher, catching her in a beam that penetrated the screen and illuminated a delicate face with large gray eyes. Sean stared at her, stunned by the feeling that cut through him. She was familiar—not just because he'd known her when they'd been children living in Ireland. It was more than that. The sight of her lovely face, those soulful eyes, roused an awareness that went deeper than mere familiarity. It was harsh and yet intimate, and it confounded him completely.

In one arm she held the vicious little canine, the other hung at her side, fingers clenching and unclenching nervously. She cast him a guarded glance and caught him staring, mouth open. He forced himself to shut it.

There was something perplexing in her expression—as if she'd had the same bewildering sense of recognition as he. As if she knew who he was and what he really wanted. As if she knew *him*. The realization unsettled Sean long after she'd turned her attention to the photograph he held.

She stared at the picture as if entranced then brought her fingers up to touch it through the screen. "Where did you get this?" she murmured.

"It was taken in Ballyfionúir, Ireland, where you're from. Where I live." He waited a half beat before saying softly, "'Tis your family."

She made a low sound and pressed her palm over the image in a gesture that at once caressed and denied. He swallowed back his conscience and asked, "Would it be possible to speak with you, Danni Jones? Without the door between us, perhaps?"

He felt her eyes boring into him through the screen and warring desires pounded in his head. There was something fragile about her that he hadn't expected. Something defenseless, despite the stiff back and level gaze. He didn't want to deceive her, and he certainly didn't want to draw her into the hell that was about to become her life.

"Who are you?" she asked.

"Sean Ballagh, as I said. I'm sent from Ireland to find you. For your family."

"Do you have ID?"

He nodded, fumbled out his passport, and placed it where he'd held the photograph against the door. The passport picture was old and grainy, and she studied it for a long time, her eyes moving back and forth as she compared his staid mug shot to his real being. Again, the recognition flickered in her eyes as she looked at him. She'd been only five and he barely a teenager when they'd last seen one another. It was unlikely she'd remember him at all, let alone place the gangly boy he'd been as the man he'd become, yet he couldn't shake the feeling that she had.

"You're very young in this picture," she said with a frown. "How old is it?"

"Old," he answered. "I need to get a new one taken."

At last she gave a nod, then the lock *snicked* back and she opened the door. The dog squirmed in her arms like a wild boar but Danni managed to keep hold of it.

"Bean, no," she scolded.

Close up, Sean was able to determine that *Bean* couldn't be all dog. Somewhere in its lineage there most definitely had been a badger. The writhing, snarling animal had a long nose, pointed ears, and no tail. There were terrier genes in there somewhere and possibly Rottweiler, too, baffling though that idea was.

"She's very protective of me," Danni said, putting her fingers around its muzzle to silence the mutant dog. "I rescued her when she was a puppy and I'm the only family she has. She doesn't like people very much as a rule."

"Grand," he said, putting on the smile again.

Having made the decision to open the door, she now stepped back and bid him enter. Sean forced himself forward and into her home.

He followed her through a sunny sitting room with a wall of bookshelves, a comfortable-looking sofa and chair, and a small television tucked in the corner. She went through an arched opening and stopped in a bright, tiled kitchen. She paused, looking momentarily unsure before regaining her composure and indicating the table and chairs.

"Have a seat. Would you like some tea?"

He nodded, still eyeing the beast in her arms. She set Bean down with a stern command and went about putting water on to boil. The dog perched at her feet, moving every time she did and then resettling, all the while keeping Sean under surveillance. Had Sean meant Danni physical harm, the dog's hostile stare would have made him reconsider. Finished, Danni took the seat opposite him and reached for the photograph.

Sean studied her face as she stared at the picture, tracing the outline of first her mother's image, then her father's with a slender, trembling finger. What did she remember?

"I can't believe this is my family," she murmured.

She spoke with a hesitancy that made him think she expected him to snatch the photo away and laugh.

"It is, I swear it."

He pointed to the little girl standing in front of her mother. "That's you," he said. "And that's your brother beside you."

Her gray eyes shimmered with a strange mixture of emotions. Hope and hurt, anger and joy. A grief that seemed to anchor all other feelings around it.

"My brother," she said, her voice thick. She shook her head. "All these years . . ."

"We've been looking for you for a long time." He cleared his throat and glanced at the picture. "Your family name is MacGrath," he told her. "You were born in Ireland. Ballyfionúir to be exact."

"Bally . . ."

"Bally-*fyun*-oor. It's on the Isle of Fennore, just south of Ireland main."

He pulled another item from the envelope he'd brought and set it down in front of her. This was a copy of a birth announcement from a newspaper. It named two babies: a girl, Dáirinn Edel and a boy, Rory Finnegan. They'd been born to Cathán and Fiona MacGrath on October 1, 1984.

"The girl's name is pronounced *Dawr*-in. And yes, it's your name," Sean said when she didn't ask.

"I can't believe this," she murmured again.

"And yet it is the truth."

That brought her eyes up and round, filled with anguish and confusion. He'd imagined a hundred reactions that his visit might elicit. They'd ranged from skepticism to elation. But he'd not anticipated this raw pain he saw now. It filled him with shame.

"Mr. Ballagh—"

"Call me Sean. We're family, of sorts."

Those eyes grew larger and took on a look of dismay. "We're family? You're not my brother, are you?"

"No," he said quickly, finding the idea just as abhorrent as she seemed to. He didn't stop to analyze why. "Nothing like that. Distant relations. Too distant to trace."

"Good." And then, realizing what she'd said, she blushed a furious red.

Sean watched the rising color stain her slender throat, her smooth cheeks, the fragile shell of her ear. She looked very small in her big blue sweater, vulnerable. Inside him, something deeply male and protective awoke and responded. He hadn't expected that either. But he was very glad not to be her brother.

She lifted the picture and looked at it again. "This doesn't make sense," she said. "If this is my family, why have I been alone for the past twenty years? Where have they been?"

"I was hoping you'd be able to tell me that."

She made a sound like a laugh, but there was no humor. "Sorry to disappoint you. All I know is one day my mother dropped me off at preschool and she never picked me up again. *No one* ever came forward to claim me. No father. No brother missing me. *No one.*"

"Your mother dropped you off?" he repeated, unable to contain the sharp edge of incredulity. "Where?"

"Cactus Wren Preschool," she said. "I do remember that."

"I mean, here? In the States?"

She nodded, a frown puckering the silky skin between her eyes. "Why?"

"Why?" Sean tacitly repeated her question as the answer he both feared and desperately wanted to believe threatened to bubble to the surface. Because that meant Danni's mother had left Ireland. And to have done that, she would've had to be alive.

He cleared his throat and said gently, "Your mother vanished with you and your brother twenty years ago. What happened to her and the children all these years has been the great mystery and tragedy of our town. Until recently, we thought you were dead. All of you."

She stared at him, trying to see through his words. He stared back without flinching. This, at least, was the truth. But beneath the open face he presented, a raging host of conflicting emotions churned in frenzy.

One day my mother dropped me off at preschool and she never picked me up again.

Here, in the U.S. Not even in Ireland.

"No one knows what happened to us?" she asked.

"There were rumors, of course. There always are, aren't there? People talk, especially in Ballyfionúir. And there's always something to say about the MacGrath family."

"Why?"

"Well, I could tell you stories about your people and mine, but tales are best saved for another time, I think. We've history, though, the MacGraths and Ballaghs, and where there's a past there's an account to be questioned. Sure and there are those who'd say the slate will never be clean for either family."

"Are you one of those who would say that?"

"Me? It's a messenger I am. Nothing more."

The look she gave him bordered on incredulous. She was smart enough to know he was more than a just a messenger.

"I still don't understand how my mother and two kids could just up and disappear without anyone seeing her or knowing where she went. How could she manage it?"

"There was talk that she had help, talk about the lover she might have been keeping. Talk that she killed herself and her kids. And still more that she'd been killed by someone else. All of you, actually.

They think you're sleeping at the bottom of the sea even now. Is that what you're after?"

"Well, people don't disappear without a reason."

"No, I don't suppose they do."

She stared at him, sensing somehow that there was more to his response than the simple words.

"Nothing was ever proven?" she pressed.

"All of Ballyfionúir was in an uproar looking for blood. They went for the easiest target—some poor wanker who had the misfortune of being in the wrong place at the wrong time. He offed himself before they could beat a confession out of him. Good riddance they all said."

"But you don't think he was guilty?"

"What does it matter what I think?" he asked. "Guilty, innocent—it's all relative isn't it? Last month, I would have said of course he did it, the bollocks. But today . . . well, here you are, obviously alive. Who's to say he did anything to be guilty of, now?"

"You have a point," she said, looking troubled.

"When was the last time you saw your mother, Danni?" he asked, leaning forward. "When did she leave you?"

The teakettle let out a shriek, startling them both. Danni rose, moving gracefully as she poured the boiling water over tea bags and set a tray with cups and saucers. He noticed she used dainty china that looked very old and fragile. It was mismatched, as if each piece had been selected for its unique pattern rather than its status as one of a set. He suspected that, like her dog, she'd rescued the pieces from junk stores or sales tables, assembling them into a new family.

She returned to the table and poured in silence while he waited impatiently for her to answer his question. When had she last seen her mother, Fia MacGrath?

With effort, he held his tongue, sitting placidly while she laid out the tea, performing the task like an elegant ritual. She had slender fingers with short nails, unadorned but for a silver ring on the middle one with the entwined symbol for yin and yang at its center. Her wrists were small and feminine, her ivory skin smooth and creamy.

Her hair hung to her shoulders in a thick, glossy veil of what seemed a thousand shades of gold and amber, russet and toffee. Like the sunrise, it defied description.

She looked up suddenly and caught him staring. At her feet, the dog growled.

"It was Wednesday, October twenty-fifth, 1989. I was four or five," she said, answering his question as she took her seat. "I don't know which. When my mother didn't come back, it was discovered that the papers she'd filled out for the day care center were all false. The address, the name, everything on it. They assumed my birth date was incorrect as well." She looked at the announcement again. "If this is real, I was five."

"October twenty-fifth," he repeated. Was there some significance to the date?

"I don't know why she picked that day," Danni said, reading his mind. "If there's a reason, twenty years of thinking about it hasn't made it any clearer to me. When did she disappear from Ireland?"

"About three weeks before that."

"Three weeks? What was she doing all that time?"

He shook his head, feeling her frustration, her hurt, that such a painful event should happen on such a random timeline. He wanted to reach out and offer her comfort, but the hypocrisy of it was too much for him to manage.

"I know even less than you do," he said. "I expected you to an-swer that for me. You and your brother," he murmured, almost to himself.

Her eyes glistened and she lowered her lashes to hide them from him. "I didn't remember that I had a brother," she said. "I think I used to talk about him, when I was little. But everyone assumed I'd made him up. After a while, I guess I thought they were right."

Bloody hell. Where was Rory? What had Fia done with Danni's brother? Had both children made the journey to the U.S. with her? Or didn't Rory make it out of Ireland alive? Had *they* gotten to him first?

"How can you be so sure?" she asked suddenly. "What makes you so certain that this is my mother? That this is my family?"

"Aside from the resemblance?"

"It could be a coincidence, nothing more."

She said it earnestly and yet she didn't believe it. He could hear it in her voice, in the way it wavered between hunger and hurt. There was too much mystery and darkness about his story—too much of the same about her own—for her to be joyous over the news of a lost family suddenly found. But he could see the longing there inside her, knew instinctively that she'd waited her whole life for someone to walk through the door and tell her she wasn't alone.

"It's no coincidence, Danni," he said, forcing the words past his guilt. "It's the truth I'm telling you. Have you not a birthmark, right here?"

He took her left hand in his, turning it as he gently pushed the sleeve of her sweater up to reveal the pale skin on the other side. There, just below the crook, was the faint pink rose-shaped pattern he sought. His grandmother had said it would be there, but some part of him had doubted it. He was a fool, to be certain.

Danni bent her head to stare at the birthmark, and the soft, clean scent of her hair seemed to wrap him in a warm and unexpected intimacy. He brushed the small mark with his thumb, thinking her skin felt like heated satin. She jerked slightly, as if she, too, had felt the electricity in the touch. Her face was close to his, their heads bent together.

"It's a family mark," he murmured, looking into her eyes. She stared back, hesitant, as aware as he of the current that traveled through that small point of contact.

He had the sudden desire to lean closer still, to press his mouth to the erratic pulse beating at her throat. To let his hands skim up and under the blue sweater to the soft curves it hid. For a moment, he considered actually doing it and the idea started a fire burning deep inside him. He couldn't remember the last time he'd been so caught up in a woman. She was blushing again; no doubt his thoughts were there in the heat of his gaze. A part of him was glad. As wrong, as inconvenient as this attraction was, he wanted her to know. Needed her to feel it, too.

Flustered, she tugged her arm free and pulled down her sleeve, hiding the pink flower. "Ten percent of all babies are born with birthmarks," she said coolly. But her breath hitched at the end, betraying her.

"Not that birthmark."

He watched the play of emotion on her face. Hope, disbelief, and that heartbreaking anguish. She took a sip of her tea, shifting under his steady gaze.

"Is this for real? Are *you* for real?"

"I am."

She gave a small nod of acceptance and then asked, "So my father . . . he's still alive?"

"Aye," he answered. "Living in Ballyfionúir."

"And does he know you've found me?"

"Not yet. I wanted to be sure first."

"And you are now?"

"Absolutely."

He paused for a moment, pulling his thoughts away from the light scent of her skin back to the matter at hand. He was here for a reason that had nothing to do with the way the sun spilling through the window turned her hair into a flame of a thousand colors or his need to touch it.

"Is there anything at all you remember about your childhood?" he asked softly. "About Ireland or the night you left there?"

She shook her head. "Nothing before my mom disappeared."

"Well, let me tell you a bit, then. You're from a very old family, Danni. And from a place that's filled with lore. It's in the air, the water. Living here, you probably can't grasp what that entails, but there are things that happen on the Isle of Fennore that happen nowhere else in the world."

A bemused smile tilted the corners of her mouth. "I come from an old family?"

He nodded. "It's thought that your ancestors—mine, too—were ancient Druids. Fearsome people. People who possessed powers uncommon to the ordinary man or woman."

The smile widened a little. "My ancestors were superheroes?"

He smiled back, but knew it didn't reach his eyes. "Have you never felt it, then? Never known something before it happened? Never felt that you were special?"

Her smile faltered and she dropped her gaze to her tea. "No. I've never felt special." Standing, she took her cup to the sink and rinsed it. Her back was straight, her chin raised, but he could almost feel the old wounds inside her open up.

"Your island sounds like a magical place," she said lightly, turning with a bright smile that cut him to the bone. He knew it cost her, that smile.

"You should come see it," he said.

It was the opening he wanted, but still he felt reluctant as he reached in his envelope and pulled out the last item. It was a thick packet of papers secured by a rubber band. On the top sheet was an itinerary with a logo imprinted in the corner of a ship and airplane emerging from a bank of clouds. Written on the top was Danni's name. Sean hadn't wanted to buy the tickets before he met Danni, but his grandmother had purchased them already and insisted he bring them. She'd insisted on everything. So far she'd been right.

He pushed the packet across the table and waited for Danni to retrieve it. She lifted the papers curiously, staring with a frown for a moment before her eyes widened in surprise.

"Are these tickets? With my name on them? Tickets to Ireland? And . . . These are one-way, for heaven's sake. For Friday. *This* Friday."

"I thought you'd want to leave as soon as possible," he told her. "And I wasn't sure when you'd want to return. It seemed easier to book that part later. We don't intend to keep you there. Unless, of course, that's what you want."

"What I want . . ." she trailed off, overwhelmed. Like a child reaching for a security blanket, she bent down and scooped up the strange dog, holding it close in her protective arms. The creature stared at her with adoration as she stroked its fur, looking somehow like a cornered animal herself, desperate to find a way out. He didn't understand this response any more than he had her others.

"Have you a passport?"

"Yes, but . . ."

"But what? Is it not what you've wished for, Danni? To know who you are and where you come from?"

Those huge eyes lifted to stare into his, giving him the perfect view into her soul. It was a lovely thing, pure and hopeful and so very vulnerable. He cursed himself, but he didn't look away. In his pocket, the jewelry box seemed to thrum, demanding he take it out and give it to her now. This was the time, he knew. But it felt too much like a betrayal and he couldn't do it.

Swallowing his shame, he simply said, "It's time for you to come home Dáirinn MacGrath. What's left of your family needs you."

Chapter Three

DANNI closed the front door behind Sean and then leaned against it, listening for the sound of an engine driving away to signal that he was gone, but it never came. Half expecting that she'd find him still standing on her porch, she cracked the blinds and peeked out. She didn't see him, but felt the need to open the door and look again. Nothing but the rustling leaves in the trees and the frantic chirping of birds waited outside. Disconcerted by the lingering sense of him, she shut the door again and locked it.

He'd been real this time. She let out a shaky breath. Very real.

And even though a part of her had expected him, anticipated and dreaded his appearance with equal measures, she still couldn't believe it.

In the flesh he'd been even more compelling than he was in the vision. She'd felt the pull of him, even as warning signals were going off in her head. Even as she questioned the fantastic tale he'd told. There was something that didn't ring true about Sean Ballagh. A subtext to his message that she hadn't been able to grasp. The sense that what he hadn't said could be more important than what he had.

For a moment the sun dimmed and she thought of the vision, of the cavern where she'd seen her mother arguing with whoever had stood in the shadows. Was her vision from the night they'd disappeared? Is that why it had felt like a memory? And what about the grave, that gaping hole in the sea of green? Her own body crumpled inside it beside the adolescent boy's? What could it mean?

Overwhelmed by her own knotted feelings and questions, she went back to the kitchen, shoving the picture, the newspaper clipping, and the tickets back into the envelope. It was nearly nine and she should have left for work already. It was her day to open the antique store she managed with Yvonne Hearne—foster mother, confidant, friend, and employer all rolled into one.

Quickly she cleared Sean's cup and saucer, adding it to the sink with her own. He hadn't drunk any of his tea. Probably he would have preferred coffee. She'd remember that.

It was this thought—perhaps more than any other—that stopped her. She'd remember because she would see him again. She was going to Ireland with him. To meet her family . . . a family she had no recollection of.

How was it she could recall the feeling of flying she'd had as a child when the air would turn and a vision would come, but no matter how hard she tried, she couldn't remember her parents, her brother, her life before Arizona? She hadn't even recognized her own mother at first when she'd seen her in the vision this morning. Danni had been five when she'd been dumped at preschool that day. Surely that was old enough to remember *something* of her life before. But she didn't. Not any of it.

In the years after her mother had dropped her off and vanished, there'd been counseling and intensive therapy. For the first six months after she'd been abandoned, Danni hadn't spoken at all. They chalked it up to the trauma of her circumstances. Decided she must have been abused before being deserted, presumed she was a victim of much more than rejection. Over the years she'd come to think they were right. What else would make a five-year-old kid shut up for half a year?

She'd never known anything about who she was. And the blank

page of her ignorance had itself become her past. She'd learned to live with it. But the shadowy glimpse Sean had given her of who she might have been had cracked that illusion. She had history. A life before Cactus Wren Preschool.

She wouldn't discount what she'd seen in the vision—the terror in the cavern or the bodies in the grave—but neither would she base her decisions on it, because she didn't yet know what it all meant. Death was a metaphorical thing, wasn't it? The precursor to rebirth in every myth she'd ever read. And besides, what Sean had said was true. Finding her family, knowing who she was—it was what she'd wished for her whole life. Nothing else really mattered.

* * *

SHE arrived at Older than Dirt Antiques a few minutes late, glad no customers were waiting to get in. Quickly she unlocked the doors, disabled the alarm, and opened all the blinds. Bright sunlight filtered in through the UV-screened windows. It was blue-hair season—the time of year when all the geriatrics flocked south to the milder climates for the winter—and it was the shop's busiest time. The sales they'd make in the next few months would keep them solvent through the long, sizzling summer when their only customers were natives who could withstand the triple-digit temperatures.

Yvonne would be in later, and Danni was both looking forward to telling her everything and dreading it at the same time. When Danni was sixteen she'd been placed in Yvonne's home as a foster child. After eleven years as a ward of the state, eleven years of being shuffled from one foster family to another, Danni came to Yvonne with the expectation that she'd soon be leaving. There was something wrong with Danni, something about her that kept her from ever fitting in. At least that's what she'd learned to believe when one family after another sent her back into the foster system. There was no reason to think Yvonne Hearne wouldn't be more than just another in a long line of disappointments.

But Yvonne turned out to be different from all the others. She'd raised six kids, outlived three husbands and two of her own sons, and seemed to know what Danni was feeling before Danni did herself. And for whatever reason, they got each other.

From Yvonne, Danni learned about trust and responsibility. She also learned the fine art of treasure hunting. Danni had come to love the antique business and the challenge of finding the lost pieces of a set. A shrink would say her affinity for the missing stemmed from Danni's feeling that they were just like her—scattered parts of a whole which had been separated, lost and alone, abandoned by families who no longer cherished them. Each time she recovered the absent chair to a dining room ensemble or rescued the last saucer in a tea set, she felt as if she were restoring a small part of herself. Stupid and a little nuts, but it was what it was.

Yvonne would be happy for her, but she'd also be worried. Who could blame her? Danni was thinking of flying halfway around the world on the word of a man who had appeared from nowhere. She touched her arm where the birthmark was, thinking for the thousandth time about the way his thumb had rubbed across it, sparking a myriad of sensations that had zinged through her veins. And the look in his eyes when he'd watched her . . . He'd known about the birthmark, he'd brought a picture of her family, and he'd already purchased tickets. If he wasn't for real, he wouldn't have gone to the trouble and expense of paying for the tickets, would he?

Working quickly, Danni balanced the register from yesterday and set it up for today's business. She tried to keep her thoughts focused on what she was doing, but she kept going over in her head everything Sean had said. She had a father who'd searched for her all these years. She had people who lived on some fantasy island where everyone was family, one way or another. It was unbelievable and wonderful.

As she replayed all Sean had told her, the man himself kept creeping into her mind, and she'd found herself staring into space, thinking of his eyes, the deep, husky tone of his voice . . . the elusive scent of him—soap and rain and heat all mixed with something intimately male and stirring. Even as he'd told her his incredible news, she'd been lost in that seductive scent.

Finally she finished her opening tasks and brought her laptop from her office to the front of the store where she could keep an eye on things while she did some research. Perched on the stool behind the counter, she launched the Internet and opened a Google window. For a moment she stared at the search box and then typed in *Dáirinn MacGrath*. Zero hits came back. She tried again, using her mother's name with a bit more success, but her quick scan of the results showed nothing more than Sean had already told her. Not surprising, really. She'd gone missing over twenty years ago, before the Internet had become the end-all source for information.

Trying to decide what to use in the next search, Danni had a prickling sensation whisper up her spine and settle at the back of her neck. She glanced up, caught a movement at the window from the corner of her eye, and nearly jumped out of her skin when she turned. Sean was standing on the other side of the glass, looking in at her. For a moment, she could only stare at him, captured at once by the harsh beauty of his features and the beseeching look in his eyes.

He wore faded jeans and a crisp white shirt that was made without a collar. It opened with three buttons in front and hugged his broad shoulders and tapered to lean hips. He wasn't bulky, like a bodybuilder. He was more graceful than that. Somehow he reminded her of a warrior from days of yore, someone whose livelihood depended on his agility as well as his might. For the hundredth time, she thought of that almost kiss in the vision.

For God's sake, she was pathetic.

He held something, a small green box, and he turned it over and over in his hands as he watched her. She didn't think he was even aware that he did it. She gave him a shaky smile and waved for him to come in, but he didn't move, didn't acknowledge her greeting. What was he thinking about? What put that dark, pensive expression on his face?

She scooted off the stool and went to the door. But when she stepped outside and looked to where he stood, he was gone.

She took another step out, scanning the sidewalk and street. No cars pulled from the curb, no taillights flashed in the distance. And no one was walking away.

The realization hit her hard. Had she imagined seeing him? Conjured his image from her thoughts? Or had he been as unreal as he'd been earlier, in the vision? Could the air have turned without her even knowing it?

Shaken, she went back inside the shop, glancing over her shoulder and out the windows as she sat down in from of her monitor. He definitely wasn't standing outside anymore, but now she was uncertain if he'd ever been there at all.

He'd been real when he'd come to her door, though, she reassured herself. She had the envelope he'd left to prove it. She pulled it from her purse and dumped the contents on the counter. *Real*, she said silently. Feeling better, she took the itinerary Sean had given her and, double-checking the spelling, typed *Ballyfionúir, Ireland*, in the Internet search engine on her computer. A jackpot of links appeared on her screen.

She began clicking and skimming her way down the list, finding tourist information about Ireland in general—complete with pictures, hotels, and pub guides, but not much about Ballyfionúir exclusively. One website displayed a map that showed the jagged outline of southern Ireland. A tiny island lay just off the coast like the dot at the end of an exclamation mark. *The Isle of Fennore* was written above it. A black arrow pointed to a star on the most eastern edge of the island and identified the location as Ballyfionúir. Below the map were a few facts about it.

The Isle of Fennore was a mixture of lush valleys and rocky terrain, surrounded by the fierce sea, which was the source of the island's main industry. An abundance of fish thrived in the sheltered coves on the island's southern shores, and some of the region's best salmon could be found there.

The people who lived on the Isle of Fennore clung to the old ways in all they did—so much so that attempts to bridge the treacherous sea between the island and the mainland had been met with fierce opposition. They didn't want strangers crossing over at will and they didn't care if that meant the convenience of going the other way would also be denied. They also refused to allow larger ships or commuters to dock in their port, relying solely on a family-owned ferry to carry them across when necessity drove them from the island. Danni got the distinct impression that nothing short of a crisis qualified as necessity.

Isolated as it was, Ballyfionúir was considered by some to be the last bastion of traditional Ireland.

There was a small photograph of a forbidding shoreline, fortified with sharp rocks and a steep cliff. In the distance the remains of a crumbling tower and disintegrating stone walls stood in the gloom of a gathering storm. She stared at it, thinking of the cold wind that had whipped Sean's leather jacket as she'd followed him to the cavern, and she shivered.

The bell over the door chimed and two women entered with children in tow. Danni gave a mental groan. Children and antiques never made good companions. Closing the lid on her laptop and storing it under the counter, Danni forced a smile and went to assist—or run interference if necessary. The women were deep in conversation and refused her offer of help, so Danni hung back, trying to appear unobtrusive while remaining watchful.

"Twenty quid says the kid with scabs on his knees breaks something before he leaves."

The deep voice speaking in her ear startled a squeak out of her. She spun to find Sean standing just behind her, close enough to touch. "When did you come in?" she demanded, hand at her throat.

"While you were busy stalking your customers," he answered with a grin.

The grin caught her by surprise. When she'd seen him standing on her porch this morning, smiling with the two dimples etched in his cheeks, she almost hadn't recognized him. He'd never smiled in the vision and it completely changed his features. But Sean Ballagh was a man hard to mistake, no matter what he was doing.

"I saw you earlier," she said. "At the window. Why didn't you come in?"

"You looked busy," he said.

She hoped she was able to hide her relief. She hadn't dreamed him up.

"Did you need something?" she asked.

"I thought you might have some questions," he said. "And I left without telling you when you'd see me again."

She nodded, tilting her head back so she could look him in the eye. He was easily over six feet, and every inch of him was packed with hard sinew and definition. She could see the muscles flexing when he moved, sensed the power that lurked beneath the casual clothing. She wondered what he did to keep himself in such amazing shape.

She realized he was watching her stare at him and felt her face flush with hot embarrassment.

"I-uh. I did think of something I wanted to ask you, how—you never said exactly how you found me."

His gaze lingered on her face for a moment longer, and she felt that familiar clenching down low inside her. That he could do that just with a glance frightened her nearly as much as the visions.

"It was a strange coincidence, truth be told. I saw you on the television."

Danni's brows pulled together. "What? I've never been on TV."

"It was the news. Some time ago. You were at hospital."

Frowning, Danni caught her lip between her teeth . . . and then she remembered. A few months ago, Yvonne had lost her eldest *and* her youngest son to the war in Iraq. Soon after, she'd followed the tragedy with a heart attack that nearly killed her, too. The media had declared her the face of the American tragedy and tried to finish her off with their cameras, microphones, and endless questions. Danni had been furious when she arrived at Yvonne's hospital room one day to find a local news team trying to bring in their cameras, uncaring that they were prying at a wound still raw and painful.

Outraged, Danni had protested the intrusion, which only led them to investigate who *she* was. They'd run their story, including a segment on Danni, the foster child who'd been saved by Yvonne

Hearne, grieving mother and widow. News had been slow that week and the feature was picked up by the channel's national affiliate and run on the *TODAY* show. The phone had rung excessively for days after and business at the store had doubled. Fortunately, by that time Yvonne's daughters had arrived from their homes in Denver and Boston to help.

"And that's what led you to me?" she said to Sean.

He nodded. It made sense and yet, like Sean himself, there was something more to his explanation than what he revealed.

"You handled those reporters very well," he said.

"I ran."

"And quite quickly," he added.

The charm, like the dimples, disconcerted her. It seemed natural enough, but every instinct she had told her it was a cover-up for what he was thinking. He'd seemed torn this morning at her kitchen table, and she'd had the sense that he didn't want to be there, though nothing in his words confirmed it.

"Where were you?" she asked. "When you saw me on TV, I mean."

"At Sulley's in Ballyfionúir. Having a pint."

"Yvonne's story aired in Ireland?" she said, the disbelief heavy in her tone.

"You're a suspicious one, aren't you now? Is it a third world country you're thinking I'm from? We get our shows piped just like you."

Piped? Did he mean cable?

"Would you like me to produce a receipt to prove my whereabouts?" he asked, misunderstanding her frown.

Danni's face grew hot again. "I'm not suspicious. It's just that in my experience things are rarely what they seem to be."

"And what does this seem to be?"

"Unbelievable, if you want the truth. I just happened to be on TV on the day you just happened to be somewhere to see it."

"Unbelievable things happen every day," he said, shaking his head. The bitterness was back. "That's how half the people I know end up married."

"That's also how 38 percent of them end up divorced," she countered.

"Well, let's just have responsible sex then and forget about marriage."

The words were said lightly. He'd meant to tease her and nothing more—she could tell by the look on his face. But somehow the humming awareness between them gave the flippant jibe a suggestiveness that made her stomach tighten. He caught her gaze with his own, and she felt like she was falling into the churning sea of his unusual eyes. The feeling made her giddy and scared all at the same time.

"I'm sorry," he said, softly, the low hum of his smoky voice brushing against her. "That was uncalled for. You've put me off with all the questions."

"You didn't expect me to have questions?" she managed.

"I don't know what I expected." His eyes had darkened to a mysterious green as they searched her face, lingering on her mouth in a touch she could almost feel. Almost taste. His elusive scent teased her senses and coaxed her to lean closer, breathe deeper. For the love of God, what was it about this man that made her so aware of him?

"You're adorable when you blush," he said.

His dark tone seemed to imply she was somehow to blame for this, but the look in his eyes said he didn't really mind. In a space of a heartbeat, the friction sparking between them caught and began to burn away any trace of common sense she might have possessed. She couldn't break the hold of his gaze. Couldn't help the ragged breath she drew in.

"Tell me again, how we're related," she said, her voice embarrassingly husky and low.

Finally, Sean averted his eyes.

"It's too distant to trace," he said. "Truth be told, I'm not entirely certain *what* our relation is. Family lines are never straight, are they now? But in Ballyfionúir, everyone is family one way or another. It's said old Collum MacGrath was a randy fellow and the girls loved him very much. He probably spawned half the town."

"Oh," she said.

"Or did you mean, are we kissing cousins?"

The question brought her gaze to his mouth and then to the silvered green of his eyes. "Are you trying to make me uncomfortable?" she asked, shooting for edgy, hoping for insulted, hitting something husky and yearning.

"Perhaps."

"Why?"

"You look at me as if you know me," he said. "I've the strangest feeling you can read my mind, though I know it's not possible. Is it?"

"No," she answered, but that wasn't entirely true and they both knew it.

"I suppose I didn't expect this would be so personal. I thought you'd be happy when I told you about your father and you'd merely come along with me."

He hadn't expected their meeting to be so personal? The incongruity of that struck her on so many levels she couldn't begin to decipher which was the most troubling. With an incredulous laugh, she shook her head and started to say something, but the prickly sensation of being watched again stopped her. She glanced over her shoulder and found the two customers standing in the next aisle, staring at her. Simultaneous "busted" expressions crossed their faces before they quickly looked away. Beside them, their children giggled.

"Hush," one of the women snapped, pulling the boy closer in a protective way.

In the next instant they were bustling out the door.

"That was weird," Danni said, moving to do a quick inspection of where they'd stood. There was only large bulky furniture there. Nothing small enough to steal, but they'd certainly acted strangely.

Sean looked equally baffled but didn't comment. The bell over the door chimed once more and an older woman with a purse the size of a carry-on bag came in. She was a regular who had a penchant for tea sets. She smiled when she saw Danni and moved toward her.

"You're busy. I should go," Sean said. "What time will you be off?"

"Five."

He gave a quick nod and headed for the door. She called out before he reached it.

"Sean, I'll see you later?"

"Yes, you'll see me later."

He left just as the door opened again to admit a couple so engrossed in conversation that they nearly ran right into him. Danni stared after him for a long moment, unaware at first that the elderly lady with the big bag had stopped beside her and was speaking.

"I'm sorry. What did you say?"

"I said no, I'm having dinner with my son and his wife tonight," the white-haired woman said with a happy smile.

"Okay . . . well that will be nice for you," Danni said. "Are you looking for anything particular today? We just got a vintage set of Shelley oleander cups and saucers. Would you like to see them?"

The shop stayed busy for the next hour and then finally a lag came. Danni knew she should be happy about the influx of business, but today she wished they'd head for the mall instead. With a deep breath, she made coffee and then returned to the counter and her computer.

The page on Ballyfionúir was still up, and she read it one more time before clicking the Back button to her original search. She continued to scan the links until one caught her eye halfway down the page. Ballyfionúir—Valley of the White Ghost. In the brief description below she caught words like *ancient*, *mythical*, and *legend*. The page opened to a panorama shot of an emerald green valley rimmed with slate gray rock, hemmed in by a frothing ocean and menacing sky. She recognized it, of course. Just this morning, she'd stood there in the vision with Sean.

She stared at the picture. She hadn't actually doubted that the place existed, but seeing it confirmed, framed by the reality of technology, made it somehow surreal, and disquiet shifted in the air around her. She looked up, scanning the still and silent store. In the back a grandfather clock *ticked* loudly. Beside it, another *tocked* on the offbeat. The effect was disconcerting.

Feeling skittish and jumpy, she returned her attention to her laptop but an instant later a sound coming from the back of the store had her on her feet. She moved down the aisle, passing mahogany cabinets and ornate side tables, crystal lamps and collectables from before the French Revolution. The sound came again, this time louder. *Footsteps?*

"Yvonne?" she called, even though she knew it couldn't be. The back door was set with a fire alarm that went off if opened. They only disabled it when there was a delivery and it could only be unlocked from the inside. Yvonne would have had to come through the front door, and even though she was engrossed in her computer, Danni would have heard the bell chime.

Again, the strange shuffling sound came. This time clearer, this time louder. Not footsteps but . . . something more fierce. Waves, crashing against a beach. Now it seemed to come from all around her.

Danni frowned, turning in a small circle, watching with growing horror as everything began to fade—the massive chests, the towering wardrobes. Tables and lamps, chairs and settees—it was as if they were thinning, becoming impossibly translucent. Danni swallowed the tickle of fear at the back of her throat, tried to pretend her eyes were playing tricks on her, but the air filled with pressure and she knew what was coming. Just as she knew that whatever was waiting beyond the crowded store wouldn't be good. She could feel it in the weight and burden of each breath.

As if released by her acknowledgment, the room wavered and the air tried to turn. Danni fought it with everything she had. She could see images moving beyond the room, but she tried not to look, afraid now that her attention would give those shapes substance.

She backed away, hurrying to the counter, watching her feet and not the pulsing transparency following her every step of the way. She reached the stool, gripping it to assure herself it was solid just as a frigid gust seeped across the floor, bringing with it the smell of brine and the damp of fog. She heard a sputtering sound, like a candle flame fighting a drizzle of moisture. The bright sun went behind a cloud, though Danni knew the sky outside was clear and blue. Overhead, the lights buzzed, became blinding for an instant before they went out. A small sound escaped Danni's lips as slowly she lifted her head.

The air turned with a sudden, plunging *hiss*. Danni couldn't move as she waited for the vision of Sean to appear beside her, unnerved by the anticipation that danced over her skin even as fear nipped down her spine. But he didn't come. Alone in the swaying world, Danni fought to breathe. Where was he? And when had she begun to feel safe by his side?

The shop vanished completely, leaving her standing graveside in the exact place she'd stood with Sean that morning. Only this time she was by herself, abandoned even by her own hallucination.

She looked around with wide eyes, taking in the harsh and rocky wall that tumbled down to the ocean, the bed of sweet grass beneath her feet, the unending horizon. It was the same sweeping view she'd seen on the website just moments ago.

Valley of the White Ghost.

In the distance, she saw a strange monument of some sort. Three enormous boulders held a fourth on top, like soldiers carting their wounded on their shoulders. Something gold glinted from their surface, but she was too far away to see what it was.

Lightning snaked from the bruised sky and the air took on the scent of sulfur. The powerful tide crashing against the rocks made the ground beneath her feet tremble. Rain pelted her face in cold splashes.

She looked down, blinking as the drops came faster and the cold reached her bones. The grave was filled in now, the dirt rusted red, an angry welt in the green pasture. Warring emotions fought inside her. She was glad the grave no longer gaped, no longer revealed the twisted bodies at the bottom, but a part of her wanted to drop down and claw at it, dig until she could see again her own face and that of the teenaged boy lying beneath.

In the distance, a flock of sheep bleated and grazed, moving like the clouds, obeying a directive that she couldn't see. Then suddenly one of the fluffy white animals stood on its hind legs and stared back. As she watched, the air around it shimmied with a silvery current that crackled and sparked. Danni tried to back up, but her legs felt wooden, nailed to the spongy ground beneath her feet.

"I want out," she said aloud. "I want out. Now."

But she had no guide this time. No one to grant her wish. The landscape before her didn't fade, didn't falter. And whatever world she'd entered held steadfast. She clenched her eyes, silently praying for escape, willing herself back home.

She felt a shift in the air that was at once alien and familiar. Slowly, with dread pulling her lower than the sinking earth, she opened her eyes.

A woman stood before her. Dressed in white from head to toe, she had silvery hair draped over her shoulder and down past her knees. It rippled and twisted in the wind. With a cold smile she pulled a sterling comb from her flowing white gown and ran it through her hair, all the while watching Danni with pale and narrowed eyes. Each stroke of the silver comb made her hair sparkle like tinsel. She paused then and held out the comb.

Danni stared at it, saw strange concentric engravings on its rim that teased the eye and exacerbated her fear until it threatened to swallow her whole. She was shaking her head, now muttering the chant "I want to go home" even as her hand lifted and the desire to take the comb brought her fingers closer. A luminescence gleamed from the white woman and the comb seemed to shudder from a power within. It lured Danni, taunted her to touch it.

Then suddenly the woman lifted her face to the hostile sky and keened, her voice a weapon that crashed with the tide in a rush of churning chaos.

Danni clamped her hands over her ears and screamed to block out the horrible sound, but the white woman wailed louder and harsher. The milling sheep stopped and turned toward the biting sound. Even the wind ceased to compete.

Danni fell to her knees in surrender. The mud from the grave seeped through her pants and sucked her deeper, becoming a quicksand that wanted to gobble her up. With the death of her resistance, the keening stopped and silence rang loud in her ears. She realized with horror that her legs were deep in the grave.

A pair of shoes stepped into sight, and like a lifeline, Danni focused on them, traveled up from them to slender legs and a wraparound skirt. She paused, recognizing the pattern and the fabric even as her mind rejected the possibility. And then she was looking into a face she knew too well because it represented every childhood fantasy.

"Momma?" Danni whispered.

And it was her mother, standing there beside her, wearing the same skirt and blouse she'd been wearing in the picture Sean had given Danni. Effortlessly, her mother pulled her from the sucking mud of the grave. Danni felt the brush of her fingers, the warmth of flesh that didn't really exist.

Taking her hand, Danni's mother led her from the grave, through a bright green door that seemed to appear from nowhere and into a crowded room packed with furniture and knickknacks. Danni looked around, one strange and distant part of her noting the amazing trelliswork on a side table she passed, the sparkle of the crystal lamps pooling light against a pair of aged leather chairs. Massive paintings crowded every inch of wall space.

She moved to a pine coffer beside the window. Hundreds of years ago, the antique chest would have held the family's treasures. Danni dreaded knowing what it held now.

Her mother used a key dangling from a chain to unlock it. She opened the lid and removed a large, canvas-wrapped parcel. It looked heavy, but she handled it like it was made of the finest glass. She set it down on the side table and began to gently remove the covering. Danni's mouth was dry, her heart pounding. She didn't know what was at the core of that bundle, but the cautious way her mother handled it made her afraid. Danni was shaking her head, wanting to stop her mother even as she finished and quickly stepped aside. Confused, Danni stared at the object she'd revealed.

It was a book. She let out a shaky breath. She'd expected something worse, something threatening.

Not knowing what her mother wanted, Danni crept closer. The book was bulky and irregular—not quite squared at the corners—easily the size of a seat cushion. Its black cover was made of leather, beveled with concentric spirals, like the comb the woman in white had held out. Jewel-encrusted gold and hammered silver twisted and twined around the edges and corners. A trio of circular lines connected in a mysterious lock fixed over the jagged edges of thick creamy paper. There were more symbols—like letters, but not any she'd ever seen before—set in a row across the front of the cover. She reached out to touch them, but her mother grabbed her wrist and stopped her. Slowly she shook her head.

Fingers curled into her palm, Danni let her hand drop down to her side. By degrees she became aware of a low hum trembling in the air. It pulled at the pit of her stomach and jarred her already stretched nerves. She felt hot and clammy, and she wanted nothing more than to back away, because suddenly she didn't want to touch the book anymore. Suddenly she wanted away from it.

The humming became a drone that throbbed and pulsated all around her. Too low to be heard, too insistent to be ignored. It rose from the floor, dropped from the ceiling, pushed and shoved from the walls until Danni thought it would crush her down like an aluminum can. A heat began to glow in her mind, a fiery coal that flared in response. Eyes clenched tight, Danni tried to force it back, pictured herself as a fist, opening against resistance, expanding and extending until she'd created a space within the confines and she could breathe again. She didn't know how or even *what* she'd done, but the pressure had eased.

She opened her eyes. Her mother stood stiffly to her left, white-faced and rigid, her gaze fixed with an emotion Danni couldn't decipher. There was fear and there was anticipation, and both were directed at Danni.

As if on cue, they turned their attention back to the black book sitting like a fat spider on the table. Danni glared at it, wanting it gone, wanting nothing more than to see it thrown into the blazing fire and turned to ash. On some level she didn't understand, she knew the book was responsible for the sick feeling in her gut.

Without warning, the three interlocking circles burst apart and the cover flew open, fanning sheaths of thick paper in a blurred arc. Both Danni and her mother gasped and stumbled back.

A dark and fecund odor filled the room, filled Danni. She tried to turn away from it, tried to take another step back, but now she couldn't move. Her eyes were fixed on the whirring pages, her mind enthralled by the creamy blur of their movement. What was this book?

The pages stopped, leaving the book opened in the middle, spread like something vulgar, something unnatural. She was shaking her head even as the first drop of red seeped from the binding to the polished surface of the table. Like honey, thick and sticky, it inched to the edge and then dripped over the side, following the intricate maze of the trellis before spilling to the floor.

Once again, the air became too heavy to breathe. Ripping her horrified gaze from the dripping wetness, Danni gave a surging mental push against the weight bearing down on her, gaining just a small space this time.

The red pool grew, bubbling up from the open spine and spreading out. It was blood, she thought. The tabletop was covered and now the liquid poured over the edge, faster and faster, spilling to the floor in a crimson tide. In moments it would be at her feet, and then it would touch her like the sticky tendrils of an inescapable nightmare. She wanted to scream. She *needed* to scream.

The pressure continued to build. Around her—inside her. It pressed against her ears, bore down on her heart, on her empty lungs, on her thoughts. She was past the point of distinguishing between reality and vision. This was happening and she couldn't stop it. This time, there was no way out.

Blackness clouded her sight, and she knew if she didn't breathe soon she was going to faint, right here, right now. And if she succumbed there would be nothing to keep that ooze from covering her feet, her legs, pouring into her mouth, her mind.

Danni took a deep, gasping breath.

Like a trigger, the sound of it shot across the room. The pages of the book began to fan again, furiously thrumming backward, forward, creating a noxious wind that lifted her hair and stung her cheeks.

Danni did the only thing she could. She loosed the scream trapped beneath her fear and hurled it across the room. She felt it ripping, tearing, shredding the invisible wall around the terrible book and then it broke free.

The book slammed shut with a *bang* that resounded, and the spiraled knots of the lock seemed to rush forward and join, mating with crude and sinister glee before it caught with a metallic grind.

Before she could take a second breath the book vanished, then the table, then the room. She was standing in the pouring rain with her mother again, and the air was pure and sweet. She gulped it in, staring at her mother as shock or cold or both wracked her body.

"What was it? I don't understand what it was," she tried to say. But the words were garbled, swallowed by the enormity of her fear. A look of agony pulled her mother's features and she began to fade. "No," Danni cried.

But in an instant she was gone.

Danni stared at the foreign land and suddenly the blaze of emotion turned from terror to frustration and anger. "What now?" she yelled at the sheep, the clouds. "What am I supposed to do now?"

And then a word took shape in Danni's head, like a sprout pushing from the black earth, becoming a green shoot and then a blooming flower of understanding. It was followed by another and then more.

Fennore. The Book of Fennore.

"What is it?" Danni breathed. "What do you want me to do? I don't even know where I am. Do you hear me? Where the hell am I?"

No one answered, her mother didn't reappear, but another trembling image poked up from a dark furrow in her mind. It wavered before snapping into focus.

Home.

This terrible place was home.

Chapter Four

THE Book of Fennore, Danni learned via the seemingly endless web pages she'd read between customers, was an ancient text thought to predate the Book of Kells—the illuminated manuscript written sometime in the eighth century. The Book of Kells was famous for its ingenious illustrations and the breathtaking artwork interwoven into the text. It told the story of Christianity, combining gospels with portraits, ornate canon tables, and intricate symbols. But where that book was dedicated to Christianity and was a historical treasure of Ireland, the Book of Fennore dealt with a darker side of Irish culture—the part seeped in superstition and born of its pagan ancestors. Its claim to fame came in the form of sinister legend and damning lore.

And the Book of Kells was real and on display in Dublin. The Book of Fennore was only a myth.

Or so the numerous pages she'd read claimed.

Danni tried to take comfort in that consensus. The Book of Fennore didn't exist. Like the boogeyman or the Loch Ness monster, it wasn't real. But she could still smell it, still sense it in the air. Still see the blood seeping from the pages and feel that dark, malevolent vibration working its way through her body.

All that from seeing it in a vision. She couldn't imagine what it might be like to *really* stand in its presence. She didn't want to even think of it. But there was a reason her mother had shown her the Book of Fennore, and Danni was afraid it had been a warning of what was to come. Of what she might be forced to face.

She rubbed her eyes. If that didn't make her sound like a raving lunatic, she didn't know what would.

Fennore, she read, was from the Gaelic word meaning *white ghost*. She noted that *Fionúir*, as in Ballyfionúir, was listed as a derivative. The white ghost. Was she the woman who'd appeared to Danni? It certainly fit.

Some experts speculated that the white ghost had been a pagan priestess before the birth of Christ. The Book of Fennore, they claimed, was her guide to the underworld of dark magic. Others thought the Book was propaganda created by the last of the Druid priests to instill fear into their dwindling flock of believers.

It's thought that our ancestors were ancient Druids, Sean's voice whispered in her head.

It was all conjecture, of course, because there was no tangible evidence that the Book of Fennore was anything but a widely circulated legend. Still, the controversy over who authored the Book raged on. Danni couldn't help but see the irony in an argument over who might have written the Book they all agreed didn't exist.

The disparity narrowed when it came to the content and purpose of the Book. All parties concurred that the Book of Fennore was believed to be a fearsome tool capable of harnessing the power of the universe. What was meant by that remained unknown. Likewise, how all that power could be utilized was a mystery as well.

What seemed clear to everyone was that the Book of Fennore should not be trifled with. All that power didn't come cheap. As with most religious myths, the gifts the Book of Fennore bestowed would inevitably bring tragedy and death—worse, anyone foolish enough to use it for personal gain could ultimately unleash on the world an evil of unimaginable dimensions. The Book of Fennore could not be trusted to obey any man's law—worthy or not.

"Terrific," Danni muttered. "So why's my mom got all the evil in the universe hidden in an antique coffer?"

It would take a historian to make sense of everything she had read, and Danni was far from that. But it seemed for every expert refuting the Book and its powers, there was another coughing up proof that it had existed at one time even if it did no longer. In the infinite realm of belief, the Book of Fennore had a great following. There was even a picture of it, drawn in a journal by a monk who'd lived seven hundred years ago.

All the skin on Danni's body seemed to pull tight as she stared at the sketch. He had the asymmetrical shape right, the pitted blackness of the leather, the entwined silver and gold, and the glitter of jewels. He'd floundered when it came to duplicating the knot that locked it tight, though. Not surprising, it had been intricate and strangely fluid.

But for something that wasn't supposed to be real, she and the monk had both imagined it in the same way.

Danni shivered, wondering if the monk had felt that screeching hum that still seemed to rattle her bones . . . or seen the thick and viscous liquid leaking from its pages. Had someone shown the Book to the monk as her mother had shown it to Danni? If so, who? And why?

She covered her face with her hands. Her head hurt. Her mind ached. But she felt like she was circling something and if she just kept at it, she would figure out what it was.

Sighing, she scrolled to the next link her search had pulled. This one took her to an article from the *Irish Times* archives, titled "The Bloody Isle of Fennore." The date on the article was October 1999. She read the first line twice, letting it sink in before she continued.

The tenth anniversary of the murders and suicide that rocked the tiny fishing village of Ballyfionúir passed with little ceremony and no closure.

Closure. There never seemed to be any of that in her world. It was something Danni had longed for and dreaded her entire life.

Although officials insist the investigation into the disappearance and likely murders of Fia MacGrath and her children will continue until they are found or their bodies recovered, they admit the likelihood of the young mother and her children being alive is slim to nonexistent. The triple murders of the MacGraths followed by the apparent suicide of their attacker was sensationalized when two additional bodies were later found in an unmarked grave, bringing the death toll to six. One of the victims was positively identified as the son of the alleged murderer, Niall Ballagh.

Stunned, Danni paused and read that again. Niall Ballagh was the alleged murderer? Niall *Ballagh*? Related to Sean Ballagh?

Rumors that the mythical Book of Fennore had been found on the island and was the catalyst to the violence that occurred that night have added to the mystery surrounding the grisly and brutal slayings, and fueled an international search for the victims, who have never been found. Cathán MacGrath, husband and father to three of the victims, is the only known survivor. MacGrath's eyewitness account portrays Niall Ballagh as a twisted and jealous man on a killing spree, which left MacGrath's wife and children dead and Cathán MacGrath seriously injured.

Using MacGrath's account of the events that took place, investigators have tried without success to uncover the catalyst for Ballagh's actions, but a head injury sustained in the attack has hindered much of MacGrath's recall and made his memory unreliable. MacGrath has never been able to offer insight about the subsequent deaths of Ballagh's son or the unidentified woman found buried with him.

When asked about the rumored Book of Fennore and its possible discovery on the island, Cathán MacGrath denied all speculations and accused the media of ridiculous sensationalism. Chief Inspector Byrne responded in like, "When so many innocent people are killed, the public seeks an explanation that will make sense of it. Unfortunately, some things will never be explained."

Evidence uncovered by the Garda supports Cathán MacGrath's accounting of what happened that night, but without the bodies of the alleged victims, much of it is inconclusive.

Danni frowned, staring at the words but seeing in her mind the vision from this morning. The boy she'd seen in the grave—was that Niall Ballagh's son? Who else could it be? But if it was the same boy, then how—*why*—had the vision placed Danni in that grave with him? He'd died twenty years ago, when she was just a child. She frowned, trying to remember more clearly exactly what she'd seen. But like a dream, it had faded into blurry bits and pieces.

And what about the rumors that the Book of Fennore had been found? Was that why her mother had shown it to her? Danni scrolled down, hoping there would be more to the article, but instead of text she found pictures.

The first was a grainy black and white. The caption read, "Niall Ballagh, only suspect in the Fennore Murders." She hesitated for a moment before meeting the eyes of the man accused of murdering everyone in her family except her father, putting off for just one more moment seeing the man thought to have committed Danni's *own* murder. Slowly, she lifted her gaze and looked into his face, knowing that at least two of the victims had been alive at the time he'd killed himself.

She shouldn't have been surprised to recognize him. He was the man she'd seen in the cavern with her mother. Niall Ballagh hadn't been threatening when she'd seen him then. In fact, he'd been just the opposite. She remembered how he'd held his hands out, palms up, trying to soothe whoever was in the shadows. Danni thought about that. The article said her father's injury had made his memory unreliable. What had he really seen that night? What had he imagined—or thought he'd seen? Danni didn't even remember him being in the cavern at all. He had to have arrived later, then. Maybe the vision had ended just before Niall Ballagh went nuts.

Niall Ballagh's eyes stared back from the sepialike picture, shadowed with despair. Like Sean, he was a tall, solid man with broad shoulders, thick arms, and big hands. He stood on the deck of a boat, dressed in a raincoat and rubber boots. She leaned closer to her screen, trying to discern his features from the many shades of ivory and gray. His gaze was direct and piercing, his jaw set. No smile or glimmer of humor in the light eyes.

As she stared at him, she was filled with a host of conflicting emotions. The part of her that had grown up in foster care, never knowing a home she could call her own—that part thought death by his own hands had been too kind for Niall Ballagh. But there was another part of her, a piece that remembered the ravaged anguish on his face as he'd stood beside his son's body, and that part couldn't help but feel compassion.

Had the murderer of Niall's son sent him into the rage Danni's father witnessed? Perhaps her family had stumbled into a show-down, had become innocent victims to violence not intended for them. She tried to piece the possible scenarios together in her mind. Niall Ballagh might have gone berserk and killed Danni's brother and wounded her father—but Danni and her mother got away—not knowing, perhaps, that her father was still alive. And maybe her father's grief and guilt over not protecting them had later filled in the pieces his memory could not.

But, if it had happened that way, why hadn't Danni and her mother returned home after they learned Niall killed himself? Why had they run to America? And why had her mother abandoned her there?

Questions. Always questions without answers.

She rubbed goose bumps from her arms and moved to the next picture. This one was of her family. They were wearing the same clothes they'd worn in the snapshot Sean gave her, but the camera had caught them unaware, each of them lost in thoughts of their own. Without the fake smiles, they appeared somehow tragic.

Danni's mother stood shoulders hunched, staring at something far off and unattainable. The breeze teased a strand of hair across her face and lifted the hem of her skirt. Beside her, Danni's father was grim and distant, hands shoved deep in pockets, chin pointed to the thundering ocean. Sandwiched in the middle, Danni and her brother held hands, each of them stoic as they quietly waited. There was resignation in Danni's expression—a mute and forlorn acceptance that made her wonder if she'd known what was to come next.

"Cathán MacGrath, pictured with wife, Fia, and their two children, victims in the Fennore Murders," was all it said beneath the picture. But the photograph itself had already said so much more.

She stared at her father's face for a little while longer, but it was the last photo, one that showed a teenaged boy leaning against a blackened boulder, that made a wall of ice come down hard around Danni's gut. The pictured adolescent was both defiant and desperate, facing a gale that chapped his cheeks and gave his eyes a glittering sheen. He was tall, wiry, not yet grown into his big hands and feet. With his dark hair blown wild and his shoulders hunched forward, he seemed to straddle the lines between youth and maturity. Still, a shadow of the man he would become stared back at her.

Torn between bewilderment and rage, she looked into those insolent eyes. What game was Sean Ballagh playing with her? What lies had he told?

Slowly she moved to the caption, feeling as if she were falling into an endless pit as she read the words printed there.

"No," she whispered, shaking her head while comprehension and disbelief battled within her. What it said couldn't be true.

And yet . . . Danni thought of this morning, how he'd appeared at her door without warning. She'd never seen a car or heard an engine, even when he left . . . and in his passport photo he'd looked so young—nearly as young as he did here. When she'd seen him standing on the other side of the window . . . the feeling that he'd been conjured from her thoughts . . . and the strange stares from the two women and their children when she'd been talking to him in the store. It wasn't they who'd acted strangely, it was Danni, talking to herself . . . and when the lady who liked tea sets had said she had plans for dinner, she'd been answering Danni's question to Sean, *Will I see you later?*

No, it was impossible, even for Danni, whose life had suddenly become so fantastic. It didn't make sense. Except in a small dark corner of Danni's heart it made perfect, horrible sense.

She read the caption under the photograph again, this time aloud, hoping the sound of her voice would bring new meaning to the words.

"Sean Michael Ballagh, picture taken days before his murder. His body and that of an unidentified woman were the only remains found."

Chapter Five

THE bell hanging over the door chimed, bringing Danni back to the antique store and sanity in a jarring instant. Yvonne strolled in, cell phone pressed to her ear. A tiny woman with short, curly hair and a round figure, she could light up the room with her smile or bring storm clouds with her wrath. She was grinning now as she said good-bye and snapped the phone shut.

"Biedermeier birchwood *vitrine*. Two grand," she announced proudly.

Disoriented, shaking, Danni didn't move from her stool behind the counter. Her mind continued to stutter around what she had just read. Sean Ballagh was dead. Her Sean. The man who'd visited her twice now . . . bearing airplane tickets. She scrambled to her purse to see if the envelope had suddenly vanished. Oblivious of anything but her own excitement, Yvonne went on about the Biedermeier. She'd been on the hunt for one of the German cabinets since a customer of theirs had raved about seeing one in Sedona.

"It's in near mint condition. One scratch down low and a broken drawer. Both can be fixed. Woman selling it is pissed off at her ex-husband and would have given it to me for less, but I didn't want some court disputing the sale later. Did you hear me? Two grand for a Biedermeier."

Yvonne dropped her purse in the drawer under the counter and crossed the store to adjust one of the blinds.

Realizing that Danni still hadn't spoken, Yvonne finally turned and took a closer look. An instant later she was beside Danni. "What happened?" she demanded. "What's wrong?"

Danni opened her mouth to speak, but where did she start? How could she possibly tell Yvonne everything that had happened? There was no way to explain without talking about the visions, and though she wanted to talk about them, wanted to tell Yvonne everything, she couldn't bring herself to do it. It wasn't that Danni didn't trust her . . . it was something deeper. Something as ingrained as the instinct to survive.

There was a reason why Danni had spent so many years being rejected by different foster families. Sean had asked her if she'd ever felt special. When she'd been younger, she'd known she was special, but she'd learned the hard way that *special* didn't mean good. It meant weird. Unacceptable.

She remembered how it felt the first time she'd casually told her foster brother not to cheat in science anymore because she'd seen him get caught. He'd looked at her like she was a freak, laughed at her, and cheated anyway. When he was caught, he'd blamed Danni. He accused her of telling lies to the teacher and her foster parents believed it.

It took other lessons—all painful, all seared in her memory— before Danni finally came to understand that as long as she had visions, she'd be an outcast. And so she quit. She didn't know how, but somehow she'd sealed off that part of her and kept it locked away in a place so dark, so deep that she'd forgotten it existed at all—until this morning's wake-up call blew the hinges off the trapdoor and opened it all up again. Now she wanted nothing more than to figure out how to reinstate the lockdown.

A logical part of Danni knew Yvonne wouldn't hold the visions against her. But logic had nothing to do with the way she felt just thinking of the disbelief that would surely fill Yvonne's eyes if Danni were to tell her the truth. *Hey Yvonne, guess what? This guy I saw in a vision showed up today to tell me I had a family. Cool, huh, except I think his dad killed my brother—oh and I think the guy is really dead.*

Yvonne would think she'd lost her marbles, and she'd be right.

"I'm not feeling that great today," Danni said. "Would you mind if I went home?"

"Of course not. I hope you're not getting the flu."

"Me, too."

"You need me to drive you?"

"No, I'll be fine. I'll talk to you tomorrow. Congratulations on the Biedermeier."

Even in her concern, Yvonne couldn't keep the grin off her face. "Bet I have it sold before you get home."

Any other day Danni wouldn't have gotten away with the ploy, but today she was grateful that the usually astute Yvonne didn't look any deeper than Danni wanted her to. Grabbing her purse and her laptop, Danni said good-bye and headed home.

Chapter Six

SEAN didn't know where else to go after he left Danni's little antique store, so he walked, hoping the activity would loosen the hard knot of tension deep in his gut. It had been burrowing and coiling since the first time he'd laid eyes on her. It ached, it comforted.

How long had it been since he'd felt anything but the grief and shame his father had brought on them all that night so long ago? How long since he'd felt more than the shattered splinters of life festering beneath his skin? Longer than he could remember.

But when she'd opened her front door this morning, when she'd looked at him with her huge gray eyes . . . He'd felt something stir deep inside him. Felt it in every pore, every nerve, every part of his being. And he wanted more.

He'd been confused when his grandmother had insisted he come here to bring Dáirinn MacGrath home. He'd understood that Danni's survival threw into doubt his father's guilt and that bringing her back might clear the family name. But there'd been another reason Nana had sent him—one he couldn't see or understand at all, one as mystifying as Nana was herself.

Whatever her reasons, though, they didn't seem to matter anymore. They'd been eclipsed by his own wants and needs. He was here for Danni. Nothing more, nothing less.

He found himself standing in front of her house again and wasn't the least bit surprised that his feet, like every other part of him, had chosen to come here. While Danni's crazy little dog worked herself into a fury on the other side of the door, Sean made himself comfortable in the chair on the porch. The afternoon breeze danced through the shrubs and grass, bringing with it the fragrance of roses blooming in a neighbor's garden. A few houses down, someone started a mower and soon the sharp scent of cut grass joined the mix. If not for the lunatic dog, it would have been peaceful, calming even. He leaned his head back against the wall, trying to block out the annoying barking. He needed some calm. He needed some perspective.

But all he could think of was the pale glow of her skin, the scent of her hair, the delicate shape of her ears. How it might feel to lean close to her, breathe her in like a fine wine. He remembered how she'd watched him with that bewildering anticipation. As if she'd been waiting for him. As if she'd expected him.

He shook his head, confused by the very clarity of the feeling.

He saw a flash of movement to his right and glanced over in time to see the yellow cat stalking him from the bushes. When it realized he'd seen it, the enormous creature bolted across the lawn and up the tree like the Hound of the Baskervilles was on its tail. Were all of Danni's animals mad? At least the dog seemed to be giving up. She gave a final, hoarse yap and then there was silence.

He didn't know how much time had passed with him sitting there, soaking in the tranquility of the place, before he heard her car turn down the street. A moment later she pulled into the driveway. He remained seated on the porch, unsure of what to do now that she was here, certain that he shouldn't have come, but convinced he couldn't have stayed away.

The day had warmed and she'd taken off the blue sweater, leaving just a thin white T-shirt and black trousers. Her hair had been twisted up and was held, he saw with amusement, by a pencil. She looked flushed, disheveled. Beautiful. As alive and earthy as the riot of flowers blooming all around him. As unattainable and mysterious as the fairies that lived beneath the hills of his homeland. He wanted to lose himself in her. Strange enough, he felt that in doing so he might actually find the missing pieces of the man he wanted to be.

She'd taken several steps up the walk before suddenly her back stiffened and her shoulders squared. She hadn't seen him yet, but she'd obviously sensed his silent perusal. Slowly she lifted her gaze to his and the look on her face, the wariness in her expression . . . it cut him to the bone.

She knew about his father—that he was the one held responsible for the MacGrath murders.

It was there in the hardening of her lips and the angle of her chin. In the coldness that seeped into the glittering gray of her eyes, turning them into a stormy sky ready to erupt. He'd seen the look before, every day of the past twenty years to be exact. When they deigned to notice him at all, the people of Ballyfionúir—*his people*—did so with the same suspicion and apprehension Danni showed him now. He'd grown used to it. Convinced himself that it didn't bother him anymore.

But on Danni's face, the look was like slivers of glass in his gut.

"Hello," he said.

"What are you doing here?" she asked. Her voice was flat, but her eyes . . . *Ah, her eyes.* They were bright with emotions she wouldn't let surface. Lightning bolts should have shot from them. Perhaps they still would.

"I wanted to speak with you," he said, taking a deep breath as she passed him on the way to the door.

She glanced back. "To explain?"

He shook his head, drowning in the condemnation on her face. It was nothing less than he deserved. He'd come to her lying. He couldn't even say he wouldn't leave that way, too. He'd do whatever it took.

"There aren't many ways to explain that everyone thinks your father is a murderer," he said. "I generally avoid it altogether."

He meant to sound mocking. Cool and unfazed by the shame

that lived and breathed with him every day. But somehow she'd captured him with those fierce eyes, and now she brought him to his knees.

"I'm sorry," he said.

There was confusion on her face now and anger, brittle and sharp. "You're sorry," she repeated. "About your father."

He nodded.

"That's it?"

He didn't know what more she wanted, but it was obvious that she expected something to follow. Some confession he wasn't prepared to make. Would he ever understand what turned the wheels of a woman's mind?

With a dismissive sound, she turned away to unlock the door. He stared at her back, noting the stiff but fine line of her spine, the soft curves beneath the slacks, the slender and shapely legs they hid.

Most of her hair had escaped the twist and curled against her shoulders. The muted browns and golds and burning reds caught in the sun and shone like some indescribable treasure. He wanted to touch it, see if it felt as soft as it looked. He wanted to press his mouth against the salt of her skin, inhale her heat, taste her.

He followed her into the house when she didn't slam the door in his face, figuring she would feed him to the rodent dog for certain. Instead she scooped the mutt up and gently put the snarling thing out the back door. Without looking at him, she moved to the kitchen, opened the refrigerator, and pulled out two bottles of water, setting one beside him before moving away. He'd have preferred a beer, but was just grateful she didn't throw the bottle at him. She perched on the kitchen counter, twisted off the top of her water, and drank half in one long gulp, all the while watching him.

This morning she'd watched him, too. He'd felt the intensity, the grudging interest in her gaze. Without saying a word, she managed to flip switches he didn't even know he had. She lowered her water, and he caught her stare, holding it a baited moment, not trying to hide the heat burning low inside him.

It was wrong, perhaps. Insane, for certain. But there it was, between them. A friction. Awareness. He saw it spark across her skin, saw her sharp intake of breath. And then she exhaled, narrowing her eyes as she did. She was still waiting, still expecting something of him he didn't quite comprehend.

He could tell her the ugly history of his family, tell her about the anger and disgrace he felt whenever he thought of his father, but he didn't have the heart to go there. Not yet, not until he had to.

Knowing it wasn't the right place to begin, but choosing it anyway, he said, "My grandmother, she sees things."

The obscure statement brought no reaction. Danni sipped her water, not answering. But she was listening.

"We're superstitious, we Irish. Half the town is afraid of her. The other half thinks she has magic. That she can change what she sees."

"Can she?"

Her question startled him. Of course she couldn't. He shook his head.

"What does she see?"

The words were absent of rancor but they held something else, something that raised the hairs at the back of his neck. They surprised him. No, they troubled him.

"She saw you," he answered softly.

The kitchen was dim, the windows shaded from outside by ancient trees. But it seemed Danni paled.

"She's seen you since you were little."

"*How* does she see me?" Danni asked.

He shrugged. "I can't be knowing that, can I now? It's her who does it."

"But she knew I was alive?"

He nodded.

"Why didn't she tell anyone?"

Before he could say, *Who would believe her?* Danni averted her face, and he knew she'd thought it on her own without any explanation from him. He'd never spoken of his grandmother's gift before, but he'd anticipated questions Danni wasn't asking. It was as if she knew exactly what he meant.

Put off by it, he said, "Well now, she did tell people she thought you were alive. But never did she know where you were or how you'd survived. And no one took her for telling the truth. Oh, some believed her, sure, but years went by without you being found."

"Did you believe her?"

"Aye. I did."

Danni's face was like a porcelain mask, beautiful and unmoving, revealing nothing of her thoughts. But he had the startling impression that behind that mask emotions raged, emotions not born of confusion but of comprehension. She understood. As strange and perplexing as it was, she understood.

"You know what I'm talking about, don't you Danni?"

She gave him a hard look. "I haven't a clue."

But it was a lie, as sure as he'd told them himself.

"Tell me something," she said, "does she see you, too?"

The question was bland, yet so pointed that at first he didn't know how to answer. What the fuck did it mean, did his grandmother see him, too? "Why wouldn't she see me? She's not blind. Just old."

Danni considered this with the same distant edge. He couldn't grasp what was going on inside her head.

"You're not drinking your water," she noted, nodding at the untouched bottle beside him.

Once again, he heard something in her voice that baffled him. Was it so important to her that he quench his thirst? He felt like an errant puppet who'd hopelessly tangled his strings. Yet she still tried to pull them. Scowling, he looked at the water bottle, but didn't lift it. "I'm not thirsty," he said.

"No?" she answered. "Of course you're not."

Before he could even guess what the hell she meant by that, she went on, jumping to another topic, keeping him unbalanced. "My dad doesn't even know you're here looking for me, does he?"

"No. He doesn't even know I'm gone." *Doesn't even know I exist,* he added silently, thinking of the cold dismissal in Cathán Mac-Grath's eyes whenever they passed over Sean. That same chill lurked in his daughter's eyes now.

Danni tipped her bottle and drained it before setting it aside. That sparking tension seemed to shiver through the room as she stared at him.

"What do you want from me, Sean?"

That he could answer truthfully enough. But what he wanted now—right now—was hot and carnal, deep and abiding. She wouldn't take kindly to him saying it.

"I want to bring you home. It's where you belong."

"If that's all, then why the lies?"

"Why the lies?" he repeated incredulously. "I should have told you the truth? Would you have opened your door had I begun with that?"

"Begun with it? I haven't heard a word of it yet. What really happened to my family?"

He made a sound that combined both pain and irony. "I swear to you, about that I've been honest. No one knows the truth of it but them that lived it. You'd have a better chance asking yourself."

"But you were there. Weren't you?"

He frowned at her and shook his head. "In Ballyfionúir, aye. But I was not with my father that night."

"Where were you then?"

The question was sharp, like a ruler rapping a desk. It commanded attention and response. He frowned at her, sensing it held more importance than the simple demand it formed. "Home, I suppose. It was a long time ago. Why do you ask me?"

She stared at him, her frustration palpable. He didn't know what she expected of him or why she'd made such an assumption about where he'd been, for it seemed she had. That much he could read in her eyes.

She said, "You told me they'd pinned the murders on someone who'd been in the wrong place at the wrong time. Those were your words."

He nodded. "'Tis the truth of it. My father was always that."

"Do you miss him?"

"My father? No, and for certain I don't want to."

"Even now that you know I'm alive?"

He shook his head helplessly. He didn't want to tell her that nothing would ever make his father innocent in Sean's eyes. Niall Ballagh may not have killed Danni and her mother, but he'd destroyed Danni's family, left it in shambles, decimated and irreparable. And it wasn't just her family he'd devastated. Before he'd wreaked havoc on the MacGraths, he'd shattered his own small and trusting unit. Niall would always be a monster to Sean.

Sean glanced away from Danni's face. "I can't know what your being alive really means, can I now? Where is your brother? Your mother for that matter? I'll not be forgiving him so easily for what he's done."

"You think he murdered my brother? Tried to murder me and my mother? You think he was capable of that?"

"I'm sorry but I do."

"Jesus," she breathed. "Jesus."

"It gives me no pleasure to say it. But you asked me."

"And you're telling me the truth?"

"I swear it."

"You used those words this morning."

"Aye, I did. You asked if Cathán MacGrath was really your father. It is still true."

"I asked if you were for real."

"As real any man can be, Dáirinn MacGrath."

She stared at him and the raw pain he saw made him want to cross the room, to hold her as he'd wanted to since the first sight of her lovely face.

"But you haven't told me who *you* really are, have you Sean? Why is it you who's come to bring me home?"

"And why shouldn't it be?"

"Because you think your father tried to wipe out my family, that's why. Can't you see how crazy that is?"

"What better reason would I need for wanting to bring you back? No one doubted for a minute that he'd done what they accused him of. Murder. Yet here you are."

"You talk in circles, Sean," she said, pushing off the counter and crossing to stand in front of him. "You just said that my being alive proves nothing but the fact that he wasn't efficient enough to kill all of us."

"And so it could be. Or maybe he told the truth all those years ago. I've no way to know, do I now? But you, Danni, you *were* there. You saw it all and you've got it locked up in that pretty head of yours."

"I was five. Until you walked through the door, I didn't even remember I had a brother."

"I've faith it will come back to you, what you've forgotten."

"You think returning to Ireland will make me remember?"

"It's certainly worth the effort."

She thought about that, and he hoped perhaps he'd distracted her, but in the next moment, she was back to him.

"How old were you when it happened?"

"Fourteen," he answered, remembering that painful year, the feeling of no longer belonging to the world of children but not yet having a place in the order of men. His body had grown, and he'd been able to see manhood waiting for him, just out of reach. Try as he might to speed it up, it would come no faster than it chose. And then his father had ended everything in one bloody night, leaving Sean neither a boy nor man, but an adolescent carrying the weight of an adult's responsibility on his too-thin shoulders. Suddenly school and the future were not so important as peat to be harvested for their fire or fish hauled from the ocean for their livelihood.

He shook his head. "I see you wanting to make this about me," he said to Danni. "But you can't. It's only ever been about you."

Her brows shot up at that. "Nice try, but no. From where I'm standing, this looks like some twisted game, and I'm just a pawn you think you can move around the board. Well, I've got news for you, Sean Ballagh. I'm not going anywhere with you until you answer my question. Why you? Why are *you* here?"

Her demand shifted the ground beneath him, pushing him ever closer to an edge he hadn't seen before, hadn't suspected lurked just in the distance.

Why was he here? Why was *he* here?

Because of her, the answer came simply enough. He'd come only for her.

It made perfect sense, and yet the *why* of it eluded him. He stood there, staring into those thunderous gray eyes and the only explanation was wrapped around his heart, bound so tight he couldn't separate it and analyze it.

He'd come for her because . . . because . . . she belonged with him. That alone was the reason he'd come to bring her home.

The simplicity of it rolled over him like a great wave. It forced him under and towed him out as it washed everything else away. He felt bewitched, bewildered, beset. The possessive need of her cast a shadow in his mind that he couldn't see past, though he knew he should. What waited on the other side? What was it that flitted in and out of the recesses of his memory?

He raised his eyes to Danni's and something of his confusion must have shown through. He sensed a softening in her, a reaching out. And like a drowning man, he grasped.

"I came for you," he muttered, propelled forward by the power of the statement. He backed her to the counter in three quick steps. Surprise widened her eyes while something else—something deep and conceding—darkened them. The moment had been inevitable; he saw it there in her face, and it charged his blood, infusing him with fire.

Slowly, deliberately, he braced his hands on either side of her and lowered his head to hers. A fraction of breath kept them apart, but the intimate rhythm of her racing pulse beating at her throat, of his heart pounding in his chest—it made them one. "I came for you," he said against her mouth.

And then he kissed her. The feel of her lips, the heat of her breath as it expelled in a rush went through him like an electric charge. He'd dived in, expecting the water to be shallow, the act painful. But if this was pain, he hoped to die of it.

Her hands came up to his chest and he knew she meant to push him away, but that surely would kill him. He did the only thing he could think to stop her. Bringing his fingers to the silken warmth of her face, he deepened the kiss, letting his tongue tease her soft, yielding lips until she opened for him. A shiver went through them both as the cold sweet of her tongue touched the hot need of his. She tasted of mint and warmth and intoxication. He was drunk from the effect. He couldn't have stopped the groan of relief, of satisfaction, had he tried.

He focused on Danni, wanting her to feel what he felt, needing her to want what he wanted. He leaned his weight against her, pinning her body between his and the cupboards, making her know how much he desired her. The hands on his chest clenched, grabbing fistfuls of his shirt as she strained against him—not pushing him away but urging him closer. He felt dizzy with the awareness of her melting softness, the surrender of her body. He slid his hands to her throat and his mouth followed, kissing, tasting, the sweet salt of her skin an aphrodisiac he'd only imagined. Her shoulders were small and fine boned beneath his hands. He felt the press of her breasts against his chest. He wanted more. He wanted contact at every point possible.

He wrapped his arms around her again and lifted, setting her on the counter so he could move between her knees and pull her closer still. The new height put her face level with his own and gave him access to the curve of her neck, the hollow of her throat and the tantalizing swell of her breasts.

She murmured his name in a low, hoarse voice. "This isn't real," she breathed.

"The hell it isn't," he said, moving back to her mouth to prove to her that it was as real as the blood racing through his veins.

It was like holding a flame, having her in his arms. She burned, she writhed, she singed his nerves and seared his control. He wanted to strip her clothes from her body and take her right there on the kitchen floor, but it seemed every inch of silken skin he touched distracted him from his goal. He slipped his hands beneath her shirt and slid them up, across the heated softness of her flesh to cup her breasts, rub his thumbs across the peaks. A small sound slipped from her lips, making his blood hotter, faster.

But then she stilled. "Sean," she said. "Stop."

The mixture of desire, hurt, and confusion in her tone did more than the simple command. It mirrored too closely the complex labyrinth of feelings inside Sean, passions raging wildly from one deceiving passage to another. There was a way to find what he wanted, but it was obscured by his pounding heart and overpowering need.

"I can't stop," he said simply, but he forced his body to do what his mind couldn't and pulled away, slowly. He didn't understand the turning point that had brought him here, but he knew there was no going back. Somehow she'd become a salvation that he was desperate to reach.

Her steady gaze felt like a spotlight, exposing what was inside him. He moved away, angry with himself. When had he become so pathetic? He'd learned to survive in a world that had turned its back on him when he was fourteen. He wasn't some vulnerable boy yearning to be loved anymore. He wasn't weak, like his father. He was a man who made his own way, alone.

He moved to the sliding door where he stared out at her garden and yard. The dog lay on the other side of the glass. She lifted her head and growled at him. He could see Danni superimposed on the surface, pale skin against the T-shirt and slacks that molded every intriguing curve of her body.

"I'd like you to leave now," she said, her voice toneless, cold when he craved her heat.

In the blurred reflection he saw her confusion and determination, and it only stoked his anger and hurt. But he could do nothing more than what she asked.

Without a word, he left.

Chapter Seven

AFTER Sean had gone, Danni didn't know what to do with herself. She had a to-do list a mile long, but the thought of hustling and bustling like her whole world wasn't shaking made her stomach hurt. Her shower did nothing to dispel the one million questions in her head. Nor did it help to cool her blood or ease her frustration. Reciting the reasons why she shouldn't be so hot and bothered over Sean Ballagh only made her feel a fool.

Because she was. It was like he'd crawled beneath her skin and was there, even now, brushing those long fingers against the curve of her spine, pressing his lips to the sensitive place behind her ear, teasing her with the hot flick of his tongue. She gave a heartfelt mental groan. How could he do all that if he was dead?

The last question stopped her as she got in her car, list in hand. Maybe she'd been wrong about that. Maybe the newspaper article was mistaken. Didn't that make more sense than the other alternative? She didn't just see him; she felt him. Could feel him even now. If he was dead, she might be able to see his ghost, but not feel it . . . right?

She bonked her head against the steering wheel three times. She was rationalizing what a ghost could and couldn't do. If that wasn't nuts, she didn't know what was.

But since the air had turned and she'd seen Sean standing in her kitchen, nothing had made sense or seemed in the least bit sane. She desperately needed someone to talk to, but who did she turn to with such a weird, supernatural problem? It wasn't something you called your best friend about. Not something she could discuss with Yvonne over a cup of coffee.

She decided she'd just pick up the necessities—eggs, milk, coffee. Everything else would have to wait. There was a Safeway in the strip mall on the corner and she pulled in, circling for a while before she found a spot. Mild sunshine streamed from a vivid sky and the warm breeze rustled the palms overhead, calming her jangled nerves. She concentrated on the warmth against her skin as she walked.

She didn't notice the young woman standing on the sidewalk watching her until she was only a few feet away. She had white blonde hair worn in pigtails and bright blue eyes with long pale lashes. Her toasted brown skin marked her as a sun worshipper. In twenty years she'd probably look like aged leather, but now she looked only young, tan, and healthy. She wore a sleeveless silk top the same color as her eyes and satiny pants with a paisley pattern.

She stared at Danni with pointed attention, making no attempt to appear casual. Danni faltered, thinking of altering her course to the store, but the woman moved quickly forward and smiled at her.

"I've been waiting for you," she said.

Danni looked over her shoulder. "Me?"

She nodded enthusiastically. "You don't remember?"

"I think you must have me mixed up with someone else," Danni said. "We've never met."

The young woman shrugged and held her hand in a "come this way" gesture, indicating the entrance to a shop called Pandora's Box. The double glass doors were painted with a gold tree that sprouted up the center. Leafless branches spiraled across the panes, reminding Danni of the patterns on the sterling comb the white woman had held out.

"I'm headed to the grocery store," Danni said, with a shake of her head. She pointed at the Safeway farther up the walk. "Sorry."

"You came to me," the woman murmured. "You asked me to help you."

Danni swallowed, but her throat was dry. The way the woman had worded the statement raised a flag of awareness. *You came to me* . . . Wasn't that exactly how she thought of Sean appearing in her kitchen? He'd come to her. . . .

"Please, let me help."

Unnerved, but undeniably curious, Danni followed the blonde into the store where the scent of incense hung heavy on the air. Soft nature music played in the background and fluted chimes tinkled from corners and nooks. The store was open and airy, with books on one wall and windows on the others. A comfortable seating area gathered around a towering bookcase and scattered displays of crystals and incense burners; charms and tarot cards stood in between. Five or six tiny black kittens scampered around a woman in a pale purple dress manning the cash register. A sign propped on the counter read "help us find homes for our kittens." There was more below it describing the dangers black cats faced from cults and other unsavory sects.

Several cocktail-sized tables had been set at intervals, each with two chairs. A thin, well-groomed man in a charcoal sweater and matching slacks sat across from an overweight woman who listened to him with avid interest. At another table, a heavily made-up older woman who looked like she might be auditioning for the role of the Good Witch Glinda sat alone. She stared as Danni followed the blonde to an empty table in the back. A pale blue cloth covered the surface and a tea light in a rose-shaped holder flickered across an array of crystals artistically arranged to one side. A deck of tarot cards lay in an arc across the center.

"Sit down," the blonde said. "I'm Alice."

"You're a fortune-teller?" Danni asked, embarrassed by the judgmental tone that housed the question. She couldn't help it, though. She looked around her, thinking these people couldn't be legitimate.

"I'm a guide," she said. "Did you know there's a spirit with you?"

Alice looked at a spot to Danni's right and all the hairs on Danni's arms stood as she glanced over her shoulder. "You mean right now?"

Alice nodded and her eyes closed for a brief moment. "He's been looking for you for a very long time."

Sean.

"He's only just found you though. Do you know who he is?"

"Yes," Danni said softly, feeling silly and scared at the same time.

Alice's eyes opened. "I don't think you do. It's not someone you know. Not yet." She didn't wait for a response. She picked up the deck of cards and shuffled it before setting it down in front of Danni. "Please cut them," she said.

Danni did as she was told, still feeling strange about being here at all. Alice gave her a sweet smile.

"Weren't you hoping for someone to talk to?" she asked.

Danni shrugged, but it was, of course, the truth. Alice began to carefully place the cards, pausing to study each one after she set it down. After a moment, she tapped the one in the center with a blue-polished nail. The card showed a person trudging over a terrain of hills and low wetlands. In the sky the moon eclipsed the sun. Cups lined the bottom of the card.

"You're at a crossroads," Alice said. "You don't see it because you've been blind for a long time, bound like a mummy by your inability to recognize what is real. But you must break free and find the deeper purpose. Do you know what I mean?"

Danni shook her head.

"I feel that you've . . . shut away some important part of yourself. But it's something you need, and without it, you're simply stumbling through your life. You're blind and you don't know how to free yourself. Even now, you think you want to stay that way."

Danni made a small sound of disbelief. "Why would I want to stay blind?"

"Because you may not like what you are forced to see if you choose to open your eyes and be whole again," Alice said with monotone certainty. Despite Danni's skepticism, a chill danced over her spine.

Alice flipped another card, this one of a tower. Fire spilled from its small windows and people jumped to escape—or jumped to their deaths, hard to say which, though the plunging fall didn't look like a good option either way.

Danni blew out an amused breath, but really, what filled her wasn't humor. "So what is that? The death card?"

Alice cocked her head, considering the question with more solemnity than Danni wanted. "In a way, perhaps. But not necessarily death of the body. Death and rebirth are part of our everyday world. If you don't embrace it, you are only living on the surface. Maybe the *old* you has to die in order for the *new* you to survive."

"That's a little too out-there for me." But she was thinking of that grave and her body at the bottom.

"If you say so," Alice answered mildly.

Alice pulled the next card from the deck, and Danni thought this one looked even worse than the last. A tall figure in gray stood with a lone lantern in hand in a dark world. Nervously, she watched Alice's reaction.

"There is someone you are looking for. This person is important to you," she said, pausing to chew on her lip. "It's a man. I think he is the reason you are blind now. You need to know what he is and to do that, you must ask."

"Ask who?"

Alice shook her head. "I cannot say. But you must seek in order to find, knock if you want to enter. The promise is found in your own heart."

"Well, that's as clear as mud."

"There are dangers in what you seek. On the surface, it appears to be everything you think you want. But there's untruth about the people you will find. I'm seeing . . ." She closed her eyes. "I'm seeing a mask that hides the true person inside. Does that mean anything to you?"

"I don't think so." Danni shifted, not liking the sense of understanding pushing its way up from her subconscious.

"But you are looking for someone?"

Danni wet her lips, unwilling to give any hints, any clues to this strange woman. "Isn't everybody looking for someone?"

Alice's smile said she knew what Danni was thinking. She flipped another card—this one of a man hanging upside down on a giant *T*. "I see a break in trust, this time within yourself. You've forgotten who you are." She fanned the deck in her hands and asked Danni to pull one out. Danni felt hollow as she did.

Alice studied the card for a long moment before placing it on top of another. "This Five of Wands. It represents strife, a struggle. I sense it's something even greater though. A battle of some sort."

"A battle," Danni repeated, with a feeling of falling in her stomach as Alice pulled yet another from her deck. "Listen, I don't know why you were waiting for me or if that's just the line you use to pull customers in, but I have a lot to do today. Tell me what I owe and—"

"Have you always run away from them?" Alice asked, unfazed.

"From them, who?"

"Your battles. Is that why you want to be blind? You are here, now, because you won't fight. But this card . . ." She tapped the last card with her blue fingernail. The card showed a man lying on his stomach with ten swords sticking out of his back. "This represents the loss of all you value. It means that in running away, you destroy yourself."

Danni pushed back her chair and stood.

"The spirit that follows you—he wants that. His aura is changing even now. I can see it. It makes him happy. He wants you to run away."

Danni looked desperately around the store, not wanting to hear what Alice might say next. Not wanting to think of the gleeful spirit over her shoulder. "How much? How do much I owe you?"

Alice stood as well. "You have the power to change everything," she said softly, and her eyes fluttered closed again. Her face was serene, but it seemed a fine static hovered around her. If Danni were to reach out and touch her, the spark of it would snap against her skin.

Danni's mouth was dry, her stomach tight as she took a step

back. "Thank you for your time," she said, fumbling her wallet from her purse.

"Take off the blinders, Dáirinn," Alice whispered. "Face what you fear."

"What did you call me?"

Alice opened her eyes and looked at her without answering. For a moment that seemed to stretch like a timeless void, the two women stared at one another. But what Danni saw was the fanning pages of the Book and the dark red that seeped from between them. If that was the thing she had to face, Danni didn't think she could do it.

"Everything all right over here?" a poised woman in a shimmering lilac dress asked. Danni had noticed her behind the cash register when she'd walked in. "Alice, are you okay?"

Alice blinked and then came out of her trance. She smiled pleasantly. "Yes, I'm fine."

Hesitantly, the woman looked back at Danni, who still held her wallet in a tight grip. "How much do I owe you?" Danni insisted stubbornly, wanting to pay—to eliminate any debt between them and get the hell out of there as fast as she could. Alice had pried loose something deep inside her, and Danni was afraid it would be blown free now. And who knew what would come out?

"Alice charges forty for a reading," the woman said in a wary voice. She was looking over Danni's right shoulder, just as Alice had. *Great.* Could everyone in this place see the invisible spirit?

Danni pulled her money from her wallet and set it on the table. Without another word, she turned and hurried from the store, aware of the eyes following her. She stepped into the bright sunshine with a feeling of escaping. But the cloying scent of the shop clung to her skin.

Focused only on reaching her car and getting far away from Pandora's Box, Danni didn't see the man watching her from the other side of the parking lot. But she sensed him, and it pulled her gaze from the ground and forced her to look around. She scanned over the people on the walkway, not even registering the familiar face until she'd passed him. She spun back around, searching for the face again. For a moment, she'd thought she'd seen her father—or at least a man who looked a lot like he had in the picture. But that was impossible. . . .

She'd almost convinced herself she'd imagined him when he appeared again. For an instant their eyes met across the busy parking lot and Danni stilled with surprise. Slowly, he smiled, and Danni was struck by the way it transformed his face. He didn't just look like the picture; he looked like he'd stepped out of it. It had to be her father. For reasons she couldn't begin to guess, her father was here in Arizona and Sean didn't want her to know it.

She hurried toward him, her heart swelling with hope as she neared. But before she could reach him, he turned and stepped into one of the other shops lining the strip mall. She followed him into the crowded store, looking up and down the aisles, but somehow she'd missed him, and now he was gone.

Chapter Eight

IT was nearly dusk when Sean finally saw Danni come into the park. She'd changed her work clothes for soft gray velour pants and a matching jacket that looked both comfortable and warm, though it didn't feel the least bit chilly to him this evening. *She is going to freeze to death in Ireland*, he thought.

He remained sitting on the park bench as she and the crazy dog came toward him, just watching her walk. The clingy fabric molded to her slim frame and accented her shapely curves. For the hundredth time that day, he wanted to touch her.

She looked tense, and he couldn't help the triumphant feeling that filled him. He'd spent the rest of the day frustrated and uptight. He couldn't have stood it if she'd been strolling happily along with her little mutt on its leash and not a care in the world.

She was a good twenty feet away before she noticed him. She slowed, and the tension became wariness. But not surprise, he noted. Once again, she'd been expecting him.

When he stood, the little dog charged him, growling and snarling, too fierce a beast for the compact little body. He'd hoped the dog would grow used to him, but at this rate he'd be an old man first.

Danni held Bean's leash tight, stopping her before she could sink her teeth into Sean's ankle. "Bean, be nice," she scolded. The dog strained at the end of the leash, ignoring her command.

To Sean she said, "What do you want?"

There was nothing suggestive in the flat tone of the question, but still it filled him with a host of very graphic images portraying exactly what he wanted. As if she'd read his mind, she blushed and looked away.

"I'm sorry about how I behaved earlier," he said, contradicting his own wild imagination. "I wanted to apologize."

She looked at him for a moment, and he was glad he could look back without fear of her seeing what was on his mind. He was sorry, but only because it had ended before he was ready.

"Don't worry about it," she mumbled.

The soft gray of her jacket brought out the flecks in her eyes and made them even more striking, more mysterious. He stared deeply into them.

"Are you here alone, Sean?" she asked suddenly.

Confused, he glanced over his shoulder, wondering what she meant. "I came here alone," he said.

"You didn't come with my father?"

He almost laughed at that but managed to control the urge. "No, I didn't. Why are you asking?"

"I saw him today. When I went to the store."

"Your father?" he repeated, unable to hide his shock. "Are you certain?"

"Yes. No. He looked just like him. Could have been his twin. His clone."

Sean shook his head, a sinking feeling hitting him hard and low. This was not good. He didn't even know why, but it was not good. "He can't be here."

"And why is that?"

He didn't have an answer, but he was almost certain she couldn't have seen Cathán MacGrath. He didn't know about Danni, Sean was sure of it.

"I don't know who you saw, Danni, but I'd swear it wasn't your father. He's a busy man and he rarely leaves Ballyfionúir these days."

She let out a deep breath. "And the man I saw, saw me back. If it was my dad, he would have spoken to me, not just walked away."

He nodded in confirmation. But he was bothered by the idea of Cathán being here.

Without another word, she started back the way she'd come, and he walked with her, thinking her silence felt like a void he couldn't seem to fill. He wanted to put his arms around her and hold her, but he didn't trust himself to stop there. He doubted she'd trust him to either.

"Who is the white ghost?" Danni asked softly. Her voice came out flat and thin, but it was her question that stilled him.

"What did you say?"

"Ballyfionúir. It means valley of the white ghost, doesn't it?"

"In a general way, I suppose," he answered carefully. "We think of it more as a spirit now. As in benevolence."

"Oh." She turned those silvery eyes his way. "So there isn't really a ghost?"

"I'm sure there are several," he said, keeping his voice level, watching the play of emotion on her face. "Ballyfionúir is at least fifteen hundred years old."

"But have you ever heard of her? Of the *white* ghost. Do you know who she is?"

"She?"

Danni hesitated, looking down at the little dog. She shook her head. "Never mind."

He wanted to let it drop. He wanted to pretend she'd never brought it up, but a strange uneasiness settled in the air between them and he knew he couldn't. They reached her front door and he hesitated on the porch, unsure of his welcome—or rather, certain that he wasn't. But she surprised him by inviting him in.

He followed her to the small kitchen, where she sat at the table and removed Bean's leash. She looked done in, and once again he wanted to hold her, comfort her.

She gave the dog a scratch behind its ear and then took a bottle of wine from the top shelf of the refrigerator. Without asking if he wanted it, she reached for two crystal wineglasses. While she filled them, Sean spied a jar on the counter with the words *Ruff Ruff* painted on the side. He looked in. Dog biscuits. He took one and risking life and limb, squatted down to hold it out for Bean.

With an expression of surprise and grudging gratitude, Bean left Danni's feet to retrieve the donation. She took it from his fingers with ladylike manners, but gobbled it like a starving wolf. He would swear it was a smile she gave him with the abrupt wag of her stubby tail.

Bemused, Sean sat beside Danni and finally asked the question he'd been holding at bay. "And why are you asking about the white ghost, Danni?"

Danni moistened her lips before she answered. A telling gesture that jangled against his already stretched nerves. She was going to lie.

"I dreamed about her," she murmured.

He didn't say what he was thinking. Instead he asked, "Last night?"

She nodded. "It was a weird dream. I don't know why I brought it up."

She pretended a sudden interest in her glass and began twisting the stem between her finger and thumb. She looked worried, afraid of what he'd say or do next. And a dark suspicion gathered in his thoughts as he watched her. A certainty that he didn't want to acknowledge.

She hadn't dreamed about it. She'd seen it. And that did not bode well for either of them.

"My grandmother has seen the white ghost," he said in a low voice.

Up and round came the lovely gray eyes. He stared into them, feeling as if he were falling into the cool mist of gathering clouds and eminent storm.

"She has?" Danni breathed. When Sean nodded, she asked, "Does she have a silver comb, when your grandmother sees her?"

"A comb?" Even as he queried, a shadowy memory poked up in his subconscious. What was it his nana said? There was a myth . . . a superstition . . . something about a comb. He frowned as the memory sharpened into focus.

"She came to me," Danni went on, but paused, frowning. "I mean, in the dream, she tried to give me her comb. It was scary, the way she held it out. It was like . . . like something I couldn't resist."

"You didn't take it, did you?" Sean asked more sharply than he'd intended.

Danni frowned. "Well, that's when she started screaming—making this horrible screeching sound that hurt to hear."

"But did you take the comb?" he demanded again, a part of him feeling foolish for the fear that backed the question.

She shook her head, watching him with those round, gray eyes. All her soul seemed to be in them. Sean forced a smile that didn't fool either one of them. He was uncomfortable with his own immediate worry and the relief that came with her denial. But the Irish were a superstitious lot and things that had been bred into a person were hard to ignore. Foolish or not, the thought of her taking the comb had brought a heavy foreboding to the pit of his stomach.

"It's good you didn't take it," he said, hoping he sounded more casual than he felt. "Sure and it's all legend. Tales that mothers have used to terrify their children into obedience for hundreds of years. But it's good you didn't take it."

She watched him, her eyes still wide, a shiver of apprehension near the surface. Her hands worked the wineglass, spinning it in idle circles without her seeming to notice. "What would've happened if I took it?" she asked.

Sean reached over to still her fingers. They were like ice and without thinking, he folded them into a warm hold. He heard her take a soft breath and it pulled his thoughts deeper into the seduction that was Danni MacGrath.

He cleared his throat, wished he could pull his hands back, but he was committed now, and his fingers seemed to be working on their own, rubbing her silky skin, bringing heat to her icy fingertips.

"My nana would say she's a banshee," he said at last.

"A what?"

"A fairy, I guess, only not the kind your Disney would dream up." He looked into her eyes, trying to make the words more gentle than they could be. "As the story goes, they appear to tell you that someone has either died or is going to."

She blinked once, twice. He could see the effort it took to process what he'd said, and he felt a slight tremor move through her. Her captured fingers curled into a small tight fist. He brought them up to his mouth and blew warmth into the shelter he'd made with his hands. She watched him with that heady combination of trust and misgiving.

"Banshees keen for the dead," he said.

"Keen," she repeated and her voice seemed to come from far away.

"Yes, that's what it was. I can't even begin to describe the sound. It was so harsh and . . . and like glass—a million glasses breaking at once."

He nodded, knowing exactly how sharp the ring of grief could be. A long moment passed and then she asked, "What about the silver comb? What was that?"

"Do you know anything about the Irish, Danni?"

"You're supposed to wear green on St. Patrick's Day and never let a leprechaun go if you want his pot of gold."

"Well, there's a bit more to us than that."

"I figured there might be."

Her voice had dipped huskily at those words and she looked away. Sean wondered what she was thinking.

"You think of leprechauns, and isn't it true we think all Americans ride horses and shoot each other in saloons? Sure and the Irish are nothing if they're not superstitious. The leprechauns my grandmother would tell you of were cruel little bastards, though. I'm not after saying most people still believe in the lore, but there are those like my nana who do. My point is, if Cinderella were an Irish tale, the Fairy Godmother would not have done her good. She'd have given her three heads or spirited her away to some dark cave where she'd be kept until the tide came in and drowned her."

"And what does she say of the white ghost?"

Sean rubbed her hand while he considered his answer. His grandmother had seen her twice and both times had brought disaster. Sean had never believed in the spirit, but he had a healthy respect for her fear of it.

"When I was a boy," Sean began carefully, "my nana used to say that I should be careful of the fairies. 'Never be too good a boy, Sean,' she would tell me."

Danni's brow's rose at his impression of his grandmother and the briefest of smiles flitted across her face. "Why?"

"Well, see, she thought that if I was too good, the fairies would come and snatch me away. I didn't have the heart to tell her that I was *never* that good. But the point I'm trying to make is that the fairies of Ireland do things like hide the money jar from a mother with six hungry children just so they can snatch the best of them and make it their own while she's out begging for food."

"That's horrible."

"Aye, well, Irish history hasn't ever been sweet and lovely."

"But what does that have to do with the comb?"

"Don't you know better than to rush an Irishman telling a tale, woman?"

Another smile—this one almost made it to her eyes.

"The comb would be something they'd thought of as a lure."

Danni grew very still and he paused, watching her. She pulled her hand from his grip and began fidgeting with her glass again. Her next words lit the kindling beneath his foreboding, and it flared up into something greater, more menacing.

"It did lure me," she said. "I wanted to touch it. I wanted to touch it very badly." Her lips tightened, her face paled. "Go on," she told him.

"It's nothing really. The truth of it is, the tale is probably stolen from mermaid mythology—the siren, tempting sailors with her beautiful hair and sparkly combs, then trapping them in the cold sea. Just don't take it if she offers it again."

"I won't," Danni said softly, and the seriousness of her tone was telling. She believed it could happen.

"What else was in this *dream*?" he asked.

Danni looked into her glass and didn't answer. He'd known there was more from the minute she'd begun to speak. She'd started in a choppy, staccato manner that implied she was editing as she went. Now his curiosity had an edge to it. Danni was scared. He could feel her anxious tension, and it triggered a primeval protectiveness in him that caught him like a hooked blade.

Danni took a deep breath and said, "I saw my mother."

"Your mother, was it?"

"In the dream," she added. "She pulled me out of the grave."

"And what grave would that be?"

"The one I saw you standing beside," Danni said softly.

Sean swallowed hard, not liking her tone. Liking the words she spoke even less.

"That was some dream you had."

She nodded. "I've always been a vivid dreamer."

He let it go, wanting to know what else she'd seen.

"This grave, it's in a valley, and I see a steep cliff. It's covered in rocks that seem like they're going to tumble right into the sea. It's very harsh. Very beautiful."

Very much Ballyfionúir.

"In the distance, there's a weird stone thing. . . . I'm not sure how to describe it, but it looks like a doorway and it has something on it that reflects the sun. Like gold."

She cocked her head and watched his face. It felt as if he'd been plunged into an arctic pool. He was suddenly very cold.

"Do you know where I'm talking about?"

He knew. He knew it well. It was a place that drew him, a place he often found himself, sometimes with no recollection of how he'd come to be there.

"What is it? The stone thing I see?"

"It's a dolmen. They're ancient and as common as castles in Ireland."

"But what is it?"

"Depends on the myth you believe. But most likely they mark burial chambers. Doorways to beyond."

She paled and nodded. "Is there one in Ballyfionúir?"

"Yes."

"I had the sense—the feeling—that there was something behind me when I was looking at it, but you know how dreams are. I couldn't look back, so I don't know. I think, maybe it's a house or . . . I don't know, something bigger, but I can't say what."

"It's the ruins," he said softly, feeling the hair at the back of his neck stand on end. "It used to be a castle and stronghold, perched up on a cliff overlooking the sea. It was built centuries ago and has stood all this time. My grandmother remembers stories of when it was whole. Your ancestors lived there before one of the walls caved in and crumbled right down to the ocean. It took the kitchen and the oldest son of the time with it."

"Oh . . ."

The breathed word shivered between them. He had a feeling of something momentous, something hovering just above them. It seemed the room dimmed, the lighting changed, became softer, though he couldn't explain it. The walls of her kitchen flickered— there was no other way to describe it. It was like seeing a home movie projected over the paint and cabinets. Distorted, out of place, but undeniably *there*.

"Now it's only ruins?" Danni said, her voice a cool breeze that blew through him.

He nodded. "There's a house just in front of it now. I've never thought it looked natural, the house standing in the shadows of the ruined castle. But they didn't ask me when they built it."

Danni stared at him, her gray eyes looking deeply into his own. The pull of her was tangible, the need for her so great he couldn't stop the hand that finally bridged the gap between them. The silk of her cheek felt hot against his fingertips. He stroked down the line of her jaw to her throat, trying to see nothing but her. Trying to lose himself in the stormy seas of her eyes. But the walls seemed to fade in and out, mocking his attempt to ignore them.

What was causing it? Did she see it, too? But he didn't ask. Asking would have made the gnawing worry in his gut too real or too ridiculous. He wasn't sure which.

"I've brought you something," he said, not realizing he'd intended to speak of it—to give it—until he heard his own words. But in the swirling mix of his confusion, he felt a pressure build. An urging that forced his hand in the same way it had from the start.

He thought, not for the first time, that somehow he'd become a pawn in his own life. A shell of the man he should be, moving mindlessly to an objective he didn't understand.

The walls around him took on a strange translucence, and for a moment he was looking out on the view Danni had just described. For just an instant, he felt the bite of the sea breeze, the salty spray of the surf. And then his fingers closed over the green box he'd brought from Ireland, and the walls were just what they should be. Staid and confining, locking him into decisions that weren't his own.

Chapter Nine

Danni felt the push of the air around them. It was heavy and thick, filled as if by sediments. She thought of an erupting volcano, spewing out ash so dense it masked the sky. The pressure of the air trying to turn was made foreign and gritty by the strange fluttering pieces of the bigger picture she couldn't yet see. Knowing it was pointless, she fought the turning, focusing just on the man beside her.

From his pocket, Sean pulled a small green box. It was what he'd been holding this morning when he'd watched her from the window of the store. It was embossed with knotted gold loops and spirals that joined in a symbol she'd never seen before . . . and yet, there was something familiar about it. It took a moment and then she realized—she'd seen similar shapes in the fanning pages of the Book of Fennore. Icy cold seeped from her scalp to her feet as she considered that.

With a brooding glance at her face, Sean thrust the tiny box at her. Again she was hit with his mixed messages. He gave it, but not willingly.

Her fingers shook slightly as she took the box and opened the lid. Inside, on a bed of white cotton, was a necklace with a fine chain of woven silver and gold. A pendant the size of an old coin hung from it. The mixture of silver and gold made an intricate weave around concentric spirals spun together without beginning or end. Again, she had that sense of familiarity and recognition. In her mind, she saw the lock on the Book, turning and spiraling endlessly. The pendant was the same.

A constellation of jewels glittered in between the strands of gold and silver. An emerald centered the piece, with sparkling diamonds, glowing opals, and bloodred rubies surrounding it. But there was no malice emanating from the necklace as there had been from the Book, only a strange jarring energy.

The walls of the kitchen continued to expand and thin around her like encapsulating lungs sucking in deep breaths. It felt like they shivered with anticipation as she stared at the necklace. They were waiting, but she didn't know why or for what. She fought the urge to look at them, struggled against the shadows moving just on the other side of the membrane.

She touched the knotted center of the pendant with the tip of her finger, and a stinging jolt seemed to race up her arm. It frightened and conversely soothed at the same time. "What is this?" she whispered.

"It's a charm," he answered in that smoky baritone, making the words seem much more than they were. "To bring you luck and keep you safe."

"Safe? Safe from what?"

He stared at her in silence, and she sensed he was sifting and filtering a myriad of responses. That he felt there were many things she needed to be kept safe from. So many things she should be fearing. Did he have knowledge of the Book of Fennore? Had he ever seen it himself?

The walls pulled and pushed at the thick air. Waiting . . . waiting.

"Just safe," he said, looking away. "It's a family heirloom. It's yours now."

"Mine?" she said, and the wall sucked in a gasp of pleasure.

"Yes. Put it on. It belongs to you."

"But where did it come from? How did you—"

"Do you want me to take it back, then?"

"No," she said quickly. "No."

The sighing walls pressed close as Sean gently lifted the fine chain, moved behind her, and clasped it around her neck. His fingers were warm against the sensitive skin of her nape, and the brush of them was as intimate as a kiss.

The walls pulsed with a dark need that terrified her.

When Sean returned to his seat, his brows were drawn, his eyes a strange golden green, a choppy pool of disquiet. He glanced past her as if something behind her had distracted him. She had the unsettling sense that he could see, that he could hear the insistent grating as the walls thinned and expanded. But that was impossible. She'd never broadcasted a vision to anyone else.

"I don't know when it was made," Sean was saying about the spiraled and knotted pendant. "I'm not sure it's ever been dated. But it's old. Very old."

It felt heavy around her neck, much more weighted than its appearance led her to believe. She lifted it with tremulous fingers, half expecting the precious piece to disappear like an illusion. But the moment she touched it another shocking bolt cut through her. Images rushed with it in a whoosh of jumbled impressions that stole her very breath. She didn't have time to make sense of any of it as it vandalized her senses.

"Are you all right?" Sean asked, taking her hand, bringing her back.

The walls warbled, and she felt that they would suck her into their swirling mass. She felt sick with the pull of it. Horrified by the lure behind it.

"Danni, what's wrong? What's happening?"

Sean's voice came from a great distance. She felt it as much as she heard it. She tried to answer him but managed only an incoherent sound that escalated her rising panic. Since the morning Sean had appeared in her kitchen, the visions had been hovering, just waiting to take her into their frightening embrace. And now this—this feeling that they would punch right through her walls and overtake life as she knew it.

Sean was standing now, pulling her to her feet. She was aware of him, the solid mass, the height and breadth of him, the seduction in those not quite green, not quite gray eyes. She wanted him to be real. Suddenly, fiercely, she wanted him to be something more than a sick twist of fate. She wanted to lean into him, have his arms around her, comforting, holding on to her. Holding back the frightening swirl of the air.

It wasn't fair, she thought. It wasn't fair that he'd come into her life this way. One more person she yearned for but couldn't have. Because even though he was a stranger, she did yearn to know more about him. To feel connected to him. She wished it could be different. Why did it always seem that everything she wanted hovered just out of her reach?

A sound echoed through her mind—a pulsating rush, a distressed groan. Destiny's train chugging up a forbidding slope. It grew louder, stronger. The air became thick and cloying, sucking at her sanity as it solidified over reality.

"Danni?"

She couldn't hear him speak, but she saw his lips move, his eyes fill with concern. He pulled her into his arms, staring at their surroundings with an expression that mirrored the fear inside her. She didn't know what was happening, but it seemed to happen to them both. Bean began to bark frantically. She circled Danni's feet and jumped to rest her paws on Danni's legs. She knew it, but couldn't make her body respond and offer comfort.

And then it seemed that the floor opened beneath her. There was no free will in her falling. No choice to obey or defy. She was simply there in the blackness, air and sound rushing past her. She clutched at Sean, both reassured and horrified to find him still with her. She couldn't bring someone into a vision, couldn't take them through the turning air with her.

But Sean wasn't like anyone she'd known before, was he?

Her own panic followed her down, down deeper into a darkness that seeped and spread. She accepted that this was not a vision. She couldn't isolate the reasons why it was different, but she felt them and she knew she was right. And still she fell—wildly pinwheeling as she plunged through impenetrable darkness. She couldn't feel Sean anymore and she wanted to cry at the loss.

Then someone grasped her flailing hand. The grip was warm, strong, the hand holding hers big and rough. He pulled her into the circle of his arms, holding her tight as they plummeted. She couldn't see him, but she could feel the breadth of him and it reassured her. *Sean.*

She wasn't alone. She didn't understand it, but she wasn't alone.

The falling became something more jarring, more aggressive than gravity. It siphoned the air from her lungs, tugged at her shoes, sucking them off, flinging them away as it stripped her down to her skin. The wind whipped her, flayed her skin, burned even as the chill crept into her bones. She clenched her eyes, burying her face against Sean's bare chest, hearing Bean barking somewhere in the confusion. She couldn't catch her breath and her head felt light. She felt light.

There was no slowing. No stopping. No fear of the bottom.

There was simply—suddenly—nothing at all.

Chapter Ten

I T *wasn't dream; it wasn't vision.*

It was some hybrid of both that held her captive. Danni rolled over and snuggled beneath soft covers, unsure of where she was or how she'd come to be there. She was warm, though, and content.

She tried to open her eyes, but her lids were too heavy and the feeling of comfort too fine to disturb. Her pillow smelled of lavender and the sheets were smooth against her bare body. She was naked. The realization lit the first tiny flicker of apprehension. She never slept naked.

In bed beside her, something—someone—moved. She felt hot skin brushing hers as he rolled and spooned behind her. He was big. She could sense the weight of him, the length of the body pressed to her own. An arm circled her waist and pulled her tighter against him. His hand spread over her stomach and then slowly moved up.

Sean. She didn't question how she knew.

Again she tried to open her eyes, tried to surface, but it was no use. Was it a vision, then? Something only in her mind?

His hand cupped her breast, his thumb moving in slow, languid circles over the nipple. He seemed to come awake in the act, slowly, sensuously, like a giant cat stretching out the tightly coiled muscles of his body. She felt awareness travel through him, and he made a sound that teased her nerve endings and made her skin feel hypersensitive.

Slowly, slowly he began to kiss her back and shoulders, moving her hair aside to reach her neck. His hands slid possessively over the edge of her hip to the slope of her spine, up to her nape and around to the curve of her throat. She felt the swollen heat of him hard against her bottom and she pressed into it, wanton, urgent.

He shifted, rolling her onto her back, and gently pinning her with his weight. His touch became demanding. He pressed his mouth to hers, hard and soft, like hot silk binding an unyielding force. She wanted to wrap her body in his kisses, wear them beneath her clothes during the hours of day when this would all be just a memory—a fantasy that hadn't really happened. His hands roamed over her as if she was his to have and to hold, the span of his fingers reached from hip bone to hip bone, his lips following every intimate stroke.

"Touch me," he said into her mouth as he caressed the flat of her belly, moving ever down to torment her with the seductive flick of his fingers. Boneless and compliant, she did as she was told.

She stroked him, eyes still sealed, inhibitions somehow locked away with her sight. A shadowy part of her mind knew this wasn't right, it couldn't be happening. But the rest of her didn't care as he dipped and circled, rubbed and toyed with her, all the while drugging her with deep, slow kisses.

When she thought she might scream from the building tension inside her, he shifted, spreading her thighs with the slide of his hips. His body was hard and muscular, gloriously defined. She felt what she couldn't see, exploring ridges over his abdomen, the tight bulge of his chest, the hard bunching of his arms.

She spread herself for him, trusting him completely as he pushed deep inside her and held. He filled her with every inch of himself, leaving no room for doubts or fears, no place for identity. She no longer knew where he ended and she began. She no longer cared. Loneliness, something that had been a part of her forever, ceased to exist.

Then he began to move—measured, sensuous strokes that brought friction and heat and a rising excitement she couldn't contain. She was mak-

ing sounds, ragged, erotic sounds that she'd never known herself to make before.

He whispered in her ear, words of encouragement, dirty words that made her hotter, wilder. Yes, she told him, yes she'd do whatever he wanted. And she would. In her blindness, she was willing to give up the control she always fought so hard to maintain. She was a vessel, begging to be filled with whatever he chose to give her.

His tongue brushed against her lips, mimicking the deliberate slide of his body. She wrapped her arms tight, not satisfied with merely the weight of him. She wanted to flatten herself until she was part of him. Her ankles locked at his back and she met him thrust for thrust. Doors to the hollow places she'd kept sheltered vanished, letting in the heat and building need he created. Like sunshine through open shutters, Sean chased back her fears, her isolation, and illuminated her darkest corners.

Still she was blind, depending on her heightened senses to guide her. Depending on Sean and his wicked touch, his demands, his rhythm. He caught her earlobe between his teeth and gently nipped before whispering a command that unleashed the pent-up excitement inside her. She climaxed with a force that rocked her body, pushing her hips up to meet his. Her fingers clutched the hard muscles of his shoulders as he braced himself above her and drove into her. And then he came along with a powerful thrust and a groan that filled her with triumph and sent her over the edge once again.

She kept him tight in her hold as his stiff body relaxed against her. He collapsed, rolling her with him so they were still connected, still linked by the hardness inside her. Unbelievably she was moving again, rousing him before he'd even yielded.

"I don't want to wake up," he said in her ear as he kissed her once more.

Neither did she. Not ever.

Chapter Eleven

"SEAN, I'll be coming with my switch if you make me call you once more. I swear it, man or no', I'll be after your arse with it."

The shrill voice penetrated the dark cocoon that held Danni tight. She frowned and tried to block it out. Some part of her knew that to acknowledge it would be disaster; some part of her never wanted to acknowledge anything again but the comforting blank of her slumbering mind. She burrowed deeper in the covers, entranced by the languorous feel of her limbs, the sated weight of her body.

"So it's royalty you think you are. Well, that's it then," the voice warned. "I'm off to find me switch." The dire words were punctuated by forceful steps pounding down the hall.

Down the hall?

Danni's eyes flew open and she was awake in an instant. Someone was walking down her hall? Who? Who was in her house? From behind her, a deep voice said, "Pay her no mind. She's always threatening me with the switch."

Danni sat bolt upright, aware of too many things at once. The room she slept in was unfamiliar. Small and sparse, the walls were painted a dull white that was relieved only by the large and gruesome crucifixion hanging over the bed. A window on the far wall had pale gray curtains that showed glimmers of a dawning and overcast sky through the gaps at the middle.

A rough wood chest of drawers with a mirror hanging above it stood directly opposite. On its surface, a small framed picture perched atop a lacy doily. And there was Jesus again, this time with a halo and long, flowing golden brown hair. The bed she lay on was in the center of the third wall. It was narrow, with four posts and a down comforter that felt heavy and warm. Bean lay curled at her feet, watching her with alert eyes that belied the dog's stillness.

And beside Danni, looking years younger in sleep, was Sean Ballagh.

She bounded out of the bed, realizing only as the cold air hit her skin that she wasn't wearing anything—not a stitch. A yelp burst from her lips as she snatched the comforter off the bed, rolling the little dog to her feet in a barking ball of fur as she pulled the length free. Sean jumped at the sounds and the sudden action, and was instantly standing, facing her from the other side of the bed. He wasn't wearing anything either.

As she stared in shock at his rumpled hair, his sleepy green eyes, his sculpted body, naked and beautiful—memories flooded in. The dream . . . the vision . . .

"My God, was that *real*?"

The changing expressions on his face told her he'd followed the same train of thought to the same, unbelievable end. They stared at one another for a stunned moment before once more, footsteps sounded in the hall. An instant later the door burst open. Sean reached for the sheet and tugged it around his waist as they faced the tiny woman standing on the threshold.

She had skin the color of bleached bone and eyes like blazing black fires. Her narrow shoulders were stiff and square above crossed arms and the line of her back was ramrod straight. She appeared to be anywhere between forty-five and sixty-five, but Danni couldn't have said which birthday loomed the closest. Her stance was somehow regal, but the lines bracketing her eyes and mouth spoke of a tired worldliness and tragic burdens. As promised, she clutched a thin, stripped branch in her hand.

"And sure look at the two of you acting like a wedding gives you leave to sleep the whole day through. Is it Buckingham Palace you're thinking I live?" She flicked a glance at Danni and then turned the full glare on Sean. "Now get some clothes on so you can eat. Yer uncle will not wait for you to dally with your woman. He'd just as soon throw you over with the hook and line."

Two things registered at once with Danni. First was Sean's expression. He stared at the tiny thunderbolt of a woman open-mouthed, neither responding nor moving. If it hadn't been so ironic, Danni would have said he looked like he'd seen a ghost. The second was the woman herself. *She* stared right back at him.

She *saw* him.

"Do you think I'm talking to hear myself?" she demanded. The black eyes swung to Danni. She eyed her from head to toe, taking in every detail in between. Self-consciously, Danni tucked the blanket tighter around her.

"And sure you've the look of one of our own." It sounded more accusation than compliment, but she didn't give Danni a chance to find out which was its intent. Bean jumped down from the bed and unbelievably, wagged her stubby tail right up to the woman's feet.

"A dog?" she exclaimed disdainfully. "Is that what this thing is trying to be? And hungry by my judgment. Another mouth to feed. Do you think I'm a fecking American with food bursting out my cupboards just for the having?" But she bent down and scratched Bean behind the ear. Bean tilted her head to give better access.

Straightening, the woman shook the switch in Sean's direction. "Are you not going to introduce me to your bride, then? Where are your manners, Sean? You were raised better than that."

Sean's mouth shut with a snap.

Lifting her chin, the woman gave Danni a sudden, beaming smile that transformed her wizened face. "I am this eejit's great-aunt Colleen Ballagh. And you would be?"

"Danni," she said, dry mouthed. "Danni Jones."

"Danni Ballagh now, so it is. You're marked as well as the rest of us, aren't you, then?"

There was no explanation for that comment either, but her eyes softened for just a moment and Danni saw something of lost splendor in them. Not too many years ago, this woman had been a beauty.

"Get dressed. Your things have yet to arrive, but from the sound of your travel, I imagine the bloody Protestants up north are tossin' them in the bogs by now. It's good the charity of the Sacred Heart lives in Ballyfionúir. Father Lawlor has provided some things to tide you over. You'll find them in the chest." She gave a sharp nod to the chest of drawers and mirror and then shot Bean a quick glance. "You come with me and I'll see what I've got to feed you."

Bean obeyed without question, stepping out as Colleen Ballagh shut the door with a force that rattled the picture of Jesus on the chest. Neither Sean nor Danni spoke as she strode down the hall.

In the shuddering silence, Danni tried to form a coherent question from the knot of confusion in her head. But all she managed was a choked, "What the hell?"

She stared at Sean, demanding he give her an answer she could comprehend, an explanation that would make this writhing chaos orderly. He hadn't moved a muscle since the door flung open, and he looked as if he'd been skewered by a hot poker. As she watched him, any hope that he'd explain this insanity vanished. He appeared at once hurt and bewildered. The second she understood, but the first was as perplexing as the situation.

"That was my grandmother," he murmured at last.

"Your great-aunt," Danni corrected him.

"No, she's my grandmother."

Putting aside for the moment everything else, Danni hauled the comforter tighter and moved around the bed. "Why did she say she was your great-aunt if she's your grandmother?"

"I can't be knowing that, can I?" he said sharply. "I don't know how we are here. It's like a dream. Like. . . ." He looked at her, and Danni knew he was thinking of the night, of touching her, of making love. But that *was* a dream—*Danni's* dream . . . wasn't it?

"Did you see that dog of yours?" Sean said. "It didn't even snarl at her."

His look of betrayal was almost funny, but the unfolding drama sapped any humor from the situation. Colleen's voice rose again, demanding that they get themselves to the kitchen before she was forced to wield the dreaded switch.

"She's not kidding this time," Sean said.

Numb, Danni moved to the window and pulled back the curtain. Outside the barest trace of a watery sun had yet to breach the horizon. The moon still glowed brightly, illuminating a patchwork of paddocks, hemmed by low stone walls and trimmed by a winding road that led up and out of the valley. She could see the steep and craggy drop to the ocean, which surrounded the island like a natural fortress. She craned her neck and looked to where the sea met the skyline in a silky blur of gray and green.

Sean came to stand behind her. She felt the heat of him as he bent forward to look out the window. A weak part of her wanted to lean back against him, to let him hold her and reassure her. But which was more crazy she didn't know—wanting reassurance from a ghost or thinking that touching him would bring anything so mild as comfort.

"Where are we?" she whispered, knowing the answer but needing to hear it all the same.

"Ballyfionúir."

It was impossible of course. Too impossible to even consider.

"Why did she call me your bride?"

Sean gave her a look filled with incredulous anger. "Why did she call you anything? Why are we here? *How* are we here?"

"We're not," Danni said with more confidence than she felt. "This is a just a dream. I'm imagining it."

"The hell you are."

He moved to the chest and yanked open a drawer. Inside were two neat stacks of clothes. He pulled out a flannel button-down, gray trousers, and a white undershirt. In the next drawer he found socks and a pack of boxers still wrapped in plastic. He tossed all of it on the bed.

Still too stunned to move, she watched him rip open the plastic and remove a pair of boxers before dropping the sheet. His back flexed as he bent and pulled them on. He was such a big man, trimmed of any fat and layered with muscle from broad shoulders to long legs. Everything solid and strong and masculine in between. She remembered how it felt to have all that power, all that hard sinew against her own soft curves, and the memory made her insides feel hot and liquid. She couldn't tear her eyes away as he tugged a white T-shirt over his head and down his chest.

He was zipping his pants when he glanced back and caught her staring. For a moment something moved in his eyes, something possessive, hungry, and burning. Something that lured her more than the white ghost of her vision. She thought of the dream that had seduced her in the night, of the words he'd whispered in her ear, of his mouth moving over every inch of her skin, telling her what he wanted, whispering what he would do to her. Freeing her of the inhibitions that had always held her back before. The memory made her entire body flush.

Quickly she shuffled past him to the chest. In the top drawer, two new toothbrushes sat beside a pack of panties and a simple white bra. Below she found a pair of light blue polyester pants and a bulky beige cable-knit sweater. She'd be making quite the fashion statement, she thought wryly. She kept the blanket around her as she fumbled into the undergarments, letting it drop as she pulled on the sweater. It hung to midthigh, and the pants were so snug she had to take deep breath to get them fastened. They fit like spandex and she was glad the sweater hid the way they clung to her hips and thighs.

While she dressed, her thoughts ran the gamut of possibilities as to what had happened. What was happening still.

She didn't know if it had been a dream, what she'd done with Sean last night. Awake, her body lacked the languid feel of satisfaction she'd had in the netherworld of slumber. There was no telltale scent lingering on her skin, no sore muscles, no intimate aching. It had to have been a dream—a very vivid, memorable dream that she couldn't shake. Every time she glanced at Sean, she thought of his mouth on her skin, his hands trailing down her body, touching her like no one had ever touched her before.

Nervous, she faced Sean across the gulf of the narrow bed. She read in his expression the same disorientated anxiety she felt on her own.

"Do you remember anything, Sean? About how we got here?"

He shook his head. "We were in your kitchen—and then it felt like we were falling."

She nodded. "Before that you gave me the necklace . . ."

Remembering, she reached for it. It still hung around her neck, but there was no prickling, stinging sensation when she touched it.

"She made it sound like we had luggage that was lost," Danni murmured. "I don't remember packing. I don't remember anything but—"

She stopped, yet it seemed he heard her thoughts anyway. She didn't remember anything but his body hot against her own, moving, sliding, making her want to scream: go faster, harder, slower, longer . . . His eyes followed the trail his hands had blazed and as impossible as it was, she knew he remembered, too. If it was dream, they'd shared it.

"I'm as confused by this as you, Danni," he said, the deep smoke of his voice low and gruff. "However impossible, here we are. Let us go downstairs before she drags us by our ears. Maybe we'll make some sense of it in time."

Neither of them believed it, but silently she tossed him one of the toothbrushes and followed him out of the room. The hall was narrow and painted the same grayed white of the bedroom. There were three doors that opened off of it. The first led to a smaller bedroom with a bed, a rocking chair, and an armoire inside. The other to a room nearly identical. The last was a bathroom. Sean waited while she used it first.

Marveling at the ancient plumbing, she washed her hands and face, brushed her hair and teeth. She rinsed before finally gathering the nerve to look into the mirror. The same Danni who'd gazed back yesterday waited in the reflection. But there was something different about her now. Something wild in her eyes, in the color that stained her cheeks.

This isn't real, she mouthed to her image.

The hell it isn't, her eyes shouted back.

She waited outside the door for Sean and then followed him through the hall. A delicious aroma wafted up and teased them down the short flight of stairs. Whatever was for breakfast smelled heavenly.

The first floor of the house had a sitting room with a fireplace, a sofa, and two chairs. There was a small television with rabbit ears in the corner. It looked to be at least twenty years old with a rotary dial and two knobs for changing channels and adjusting the picture. A tall clock in the corner chimed the half hour, and Danni was shocked to see that it was only four thirty. What in the world were they expected to do so early in the morning?

A half wall with spindly wooden rails divided the room from a dining area, packed with a long battered table, eight chairs, and a china cabinet. Sean didn't give her time to examine the set, but it was obviously old and cherished. The wood gleamed with a deep, burnished sheen, and the cabinet displayed a full assortment of crystal and china.

A doorway led through to a good-sized kitchen done in linoleum and papered with yellowed flowers. Open shelving covered only by a gauzy curtain of lavender took up the far wall. Through the diaphanous fabric, Danni saw a few store-bought canned goods among rows of jarred preserves, fruits, and vegetables. Something that looked suspiciously like pig feet floated in a pink brown fluid.

Colleen stood at the stove, stirring potatoes that smelled greasy and completely wonderful. Bean sat at her feet with a watchful and adoring look on her face. Every few minutes Colleen would flip a sliced potato out of the skillet to a paper towel where it would cool before she tossed it to Bean, who caught it like a show dog in the circus.

Sean moved to a kettle on a back burner and poured two mugs of tea. He added milk to one and several spoonfuls of sugar to another.

"There now," Colleen scolded, reaching over to crack his knuckles with her wooden spoon when he tried for another scoop of sugar. "Do you think I'm the fecking queen of England?"

Sean's head jerked up and he stared at his great-aunt—*grandmother*, Danni corrected herself—with even more surprise than when she'd burst into the bedroom. Danni had the sense that this was a ritual, something that had played out with them before—Sean shoveling sugar into his mug and Colleen admonishing him with a smack of her spoon—and that somehow this familiarity had done what the *being*, what the *seeing*, had not.

His surprise faded into a look of such gentle affection that Danni's heart contracted with it. The harsh lines of his face smoothed into a faint grin, his dimples no more than a hint in the stubble on his cheeks. He leaned over and kissed his grandmother's brow. "It's not the fecking queen I think you are, Nana. It's a beauty star from Hollywood."

To Danni's surprise, Colleen blushed like a young girl.

"It's good for me eyes to see you, Sean," she said softly.

Sean handed Danni the tea with milk. Gratefully she held it between her palms and breathed in the aroma. "How did you know the way I like it?" she asked, taking a sip.

His mouth quirked at the corner, and his gaze traveled slowly over her face and shoulders, leaving a hot tingle in its wake and a warm flush on her entire body. The Sean she'd awakened with was even more disarming than the one who'd appeared at her door. She felt wary and defenseless, jittery and needy in his presence. She stared determinedly into her cup, refusing to respond to the demand she felt in his eyes.

"What kind of husband would he be if he didna know the way his wife takes her tea?" Colleen asked, piling two plates with shiny potatoes speckled with course pepper, thick square sausages, and heaping mounds of fluffy scrambled eggs. Beside the eggs was a circle of something that looked like a sausage, but not one Danni had ever eaten before. Colleen put a plate in the center of the table, filled with hunks of fried bread. Danni's arteries hardened just looking at the feast, but her stomach growled eagerly.

Colleen stood beside them, waiting impatiently for them to lift their forks. Danni took a bite of eggs and smiled in appreciation as she chewed. Colleen beamed and waited for Sean to do the same.

Sean picked up his fork and stared at the mound of food on his plate. He took a bite of potatoes then stilled, holding it in his mouth as his eyes closed for a moment. Slowly he chewed and swallowed. The look on his face made Danni wonder what Colleen put in the potatoes. She took a bite and found them delicious, but nothing that warranted the ecstasy she read in Sean's expression as he tucked into his breakfast, savoring each bite and following it quickly with another. Like he was starved.

No. Like it had been years since he'd really tasted food . . .

"What are these?" Danni asked, tearing her eyes from that almost sexual look of pleasure on his face and pointing to the round sausagelike things on her plate.

"Do you not know?" Colleen asked, surprised. "White pudding, that is." At Danni's blank look, she explained, "That'll be pork, bread, spices of course, oatmeal, and onion. Would you rather the black pudding? Sean doesn't yearn after it as much as the white, but I have both."

"Oh no, this is fine. I just wondered."

Colleen eyed her for a moment, as if seeking deception. Then, satisfied, she returned to her skillet. At her feet, Bean gave a small, apologetic woof.

"And sure I know you're there, little beastie. Wait your turn like a lady, though," Colleen said.

The back door opened, and a man and an adolescent boy strolled in with a damp breeze and murky predawn light. Thinking the morning could not be any weirder, Danni felt all the breath leave her lungs as the pair turned their eyes to her and Sean.

The man stood tall, as tall as Sean and every bit as fit. He wore his hair military short, and the cut gave the graying strands at his temples a salt-and-pepper look. His eyes were a bluer green than Sean's, but the face was put together in the same strong, square manner. He was the man she'd seen pictured in the article she'd read. The man accused of killing her family.

Sean's father.

The shock of seeing him nearly equaled the one she'd awakened to. This man had killed himself twenty years ago. Was he another ghost? Were *all of them* spirits in this alter-reality? If so, what did that make Danni?

Before she could even begin to think through it, to reason it out, the boy beside him drew her attention and shock trembled through her body. Wanting to turn away, wanting to run away, Danni stared at him.

Next to the solid mass of his father, the teenager looked like a willow sprouting tall with shoots of young growth. He was narrow and lean, corded like a thick rope, but a boy still by the breadth of his shoulders and the soft fuzz on his chin. The eyes though . . . The eyes that stared at her with a combination of banked resentment, bright curiosity, and masculine appreciation . . . Those were Sean's eyes.

The slow tick of the clock grated against her stretched nerves as thoughts burst in her mind like explosions. It was Sean as he'd looked in the photo from the article she'd read. Sean, as a boy. Sean, twenty years ago.

"Say morning to yer cousin Sean and his wife, Danni," Colleen told Niall and his teenaged son. Continuing with her baffling ruse about their relationship to one another, Colleen turned to the grown-up Sean and said, "This strapping lad would be your third cousin on your father's side, named Sean Michael for your great-grandda, same as you are. He answers to Michael, though. A blessing that is, or we'd be tongue-tied with the two of you Seans running about." She ruffled the boy's hair to his obvious annoyance and then looked at Sean's father. "And this fine man is your second cousin, Niall."

Danni felt sick as the scene played out in front of her. In a realm of impossibility, this latest twist put her over the edge. The young

Sean—Michael as he was called—and his father were standing in front of them looking exactly as they had twenty years ago. At the same time, grown-up Sean was sitting right beside her. And none of them could possibly be real.

Except, before they'd awakened here, people only looked through Sean without ever seeing him. Suddenly these people—these people who couldn't exist—were looking right at him. And not with fear, misgiving, or confusion. But with curiosity. With friendliness.

Like the ghost she knew him to be, Sean was pale and solemn as he came to his feet. What he was thinking, she didn't know, but he stood unsteady and silent as he faced his father and, impossibly, the young version of himself.

Niall said, "Sure and Mum's been talking about your coming for weeks. You'd think you were the Sainted Peter for all her fuss. Michael has been eager enough to meet you, that's a certainty." Niall gave Michael a playful punch in the arm as he spoke. The boy shot him a poisonous look and swatted his hand away.

"You've come from America, haven't you?" Michael said, speaking to Sean, but staring at Danni like she was something he'd dreamed up for his viewing pleasure.

She felt awkward and exposed beneath the steady eyes that were so like Sean's. *Not just* like *Sean's*, she whispered to herself. *One and the same.* In twenty years, those very eyes would be turning her bones to putty. She frowned at an idea embedded in that elusive thought. In twenty years . . . In twenty years . . . She pulled in a deep breath. It couldn't be . . . but in some twisted way it made sense. Crazy, but . . . was it possible they could have awakened in a different time as well as a different place? Could they have opened their eyes twenty years *in their own past?*

"Yes, we've come from America," Sean answered, still standing, still looking like he'd been carved of stone.

"And you're a Yank, true enough?" This to Danni.

"I guess. I mean, yes," Danni answered. They were all staring at her and waiting with expectant expressions. Feeling like an idiot, she mumbled, "I live in Arizona."

"Lived you mean," Niall said cheerfully. "You're settling here, isn't that the way of it?"

"Do you know any Indians?" Michael asked.

"Uh, well yes, there are quite a few Native Americans who live in Arizona."

She reached for Sean's hand, wanting to squeeze it hard. Wanting to ask him what was going on. Why did they all act like it was perfectly natural for Danni and Sean to be here—and married on top of it? How could these people have anticipated their appearance? How could they be here at all?

She stopped herself before she went any further. Only madness waited down that avenue of pursuit.

Michael took the seat to her right, his attention riveted. Colleen shuffled over with more plates of food. "Don't be pestering her now. She's trying to eat her breakfast."

Eating suddenly felt like an impossible chore, but Danni dutifully lifted her fork again. Sean sank to his seat on her left. He couldn't seem to stop staring at his father and grandmother, but he avoided looking at Michael at all. She couldn't blame him, couldn't even imagine what must be going on in his head, through his mind.

Michael picked up his fork and began shoveling food into his mouth.

"Look at you, eating like ye was starved. It's ashamed, I am," Colleen said, with a quick slap to the back of the boy's head. "Are you thinking the dog will have your breakfast if you doona wolf it yerself?"

"What dog?" he asked around a mouthful of potatoes.

"Why the one sitting on the floor, you blind fool," Niall said.

Though the words were delivered with a teasing tone and a gentle smile, Michael's head snapped up and he glared at his father. A deep, angry flush stained his face.

"The wee beastie came with your cousin's bride," Colleen said, tossing a cooled slice of potato to Bean. Bean jumped and snapped it from the air. When had she learned to do that?

Michael frowned and then glanced back at Danni. "Why did you get such an ugly dog?" he asked.

His expression so perfectly mirrored one his grown-up counterpart had used that for a moment, Danni was too unnerved to speak. "I don't think she's ugly," she managed at last.

"Aye, isn't that the way of it?" Colleen agreed, nodding over her skillet. "It's not the bones that are beautiful but the flesh on the shoulders."

With equally baffled expressions, all heads swiveled to take in Bean's little body.

"'Tis a truth," Niall interjected. "'Tis a truth."

"Are you messing with me?" Michael said, frowning. "Dogs don't have shoulders."

Niall grinned, but continued to demolish his breakfast, only pausing between bites for a gulp of tea. After he'd swallowed the last bit of sausage, he wiped his mouth on his napkin, leaned back, and let his gaze move from Danni to Sean and back again.

"You've a look of the Irish, Danni," he said. "Have you family from here?"

Danni cast an uncertain glance at Sean, not sure how to answer that one. Honesty didn't seem the right response given the situation. Sean sat rigid and silent beside her, offering no help. On her right, Michael finished his eggs and scrutinized her with guarded eyes. Being sandwiched between the two of them gave Danni a shaky sense of vertigo.

"Maybe up north?" Niall asked, still shifting his eyes between them, now with a bit more curiosity.

"Who doesn't have family from Ireland?" Sean finally answered.

Niall laughed and leaned forward to wink at Danni. "We're a fertile lot, that much I'll give you. Self-preservation is what we call it. If they won't take us for what we are, what choice have we but to breed ourselves in?"

Danni managed a weak smile.

"Ah, you're a lovely thing and a jealous man I am," he said, grinning as he pushed himself to his feet. "So, cousin, are you ready?"

As Sean looked up with dull surprise, there came a knock at the front door.

It was like being in the center of a tornado, Danni thought. Everything spinning around them so fast they didn't stand a chance of understanding it before it was gone. She wanted to stand up and shout, "Stop everything," but of course she couldn't, wouldn't.

Colleen wiped her hands on her apron as she crossed through to open the front door. Danni could hear the warm smile in her tone when she greeted her visitor.

"Good morning, Mrs. Colleen," a lilting childish voice answered her.

"And how are you this morning, my wee missy?"

"I'm very fine and thank you for asking, Mrs. Colleen. My mother sent me to ask Mr. Ballagh if he thinks there will be salmon today."

"God willing there will be," Niall called from the kitchen.

"That is good, because cook has a new recipe to try and would like it for tonight."

"And so she'll have it," Niall said, standing to take his plate to the counter.

"Thank you."

The girl's voice was young and sweet and it drew Danni like an elusive melody. While Sean stood awkwardly at her side—Danni swiveled to face the door.

"My mum says you have company from America. Is that so?" the girl asked.

Colleen and the young girl stood in profile, facing each other with a formality that would have struck Danni as odd if she hadn't suspected it was a game the two played. The girl wore a big T-shirt with a bright pattern of pink flowers on it over pale blue stirrup pants that ended with white high-top sneakers. Her hair hung to her shoulders in a feathered style that would be considered big in today's fashion of smooth, flat hair.

Danni took a step closer, frowning, wondering why the child seemed so familiar.

"Well, yes," Colleen was saying in the same formal singsong she'd used to greet the girl. "We do have guests from America. Would you like to meet them?"

"Oh, very much, thank you."

Colleen held out her hand and the young girl took it. Danni watched them approach, feeling each step closer like a drumming in her head. She stumbled back, toppling her chair, aware of it only when Sean moved to right it. But she didn't turn around. Couldn't pry her gaze from the child's face. As if from a distance, she felt his arm circle her waist and pull her against his solid warmth.

"Easy now," he breathed against her ear.

But she couldn't take it easy. As she drank in the site of the shiny golden-brown, the clear gray eyes, the sprinkle of freckles across the child's nose, a feeling beyond shock locked her jaw and knees in the same instant. Like a statue, she stood frozen as the girl stopped in front of her and smiled up with heartbreaking innocence.

"Sean, Danni, this little darling is Miss Dáirinn MacGrath. Dáirinn, this is my great-nephew and his new wife."

"From America?" she asked.

"True enough," Colleen answered.

Danni couldn't speak. Couldn't think. It had been one thing to see Sean mirrored in the boy, but this. . . . She hadn't expected it. She couldn't comprehend it. How could she be standing here, facing *herself* for God's sake? Dáirinn's smile wavered and she shuffled her feet, obviously uncomfortable under Danni's distraught gaze. But what could Danni do? What could she say?

"It's a pleasure to meet you," Sean said, reaching down to shake the girl's hand. Dáirinn gave a relieved sigh and her smile brightened again.

"I'm pleased to meet you, too," Dáirinn said with a small curtsy.

Danni had a sudden, vivid memory of practicing the curtsy in front of an ornate mirror in her mother's room. She'd made her brother bow to her while she rehearsed it over and over and over . . .

From outside, there came a brief blast of horn. "I have to go," Dáirinn said, but her puzzled gaze lingered on Danni's face a moment longer before she gave a small wave and turned to the door.

"Tell your mum I'll save the best of my catch for her," Niall said before she stepped out.

Like a puppy on a leash, Danni trailed behind, silently stopping on the porch to watch her go. A car idled in front of the house with a woman sitting in the driver's seat. She stared out the windshield, deep in thought. There was a boy in the backseat, nose pressed to the window. *Her brother . . .*

Dáirinn opened the car door and the woman in the driver's seat jumped—startled by the sound. Dáirinn said something to her as she climbed in the car, and the woman turned her head to stare at the people on the porch with such intensity, Danni wondered at her thoughts. Her eyes seemed to snag on Niall and hold for a long moment before moving on to study Danni and Colleen. Then, as if realizing they were all staring back, she pasted a smile on her face and the strangely focused look vanished. As the car began to pull away from the house, she leaned out of the open window and waved good-bye.

Numb, Danni lifted her hand in response and watched with stunned disbelief as her mother drove away.

Chapter Twelve

For reasons Danni didn't know and couldn't find a way to ask, Sean was supposed to assist Niall and Michael on his fishing boat this morning while Danni was expected to work at the MacGrath house. It seemed the arrangements had been made weeks before, when Colleen had first received word that Danni and Sean were coming to Ballyfionúir. How or from whom the notice of their eminent arrival had been delivered, she didn't say. Again, Danni found it impossible to ask without revealing the reason for her ignorance. And wouldn't that go over well?

Could you explain why I'm here, because the last thing I remember, I was standing in my kitchen lusting after your dead grandson . . . .

She watched Sean finish his tea and prepare to leave with panic burning in her stomach. How was this happening? How could it be that one minute she was safely in her own home and now she was here in a time and place of strangers where Sean's was the only familiar face?

And how could he even consider leaving her to go off and do God knew what on his father's boat? Couldn't he see the absurdity of it? However they'd come to be here, this wasn't their time, their place, and the only thing they should be doing was trying to figure out how to get back. But even as she seethed over the situation, Sean was rising and following his father and his younger self outside. He truly intended to keep up this pretense.

Her throat tightened as the door clapped shut, and she rushed forward, pushing it open and stepping onto the porch. She heard Colleen come out behind her, and Danni had an instant mental picture of the older woman grabbing her and wrestling her to the dirt. Danni quickly moved away before she had the chance.

A part of Danni recognized the hysteria rising up inside her, understood that it was the being *left behind* that triggered it. Abandoned. Deserted among strangers in a strange place—just as she'd been as a child. But the cold logic of it did nothing to dispel her fear or ease the tightness gripping her chest so hard she couldn't breathe.

"Sean, wait," she said, hating how weak and frightened her voice sounded.

You're not five anymore, Danni. And Sean was the last person she should be counting on to save her. She squared her shoulders and lifted her chin—silently scolding herself for the way it wobbled.

Sean turned at the sound of her voice. For a moment, he simply stared at her and her fear ratcheted up a notch. He didn't understand—how could he? She was a fool to think anyone could grasp how this scenario mirrored her darkest nightmares, her worst fears. He was probably glad to be going—would be running to leave her behind if he thought he could get away with it.

But instead, he backtracked to her side, took her hand in the strong warmth of his own, and pulled her a few steps away where the corner of the house shielded them from their rapt audience.

Close to tears, Danni bit hard on her lip and stared at her feet. *You're not five anymore, you're not five anymore, you're not . . .*

He lifted her chin, forcing her to look into those deep-sea eyes.

"Are you just going to *go?*" she demanded, but her voice betrayed her with a painful hitch.

"What would you have me do?" he said softly. "Until we figure out what's happened, we can only play along. Whatever this is, it's no dream."

"I know that, but . . ."

She couldn't finish. Couldn't risk bursting into tears as she tried to find the words that would aptly describe her fear.

"But what, Danni? What is it?"

"I just thought we should stick together, in case . . ." In case one of them was suddenly zapped back to reality. In case it wasn't her. In case it was.

Sean seemed to hear her unspoken thoughts. Gently, he cupped her face with his hands and pressed his lips to her forehead.

"Don't be afraid," he murmured, his deep voice soft against her skin.

"I'm not afraid. It just makes sense that we shouldn't separate. . . ."

"It does. But if we huddle together like children afraid of a storm, won't there be questions? Questions we haven't a way to answer."

"So what?"

"So what if we can't find our way back? What if we are stuck here for some time? What will we do when everyone thinks we are daft? I've seen what happens to the lunatics. It isn't pretty."

Danni's eyes widened. She wanted to ask what he meant by that. Did they torture them or lock them up in the asylums of Dickens?

"But what if . . ."

"Don't be worrying that I'll not be back, Danni. I won't leave you here."

That he'd guessed the source of her fear so accurately unnerved and unraveled her at once. She felt transparent and ridiculous as she stood there shaking in her shoes over the thought of being left alone.

"I mean what I say. I won't be leaving you." He waited for her to acknowledge that simple statement. She gave a small, unconvincing nod. "Just go with Nana and do whatever it is she tells you to do—sounds as though you'll be scrubbing floors for the day. Whatever it is, you can handle it. It's all just minutes to pass until the world rights again, isn't it? And maybe you'll learn something that can help us make sense of this mess while you're there."

It was true, everything he said. But it didn't make it better.

"I'll be returning before suppertime and then we'll sort it out. I'll be back for you. I swear it."

He didn't intend to dump her in this strange place and leave her to survive on her own, she lectured herself sternly. He'd be back. He swore it.

"Do you hear me?" he asked.

She nodded again.

"Do you trust me?"

She nodded once more, realizing she meant it even as surprise rolled over her. She did trust him, crazy as it might be, and Sean rewarded her for it with a dimpled smile that knocked her heart sideways. It was teasing and serious all at the same time, as complex and mystifying as the man behind it and the emotions churning inside her.

"Danni," he said softly. "Have you any idea why it is they've been expecting us?"

"No. I thought maybe you did."

He shook his head. "I don't understand it all. It's like she had it all planned out, isn't it though? Calling herself my great-aunt, introducing me as a cousin. . . ."

"I know. All I can think is that we must be here for a reason."

"And what reason would that be?"

"It's twenty years ago, Sean. Don't you get that? And if it's *exactly* twenty years ago, then in a couple of days my mother is going to vanish with me and my brother, your dad is going to kill himself and . . ."

And someone is going to dump your young body in an unmarked grave with mine. . . .

She stilled, thinking of it with an aching pain in her chest. If the vision had been true, then Danni—adult Danni—would be buried in the same grave as Michael. "Are you coming, cousin?" Niall called politely.

"One minute, please," he answered. To Danni, he said, "I need to go. Are you going to be all right?"

"Yes." But it was a lie and there was no way she could hide it. She wanted to cling to him and beg him not to leave her. She steeled herself not to do it.

Gently he tilted her chin so he could see her eyes.

"G'wan with you now," Colleen chided. "Give her a kiss, Sean, and be off. Herself won't be going farther than the MacGrath house while you're gone."

Danni caught her breath as he lowered his head to do as he was told. His lips brushed hers in a shock of sensation that traveled her skin like a shiver. When he'd kissed her before it had been exciting and hot, but now . . . his touch was electric. It galvanized her and wiped her mind clean of everything but responding.

The kiss began as a gentle comfort, but her hands were on his chest, her fingers curling into his shirt to hold him as her mouth opened beneath his and she kissed him back. She did cling then, urgently. Begging that he not stop, not step away. Not leave her. He made a deep sound, a groan of reluctance as he pulled back, and despite her fears, despite her worries, she felt the flare of victory when she saw the hunger in his eyes.

"We'll finish this later," he promised softly. "It will not be long before I'm with you again."

There was so much said—so much *un*said—in the simple statement that she could only nod in answer. But which Sean would be returning to her? The ghost or the man? And where would *she* be when he walked through her door once more? Back home in her lonely little house? Or here in this world she didn't understand?

With a feeling that surpassed panic, she watched as he followed his father and Michael down a winding path toward the sea. As they went, other men stepped from the haphazard scattering of bright yellow and garish pink homes into the gray light of dawn. Niall introduced his cousin and welcomes rang out as the others greeted him with laughter and good-natured banter.

As Sean shook hands with them, she saw him glance back at

her, and though she was too far to see it, she knew there was surprise in his eyes. He was as baffled by their friendliness as he was by his own confusion. What had he been thinking all these years when others looked right through him? Had he somehow managed to block it out, pretend it was common to be ignored? But now that he was faced with true normal behavior, he couldn't help but see the difference.

"Come. Come now," Colleen urged. "Ye'll be seeing the lad again when he's worked his day. You're due at the big house and you'll not want to be late."

Turning, Colleen looked at Bean who waited dutifully just inside the door. What was it with Danni's dog and Sean's grandmother? "Don't be jumping on me furniture, now," she said gently and Bean immediately signaled her understanding by curling up on the worn rag-braid rug by the door.

Amazed, Danni could do no less than obey as well when Colleen ushered her away.

Chapter Thirteen

As they walked, Colleen chattered about Ballyfionúir, Ballaghs, and MacGraths. In a morning that had been no less than astonishing, hearing Colleen speak of Danni's family history—of the heritage she'd never imagined—took Danni to a whole new level of amazement. She was from an old family—an ancient family, if Colleen was to be believed. And they'd all been living here on the Isle of Fennore while Danni had been on the other side of the world unaware they existed at all. Listening helped assuage her fear and calm the aching part of her that wanted to turn and run back the way Sean had gone.

But beneath the chatter, Danni had the sense that Colleen was playacting. Pretending to be a grandmotherly figure when in fact she had a set agenda. She was leading Danni to something—something other than the "day job" at the MacGrath house. Wary, Danni followed, aware that each step might be the one that plunged her deeper into obscurity. Aware that in this time and place, the point of no return was literal. There was a ticking clock over her head, one set to countdown to that grave she'd seen in her vision.

"Now Fia MacGrath is an outsider," Colleen told Danni with a sad shake of her head. "From County Cork, they say, God bless her.

And didn't it cause such an uproar when Cathán brought her home and declared she was his wife? Many a girl *and* her mother cried into her pillow that night. 'Beauty won't make the pot boil,' 'tis what they told each other. But Fia is a good-hearted woman, and not a one of them can deny the luck she brought with her. Isn't Cathán living like a king these days? Soon enough they'll be blowing fecking trumpets when he passes them on the road."

"He's rich, then?"

"Or doing a fine job of pretending. 'Twasn't always the way of things before Fia, though. After himself passed on there were gray days a plenty."

"Himself?"

"Well, Brion MacGrath of course. Cathán's father. He kept the island afloat with just his will alone. With him gone, didn't the taxes come due and the storms hit hard, as if just waiting for the master to be out? And wasn't poor Cathán always in the field when the luck was on the road?"

Colleen nodded in agreement with herself. Danni wasn't quite certain what she'd be agreeing with so she stayed quiet.

"And poor Mary O'Leary's son, swept out to sea and not found for a week. Washed up in Kinsale, he did. He looked like a rotten sausage burstin' from his skin after seven days and nights in the ocean."

Danni grimaced at the visual. "That's terrible."

"Ah, sure it is. It was a wonder there was as much left of him as they found. A wonder it was, I told Mary. She was just glad to have anything at all to pour into the casket for Father Lawlor to bless."

Danni was glad Colleen didn't seem to expect a response to that.

"But isn't it good fortune for you and your husband to be coming at just this time? With Cathán living like a king and the jobs being handed out like potatoes in heaven? Work is not so easily had in Ballyfionúir as it is in America, or at least it wasn't before Cathán brought his bride home to his island."

As Colleen talked, they came upon a cluster of houses lining the rough dirt road and neighbors bustled out to meet them, sometimes waiting at their gates for their arrival. It was like a bell had been rung announcing visitor's hour, Danni thought, overwhelmed by the friendly faces and endless jabber. Had she and Colleen stopped for tea each time it was offered, they'd have been waterlogged and hours late to their destination.

"Isn't it grand to have visitors from America?" one freckled and plump woman told them. She had a baby on one hip and another tight by the hand. "A wonderful place, is America, though the streets are fearful I hear. But isn't that President Reagan a handsome man, God bless him. Did you know that Tom Quinn's niece moved to Detroit a few years back? Do you know it, Detroit? Is that near your Arizona, Danni?"

Danni smiled politely, not certain any of the lilting questions were actually meant to be answered.

"Unfortunate girl was killed by a Ford Bronco in a Mac-Donald's parking lot, poor lamb. Have you ever eaten at a Mac-Donald's, Danni?"

"Yes," she answered solemnly. "And if the Fords don't kill you, the fat will."

"Oh," the woman said, pulling her baby closer.

At last Colleen led Danni away and they left the houses behind. Danni couldn't help the glance over her shoulder. As she suspected, the neighbors had gathered to talk amongst themselves about the Arizona stranger.

"Not much excitement around here, is there?" Danni asked.

"You'd be surprised," Colleen answered.

They rounded the base of a hill and a new sight grabbed Danni's attention and made her pause. The ruins . . .

It had been a castle when it was whole and functional. Not the sparkling imagery of Cinderella, but something dark and solid, meant to withstand the blood rites that came with holding land and ruling people. From another time, another world, its existence seemed as unlikely as Danni's presence in its shadow.

Staring up at the weathered stone walls rising like an illusion from a sunken flat terrain at the top of a massive knoll, Danni shivered. In the vision, she'd stood in the valley with the remains hunkering behind her, perched so precariously close to the steep crag that a strong wind might have pushed them over into the angry and churning sea.

Gray and crumbling, the ramparts were a weak sentry to the elements of time. Pieces of walls and fragments of corners stood within the remains of a broken enclosure. Rough-hewn stones fit like puzzle pieces up the round tower to a gaping hole where once a roof had been. Danni could hear the wind whistle through the sculpted openings and collapsing partitions that gave only a hint as to the shape and size of the original structure. The sound made her cold to the bone.

The road she and Colleen walked split here, with one branch twisting up to the desecrated ruins and the remainder of what must have been an enormous gateway; the other circumvented the hill and curled back around it. She turned, putting the fortress behind her, and took in the valley below that she'd seen so vividly in the visions. There in the distance were the flocks of grazing sheep, the sharp rocks of the sea cliff, and the emerald carpet that held it all together. Beyond and to the right where the path twisted, she saw the house—a beautiful Victorian creation that looked the anomaly it was with the decaying castle for a neighbor.

She scanned the horizon again, looking for the last piece of the puzzling vision. Then she saw it. There, made smaller by the distance, was the arrangement of three enormous stones, balancing a fourth like a giant house of cards.

Wishing she could stop herself, she imagined the steps she'd taken in the vision—reliving the anxious fear now as she gauged the interval between ancient dolmen and the unmarked hole where she'd seen her own body laying beside the boy—Michael, she now knew. Her eyes were drawn inexorably to the very spot where she and the grown-up Sean had stood. To the grave . . . a grave that had yet to be dug.

Ahead, Colleen slowed and turned to face her. "It's all right now, child," she said. "'Twill be all right now."

Her voice pulled Danni's gaze away from that awful place. She stared at Colleen, hearing those murmured words echo in her mind.

'Twill be all right now.

"What do you mean?" Danni asked, hurrying to catch up.

Colleen started walking again at a brisk pace. Danni repeated the question, refusing to let her ignore it.

"Oh, just that ye look so distraught. Sure and yer missing your husband as a young bride should."

She sounded sincere enough, but all the years of Danni's childhood when she'd been shuffled from home to home never knowing what to expect had taught her to read people. And she knew without doubt that there'd been more behind Colleen's comment than thoughts of Danni missing "her husband."

An uneasy suspicion filled Danni as she fell into step beside Colleen. "Do you know who I am, Colleen?" Danni asked softly. The question stiffened the older woman's back, but didn't slow her. After talking nonstop thus far, Colleen was suddenly silent. Danni watched her face, noting how her mouth tightened and her brows drew close. "Do you? Know who I am?"

"Oh aye," Colleen answered with feigned gaiety. "You are Danni Ballagh from America and welcome you are to our island."

Danni reached out and grabbed Colleen's arm, halting her quick steps. Colleen tried to look past her, but Danni wouldn't let her go, wouldn't move until the older woman met her eyes. Silently they studied one another.

Age had taken a toll on Colleen that exceeded the mere passage of years. It mapped a trail on her face, sagged the narrow shoulders. But it had also put steel in her spine. She exhaled and gave a weary nod. The sweet little grandma persona left with the pent-up breath. In its place stood a woman who'd endured and survived a life Danni could only guess at.

"Aye, I know," Colleen said at last. "But you, child, I'd wager you've not a clue about who you might be."

Danni sensed they'd reached the brink Colleen had been leading her to all along and though it suddenly frightened her, retreat would only delay the inevitable. Feeling the truth of Colleen's simple statement settle down low in her gut, Danni asked, "Do you know why I'm here? Did you bring me?"

"Me?" Colleen shook her head. "You think me a conjurer who can wave a wand and make a thing so?"

"Are you?"

Colleen grinned, but shook her head. "It's a fair enough question, though. A question our people have been asked before."

"*Our* people?"

"The people of Ballyfionúir. Is it just another island you think you've come to?"

"Could you be a little more cryptic?"

Colleen scowled. "I've no liking for that tone you're using, miss."

Embarrassed, Danni dropped her gaze to her feet and took a deep breath. "I just want a straight answer, Colleen. That's all."

"That's all, is it? Well, there are no straight answers. Not here anyway. Not where you're concerned. Ballyfionúir isn't just a village. This," she said, gesturing wide with her arms. "*This* is the Isle of Fennore. Do you know what that means?"

Danni shook her head.

"Well then, I'll tell you. The very earth beneath your feet is steeped in lore. Sure and the rest of Ireland talks of fairy hills and what have you, but here the magic is in the air we breathe. In the land and the skies, in sea and the stars. It's real and it's a part of us. Only a fool denies it."

Danni wanted to scoff, she wanted to rail at this slight woman who toyed with her. She'd asked for a straight answer and Colleen was giving her *magic*. Did she think Danni was an idiot? That she would believe such utter *crap*? But even as anger built inside her, Danni could hear Sean's deep, smoky voice telling her that magic was no joking matter in Ballyfionúir, and she knew Colleen was serious. She meant what she said.

Colleen tilted her head and let out a snort of wry laughter. "You're a fine one, aren't you now? Here you stand yet still you don't believe.

Is that what living in America does to a person? Makes them doubt what's right before their eyes?"

Maybe it was. She'd dismissed Sean's statement the same way she wanted to dismiss Colleen's. She'd thought him crazy. No, she corrected herself, she'd thought him dead. Who did that make the crazy one?

Danni swallowed and said, "So you did bring us here."

"No," Colleen answered and started walking again.

"But . . ." Danni sputtered, following. "But Sean told me you see things."

"Did he now?" she said, black eyes flashing. "I've not known him to tell tales before."

"How have you known him to speak at all, Colleen? He's—" Danni stopped herself before she said, *He's a ghost.* Because he wasn't one—yet. But in a few nights that would change. There wasn't a way to gauge what Colleen knew about Sean, though. About things that hadn't happened yet. Danni had to be careful what she blurted out. "Do you see things Colleen?"

"Aye. And doesn't everyone? Or is it blind you think I am?"

"Did you see me? Before we came?"

The question was too direct to dodge, and they both knew it. Danni waited tensely for her answer, but Colleen's lips thinned stubbornly.

"How did we get here?" Danni insisted.

"It's a burden, knowing what may come," she said so softly Danni had to lean in to hear. "Knowing what, but never why. Never how or even if."

Warily, Danni nodded. "Never everything."

"Aye," Colleen said, understanding. "Never everything. Isn't that the worst of it? Like a cyclone, the sight is. It goes though and picks and chooses what it will skip and what it will unearth." Colleen stopped and faced the valley. "It was years ago that I saw you for the first time," she murmured. "Right there, you stood next to my Sean."

Danni didn't have to look to know she pointed to the grave.

"Why . . ." Danni began hesitantly. "I mean, when you saw me . . . what did I want?"

Colleen cocked her head to the side and stared at her curiously. "Want is it? Is that how it is for you, then, when you see?"

"I think so. I haven't—I didn't have visions for a long time. I don't remember how they were before. Until I saw Sean in my kitchen, I didn't remember them at all. But I knew what it was as soon as I saw him. And I knew he was there for a reason."

"And what is it that my Sean would be wanting from you?"

"I don't know yet."

"Do you not?"

The question was baited, but Danni didn't bite. After a moment, Colleen sighed and glanced away. "I can't say what you wanted in the visions. Could be you just wanted me to know you. To recognize you when you finally came." She paused, eyed Danni, and then went on. "It's not the answer you're looking for, but it's all I can tell you. I saw your coming and I have waited, waited and hoped. Now here you are."

"Hoped for what?" Danni asked.

"For you to put things right, of course."

"What . . . why would you think *I* could put things right?"

Colleen's smile was again grandmotherly, only now the façade was gone. There was love and tenderness in the look. She reached out and patted Danni's arm.

"Time will answer that one, lamb."

Colleen started back down the trail, talking as she went. Danni hurried to follow.

"I was just sixteen when I came to Ballyfionúir," Colleen said. "It was a different time, then. Back in those days, the house had just been built and the family was very powerful, very wealthy—before the hard times, you understand. It's the whole island they own, did you know that? It's gifted, the lands we live on."

She nodded to herself for a moment and then went on. "Me mum, she had the sight herself but she never took to it well, and in the end it drove her crazy."

"Your mother had it?" Danni said, surprised.

"Oh aye. You'll find it's not uncommon on the Isle of Fennore. I'll never understand why my mother left to live in Dublin, among people who were different. We're all family here, one way or another. And the gift, it's hereditary. Did you not know it?"

"No, I didn't."

"Ah, and now you do." Colleen looked blatantly satisfied by this revelation. Danni wondered if her own expression was as transparent, if Colleen could see just how lost Danni felt.

"The sight drove my mother to her death and left me penniless, living on the streets. I knew she had family here so I came to Ballyfionúir hoping they'd take me in. My uncle gave me a home and got me a job in the big house. It was a fine job and it's lucky I felt to have it. On the streets the offers of employment were not so honorable, if you get my meaning."

Danni nodded. She could imagine the propositions that a young and beautiful Colleen might have garnered. She must have been stunning in her youth. The kind of girl men longed to possess . . .

"When I first came, there were some living here that could recall the days when a MacGrath had always been laird of Ballyfionúir."

"Laird? Is that like a king?"

"I suppose in some ways, but more like the head of the family. MacGrath land. MacGrath people. Brion MacGrath was of the old ways, and the people, they loved him. No one on his island went hungry nor did a one of them shirk their responsibilities. We took care of his island and he took care of us. You see how it was?"

"Codependent," Danni said.

"*Coda* what?" she asked, frowning. "'Tis no matter. I see you understand what I am saying. I'd lived here some months before I met Brion MacGrath. I remember it like it was yesterday. I was at his house, upstairs changing the sheets, thinking I was alone as I worked and sang when suddenly himself is standing on the other side of the bed dressed only in a towel and smelling of his bath. He smiled at me and told me I had the voice of a lark. I had never seen a man without his clothes. Me mum was a widow and a stricter woman I've never met. She didn't go for shenanigans."

Colleen took a breath and went on with the manner of someone taking a plunge into icy waters. "I tried to hurry from the room, but Brion, he tells me to go on about my business. 'I'll be no bother,' says he, and took himself to the changing room, leaving the door as wide as the gates to heaven. I didn't look, but I knew from the sounds that he was dressing, right in front of me. I finished with the bed and hurried out. Later I was scolded for the sloppy job I'd done."

Danni tried to interrupt then, wanting to ask why Colleen was spinning this tale. What did it have to do with Danni or Sean and how they'd come here?

But sensing Danni's intentions, Colleen said, "I've a point, child. Let me get to it in my own way." Danni nodded and Colleen went on. "After that, Brion MacGrath, he was everywhere I was. At first I thought it was chance that brought him to my path. But I soon came to see it for what it was. Even so, I didn't realize what it meant until he found me one day out in the pastures, by yonder dolmen. It was my special place to sit and think. It was where I had the sight for the first time."

"You didn't see things when you were a child?"

"No," she said, looking surprised by the question. "Not as a child." Something that crossed superstitious fear with curiosity gleamed from her eyes as she stared at Danni. "I've never heard of anyone who had the sight as a child. Until you, that is."

Danni felt goose bumps rise on her arms. "What did you see, when you were sitting there?" she asked, nodding at the dolmen.

"It was Brion, come for me. I was swollen with child and he declaring his love. In it, he said he'd be done with his wife and he'd take me as the mistress of Ballyfionúir."

Danni's mouth was dry and her nerves felt raw. If this was true— if any of this was true—then Colleen was talking about Danni's grandfather.

"He was going to divorce his wife?"

"No, lass. 'Twas no divorce in Ireland those days. That was a sin against God and government alike."

"Then how . . ."

"'Twas my very question. *How?* And then I saw, in this dream of mine, what he meant to do. He meant to kill her."

"Wait," Danni said, holding up her hand. "He wouldn't divorce her because that would be a sin, but killing her wasn't?"

"Oh sure and it was. But who would say it was him? Who would dare point a finger at the man who allowed food to be put on the table? Would be like cutting off your own hand."

Danni shook her head, unable to comprehend life with such loyalty and dependence.

"Brion was loved in this town and none would stand against him. All of this I saw. And then lo and behold, there's the man himself, the real man, casting his shadow over me. I wanted to run, but I couldn't move. 'You know I'll have you,' says he. And I did know."

"You didn't try to stop it?"

"Are ye not hearing me, child? Yes, I tried to stop it. I didna want to play my part in it all. I swear to y' though, the man had some of the gift himself, for he seemed to read what I thought. He kissed me until my young toes curled right into my shoes. A kiss that was as sinful as the man, it was. And then he left me on my own to think about it. I would not be female if I'd been able to forget such a kiss. My first, it was and from a man who knew how to give it."

"Why are you telling me this, Colleen?" Danni asked at last, watching the obvious discomfort in the older woman's face and bearing. She didn't like relating this story, but for some reason, she felt compelled.

"You asked me if I know who you are. I do. Listen so you can know, too." She paused, took a deep breath, and continued. "He said he'd have me for his own and have me he did, though I kept him at bay for longer than most women could have. He was beautiful, Brion MacGrath, and he was gentle. I began to think that he loved me. I think it still. But that was a terrible thing, for I'd seen what he had not yet thought of—I'd seen where this love would lead us. When I realized I was with child, a horror it was for me to face. I'd fooled myself into thinking it would not happen the way I'd seen. But there

I was with a bastard child in me and no place to go but back to the filthy streets."

"What did you do?"

"It was his wife who offered me salvation."

"His wife?"

"Aye. She called me to her rooms, and I knew exactly why. I knew she'd seen us or heard the servants' gossip. I was shamed to my soul as I stood in front of her. She said that I was one of many women before and would be just one of many after where her husband was concerned. She said that he would lose interest and cast me aside, and I would be destitute. She'd seen it before; she'd see it again. And then she offered me a choice—a terrible choice." Colleen's voice faltered for a moment. "She told me that for years she'd tried to conceive and had been unblessed. She needed a child to keep her husband with her. I knew what it cost for her to tell me this, though she spoke like she was made of stone, all pride and disdain.

"She told me she knew of a man in Limerick—where she herself was from. This man's wife had died in childbirth. He needed a woman to care for his babe and his home. If I would get myself with Brion's child, she would see me wed to this man before I showed my condition. She would pretend to be pregnant whilst I was carrying and when my time came, I was to send for her and we would say the baby had come dead. She would take it home, though, and say she'd delivered it herself."

"What? That would never work," Danni said. "What about the doctor? What about the body of your stillborn? How would you explain there being no body? And what about the man you married? Surely he would know? Not to mention her husband—how did she think she could fake being pregnant to him?"

"She'd thought of it all down to the last detail—the very last detail. My new husband and I were to be given a house with land enough to work. A few sheep. A cow. A boat, for my husband-to-be was a fisherman. A life of respectability. She built us a past with a means to explain all we had. If I did as she asked, I would have a future of sorts. If I did not, she would have me exposed as an adulteress, and she would tell the authorities that I'd been stealing from the family. My aunt and uncle who'd taken me in would be disgraced along with me. I could see all too clearly what lay down that road. If she succeeded, I would be jailed, my child taken away. If she failed, Brion would have her murdered, and I would wear the stain of her blood on my heart for the rest of my life—and everyone in Bally-fionúir would know of it. I'd already lived on the streets once in my young life and I couldn't face going back there. It was no choice for a girl to make, but I could see that I hadn't an option. I was carrying Brion's child already and alone I had nothing to offer it. I agreed to her proposition."

Danni's eyes widened as she waited for the next words.

"And so I married a man with a kind soul and a needy babe who'd also made a pact with the devil, for he lacked all choice as well. In that day, you didn't turn down a house and property for principle. Michael took me as his wife, but he knew what I had bargained and he found me disgraceful. As for Brion's missus, she played her role beautifully. She blossomed with her pregnancy, and the town cheered her along. I turned Brion away, and she gathered him up like a bouquet with her promises of a baby. But she did not get all she wanted, for he never stopped loving me."

Colleen shook her head sadly. "I was small and able to hide my baby until I was far along while she exaggerated her condition so that when I reached my nine months. Most thought I was only five or six and she was ready to deliver any day. She played midwife to me and I think in her heart she hoped I would die giving birth. She and Michael both. But I delivered a squalling baby as if I'd done it a hundred times before. I put that bundle of humanity to my breast just once, and then she took him away, leaving me alone with the pains of my milk and another woman's child to fill the place in my heart my own babe had left. If I'd been a stronger woman, I'd have killed myself."

Danni stopped walking as those trailing words washed over her. She grappled with the reality of Colleen's story, not able to bring it into focus. Not able to process what Colleen was saying.

Colleen went on. "It was the worst kind of torture, watching her and Brion parade my baby in their pushcart. But the Blessed Jesus has a wry wit and a cruel sense of irony. Though they looked the happy family, Brion never could adjust himself to the miraculous birth, and he was convinced that Marga had been unfaithful to him. That I had never conceived by him only made him more convinced that he was not able to father a child."

"But the baby was his," Danni said, "and yours."

Colleen nodded, watching her. And suddenly Danni comprehended what her mind had refused to grasp before.

"Wait a minute. Are you saying . . . ?"

"Aye, lass, I am. Your father was my baby."

"But that would make you . . ."

Colleen nodded. "Yes it would."

"But what about Niall?"

"Michael's babe by his dead wife, though he is the child of my heart as well."

Danni couldn't stop the shaky breath of relief. Not her uncle, then. No blood relation between her and Sean.

"So now you know who you are and where you come from," Colleen said softly. "You are a child of the Ballagh and MacGrath lines—families whose histories go back to a time before memory."

Danni frowned, overwhelmed by all she'd learned but bothered by what she sensed was still missing from Colleen's story. "Why did you feel it important to tell me all this? There's more to it than just knowing who my grandparents are, isn't there?"

"Aye, that's true enough. You asked how you came to be here. To answer that, you must know that your bloodline is filled with people who have seen the future, people who have changed their own destiny."

"And how have they done that?" Danni demanded.

"That I cannot tell you, child. If I knew how it was done, wouldn't I do it myself?"

"You brought me here because you think I can change—"

"I told you," Colleen snapped. "It was not I who brought you. But here you are, all the same. It is up to you to figure out how and why. Only you can know what to do next."

"You make it sound like I should have all the answers. I woke up this morning and it was twenty years ago. How the hell should I know what to do with that?"

"Something inside you knows it already, Dáirinn MacGrath. I suggest you figure out what part of you it is and start listening to what it has to say. There are worse places to awaken than your past."

Chapter Fourteen

THE MacGrath house seemed to be in a state of chaos when Colleen led Danni through the gates. Men worked the grounds, planting flowers in the beds, pulling weeds, trimming trees, mowing the lawn that stretched like a carpet amongst the wild pastures. Others were at work washing the many windows and cleaning out gutters, putting a fresh coat of yellow paint on the outside walls.

Colleen took her around to the back door, and following, Danni was suddenly swamped with an aching loneliness. She didn't want to go inside—didn't want to step into the house where she'd spent her first five years and face the fact that she had no memory of it. She couldn't do it—not alone. She wished Sean were here with her, ridiculous as that sounded even to herself. He would hold her hand, though. He would share his warmth, his strength.

But he wasn't here and Danni had no choice but to follow Colleen inside.

The back door opened onto a bright, cheery kitchen with pale blue walls and tiled counters. Stonework to the right framed an old coal-burning oven and made the massive room seem cozy and welcoming. In front of it, a long pine table with benches tucked beneath it and chairs on either end sat empty but shining from a fresh polish. Behind it was a pine coffer with a round lock centered in front.

Danni glanced away and then quickly back as recognition hit her. The chest wasn't such an unusual piece, and yet she knew she'd seen that particular one before—in the vision when her mother had shown Danni the Book of Fennore.

But this wasn't the same room she'd seen it in.

Danni swallowed hard, unconsciously bracing herself for that terrible hum, the fecund odor, the oozing blood.

"Are you ill, child?" Colleen asked, touching Danni's arm and bringing her back to the sunny kitchen.

"I'm fine," Danni answered, pulling her gaze from the coffer.

A window over the sink looked out at the gardens and breath-taking ruins. Bundled spices dangled from strings around it, and a rack suspended by chains from the ceiling displayed an assortment of copper kettles and pans above it. The kitchen smelled of cinnamon and some other sweet and elusive aroma she didn't recognize, yet deep within her it stoked a memory and made her feel simultaneously comforted and bereft.

Two women stood at the counter with a pile of dough between them. They chattered and laughed as they rolled it into ping-pong sized balls and stuffed them with a dark sticky concoction Danni couldn't begin to guess at. Another woman entered from a swinging door that probably led to a dining room. She carried a tray of crystal stemware to the sink for washing.

As Danni and Colleen hovered just inside, a stout woman with black hair and sharp blue eyes approached. Danni caught her breath as another bite of recognition nipped at her memory and associated the woman with tasty treats and warm hugs.

Colleen beamed at her and said, "Morning to you Bronagh. This is Danni Ballagh, come all the way from America to help you this fine day. A blessing she'll be. Danni, this fine woman is Bronagh Dougherty."

"*Danni*? And isn't that a strange name for a woman to be calling herself? Is it your father you're named for?"

"I don't know," Danni answered honestly.

"Well, no matter." She shifted her attention to Colleen. "'Tis late you are. I'm not of a mind to call that a blessing."

"Oh no and sorry we are for that. But the poor child dinna arrive until the wee hours of the morn, and without a bit of sleep, she'd have been no use to you. She'll not be late again."

Bronagh's tight mouth eased and a quirk of her lips told Danni she might be smiling, but it pained her. "Well then, I'll let it go this time. Have you had your breakfast?"

Danni opened her mouth to say, "Yes," but Colleen cut her off.

"Well, what do you take me for not to feed the girl a hot meal for breakfast?" she demanded.

"No offense meant, but Americans are peculiar. How am I to know if she only ate just enough to smooth your feathers? Could be she's still longing for a decent meal."

"And what would you be knowing about the peculiarities of the fecking Americans' appetites?" Colleen challenged.

"Are you thinking you're the only one who knows Americans?" Bronagh sniffed and put her nose in the air. Two steps took her to a shelf beside the oven that was packed with cookbooks. "My own brother was recently in the lovely state of Nebraska and didn't he bring me both of these lovely American recipe books?"

With much ado she held up a red and white checked Betty Crocker cookbook in one hand and *Omaha's Best Recipes*, with "potlucks for any occasion," in the other. Danni hid a smirk, wondering if Bronagh had ever cracked the cover on that one.

She quickly interrupted before Colleen could spit out the words she seemed ready to choke on. "Thank you, Mrs. Dougherty, but Colleen made a delicious breakfast this morning. I couldn't eat another bite."

Bronagh's painful smile tightened. Colleen gave Danni a loving pat on the arm.

"Well then, I supposed there's nothing for it but to put you to work. Are you one for the kitchens?"

As a matter of fact, Danni loved to cook. When she'd lived with

Yvonne, Danni had made all their meals. But once she'd moved into her own home, cooking had lost its appeal. She and Bean made do with fast food or simple fare most nights. Occasionally she'd dig out her own cookbooks and surprise Yvonne with a home-cooked meal. When she got back home, Danni silently promised herself, she'd plan something special. *If* she got back home . . .

Danni blinked, finding both Colleen and Bronagh staring at her expectantly. Even the women at the high table had paused to listen.

Danni cleared her throat. "I'm no Rachael Ray, but I can hold my own."

They all exchanged looks at that, and Danni cursed herself. Of course they wouldn't know who Rachael Ray was. Had she even been born yet?

"Well, I'm off myself. I'll be leaving our Danni in your care," Colleen said to Bronagh.

Leaving? Why had Danni thought Colleen was to work here as well? She bit hard on the inside of her lip, tamping down the panic she'd only just managed to quell after Sean's departure.

Colleen patted her again and was gone in a moment. Bronagh didn't give her a chance to indulge in her worries, though. She put Danni to work preparing a baked herring after laboriously going over the recipe with her not once, but three times. It seemed dinners at the MacGrath house were no casual affair of late, and tomorrow there'd be a special dinner in honor of the twins' fifth birthday.

Danni swallowed hard but tried to keep her composure as she thought of that. In addition to the fish, Bronagh told Danni with pride, there would be crisp salad with tomatoes and watercress, seafood chowder, colcannon with curly kale and spring onions—which Danni gathered from the recipe was an Irish mashed potato dish—asparagus braised in butter, leek bacon tarts, and black pudding. Bronagh would top it off with rhubarb tarts for dessert.

Rhubarb . . . that was the other scent in the kitchen . . .

While she worked, Danni dwelled on all Colleen had told her. Colleen was her grandmother. Her fraternal grandmother. Colleen hadn't answered her when she'd asked if she knew why Danni and

Sean were there. Maybe she didn't know. But her final words still hummed in Danni's head. Why did she think Danni knew the answer to this riddle she'd stumbled into?

There are worse places to awaken than your past. . . .

Lost in thought, Danni didn't notice the kitchen door open until Bronagh said, "Why good morning to you Mrs. MacGrath. And how can I be helping you?"

Danni's gaze snapped up. There, smiling in her direction, was Danni's mother.

"Oh, don't trouble yourself with me, Bronagh," Fia MacGrath said with a shy smile. "I only wanted to see what was about here."

Danni stared as Fia moved from place to place, eyeing the creations in progress, tasting the rhubarb concoction for the tarts, and exclaiming that Bronagh had outdone herself. Bronagh beamed with pride.

Up close, Fia was lovely in an ethereal way. She moved with grace and poise, as if she'd never known a reason to rush or a cause to fret. Her features were delicate: a small nose, perfectly arched brows, wide eyes, and long lashes. She wore little makeup, just coral lipstick that accented her full mouth and a light dusting of blusher on her pale cheeks. Her clothes were crisp and pressed, and when she went by, Danni caught a whiff of a rich cologne, light but exotic. It caught her unaware and brought a rush of memory—a feeling of contentment, of happiness. She imagined herself as a child, breathing that wonderful scent.

"Have you everything under control, then?" she asked after she'd finished her perusal of the kitchen.

"Oh aye, just like clockwork."

"Then I wondered"—Fia began looking suddenly very young and unsure—"might I borrow one of your girls for an hour or so?"

Bronagh's mouth tightened, but she said pleasantly enough, "Sure and they're your girls, are they not? You may take one or all."

"I wouldn't want to cause you trouble if—"

"Not to worry. Take Danni, she's not much help to me anyway. American."

Stung, Danni looked at Bronagh, but there was no malice on the stout woman's face, and Danni realized she was just trying to put her mother at ease. Fia didn't just look young; she couldn't be older than twenty-two or twenty-three. A few years younger than Danni was now.

Fia smiled. "Thank you, Bronagh."

Nervous at the thought of being alone with her mother—being *older* than her mother—Danni washed and dried her hands before following Fia out of the room. Obviously, Fia felt just as uncomfortable alone with Danni, although for different reasons. Danni didn't think she was accustomed to directing servants or asking for anyone to do her bidding. She kept glancing over her shoulder, as if to reassure herself that Danni still followed. Each time she gave a breathy little laugh that revealed how uneasy she was. The sophisticated clothes it seemed were just a ruse, armor for a battle she had no weapons to fight.

An awkward silence followed them into a foyer with graying walls and massive portraits. A large settle dominated one wall and Danni couldn't help pausing to admire it.

Fia waited, looking at her with curiosity. "Sorry," Danni said. "It's just, I have a thing for antiques."

"Really? And is that one?"

"Well, yes. It's a settle. They were used for seating in the great halls. And see how it opens?" She demonstrated by lifting the bench seat. "Inside was used as a guest bed."

Fia smiled. "But it's so short."

True, though the settle was a good five feet long, it would have made a short and narrow bed. "Remember back then, your host would have thought nothing of putting you in bed with five or six others—so having to pull your knees up when you slept wasn't really such an inconvenience."

"How d'you know that?"

Danni shrugged. "My . . . mother is a history buff."

Fia looked intrigued as she started walking again. "My mother liked old things, too—as long as they were expensive. We were very poor when I was young, before. . . ." The nervous laugh tittered out. "Before my grandmother died and we inherited. After that, she wouldn't have anything old in the house unless it was worth its weight in gold. Not even the quilts that had been handed down for generations. I'm still sad when I think of her throwing them in the bin."

The very idea of it made Danni's stomach hurt, but she kept quiet as she followed her mother up a staircase to a long hall.

"After mum died, I brought some of her pieces here."

"Was the coffer in the kitchen hers?" Danni asked.

"The what?"

"The chest, in the kitchen."

"Oh yes."

Fia opened a door toward the end of the hall and led Danni into an enormous chamber with walls painted dark red, complemented by a burnished gold chair rail which ran chest-high all around it. A gorgeous king-sized half-tester canopy bed with a shiny satin comforter should have dominated the room—but it was too spacious for that. Not even the mahogany armoire gleaming by the window, the elegant marble fireplace—with hearth stretching at least eight feet—or the twin glass cabinets facing off from the corners could come close to filling it. Even with the damask-covered settee and two matching chairs cozied up to the fire, there was enough open space to harbor an echo. Though exquisite, the room was overwhelming. Her mother looked like a child playing grown-up in it.

"Like a museum, isn't it?" Fia said with an embarrassed smile. "Cathán's—my husband's—latest project. He had the wall torn out of the nursery and made it all one room. I don't know why we need so much space, but he seems to like it."

"It's beautiful."

She shrugged and indicated the grouping of chairs and settee. A basket sat on the floor between them. "I'm making costumes for the twins," she said. "They've been invited to a costume party in a few days. Dáirinn wants to be a kitten and Rory wants to be a horse."

The words struck a chord somewhere in Danni, and a memory

exploded in her mind. She saw her five-year-old self racing into this very room, squealing with delight in her orange-and-white striped kitty-cat costume. She'd meowed like a maniac while Rory whinnied and snorted at her side.

"Are you all right?" Fia asked.

"Yes," Danni answered, though it was far from true. Her stomach had flipped and knotted, and her insides felt watery.

"Please sit down while I show you the costumes." Fia bent and pulled the first from the basket. "I just need help with the final touches. I'll never get them done in time for the party on my own."

"I'm not very good with a needle," Danni confessed.

Fia grinned. "Can you hold one?" Danni nodded. "Then you'll do fine."

She indicated one of the chairs and handed Danni a metal box filled with pink and white sequins. "Dáirinn wants her kitty to wear a tutu," she said, still grinning. "I need you to add some sequins to the ruffle."

Fia shook out the costume to show her, and Danni felt another rush of memory as she watched. Fia'd made the body of it from a soft white fabric with hand-sewn stripes of orange felt around it. A gauzy pink skirt flounced at the waist, and Danni was swamped with thoughts of how it had felt to twirl like a ballerina as she swiped the air with her kitten paws and meowed at the top of her lungs.

Unaware of the turmoil she'd caused, Fia threaded a needle and showed Danni how to attach the sequins to the ruffle.

Next she pulled out the black and white horse costume she'd made for Rory. Another flash, another exploding memory of Danni and her brother racing down the hall, laughing in their joy. Fia had added a yarn mane and tail to the costume and now she was working on the long muzzle and hooves. From the tufts of orange fur that came to a point at the kitty's ears to the black mane of the stallion, Fia hadn't missed a detail in either costume.

"These are amazing," Danni said.

Fia smiled with pleasure. "Thank you. I've been working on them for weeks. You'd be surprised how difficult it is to sew a horse."

"I don't think I'd be surprised at all. I have to warn you, sewing on a button is a challenge to me."

"Don't worry, those don't need to be straight, and my little Dáirinn wouldn't notice a flaw if it bit her on the nose."

The love in those few words nearly wrenched a sob out of Danni. She fought to keep her composure though. It wouldn't do for Fia to think she was unstable.

They sat side by side for a few moments, neither speaking. Danni had a thousand questions, but they were all too personal to blurt out and so she sat, tongue-tied and miserable, as she attached the sequins to the tutu.

"Michael told me that you had only arrived from America last night. It's a long way to come. You must be exhausted," Fia said.

"I've got a bit of jetlag, nothing a Starbucks wouldn't cure."

Fia cocked her head and frowned. "A what?"

"Never mind," Danni said quickly, unsure if the coffee shops even existed yet.

Way to blend, Danni.

Fia's eyes were curious but she let it go. "Where in America did you live?" she asked instead.

"Arizona. Have you ever been to the States?"

"No. I've never been anywhere but here. My sister moved to California, though."

"Really? Where?"

It was Fia's turn to look like she'd stepped in it. A small, uneasy laugh bubbled out of her and she shook her head. "Oh, I can't remember the exact place. We don't talk much anymore."

"I'm lying" was practically stamped on her forehead, Danni thought. Why would she feel the need to fib about something like that? Danni wanted to press, but Fia's entire body had grown still as if she was testing the air for danger.

Looking back at the sequins, Danni said casually, "California is beautiful. I've been a couple of times. You know, to Disneyland and Hollywood. I always wanted to go to San Francisco, but never made it."

"I always wanted to travel, too. But then I met Cathán, and here I am."

There was a sad finality to her words. "You must have been very young when you married," Danni murmured.

"Seventeen. A hundred years ago, it feels like sometimes." She sighed, pulled a stitch, and then added another. "And you and your husband Sean, how did you meet?" she asked.

Caught off guard, Danni quickly averted her eyes. "We just kind of ran into each other one day."

"He's very handsome."

Dry-mouthed, Danni nodded. Didn't she know it. "What about you? How did you meet your husband?"

"As you say, we just kind of ran into each other one day. He says he took one look at me and knew he was in love. After that there was no stopping him until I was his."

She smiled, but her words sounded too bright. A happy story without the happiness.

"He must have swept you off your feet," Danni murmured, the little girl in her hoping it was true, that her mommy and daddy had fallen madly in love and would live happily ever after.

"Yes, he did that," Fia said, but a dark flush crept over her face. "I was pregnant with the twins before we married. I'm sure you've heard it already. I was quite the scandal of Ballyfionúir."

"Oh," Danni said. "No I hadn't . . . I mean . . ."

"It doesn't matter. I love my children." This said fiercely, almost angrily. As if she expected Danni to deny it. "I would do anything for them."

There was subtext in the last statement, but Danni couldn't decipher it. She watched her mother, watched the play of emotions on her face. Tried to understand what was going through her mind.

"What is your husband like?" Danni asked, and now it was she who sounded wistful. *Tell me about my daddy . . .*

"Oh, Cathán is very . . . determined. I remember thinking that the first time I met him. *My, what a determined man.* He never does anything halfway. I don't think he knows how." The nervous laugh came again. "When he was courting me, I felt like I was a goal, an objective. I mean that in a good way of course. He wanted me—loved me. Loves me, I mean to say."

There was something childlike about her mother. Something endearing and vulnerable, and Danni wanted to reach out and hug her. She seemed so unsure of herself and of her place in the world.

"He must be proud to have you for his wife," Danni said. "You have such a lovely family."

Fia nodded vehemently. "I do, don't I?"

"Before we came, I did some research on Ballyfionúir. I read that it's named after a spirit. The white ghost."

"Really? I didn't know that." Fia frowned, shifting uncomfortably.

Danni hoped her mother didn't have the need to tell too many lies in her life, because she was really bad at it.

"I looked it up on the web and there was a ton of information."

Fia was giving Danni that blank look again. Danni thought back. The web—dammit, she had to pay better attention to what she said. Danni hurried on before Fia could ask what *web* Danni referred to.

"There was also some interesting stuff about an old book. The Book of Fennore, I think it's called."

"Oh," Fia said with another of her shaky, nervous laughs. "It's quite a myth, isn't it?"

"It's not real?"

"A book that can change the world?" The nervous titter came in a burst. "I wouldn't think so."

"No, me either. But I wonder where the myth began."

"What d'you mean?" Fia asked, paling.

"Just that so many people think it's real. There was a picture of it."

"A picture you say?"

Danni nodded, noting the distress on Fia's face. "It looked like it was made of leather—but I don't think it was. Too black, too shiny, too slick. And there were jewels on it. And silver trim on the edges."

Fia stabbed herself with her needle and cursed. "Jesus feck. Look at that, I'm bleeding," she said, sucking her finger between her lips.

Just then the door to the bedroom opened, and a tall, heartbreakingly handsome man walked in. He had sparkling blue eyes, a strong, square jaw, and a wide smile. He wore athletic clothes covered with dirt and grass stains, and he smelled of sweat. Even so, the man was as good-looking as any movie star Danni had ever seen.

At his abrupt entrance, Fia's eyes widened and she jumped to her feet, the anxious titter escaping yet again. The man looked equally surprised and paused, looking from Fia's guilty face to Danni's shocked expression. Straight on, Danni noticed that his blue eyes didn't sparkle as much as they gleamed. She stared into them, the moment as surreal as it was uncomfortable. She should have known this meeting would come, but Danni was not prepared to be standing face-to-face with the man who was her father.

Chapter Fifteen

THE silence seemed to stretch and pull, curling up the edges of time and rolling them tight, until the three of them were trapped by it. Danni knew this was the same man she'd seen in the parking lot in front of Pandora's Box, even though it was impossible.

"Cathán, I didn't know you'd returned," Fia said at last. She cleared her throat and took her seat again. Her smile faltered, and there was a slight tremor in the hand that held her needle. Had it been there all along? Danni wasn't sure.

"Only just got here," Cathán MacGrath said with a wide smile that showed big, slightly crooked teeth. He was even more attractive in person than he'd been in the pictures. Still shots hadn't captured the sun-kissed strands of hair that glinted golden in the reddish blonde or the long lashes of the same shade. The glimpses in Arizona had been too brief to form a complete impression.

He moved gracefully, confidently, as he crossed to Fia's side. His eyes roved over her delicate features like a hungry wolf. It was a look that mixed love, lust, and possession in a way that would melt most any woman. Danni drank in the sight of him as he bent to kiss his wife's cheek. This was her father. The man who'd stood smiling in the pictures, who would be grieving in just over forty-eight hours for the loss of all he held dear.

"Ew," Fia laughed, waving a hand in front of her nose. "You're ripe as a pig."

He grinned, unabashed. "And the master of the hurling match," he proclaimed proudly.

Feeling her fixed stare, his eyes shifted to Danni. Flushing, she shut her mouth and tried to pretend like she hadn't been gawking, but he'd obviously caught her in the act. For a moment he simply studied her, his expression thoughtful. Danni held her breath, wondering what he saw in her. A part of her begged for recognition. The pain of being here with her parents but still being alone—a stranger—went too deep to bear.

"Who is this?" he asked.

Of course he hadn't recognized her—no more than her mother had. She couldn't really have seen him in Arizona—no matter how much he and that man resembled one another. As for any familial recognition, he'd have to be insane to make the leap from kitchen help to time travel daughter.

"This is Danni Ballagh," Fia answered. "She's helping me with the costumes. Danni, this disreputable character is my husband, Cathán MacGrath."

"Ballagh?" he asked, and the glittering eyes narrowed. "A relation?"

"Not to me, but to Niall," Fia said, confusing Danni.

"Is that so?" Cathán asked. "You're related to Niall, then?"

"Yes. Sean, my h-husband, is a second cousin I believe."

Cathán frowned. "Who is his father?"

Danni didn't have a clue, and his sudden scowl confused her even more.

"Don't interrogate the girl, Cathán," Fia said, saving Danni. "She's a great help. They just arrived from America."

Cathán turned that unhappy look to his wife. "Don't say it like they've come from fucking heaven."

"I didn't," she protested.

His sigh held a host of feelings—sorrow, hurt, disappointment, hope. He looked down for a moment, and then he lifted his face again. The smile was back on, filled with chagrin for his words. "No, just me being jealous I suppose. What can a poor Irish lad offer to a beautiful lass who yearns for America?"

Fia's forced laugh was beginning to feel like nails on a chalkboard. Danni wondered if she was the only one who noticed.

"Why, his heart, of course, my love," Fia murmured, looking down.

There was something needy in the way Cathán gazed at Fia, begging for it to be true. When Sean had told Danni the story of her mother disappearing, he'd said that some suspected marital discord between her parents. Clearly, her father adored her mother, but what was the weird vibe she picked up from Fia?

"Are you almost done, then?" Cathán asked. "I want you to myself for a bit before the children are home again."

Embarrassed, Danni began to fold the costume and beat a hasty retreat, but Fia halted her. "I am sorry, Cathán, but I must finish these before the party. I haven't the time just now."

"No?" he said, and there was a wistful note in his voice.

Danni wanted to snatch the horse costume from Fia's hands and insist she go with him, give him the few moments he so obviously longed for. There was shadowed sadness in Cathán's bright blue eyes, and something else. Something Danni didn't understand.

"And look at the time," Fia went on. "I'll be off for the children at half three anyway.

He let out a deep breath and shrugged. "That's it, then. There's nothing left for me but to shower away the pig smell, I suppose."

"'Tis the lye soap I'm fearing you'll need. A layer of skin may be required to rid it."

"And willing I'd be to give it if you'd come along and wash my unreachables," he countered.

"Cathán," Fia exclaimed with shock, giving Danni an embarrassed glance. Cathán's laughter held no apology as it followed him out of the room.

Chapter Sixteen

L ATER that afternoon, Danni was in the kitchen scrubbing what seemed a thousand pots and pans. The day had passed without a sense of time. It seemed to loop and swirl back on itself, stretching the moments of a lapsed hour into the slow tick of an entire day. It should have been weeks ago that she woke up naked in bed with Sean, his skin like hot satin down her back. The memory of his kisses, the power of his lovemaking as fresh in her mind as the morning chill in the air.

She turned on the faucet and pulled the spray nozzle over the deep sink to rinse the pot she'd just washed. The sound of water against the stainless steel reminded her of rain pelting against windows. There were no showers today, but as she rinsed the soap from the steel, the hollow patter of it came with scent and damp chill. Pausing with the pot still in her hands, she shut off the water and looked out the window over the sink. Sunshine spilled brightly over the garden and the valley beyond.

It wasn't raining, but she still heard the drops pelting the window and roof. Frowning, she looked around. It wasn't rain, no water was running, so what was making the sound?

Even as the question formed, she felt it. . . . The air. It was changing, thickening, pressing outward. She had only an instant to catch her breath before, like a puff of steam from a hissing iron, it turned.

Without warning she found herself outside in the dark of night. She stood on a cobbled street among stately homes set back behind ornamental gates. Long drives curved up to massive front doors. Porch lights glowed like beacons in the gloom. Above, a cast-iron sky rode low and heavy. Not a star twinkled, not a beam broke the churning layer of clouds.

Danni still held the pot she'd been rinsing, and she looked at it stupidly, as baffled by its presence here as she was by her own. There'd been no time to prepare—no way to know what she should have prepared for.

A light came on in the house ahead of her. It spilled a yellow beacon out to where she stood.

With no conscious decision made, she followed it. The streaming rain made crossing over the cobblestones treacherous and blurred her vision. She slipped and skidded up the drive, clutching the pot in one hand and waving the other for balance. She reached the house and pushed through the bushes to a window, where sheer curtains gave her a hazy view inside.

The room was large but crowded with heavy furniture. It seemed that every inch of wall had a table or chest pushed up against it or a massive painting hanging in the gap. Not one, but two sofas sat in front of a crackling fire with a heavy coffee table in between. Matching chairs of rich leather flanked them.

There were expensive candy dishes and figurines on the surfaces, some still in boxes, and shopping bags strewn on the floor. As if the occupants had just returned from making their purchases.

It took only a moment to realize where she was. Her mother had brought Danni here when she'd shown her the Book of Fennore in the vision. Danni leaned closer and peered through the window at the pine coffer pushed against the wall.

Just then three women entered the room. The first was older and portly, wearing too much makeup and jewelry. It hung from her earlobes, dangled around her throat, and glittered on every finger.

The other two were both young and slender, dressed in jeans and sweaters.

The eldest girl looked to be nineteen, maybe twenty. She wore ghoulish makeup with dark lines circling her eyes and garish pink lipstick on her mouth. The younger girl might have been seventeen. She was soft and curvy, a golden blonde with pale skin. She wore no makeup—she didn't need to. There was a quiet beauty about her, a serenity that seemed to glow from within.

She looked up and Danni swallowed hard. It was Fia. Her mother—her mother at seventeen . . .

The many lamps in the room cast the older woman's face in bright illumination, giving her prominent brow and deep-set eyes a sinister look as she stalked the room, fingering the things she saw with a possessive hunger. The girls watched her warily. They were uneasy. Danni could feel it. The absolute quiet in the room was unnatural, and it only served to magnify the disturbing atmosphere.

Danni was inside now, though she had no recollection of moving, of crossing through a threshold to enter the room. She simply found herself in the corner, dripping on the floor behind the group of women.

"It's time," the older woman said to no one in particular.

"Mum, no," Fia said. "Not tonight."

Fia's mother ignored her. She went to the coffer, unlocked it using a key she wore around her neck, and lifted something out. Danni braced herself, knowing what it was even before she saw the canvas wrapping.

The Book of Fennore.

Danni waited for the vibration, for the sickness that would spew from the evil thing once the canvas was removed. Fia's mother didn't hesitate to unveil the dreadful thing. She laid it bare and gazed upon it with a cold smile. The black of its cover seemed to gleam while absorbing any light that touched it. But it didn't move, didn't open as it had in Danni's vision before.

"Edel," the mother said, snapping her fingers at the older girl.

"Yes, Mum."

The reluctance with which the girl approached made Danni's stomach knot tight. Edel shuffled to her mother's side and turned. Danni stared into her face, noting the deep chocolate brown of her hair. Her eyes were the same rich color. They sparkled brightly in the muted light.

Against her will, Danni's feet shuffled closer. There was something strange about those eyes, something . . . Edel looked up then, as if she'd seen Danni stir. For a long, chilling moment their gazes locked.

Danni tried to recoil but she couldn't move now. Not an inch. Not a muscle. She could only stare back into something so cold, so bottomless it seemed to plunge for eternity. She managed to suck in a deep gulp of air and let it out. Her breath turned to frosty mist before her.

Those eyes, they weren't human.

"Come on now," the mother urged. "I'll not be changing my mind no matter how long you dally."

The icy, eerie eyes shifted and Danni slumped with relief.

"It won't fucking work," Edel snarled at her mother.

"Not with that surly attitude it won't."

Edel bared her teeth and snapped them together with a sharp click. Her mother sprang back a step. "Are you afraid Mum? Afraid of what I've become? You should be. Fia is, aren't you sister?"

"I've a mind to throw you on the street and let you beggar yourself," the mother said sharply.

"Fecking Christ, and who will do your bidding, then? Fia? Look at her? She's scairt."

Both of them turned to glare at Fia, stone-still as she perched on the edge of her seat. She looked small and lost, her big eyes swallowing her face. She was shaking her head, her lips moving silently. Her entire body trembled.

Edel made a sound of disgust.

"You'll go because I say you'll go," the mother warned, drawing herself to her full height.

"I'll go because *I've* a mind to leave this stinking hovel. I won't be coming back with the bacon, mum. I won't fucking be coming back at all."

The look of horror on the mother's face made Danni want to turn and run. She clutched the pot she held over her chest, like a shield.

Edel stepped forward deliberately, staring her mother in the eye as she'd done with Danni. Mesmerizing her with the deadly intent in their depths. Slowly Edel lifted her hand, holding it spread above the black cover of the Book. A smile teased her lips, a ghastly grin of terrible pleasure.

"I've a mind to see someplace new, haven't I? Someplace where it never rains, where there's sun all the fecking time."

California . . . Fia said she had a sister who lived in California . . .

"There's no such place," the mother snarled. "Now you do as I say, and no coming back without the money. All of it this time. You do that and you'll not have to go again."

The look on Edel's face made Fia gasp and Danni stumble back. She closed her eyes tight against it, not wanting to see what happened next. Not wanting to know why Edel's eyes were those of a monster.

Danni felt the hum before she heard it. Low and terrible it rose like a sonic boom, rattling the windowpanes, shaking her to the bone. "No," Danni whispered, eyes snapping open again, having to look no matter how she dreaded it.

Edel's hand hovered above the cover, and the Book began to jerk against the table. It rumbled and quaked, as if preparing to jump up to meet her flesh.

"No," Danni shouted this time.

The sound of her voice seemed to echo all around her. Edel's head turned and her gaze skimmed the room.

She'd heard it.

"No," Danni said again, though now she was unsure if it was a plea or a denial.

Edel's face pulled tight in a scowl as she peered from corner to corner. "Someone's here," she said.

The mother swung around and took in the room. "Go check the kitchen," she ordered Fia. Fia scurried to do as she'd been told. A few moments later she was back.

"There's no one. I checked upstairs as well."

Edel continued to flit her gaze around the room. Danni felt it slice over her and move on without pause. Then suddenly Edel stopped and stared at the window. Like puppets, Danni, the mother, and Fia all turned and looked, too.

There was a man standing on the other side. The rain, the darkness, the shock, all masked his face so he appeared as nothing more than a pale orb with dark blotches for features. He stepped back, disappearing before they could focus. The mother rushed to the window then to the door where she yanked it open and stepped onto the porch. Enraged, she let forth a string of crude and violent curses.

"He's gone," she said when she came back.

But who was he?

"Who was it?" Fia echoed Danni's thought with a tremulous voice.

"The fucking devil," Edel said. "Coming for the rest of my soul." Fia's eyes grew larger still and she made a sound of fear. "Watch and learn, little sister. Your soul is next."

The humming had receded but now it flared again like a stanza in an overture. It grew in size and volume, becoming a thrumming harmony that shredded Danni's will, churned her thoughts, and tormented her senses. She gripped the pot so hard her fingers ached. The need to run, to hide, to *escape* became overpowering but still she stood. Still she watched.

Edel turned back to the Book. Closing her eyes as if in prayer, she lowered her hand to the tooled black cover. For a moment nothing happened, and then the leather began to bubble like oil and her fingers began to sink into it. Danni was shaking so hard her teeth began to chatter.

Edel's hand disappeared up to her wrist in the blackness of the Book. Slowly she opened her eyes again, and the deep chocolate irises had turned the same midnight shade as the leather cover. They gleamed and sparkled like polished obsidian. Edel threw back her head and screamed—like the banshee. Like the winds of hell.

Danni dropped the pot, knew it clanged to the ground as she clapped her hands over her ears, and shut her eyes tight, trying to block out that horrible sound, the gruesome sight of Edel's hand immersed in the foulness of the Book. But her screams permeated the air, the walls, the moment. An endless shriek that she would hear for the rest of her life.

And then suddenly there was silence.

Afraid to look, afraid not to, Danni opened her eyes. Edel was gone. The Book was once more a mere object, unmoving on the table.

Fia and her mother shifted in place. Neither spoke. Neither searched for the missing girl. They just waited. Waited, as a gold clock on the mantle ticked away the seconds.

"Will she be back?" Fia asked.

The mother didn't answer. She just stayed where she was, watching the second hand circle the large black numbers on the clock.

A minute went by. Then another and another. Fia's shaking hands went to her mouth and covered it. Ten minutes, and still the mother hadn't moved. Twenty and then thirty.

"She's not coming back, is she?" Fia whispered.

Moving like a robot, the mother went to the Book, covered it in the canvas. Careful, Danni noted, not to touch it. Then she took it to the chest, stowed it, and locked the lid.

When she turned to Fia again, her face was hard and set. She stared at her remaining daughter for a long, troubling moment.

"Mum?" Fia said, and Danni felt her fear like cold and bony fingers clutching her throat.

"Tomorrow you'll go and bring the little bitch back," the mother said.

Chapter Seventeen

NIALL'S boat, the *Guillemot*, waited at the dock for them as it had a thousand other mornings of Sean's life. The boat was as much a part of his childhood as his family. His home.

It was a small skiff, rigged with poles and multiple lines for trolling. Weathered, but still seaworthy, it didn't look like much—and to the average fisherman, it probably wasn't. But Sean's father had never been an average fisherman. If fishing could be considered an art, his father would have been a revered master. The moment he stepped on board, Niall knew exactly where to point his bow and go—he had a damned beacon in his head that rarely failed to hone in on his catch, no easy task on the waters around the Isle of Fennore.

For centuries the unpredictable current, the treacherous undertow, and mean riptide had been chewing up the unwary sailor and spitting out the remains. Long after mainland Ireland had been settled and warred over, the Isle of Fennore remained untouched by man. Not even the Vikings were able to reach the shores. Legend said the seamen who'd finally made it to Fennore had a sixth sense without which they, too, would have died trying. Sean believed it and understood his father possessed perhaps even a seventh sense when it came to the dangerous sea.

Before Sean's mother and brother had died, before the disappearances of Fia MacGrath and her children, which came five years later, Niall was an admired man in Ballyfionúir. A sort of celebrity among fisherman. Sean's mother had found that laughable. "Famous for the stink of the sea," she'd snarl whenever someone would comment on it.

Time and distance seemed to have sharpened Sean's memory of his father, but mellowed it as well. Being with Niall again was like meeting a distant relative. He was familiar, and yet he was very much a stranger. For all the years since Niall's suicide, Sean had convinced himself that he hated his father. But now, standing beside Niall, Sean couldn't pretend that was true anymore. He could see Niall through eyes untainted by the black-and-white judgment of youth, and what he found was that his father was just a man. A man trying to do his best to raise a son who would never forgive him his mistakes.

Since the moment Niall had walked through the kitchen door, the knot of feelings inside Sean had begun to unravel, stretching out into a longing. An aching sense of loss.

For twenty years Sean had believed he'd never see his father again—how could he? The man was dead. But here Niall was, moving aboard the *Guillemot* like he'd done in nearly every memory Sean had of him. It was impossible for Sean not to see this as a second chance. A chance to reconcile all his bitter feelings to the joy he felt now as he watched this gentle giant commune with the deck beneath his feet and the lapping waters of the ocean.

All the anger and hate Sean had locked inside himself for so many years, all the rage he'd directed at the memory of his father . . . it was time to reexamine it. To compare the man to the memory. Sean blamed his father for the deaths of his mum and little brother even though the Garda Siochana had called it accidental and cleared Niall of any responsibility. Sean had seen it happen, though. He'd stood on the fringes of the erupting violence and watched his worst nightmare become a terrible reality.

His mother had been drunk the afternoon she died, but that was nothing new. Usually Sean and his brother would come home from school to find her passed out beside an overflowing ashtray and an empty bottle of Connemara. But that afternoon she'd been awake and on a tear, ranting at Sean's father, talking crazy like she so often did. Niall had tried to calm her, but she'd have none of it.

She'd charged Niall with a butcher knife in her hand, meaning to wound him if not kill him. But Sean's little brother had tried to stop her, and the knife had found him first.

What came next was still a painful and jumbled blur to Sean. And yet parts of it played with excruciating slowness . . . the glint of light on the blade of the knife . . . his mother's scathing shrieks of fury . . . the sickening, sweet smell of blood as it spread across the kitchen floor. . . .

It had been an accident, born of self-defense—that's what the Gardai determined. But when it was all said and done, Sean's mother *and* his little brother lay dead on the kitchen floor, and his father's hands were stained with their blood.

For years following that day's violence, Sean had played those hellish moments over in his head, turning them and twisting them until the outcome was different. Instead of standing frozen by fear, cowering, Sean's imagination heroically thrust him into the middle of the conflict, where he saved both his mother and brother. Sometimes it would be his father who died instead. Often it would be Sean himself. He'd been filled with self-loathing for not protecting them, for being too cowardly, too stunned, to do *anything* but watch in horror as they died. His guilt and grief warped all the pain inside him, leaving Sean to slowly self-destruct, dreaming of death as absolution. And Sean made sure Niall felt every bitter moment of his anguish.

And then five years later, Niall had taken his own life in the cavern beneath the ruins where Danni's mother had disappeared with her children. Niall had chosen death rather than face the authorities about murders Danni's very existence proved he hadn't committed. Was it because Sean had drained him of the will to live with his scorn, his accusations, and his hate? Had Niall simply succumbed to the temptation to end it all rather than face his only living son and look into his unforgiving eyes?

Sean hoped it wasn't so, but he feared it was. He still remembered the morning after Fia and the children disappeared, when the authorities had come to see his grandmother. He'd awakened to voices downstairs and stumbled into the kitchen just as they'd told her about finding Niall dead in the cavern. Sean would never forget the raw agony in Nana's sobs, nor the way the inspector looked right through him as they explained what Niall had done.

It was that day he'd stopped answering to Michael and become Sean. He hadn't thought of it too deeply at the time, but now he saw it as a symbolic shedding of his old self—an attempt to leave behind his tormented past and become a different person—a new man from that point on. He hadn't managed to do more than change his identity though. The damaged boy had continued to grow inside him.

Sean felt like he was torn in two now, as he watched Michael—himself—jump on board with the fluid grace of practice. Michael began to pull in the lines and prepare to cast off, but Sean could feel the burning, bitter emotions inside the boy. Michael's sullen glances at his father added a bite to the morning, and Niall's mute acceptance of his son's resentment spoiled the fresh spray of salt and sea. Sean could see the pain in his father's eyes, the bewildered hopelessness that lurked behind them as the *Guillemot* got underway.

"Ever been on a troller before, cousin?" Niall asked him as they pushed off from the dock.

"Once or twice."

"Have you now? I hoped you weren't a city boy. Mum couldn't say much about you other than you were coming."

Sean had wondered what Nana told Niall about them. Apparently, as little as possible. "I worked a boat that sailed out of Cobh," Sean lied.

"Cobh? Very good. Then I'll not need to hold your hand. I've got a fine spot in mind for us today. We'll loop around to the north and catch them unaware."

Niall's smile didn't reach his eyes, but still it transformed his face and made him look years younger. Sean felt a lump of emotion lodge in his chest at the sight. There'd been a time when Niall's smile had been the sun that Sean and his brother rose to. He hadn't realized how much the loss of it had clouded his world.

"Have you tried the western coves of late?" Sean asked casually, looking away.

"Not that I recall. The others fished it out a year or so back. I warned them about it, but the fools never listen. They find it plentiful and take until they've depleted every fecking fish in it. They've not the imagination to look elsewhere and give the poor scaly beasts a chance to replenish. Why do you ask?"

"Just curious," Sean said.

"Not a feeling, is it?"

Sean paused, remembering the numerous times his father had queried him just so. Niall felt the fish, followed his instincts to where they led. When he'd been younger, Sean had developed a sense of it as well. He could feel them moving beneath the choppy waves, a shimmering force that called to him. But after losing both his mother and his younger brother, Sean had ceased to listen to that feeling and never shared it with his father again.

"Could be a feeling," Sean answered now. "Could be they've come back to the coves."

Niall narrowed his eyes. "Could be indeed. Could be we should check."

Another flashing grin and Niall was adjusting his course and following the island's curve to the west. Smiling, Sean turned away, only to stop when he caught Michael watching him with a canny and unsettling gleam in his eyes. He realized his younger self had felt the school of fishing growing and swarming in the cove as well.

Quietly Sean began to ready the lines and bait the hooks. There was a trick to it Sean had perfected years ago. Salmon had three senses—sight, smell, and what was known as lateral line response. For salmon to see bait they had to be right beside it, because their vision was poor and the waters often murky. They had a sharp sense of smell and might catch a whiff of the bait, but again, if it was at forty feet down and the salmon at fifty, he'd have to be right behind it to catch the scent.

The most important sense came from tiny hairlike projections on a salmon's back and sides. The tips of each of them could pick up vibrations in the water, and it was this that the bait played to. If the bait just hung on the hook, it did no good. It had to be cut in a special way and mounted so that it quivered and spun, rolled and wiggled, tricking the salmon into thinking it was a wounded fish—supper waiting to be served. It pulled them like a magnet.

Michael watched him work for a moment before he came closer. "Where did you learn that?" he demanded.

Sean looked up and shrugged. He couldn't remember who had taught him. He'd assumed it was Niall, but from Michael's expression, he thought it might not be so. Michael pulled some bait from the cooler and tried to duplicate how Sean hooked it.

"Almost," Sean told him, showing him how to twist it at the end. "It will squirm like a wounded minnow that way."

Niall cut back the engine and slowed to a trolling speed when they reached the coves. Sean and Michael dropped in the lines one by one. He saw his father looking over his shoulder as they did it, a curious frown on his face.

"Something wrong?" Sean asked.

"Not a fecking thing," Niall answered. "Doesn't it look like you've been doing that your entire fecking life?"

Sean was saved from answering because his hunch had proven right and the salmon were everywhere. The day passed in a blur of slick silver fish and baited lines stretching out from the hull. It was soothing, the work, yet demanding enough to keep his thoughts occupied—to keep him from dwelling on just where the hell he was and how it could possibly have happened. By the time Niall turned the *Guillemot* home, Sean was exhausted, his face was burned, his body sore. He'd used muscles he'd forgotten he had and ached in places he hoped not to remember again. But his head felt clear— clearer than it had in as long as he could remember.

"I must confess, I expected you to be more bother than help, but it's like you were born to it," Niall told him as he shared a thermos of tea Colleen had packed. Michael sat on a pile of nets, brooding. His simmering antipathy was like a rancid stink in the air.

Niall went on, pleased with the weight in their hold and the drag of the current beneath the boat. "Sure and it's rarely enough, what I catch each day. But I can only do what God made me capable of. I know fish." Niall barked a laugh. "A good thing for a fecking fisherman to know, eh?"

"That it is," Sean answered. But he was looking at his younger self, wanting to shake him, wanting to tell him not to waste these precious moments with his father, because they would be his last. If Danni was right, only days separated this one from the morning when the Gardai would be waiting in the kitchen. He finished his cup of tea and left Niall at the wheel to wander over and sit beside Michael.

"It was a good day," Sean said. "You're a fine fisherman."

The boy shot him a resentful glare. "I hate fish. I hate the sea."

Sean stared out at the glittering green waters and could only think how he loved it. Now. With the insight of years and experiences to show him how beautiful and simple life could be on the sea. But he also remembered that tight anger he'd held in his chest when he was young, the feeling that the waters surrounding the Isle of Fennore were a prison.

"Your da has a good setup," Sean tried again, knowing it was pointless but somehow compelled to at least try to change the tides that would wash this life away.

"It's a fecking wreck," Michael said. "One day it'll end up at the bottom of the ocean, and I'll be standing on the fecking shore clapping."

Sean raised his brows. "What will you do then, if not fish?"

"Anything. I'm not a wanker like my da. I can do more than bait a hook and gaff a fish."

"Like what?" Sean pressed, genuinely curious. He had no recollections of ever dreaming of being . . . anything. He frowned at that, wondering why, wondering how it was that he'd never realized it before.

"Why do you fecking care what I do?"

He shrugged. "Didn't realize it was a secret."

Michael shot him a suspicious look but he answered. "I could build things. I'm good with my hands."

"Are you, now? What kind of things would you be building?"

"Maybe a castle," Michael said, looking down.

"A castle is it? Will you be king of it?"

The boy's eyes narrowed. "I mean make them like they were."

"You're talking about restoring them? Rebuilding?"

"One day I want to do that one. The ruins."

Sean swiveled around and looked at the seawall jutting up in the distance like an illusion . . . like a shadowed memory. The ruins perched on top in a tumbled heap of darkness and light.

"Mum," Michael began, stopped, took a breath. "Mum used to talk about how it was . . . before."

Sean faced the boy again, unsettled by both his tone and the words he spoke. "Before?"

Michael nodded and for a moment, Sean found himself staring into his own eyes, falling down a well of his own hopes and dreams, remembering, remembering. . . . His mother had talked about the castle, painted it with her entrancing tone. When he'd been young, her words had guided him through the gatehouse, the bailey, into the great hall, up to the battlements. She'd known so many details, from the lard candles to the smoke-soaked tapestries and greasy shanks spitted over the blazing fires. She'd talked as if she'd been there, walked that drawbridge, woken to the sounds and sights of life in the castle.

"Where is your mum?" Sean asked casually, knowing he was a fool for going there. Asking the question was like peeling the scab off a festering wound. But he needed to hear what Michael would say. Needed to remember why he'd been so convinced the Gardai were wrong and his father could have prevented the deaths if he'd really wanted to.

"Dead," Michael said, shooting a glare at Niall.

"I'm sorry."

"Don't be. He's not—unless boinking Fia MacGrath is the way to grieve, that is."

Sean tried not to react, but he couldn't stop it. Staring into his own face, he felt the surge of the boy's rage rise up, and with it came other memories. His mother had hated Fia MacGrath from the first day Cathán had brought her home. She'd been convinced Niall was in love with her, though Niall denied it. Sean couldn't remember ever seeing his father in Fia's presence, didn't know what had made his mother so certain there was something going on between them. But here was Michael saying it was true.

"How long has your mother been dead?" Sean asked, though he knew the answer.

"Five years."

"You want your father to mourn her still? Not live his life?"

"Why should he have a life to live? He killed my mother and my brother, both of them."

Sean looked at him sideways. "How is it he's not in jail, then?"

"The bloody Gardai called it an accident."

"But you know different?"

"I fecking saw it. I—"

But whatever he was going to say was cut off when Niall shouted for them to look alive. The shore was dead ahead and Niall was cutting back the engines. Soon the *Guillemot* glided to the dock. Sean and Michael moved to secure the boat while Niall cleared the hold and took his haul to the market.

It was Michael's job to scrub the deck and put everything in order for the next day, and he went to it with determination, effectively closing the door on their conversation. Sean understood. It was too painful to dredge up. He'd been a fool to force it.

By the time Niall returned, they were finished with their tasks. "That's it, then," Niall called as he came on board. "Check the lines one last time and we're off."

In unison, both Sean and Michael moved to obey. When they'd

checked that all was secure, they both gave Niall a thumbs-up. Niall stared from one face to another, his eyes shifting back and forth and then widening with something very close to fear.

"Jaysus God," he murmured and turned abruptly away.

"What the feck is his problem?" Michael muttered.

Sean could only shake his head and wonder.

Chapter Eighteen

"Have they left you, Danni?" a male voice asked, pulling Danni from the vision and back into the MacGrath kitchen. She gave a yelp of surprise, releasing the stainless steel pot in her slippery hands. It splashed into the sink.

The sink. The dishwater in it was still hot, the suds still fluffy. The pot she'd carried into the vision bobbed, sloshing water over the side.

Disoriented, she spun to find Cathán MacGrath standing at the doorway, staring at her with a humorous expression. But in her mind, she could still hear the echo of Edel's screams, still see her blackened eyes and the fear on Fia's face.

"Sorry, I didn't mean to sneak up on you," Cathán was saying, tilting his head curiously.

"I guess I was daydreaming," Danni managed, but her mouth was dry, her throat tight. She blotted the puddled water from the counter and dried her hands on a towel. "I'm not usually so jumpy."

"Ah well, new place and all that. Do you need to sit down? You look a bit pale."

"No, I'm fine. Thank you though."

Cathán smiled again, moving to lean against the counter beside

her. His eyes sparkled and there was open friendliness on his handsome face, but there was also something shadowed in it—as if he was
presenting a front. She thought of her mother and the hollow ring
there'd been to the happy story she'd told of their meeting.

"Can I help you with something?" she asked.

He shook his head, still watching her. "Where are the others?"

"Bronagh went to the market. I think Brenda and Maureen are
polishing silver in the dining room."

His smile took on a devilish quality, and for a moment she thought
she must have mistaken that desolation she'd seen lurking in his eyes.
He straightened and crossed to the refrigerator. "I'm a lucky shite," he
said, sticking his head inside and rummaging. "I missed lunch, but I'd
rather starve to death than battle it out with Bronagh for a snack."

Danni stared at his bent back with surprise. Her dad was afraid
of the cook? She'd never have guessed it.

"I think I saw some lamb chops in the back," she said.

"Yes!" With a triumphant grin he pulled the container out. "You
are an angel, Danni."

"I didn't cook them," she began awkwardly, but he was smiling
and shaking his head as he took a bite.

"Doesn't matter. You guided me to them. Shout a warning if you
see Hitler coming though."

She nodded, gazing at her father, wanting to drink in the sight of
his features. This was her dad, a man she'd longed to meet her entire
life. And now here he was, striking up a casual conversation with
her. Somehow the scenario was nearly as hard to believe as traveling
through time.

She forced herself to go back to washing the dishes while he ate.
She felt a mess. She was tired, dirty, and probably as ripe as her
father had been after his match of hurling, whatever that was. Her
ponytail hung loose and lank down her back and her skin felt coated
with flour and oils, perspiration and cooking smells. She wanted a
shower. A long one.

"You look so familiar, Danni," he said, making her glance over
her shoulder at him. "Is there a chance we've met before?"

A small laugh escaped her, reminding her of her mom's habit of tittering when nervous. "I doubt it, but I've heard that I look famil- iar more than once today," she said, keeping a smile in place even though her heart was stuttering in her chest. "The general consensus is that I must have ancestors from here."

"That would be quite a coincidence, wouldn't it now?" At her frown, he went on. "Meeting a husband in America who is from the very place your people haled."

Only unbelievable, she thought. She said, "Not so much. Everyone claims to have some Irish in them."

"You do have a point." He'd polished off the first lamb chop and started on a second. "You seem to have made good friends with my wife in a short time."

His tone was still casual, barely curious. But her nerves had been stretched too far in the past twenty-four hours. She felt defensive as she said, "She's very nice."

"That she is. Too nice, I fear. People take advantage of her."

Danni looked up to see if he'd meant that to be a warning of some kind. Did he think Danni was going to take advantage of her? But he was focused on his food and didn't even glance at her. Decid- ing she was being paranoid, Danni began drying the pots and pans and putting them away.

"I guess I was wondering if you'd known each other before you came here," Cathán went on. "She's usually much more reserved with people when she first meets them."

"Oh," Danni said, suddenly wondering if her mother had sensed a kinship with Danni on some subconscious level. She felt pleased by the idea of it, no matter how far-fetched it was. "No, we've never met before."

"Of course not . . ." He paused, seemed to consider his next words carefully; the dark look was back in his eyes and Danni could see it was worry by the pull of his brow and the line of his mouth. "This is going to sound a strange thing for me to be asking you under the circumstances, but . . . does she seem . . . all right to you?"

"I'm sorry?"

He shrugged and a flush turned his fair skin red. "I'm not in the habit of grilling the servants about my wife's well-being, I swear it. It's just, she . . ." He cursed under his breath. "She was laughing and smiling with you. It's been forever since I've seen her laugh and . . . she's been so miserable and I don't know why. I'm at my wits' end over what to do about it."

Danni watched him, moved by the distress she saw in his eyes. He must feel desperate to be asking Danni, a kitchen helper he hardly knew.

"She seemed fine to me, Mr. MacGrath," Danni murmured. "More than fine."

"Happy?" he asked hopefully.

Danni's hesitation answered for her. He exhaled and wiped his hands on a paper towel he jerked from the roll. Finished, he looked up, and the pain she'd seen was once more hidden behind a calm mask.

"How long have you been married to Ballagh?" he asked suddenly, catching her off guard yet again.

"Not long."

"A week? A month? A year?"

"A few weeks."

"Was it love at first sight?"

"Something like that."

"Ah," he said in a knowing tone.

"Ah, what?"

"That was just a telling answer," he said. "Something *like* love at first sight isn't exactly one and the same with the real thing. Is it? Did you have to get married?"

Danni frowned at him. "Have to . . . ? No, of course not."

He held his hands up at her sharp tone. "No offense intended. I'm sorry—I have no tact. Fia is always scolding me for it. I think the circuitry from my brain to my mouth was damaged during birth. It's always the wrong thing I'm saying."

"Don't worry about it," she mumbled.

"But now you're irritated with me, and we were getting on so well."

She glanced at the door leading to the dining room, wondering when the other girls would come back in. But the door remained closed. The kitchen isolated.

"You seem a bit anxious," he noted. "Am I making you nervous?"

She managed to stop that annoying titter of laughter that wanted to erupt before it reached her lips. But suddenly he *was* making her nervous. She hoped he'd stop with the questions.

He finished his lamb chops, put the leftovers back in the refrigerator, and washed his hands. She dried and put away the last of the pans and turned to find him standing just behind her, boxing her into the corner. For a moment he stared at her, his blue eyes probing. Then he pointed at the necklace Sean had given her last night.

"That's beautiful," he said. "It looks very old."

Her fingers came up to smooth it against her throat. "Thank you."

"Where did you get it?"

She wanted to sidestep, but unless he moved that would bring her closer to him. It wasn't that he had her pinned, but she was uncomfortable. He'd stepped into her personal space and now seemed determined to stay there.

"Was it a gift?" he asked.

"Yes," she answered and then pushed forward anyway, forcing him to move back.

"From your husband?"

She frowned at him. "Why do you want to know?"

His smile was guileless, his blue eyes wide. "I'm a collector of sorts. Amateur, of course, though I'm fascinated by the history." At her blank look, he said, "Celtic spirals. The symbol on your necklace—do you know about them?"

She shook her head, relaxing a little. She wasn't sure what had made her so uptight. Perhaps her own paranoia. Her own dislike of tight places. He was just being friendly, and she was acting like a woman who had something to hide. *Surprise, surprise.*

"No one really knows what they mean," he went on. "Some think the symbols have to do with the constellations, others think they have to do with balance and harmony." He pointed at the spiral pattern. "This one—the tri-spiral—is thought to be the spiral of life."

Danni looked down at the intricate pattern with new curiosity.

"But see," he went on, "that's only one school of thought. There are others who say it represents the triple goddess. Three is a sacred number."

"Which one do you think it is?"

Cathán touched the pendant with his finger and then quickly jerked it back. "I'm sorry, may I?" She gave a tight nod and watched as he lifted it from where it rested against her skin. "There is no way to prove one theory over the other. So much of our history was oral that we can only guess at it. The spirals are ancient so they could be the circle of life—life, death, and rebirth. It's a mystical symbol though. Seems it should be something beyond life and death. To me anyway. It could also represent eternal truth."

"Eternal truth? Interesting. How do you know so much about them?" she asked, looking up. He was standing very close again, and she tried to be calm about it. He seemed completely focused on the necklace and probably wasn't even aware he was crowding her.

"I'm a bookworm as well as a history lover," he said. Another flush crept up his face, and his smile had a shy quality that she found endearing. She had a sudden mental image of him as a boy, reading under the covers long after bedtime. "I'm . . . what do you Americans call it? A nerd."

She laughed. Her father was anything but a nerd. Complex, yes. Confusing—one moment concerned about his wife's emotional well-being and the next focused completely on a necklace a new servant wore—absolutely. But he was far from the horn-rimmed stereotypical nerd.

"It's a personal obsession of mine, I guess," he was saying. "Ever since I was a boy. I suppose it's the mystery of it. These symbols are everywhere and yet no one has ever cracked the code. What do they mean? Why do some spiral clockwise and others counterclockwise— like this one. It's significant, you know. Many believe the spirals that curl this way are connected to pagan spells. They were used to ma-nipulate the natural order of things."

"Spells? Like magic?"

He raised his brows and grinned. "Aye. You could be wearing a powerful charm around your lovely neck, Danni. Have a care what you do with it."

He laughed and finally stepped away. Danni smiled back, but his words unsettled her. Sean had called it a charm as well, but she hadn't though much of it—not in the way her dad meant it. A charm . . .

She'd been touching the necklace when the walls had thinned and the floor beneath their feet vanished. Coincidence? Wasn't Danni and Sean being here proof that magic was at work?

There was a knock on the back door and it made her jump. Grate-ful for the distraction, she hurried to it and flung it open to find Sean on the other side. His very presence—tall and strong and . . . fasci-nating, if she was honest—took her breath away. If he'd really been her husband, the sight of him would have made her pulse race every day. He was little more than a stranger to her now and look what he did to her equilibrium.

Aware of her father's watchful eyes, she gave Sean a tight smile and stood back so he could enter. "I was just finishing up," she said, hurrying back to wipe the sink and fold the towel. Bronagh expected the kitchen to gleam at the end of the day, and Danni didn't want to incur her displeasure.

"I'll wait on the porch," Sean said. "Don't want to dirty your floor." Then he noticed Cathán leaning so casually against the coun-ter and frowned.

"Sean, this is Mr. MacGrath." Danni said. To her father, "This is my h-husband, Sean."

Cathán gave Sean a nod, but didn't move closer. Didn't offer to shake hands. In his eyes, there was something wary, guarded. A sense that he was missing the bigger picture and knew it.

"Danni tells me you're second cousin to Niall," Cathán said.

"That's right," Sean answered.

"Who is your father?"

Sean blinked, lifting his chin so he could look Cathán in the eye. "Why do you care who my father is?"

"I only wonder that I never heard of you."

"Well, I've never heard of you either."

This brought Cathán's brows up in surprise. "Truly? Where did you grow up?"

"Killarney."

"And what brings you to Ballyfionúir?"

"Work."

"There's none to be had in Killarney?"

"I'm sure there is. But my—Colleen—is getting old. She's all the family I have left, so I wanted to be near."

"What about Niall?"

"What about him?"

"He's family, too, isn't that right?"

Sean shrugged, taking Danni's hand as she reached his side. His touch was warm, his grip big and encompassing. It steadied her—made her realize just how off-kilter she felt. Surprised, she shot him a grateful smile.

The exchange was not lost on her father. He continued to study them for a while longer and then said, as if conceding, "Well, there's plenty of work here. At least for the time being."

"I'm ready," Danni said abruptly. "It was nice talking to you Mr. MacGrath."

She took Sean's arm and turned him away from the house. But before they'd taken a step, Cathán said softly, "You still haven't told me who your father is, Sean Ballagh. Is it ashamed, you are?"

Sean stilled and faced him again. There could be no misinterpreting the intent of Cathán's comment, though Danni couldn't understand what compelled him to taunt Sean that way. Cathán meant to insult, and from the look on Sean's face, he'd succeeded.

"Now why would you think that?" Sean asked tightly.

The slow smile that spread over Cathán's face was cool. "Just a feeling," he said lightly. "No offense intended, of course.

Sean's answering smile was equally cold. "None taken . . . of course. You're not the first MacGrath to be jealous of what a Ballagh has, are you now?"

Cathán's face flooded with color, but before he could sputter out his denial, Sean had closed the door behind them.

Chapter Nineteen

"WHY should he care who my fucking father is?" Sean snarled as they walked away. "What did he say to you? Do I need to go back and teach him some manners?"

"No," Danni said hastily, catching the anger glinting in Sean's eyes. "He was very polite and nice."

Sean made a derogatory sound. He looked tired and dirty, and his face was flushed from the wind and sun, though there'd been a layer of clouds for most of the day. She wondered at that—at his burning under the watery rays. He'd been a spirit until yesterday morning and his skin hadn't seen the sun since . . .

It boggled her mind, thinking of that, of them really being here, twenty years ago. Meeting themselves in a parallel time before their lives would be changed forever. It was the stuff of movies and science fiction novels.

"I'm to believe he didn't say a thing about me, then?"

"He wanted to know how long we'd been married."

"Why?"

"I don't know. But earlier when Fia told him my last name, he just got . . . curious I guess. It seemed to set him off. Are there bad feelings between your family and his . . . mine?"

Sean glanced at her from the corner of his eyes. "You could say that."

"But you said my father sent you to get me."

"I never did."

"You certainly implied it, and you know that's what I thought. That's as good as a lie." When Sean didn't answer, only continued to walk with his eyes staring stiffly at the ground, Danni asked quietly, "Is anything you told me true?"

He stopped in the middle of the path and faced her, taking her shoulders roughly between his big hands. "I came for you," he said, but his tone made it clear he wasn't happy about it. "That much was true."

She swallowed hard, feeling anger and betrayal mix into her confusion. A part of her reasoned that Sean couldn't be expected to tell the whole truth about why he came to her house that morning. Chances were good that he didn't know himself.

But she couldn't deal with the lies—not from Sean. They were in this together, and she needed to know that she could trust him. Depend on him.

He's a ghost, Danni. And your being here is impossible . . .

She shook her head. *Impossible* had become quite the norm lately.

"I came for you," he repeated, this time with less anger.

The grip he had on her shoulders eased, and his fingers moved in a gentle caress. It would be easy to let it go, to lean against the solid warmth of his broad chest, let those strong arms wrap around her. But Danni knew better than anyone that *easy* rarely meant *good*.

She pulled out of his hands and started walking again. "Well, next time you come for someone, make it someone else," she retorted over her shoulder.

He mumbled a response she didn't have to hear to understand. He was pissed off again. Well, so was she. Fueled by her righteous anger, she kept walking. After a moment, he fell in step beside her.

"I'm sorry," he said. "I should have been more honest about why I wanted you to come home. The years after your mother disappeared with you and your bother were not . . . pleasant. Most people loved Fia and hated my father for what they thought he'd done. Since he wasn't around to face them, I became his stand-in."

"But you didn't do anything. And you were just a boy."

"A surly one with a pissy outlook on life. It wasn't hard to hate me, too."

Danni looked at him from the corner of her eye, knowing this must have been how he'd interpreted his existence in Ballyfionúir after his death. Friends and neighbors had turned their backs to him, not because they hated him, but because they couldn't see him. And the few that sensed his presence mostly feared him. What a sad and lonely existence it must have been for him. He didn't know he was a spirit; he only knew that he was outcast.

Not for the first time she wondered what he would say, what he would do if she were to give up her own secrets and tell him the truth. Would he believe her if she told him he was a ghost—or at least had been a ghost when he'd shown up on her doorstep? Of course not. But what if he did believe her? What if telling him pushed him to accept that he was dead? What if all he needed was to acknowledge the fact to make the transition from spirit to the beyond? Would he still be here with her, or would he simply vanish like a drop of water into an ocean? There was no way to know, and she was too much of a coward to risk it. To risk him leaving her here, alone.

She took a deep breath and slowly let it out. "It's been a long day," she said.

"Aye, that it has," he agreed, accepting her peace offering with a tight smile.

"Did you learn anything? Any clues about how we got here?" she asked.

He shook his head. "I spent the day with my father who's been dead for twenty years. I learned that I was a stupid boy."

She waited for him to say more about that, but he didn't. He just kept walking, hands shoved in his pockets now, eyes turned to the ground beneath his feet.

"What about you?" he asked, not looking up. "Did you learn anything?"

"Maybe," she said. "What do you know about the Book of Fennore?"

That did draw his attention. He finally glanced up, surprised. "No more than anyone knows of it."

"Very enlightening," she said, feeling her frustration rise again. "Could you be a little more forthcoming?"

He let out an exasperated breath. "It's a legend. No one's ever seen it, but that doesn't stop people from believing in it all the same. I would guess the same people believe in leprechauns as well."

"And probably time travel, too?" she said sweetly.

He gave a conceding shrug. "You have a point. Why are you bringing it up? What do you know of it?"

"It was supposed to have powers. Magical powers," she said.

"So do fairies, if it's fantasy you're wanting."

"I don't appreciate the sarcasm, Sean. Something brought us here and it wasn't a 747. We are a walking paradox right now. You get that? You had breakfast with your*self*, remember. If you have a reasonable explanation for how that could happen, I'm all ears."

He didn't say anything.

"I didn't think so," she muttered.

"What is it you're thinking about the Book of Fennore?" he asked.

She thought of quipping back with his own "no more than anyone else," but managed to refrain. She didn't want to fight—she was too tired for it. But her temper didn't seem to understand that.

"Well, I think it's real, for one." She waited for him to deny it, but he didn't.

Instead he gave a sharp nod and reluctantly said, "When I was a boy, I heard it had been found."

"Here?"

He nodded. "There were rumors about it the night you disappeared."

"I read that on the Internet. Do you believe it?"

"It's not something I ever wanted to believe. If it is real, it's a terrible thing, the Book. Worse than any evil ever born. We grew up fearing it—fearing whoever might use it, like a boogeyman."

Danni swallowed and looked away. "When I mentioned it to my . . . to Fia she acted . . . strange. Not frightened as much as . . . uneasy. I don't know how to explain it. But I thought, if it wasn't a myth—if it really existed, this would be the place for it, right? This is where the legend put it, in Ballyfionúir. And if it *was* here before then . . ."

"Then what?"

"Well then, maybe it had something to do with *us* being here now. I know it sounds nuts, but this *is* nuts, Sean, and we're not going to find a rational explanation for how we just lived through a day that happened twenty years ago."

"All right, so say it is true and we're here because of the Book of Fennore. What then? Are you thinking we might find it?"

She shot him a look, seeking out any sign of mockery in his eyes. He held his hands up. "I swear, an honest question is all it is. You want to find it and use it, is that the way of it?"

"Maybe."

"That wouldn't be wise," he said.

"Especially when we have so many other choices."

"Even if we have *no* other choices."

His tone was so serious she glanced at him and stumbled. He caught her arm, keeping her from falling. When she tried to pull away, he kept his hand on her, holding her still.

"For every tale told about the Book of Fennore, there is a lesson of doom surrounding it. For every voice that says it's just a myth, there is the fear that it's real. Do I believe it exists? Yes. Does it scare me to say it? More than you know. Can you understand that, Danni?"

She nodded.

"It cannot be used."

She knew that, too. She'd seen it, hadn't she? The black seeping into Edel's eyes, turning them into sparkling pits of pitch. Whatever had happened to her when she'd touched the Book, it wasn't good. It wasn't right. And it most certainly wasn't natural.

"What if it's been used already, Sean? What if it brought us here?"

He didn't answer, but his face paled and his grip on her arm tightened.

"I get that it's not a good thing, Sean. But if you're thinking we should just sit around and wait to see if it plans to send us back, then I have to tell you, I'm not thrilled with that plan."

"It cannot be used," he repeated, stoically. He took a deep breath, released her arm. The chilly air rushed in where his warmth had been, and goose bumps traveled over her skin.

"We could argue about it all day," he said. "But it doesn't matter, does it, when neither of us knows where it is anyway. The only way we'd find it is if it wanted us to. That's what the legends say. It chooses you, not the other way around. You can look for it all you want, but I for one would rather be a living *paradox* than a tool for the Book of Fennore."

The hard cold tone made Danni shiver. She rubbed her arms and nodded. Taking this as agreement, Sean started walking again. Slowly Danni followed.

"My fa—Niall tells me there's a cottage that Nana has rented for us," he said, shortening his stride to hers.

"How do you think she knew we were coming?" Danni asked.

"The woman is a mystery. She always has been. Better to ask the sun why it rises."

"My necklace," Danni said. "Where did she get it?"

He gave her another sideways glance. "Why?"

"My . . . father said it was old."

"I told you it was a family heirloom. That generally means old."

"You said it was a charm. To keep me safe. Safe from what, Sean? That one you didn't answer."

And he didn't answer now. Looking straight ahead, he kept walking.

"Okay, how about this one. If it's a family heirloom meant for me, why did your grandmother have it?"

"I've no idea."

She watched him, looking for a sign of another lie, but he was either a great actor, or he really didn't know. "Do you know what it is, this charm?"

He glanced at where it rested against her chest and then away. "The Spiral of Life," he said.

Perhaps it was the bland tone of his deep and smoky voice or maybe it was the chill breeze, but the words hit her with a physical force. Her father had said life, death, and rebirth, and she'd thought it interesting. But walking beside Sean, *Spiral of Life* took on a whole new meaning. She swallowed hard. "Colleen knew we were coming," she said, returning to the topic.

"Aye."

"Do you think she knows more than that? Like what happens next?"

"Do you?" he asked, looking at her from the corner of his eye.

She shrugged, but she felt guilt crowding in. She'd blasted him for lying, yet wasn't she doing the same? Withholding information because she was scared of being left alone?

"I don't know the first thing about what your grandmother does or doesn't know."

"That's not what I'm asking," he responded flatly. He stopped, pulling her to a halt as well. "I'm asking, do *you* know what happens next?"

"How could I?" she asked.

She felt his gaze on her, but kept her face averted, refusing to let him see deeper than the surface. He'd asked her the same question last night, in her kitchen, before . . . before they'd fallen through a hole in time. But she didn't know what happened next, only that it ended with Sean and his father dead and Danni's family shattered.

She lifted her chin and steeled herself to meet his eyes, presented a blank expression she could only hope hid the turmoil behind it. Sean continued to stare, and she saw something move in his steady look. A doubt, a suspicion.

"Why did your grandmother send you to get me?" Danni asked softly, deflecting those prying sea green eyes with a counterattack.

He let out a deep, harsh breath. "I can't tell you the why of it, Danni. I don't know it myself."

"Does it have to do with Niall? With your father?"

It was a shot in the dark, but it hit. Sean shoved his hands back in his pockets and scowled.

"Does it, Sean?"

"Why should it?"

"I don't know . . . it's just a feeling. You—I mean, Michael—I see how you used to act around your father. When you were young, you looked at him like you hated him and it seems . . . more serious than just teenage angst. Like you had a reason. I know what you said about how you were treated after Niall killed himself, but that hasn't happened yet—I mean, not in this time we're in now."

Sean didn't say anything, but he held himself stiff and away.

"Talk to me, Sean. Help me understand what's going on here."

He let out a pent-up breath, shook his head as if trying to deny what needed to be said. Then, finally, he spoke. "Do you know why—when your mother disappeared with you and your brother—do you know why the people of Ballyfionúir were so quick to say it was murder and so eager to condemn my father, a fisherman who'd lived here peacefully his entire life?"

"I thought it was because my father saw him do it. . . ."

"Sure and they'd believe a man who's never done an honest day's work over one of their own?"

"But the evidence . . ."

"Not enough to convict him, dead or no. They'd have done it if they could."

"Then why?"

"Because they all thought he'd gotten away with it once before—when he killed *my* mother. He'd already taken the life of his own wife. It was barely a stretch to think of him taking another man's."

"Your father killed . . . ?"

"Yes, it's what I'm telling you." In his anger, in his grief, emotion dragged out his lilting words into a long, painful softening of consonants and sharpening of vowels. "You want to know why I hated him at fourteen? Well, there is your answer. He killed my mother when I was nine. I saw him do it with my own eyes, though even now I can't tell you how it happened. They called it an accident. Maybe it was—I don't fucking know. But who do you think suffers for a thing Danni? Not just him who did the deed. Not just him. If my grandmother brought us here—which I don't know to be the way of it—but if she did her reason wouldn't have been my father."

Danni stared into Sean's eyes, looked into a sea of churning and conflicting hurts and rages, confused memories and blurred facts. She saw in that tempest the young child who wanted to believe in his father, and she saw the grown Sean, who'd lived his life as a ghost because of the same man. It was tearing him apart, the warring emotions.

"I don't know what the fucking hell we're doing here Danni. You think it's for a reason? Well, I can't see it that way. I can't see how we'll make a damned bit of difference no matter what we do. The past can't be changed. Surely you know it's the truth?"

And with that, he walked away from her.

Chapter Twenty

S EAN and Danni arrived at Colleen's front door in a strained silence. His jaw was set and his lips tight, his expression as closed
as a bolted door. With his tormented words still ringing in her ears,
Danni didn't dare ask him any more questions. But she had many.

Colleen cast a curious glance between them when she opened the
door and ushered them in, but she saw the tension in Sean's bearing
and she refrained from questions, too. Bean sat at her feet, watching
nervously. Michael looked up from his plate at the table and stared
at them with guarded interest.

"Sure and it's exhaustion I see on your faces. I knew you'd be
worn out by the time they were through of you. I've packed up yer
supper, and Michael will be taking you on to yer new home. The
good Father has managed to gather some more donations, seeing
how your things are lost. I've left them for ye inside."

Like obedient children, they thanked Colleen for her trouble.
Sean hefted the box she'd packed for them and followed Michael to
the door. Danni paused and called to Bean, but the little dog yawned
and put her head between her paws with a sheepish expression on
her face.

Colleen blushed as she hurried to explain. "I fear I might have spoiled her a bit. It was such a comfort having her with me that I couldn't help myself."

"It's okay," Danni said.

"Sure and tomorrow she'll be sick of me and ready to go back to her master."

Danni nodded, trying not to show her hurt. It felt like betrayal. Dejected, she followed Sean out the door.

"I knew the little rodent was possessed," he muttered.

They took the same road Sean had walked that morning, snaking down the hillside toward the sea, weaving around enormous boulders and fragrant heather. As they descended, she could hear the beat of waves against the rocky shoreline and smell the spiced sea air as it cloaked the dusk with its pungent perfume of fish and tar and storm.

The path split then, with one side leading down to the beach and the other running parallel to the embankment. Michael led them on the second.

"The pier is just down there. It's where our boat is docked. It's a fecking pile of shite, if you want to know the truth. I wish it would sink."

Danni bit back a question about how, then, would his father put food on the table. After hearing Sean's story, her heart could only go out to the young boy who'd seen his father kill his mother.

After another few moments, Michael pointed behind them and said, "You can see the castle from here."

Danni turned and caught her breath as she gazed at the steep and rocky plateau and the ruins perched atop like a cornice on a spire. From this distance, she could get a better sense of what it had looked like whole. The crumbling walls had been anchored by four round towers with another set of walls inside the stronghold. Gray in the twilight, the stone glowed like something from another world, representing a life so long gone it could barely be imagined. The picture of it stayed seared in her memory long after she'd turned away.

The cottage was more a thatched shed than a house. A bright purple front door gleamed with fresh paint against the faded yellow walls. Two windows made eyes into the deep darkness on either side of it and a small porch confined them to crossing the threshold one at a time.

Michael opened the door without a key and flipped on a switch. A single lamp on a single table cast a dull and clouded glow on a single room divided by two curtains into a kitchen, sitting area, and bedroom. The bathroom had a door, but it was so tiny that Danni thought it would take maneuvering to close it while standing inside.

"Used to be Court O'Heaney's," Michael told them. "But he died a month back. Stranger things I've never seen. His dog died on the very same night. Both of them, gone. He was sitting in a chair by the fire and the dog was at his feet. Have you ever heard of such a thing?"

Danni and Sean had not. Michael waited for their exclamations of amazement with a hopeful expression, but the pair were too tired, too confused to give it.

"Well now, I'll be taking my leave. I'll see you in the morning, cousin," he said. "There'll be a need for fresh salmon and Da will be trying to catch it."

"You work on your father's boat?" Danni asked.

"Aye, and isn't it a crime. Child labor, I say. But it does no good. He'll have me out of bed and swabbing the decks by dawn. A waste of a day."

"It's an honest day's work," Sean said, eyeing the teenaged version of himself with a combination of humor and impatience. "And what else would you be doing with yourself but looking for trouble?"

"I'm man enough to spend my time without reporting to the likes of you," he said with defensive pride and a pointed look at Danni. His gaze was at once pleading and sexual, begging her to see beyond the boy to the man he would become. It disconcerted her, staring at this young echo of the man beside her. Worse than double vision, it made her dizzy and slightly nauseous.

Sean, apparently, had no such confusion when it came to Michael. He put himself directly in front of her, blocking Michael's line of sight. *Jealous of himself*, she thought with insanely dark humor.

"We'll be seeing you in the morning, then," Sean said as he ushered the boy to the door.

"Michael," Danni asked before Sean shut him out, "have you ever heard of the Book of Fennore?"

Michael paused and looked back at her. His expression was shocked.

"Aye, everyone has. Do they talk of it in America, then?"

"No," she said, trying for a casual tone, a natural smile. "I just read about it. Do you think it's real?"

"Why wouldn't I? No one can say it isn't, can they now? Nana has seen it with her own eyes, she has."

"I thought no one had ever seen it before?"

"No one has," Sean said firmly. "Your nana is filling your head with tales, she is. She'll tell you she's seen purple elephants in Dublin next."

A dark flush stained Michael's face as he glared at Sean. "I'm not some fecking imbecile."

"Of course not," Danni said, shooting Sean a warning look. "Thank you, Michael, for showing us the way here."

Mollified, Michael nodded and said good-bye. When the door finally closed behind him, the air inside felt thick and damp. There was a musty scent and a chill that only intensified her weariness. Danni needed some space. She needed to be alone. She needed to cleanse herself of the day's grime and her mind's confusion.

"I'm going to take a shower," she announced to the quiet that followed Michael's departure.

Sean had moved to the fireplace and set chunks of what looked like mud bricks on the grate. At her words, he glanced back at her. His gaze glittered over her face like the reflection of sun on choppy waters. It burned a trail down her throat, lingering on her breasts, whispering over her knotted belly. She had an immediate, intimate image of him there, in the shower beside her, arms locked behind her back, slick wet skin pressed to her own. A shiver tickled down her spine and gathered in the pit of her stomach.

"I'll get the fire started, then," he said, his voice sinfully deep and soft.

Danni nodded thinking, *Oh, but you already have.* She stood for another awkward moment and then said, "I won't be long."

Turning, she went to the bathroom, scooting past the toilet and sink to the small gap between so she could close the door. She locked it even though Sean wasn't likely to barge in on her, and if he did, she wasn't entirely sure she'd be sorry. She undressed and stepped into the tiny stall under a pitiful stream that sputtered and spat. But it was hot and there was soap and it was more than she'd hoped for.

She had the sense of time running out but no idea how to stop it. It seemed showers and meals and sleep should be foregone. She should be making decisions and taking actions—but to what end? A whole day had passed and she was no closer to understanding why she was here or what she should be doing.

She had her hair in a full lather of shampoo that smelled surprisingly of lavender when the sound of the water grew louder, more insistent. It roared from the faucet and seemed to crash against the tiled walls, yet Danni could feel the weak drizzle, unchanged as it streamed down her back. Wary, she rinsed the soap from her eyes and looked at the nozzle. But instead of the shower, instead of the speckled tiles and rusted fixtures, she found herself staring at the gray smudge of the sky meeting the ocean.

She turned in place, taking in the fat clouds overhead, the two o'clock sun stretching her shadow out in front of her, the rocky beach. She hadn't even felt the air turn but turn it had, and now she waited—naked, dripping wet, and bone cold—for whatever would happen next.

The waves churned and frothed at her feet and seagulls cawed as they scurried and soared, looking for tasty snacks in the tide. To her left, she glimpsed a small bay with ships anchored in its harbor.

She heard a rock bounce down the side of the sloping cliff and looked up. On the plateau overhead, she saw the backside of the crumbling ruins. Great mortar blocks mingled with the giant stones cascading to the sea from above. This must be where the castle wall had given out and taken the MacGrath child all those years ago. God, what must it have felt like to plummet down that jagged side to the merciless sea?

The sound of music drew her attention and Danni looked away, glad to be distracted from the horrible images in her head. It seemed to be coming from the other side of the boulders to her right. Still naked, Danni gingerly picked her way over a jagged outcropping, leaning down to hold the edges of the massive rocks as she carefully navigated her way across the natural barrier. The ocean sprayed her with freezing water and she trembled with cold.

She reached an isolated beach and paused to catch her breath. The song she'd heard was louder here, and she saw a rough opening cut into the cliff side. *A doorway*, she thought, *nearly invisible from any other angle.* Looking closer, she noticed something else. Where the water met the rocky wall leading up to the castle's plateau, there was a low arch, visible only when the tide withdrew.

Frowning, she climbed to the narrow entrance and stepped through.

The dark here was like crushed velvet, thick and soft and yielding. She moved through it in silence, following the melody to a cavern lit by alternating brightness as the tide rushed forward, blocking the sun, then pulled away to let it back in. The ground beneath her bare feet was made of gravel and shells layered over stone. The walls were roughly hewn, carved out by the sea and worn by the grit of the unceasing tide. But as she looked closer, she saw a pattern etched onto every surface, repeated over and over on the walls and ceiling. Even on the boulders that crouched defensively around the churning pool in the middle. Spirals. They were everywhere.

She fingered the pendant at her throat and shivered before cautiously moving on, past the tide pool to the back, where another door opened into the darkness. The song was coming from there. She stepped closer and looked in to see rough-cut stairs making a circular route up.

Surprise made her breathless. She was in a cave beneath the castle. And perhaps the stairs led to a secret passage. A hidden place that offered escape, though at no small peril.

The haunting song grew louder, and Danni backed up, tucking herself into the shadows, though a part of her knew she wasn't really here. But the instinct drove her as the woman with a voice more beautiful than the stark scenery emerged from the stairwell.

It was Fia. Danni shouldn't have been surprised.

Fia carried a small lantern and a blanket in her hands. Honey brown hair hung loose and silky to swing against thin shoulders. Her song was in Gaelic, and she sang it with feeling, closing her eyes as the wrenching notes echoed against the cavern walls.

Danni swallowed a lump in her throat.

The song ended, and Fia stood very still for a moment, as if it had drained her strength with its sadness. She stared at the rippling water, nearly black where it lapped the rocks, gray green where it surged out of the arched opening. Her expression filled Danni with unease. The look in her eyes seemed to beg for miracles. As if she hoped for a ship to suddenly appear in that opening and whisk her away. Was that what she wanted?

Unable to help herself, Danni lifted her hand and brushed an errant strand of hair back from her mother's face. Fia turned, without noticing.

Still naked, still cold, Danni followed her mother to a flat, smooth area where she set down her lantern and spread the blanket.

Fia seemed oblivious to the cold as she stripped her clothes and folded them neatly. Danni saw the mottled greens and yellows of bruises on her back and ribs. She'd seen them before, that first time when Sean had guided her through the vision. What had happened to her? Had she been in an accident? Had she fallen?

Lower, on the pearly white skin of her forearm, Danni saw the rose-shaped birthmark, just like the one on her own arm.

Fia turned away, and with only a moment's hesitation, she stepped into the pool. Danni followed her in. The water was bracing, icy even, but Fia didn't seem to mind. She swam and splashed like a mermaid, freed from the boundaries of gravity. Danni watched her, thinking how young, how beautiful her mother was. Lost in the magic and the mystery of this stranger who she longed to know, Danni didn't hear the footsteps until they stopped just behind her. Frowning, she glanced over her shoulder.

Niall Ballagh stood against the backdrop of the ragged and harsh cavern walls. What was he doing here?

Like Sean, Niall was a big man. Broad of shoulder, lean of hip, long of leg. In the photograph she'd seen, Niall hadn't seemed so large and solid. But here, now, he was all muscle and sinew, looming and somehow frightening.

In her head, she could hear Sean's pained and angry words. *He killed my mother. . . .* Was he here to do the same to Danni's? Stalking her as an overture to the final act?

Fia hadn't noticed him yet, and he moved in, his gaze riveted on the flashes of pearl skin streaming with water, dipping beneath the surface. He stopped when he reached the flat boulder and sat beside her blanket and clothes, waiting.

Frightened, Danni swam to her mother's side, wanting to alert her. To warn her. *Momma, there's a man here and he wants to hurt you.*

As if hearing her daughter, Fia came up for air and turned to see Niall sitting patiently beside the pool.

They stared at one another for a long, bated moment as Danni watched from the freezing water. Neither spoke.

Then slowly, with a deliberation born of intent, Fia moved to the side of the pool and climbed out. Danni followed, dismayed by her nudity even though she knew Niall couldn't see her. Fia seemed to have no such compunctions. She crossed to stand just in front of him, breasts heaving with ragged inhalations, skin puckering with a thousand shivery goose bumps. The water ran down her body, pooling in the hollow of her throat, tunneling through the valley between her breasts, sluicing over her rounded hips and thighs. Niall's look should have made all that wet turn to steam. He stood slowly, gracefully, one small step away.

A deep breath from Fia would have brushed Niall's hard chest in a whispered touch. But neither moved. They only stared at one another, absorbed, transfixed. Fia's gaze traversed his face, lingering on his strong brow, shadowed eyes, and sculpted mouth with something akin to anguish. Then tears turned her eyes shiny before overflowing to mix with the sea drops that clung to her skin.

Watching them, a burning anger and crippling sense of betrayal filled Danni's gut. She wanted to launch herself at Niall Ballagh. She wanted to scratch his face, kick and pull and push him away from her mother. In a moment of clarity, she understood that this—the magnetic force that seemed to hold the two captive, not merely Niall himself—was the prelude to doom. She knew without a doubt that Niall was to blame for the tragedy that would take place tomorrow night. Niall had been obsessed with her mother. He'd destroyed his own happiness and family and then moved on to Danni's.

She thought hard at Fia, tried to move her mother by will alone. She wanted to believe that Fia was too frightened of Niall to even scream. That's why she stood so still, bare and trembling. That's why she didn't tell him to leave.

Danni moved forward, tried to grip Niall's arm and drag him away. Tears of rage filled her eyes as she shouted at him to leave her mother alone. But it was no use. She wasn't there. Not for Niall, not for her mother.

Niall made a sound deep in his throat—one of resistance overcome, one of barriers brought tumbling down. And then he breached that tiny gap that held them apart and pulled Fia's dripping body against him. His hands skimmed her wet skin, sliding over her silky curves then up to cup her face.

"I can't stay away," he said, and the words were demand, apology . . . defeat.

Danni felt his agony, his yearning, and it fired her helpless fury. "Try harder," she shouted. "She's not yours. My father loves her. *I* love her."

And Niall would destroy all that.

He trailed his fingers over the flat of her breastbone to the valley between and down to settle on the small rise above her pelvis. He dropped to his knees, his big hands circling her hips, holding her there as he subjugated himself at her feet. Pressing his face to the swell just over the tight mass of red gold curls, he whispered, "I will be this baby's father in more than seed." Then, fiercely, "Please, Fia, please let me."

Danni came back to the shower with a gasp that burned her lungs and made her choke on the sudden spray of water in her face. She coughed, bending with the force of emotion, the need to clear her lungs, her heart.

He'd said *father.* He'd said *baby.*

The implications of that rolled over her like the unharnessed power of the sea. Danni quickly rinsed the soap from her hair and body. She fumbled with the faucet, turning off the water as she sank to the floor of the shower and pulled up her knees.

He'd said *father.* He'd said *baby.*

The words repeated in her head, a screeching echo that shredded her beliefs, her hopes and dreams. Niall Ballagh was the father of the baby Fia carried. Not Cathán. Not her husband.

She stood on trembling legs, pulling a towel from the rack and wrapping it around her. She was cold and shaky and sick to her soul. Sean said that after Fia and the children disappeared, there was talk of an affair, and Danni had defended her. Said she knew, in her heart, that there couldn't have been another man. The bitter truth burned her like an oily flame.

While Cathán was trying so hard to please Fia, to make her happy—Fia was sleeping with Niall Ballagh, a man who'd killed his own wife.

Danni clenched her fist in hurt and anger. She tucked the towel around her, realizing she'd forgotten clean clothes when she'd come in. With a growl of frustration, she scooped up the pile on the floor and yanked open the door.

Sean looked up from the fireplace with surprise and stared at her. For a moment, she could only stare back. The fire gilded him in warm gold, making the dark of his hair into a glittery cap of silken light.

It gleamed with hues of blue black and starlit velvet. His face, wind burned and sun touched, glowed with an inner luminance, turning his eyes into bright green and silver orbs surrounded by sooty lashes and shifting shadows. In that moment, he looked nothing like his father, nothing like the man who would destroy her world, and Danni was more grateful than she could say or even understand.

He stood, graceful even in the small action. She watched his tall body unfold and stretch. Drank in the sight of his broad shoulders, the power of his strong arms flexing, the lithe beauty of his form. He watched her watching him, an unfathomable gleam deep in his shining eyes.

"That was a quick shower," he said.

It felt like days had passed while she'd waded through that icy pool of betrayal with her mother.

"Are you okay, Danni?" he asked, stepping closer.

She caught his scent. Bracing wind, salty ocean, man. Even after the long day, he smelled good to her. She inhaled, letting him chase away the lingering memory of the cave, the steaming scent of dark secrets. She wanted to bury her face against Sean's chest and breathe him in, forever.

Tentatively Sean reached a hand out and touched her shoulder. Danni stared into his eyes, helpless to fight the pain eating her from inside out. He seemed confused and yet he knew just what to do. He pulled her into his arms, cradled her head against his chest, and held her while she cried.

Chapter Twenty-one

S EAN didn't ask why she was crying. Some part of him knew to do so would be to invite an even greater breakdown. Somehow Sean sensed that Danni's tears sprang from a deeper well of emotion than fear and confusion over how they'd ended up here. Her pain came from a part of her as hot and central as the core of the earth. She didn't just cry, she wept as if wounded to her very soul. Her misery could not be mistaken for anything less than grieving. But what did she mourn?

Everything that made him a man wanted to demand an explanation. Wanted to fix whatever was wrong and make her world right again. He managed to control the urge, perhaps because the same man who drove it also recognized the fault in it. He couldn't fix anguish. No matter how he wanted to, he couldn't. And in this, trying and failing her would be worse than not trying at all.

So he did what he could. He held her. Tried to give comfort through strength. Weathered her storm. His shirt was wet with her tears and still they flowed, a river of loss that had become too much to dam. He'd taken her bundle of clothes and set them aside then rocked her slowly, gently. Rubbed her back, his hands occasionally slipping higher than the towel to meet warm and silky skin. The contact was electric and it distracted him, but he stayed the course, offering nothing more than his strength and his embrace.

He couldn't have said how long he held her before her sobs became sniffles and her tears finally ceased. He'd become lost in the feel of her, lost in her scent and the warm vibration of her body. She lifted her head from the hollow of his shoulder where it fit so perfectly and looked at him with those tear-soaked eyes. Her lashes were dark and spiky, her pupils huge and black, ringed by a circle of smoky light that shimmered with her pain.

He wanted to kiss her. He wanted to touch her as he'd done that morning—if in fact it had been more than a dream, more than a fantasy that played endlessly in his mind. But she looked embarrassed now and vulnerable, and he couldn't bring himself to cross that line of trust. With a control he didn't know he was capable of, he pressed his lips to her forehead and stepped back.

"I'm sorr—" she began.

"Don't, Danni," he said.

Those beautiful eyes rounded and she nodded once. Quickly, curtly.

"I was going to unpack the supper Nana sent," he said, turning, giving her a moment to compose herself. "Why don't you put some warm clothes on?"

She gave another jerky nod. "I will. Go ahead and shower. I'll unpack the food when I'm dressed."

He sensed her desperation for a task to fill her mind and nodded.

"I hope I left you some hot water," she said, turning toward the curtained bedroom.

"You did, I'm sure. I thought I would have to drag you out to get a turn, but you were only in there for a few minutes."

She paled at this, and he glanced into the tiny room wondering again what had sent her out in such a state of shock. What thoughts had poured over her with the spray of water? But he didn't ask.

His shower was considerably longer than hers, and the hot water lasted nearly to the end. As he seemed to be doing with everything of late, he found himself entranced by the feel of the spray against his skin, the sensation of lather in his hands. Why did everything feel so different here? So vivid and tangible. Since waking that morning, it seemed even the act of breathing—of existing at all—was like a seduction in itself.

Dry, he dressed in clean boxers and a pair of worn jeans that were only a bit too big. They hung low on his hips, and he thought of the rappers who wore them around their thighs as a fashion statement. A fashion statement that was years from being made in this time or place. Colleen had sent several shirts, but most were too small. Left with only two that fit, both too heavy for indoors, he opted to go without.

He felt like a new man when he emerged to find Danni sitting in front of the fire he'd started. Her golden brown hair had almost dried and it shone in the muted light. She wore an oversized man's T-shirt—one that would have been too small for him—and a pair of stretchy pants that ended at thick white socks. She glanced at him over her shoulder with wide, shell-shocked eyes.

"Hi," he said.

"Hi."

Her gaze moved from his face to his chest, slowly down then quickly up again. She blushed, and something within him, something deep and male, growled with satisfaction.

They ate the cold meal Colleen had sent and cleaned the dishes afterwards. They spoke very little, but between them there buzzed a tension as real as the air in their lungs and the food they'd consumed. It was full dark outside, but Sean suspected it was no later than seven or eight. He was bone tired, but also alert, attuned to the woman beside him.

"Have you ever been married, Danni?" he asked her suddenly.

"No."

"Why is that, do you think? Are the men of Arizona entirely daft?"

Her smile was tight and sad. "I came close—twice."

"What happened, then?"

He thought she might not answer. He was prying, and she didn't owe him any explanations about herself or her past. But he hoped she'd tell him. He wanted to know about the other men in her life. He wanted the power to drive them from her memory.

"The first time, I was very young. My . . . Jack. That was his name. He met someone else." She looked down at her white socks. "He didn't tell me though. I think he might have actually gone through with the marriage rather than face up to what he was doing if I hadn't caught him at it. I don't understand it. To this day, I don't. But I saw them together."

He waited, wondering if she'd seen them in person, or if she'd "dreamed" them like she had the banshee. She hadn't said as much, but he suspected she saw things the same way Nana did. He wondered if her sudden questions about the Book of Fennore had been spurred from such a sighting.

"Jack tried to deny it when I confronted him," Danni was saying, "but I knew too many details. He said he didn't love her and it was a mistake." She looked up at Sean with another tight smile. "I wanted to believe him. I wanted it so badly that I forgave him, even knowing that I could never forget what he'd done. Yvonne thought I was nuts. I guess she was right. But getting married, having a family. Being *part* of a family . . . It's all I've ever wanted."

He swallowed hard, remembering how he'd used that very lure to bring her back home. *Is it not what you've wished for, Danni?*

"The second time I caught him, I knew that even if I married Jack, we'd never be a couple. We'd just be two people who shared a last name and liked to pretend they were together. That probably doesn't make sense, but it's how I felt. But even then, I still couldn't bring myself to kill my dream. I waited for him to do it."

"He left you?" Sean said, surprised.

"Yes." She took a deep breath, pulled her knees up under her chin, and wrapped her arms around them. "He left me."

Sean wanted to move closer. He wanted to hold her again, to smooth out the silky skin puckered between her brows. "What about the other guy you almost married?"

"His name was David. He didn't cheat on me, but he didn't want me either. He said I was too reserved, too cold. He wanted a woman he could love, not just admire." She blinked, and Sean suspected tears would have been in her eyes had she not already cried an ocean. "I never understood what he meant by that. Do you think I'm cold?" she asked.

Hell, no. She was a flame, and he felt raw and open from the burn of her. "I think he was a fucking idiot."

She studied him, looking for something false in his words, in his eyes. Something she wouldn't find. She smiled then. It was but a whisper of the real thing, but it was for him and only him.

With the kitchen cleared, she poured them both tea and sat at the table. She looked small in the man's shirt, fine boned and pale as the moonlight. Once more she drew her knees up, wrapped her arms around them.

"How about you?" she asked after a moment. "Have you been married?"

"No. Not even close."

He saw something in the look she gave him that nudged a dark place in his mind. He sensed there was a purpose behind it, but he couldn't begin to fathom what it was or how to question it.

"Why not?" she asked. "Don't you want to get married? Have children?"

He shrugged, realizing he hadn't thought of it for years, hadn't even considered it a possibility. The reason why eluded him now though. "I never met anyone I trusted enough, I guess," he said, answering both himself and the woman across the table from him.

"Trusted enough? What about loved enough? They go together, don't they?"

"Not always. I've known men who didn't trust their wives alone in the next room, but they loved them anyway."

Danni set her jaw and shook her head. "It has to be both for me. Doesn't it for you?"

"Yes."

She stared at him again with that same probing look. He felt like he was under a spotlight, a glaring search beam that rousted out the slumbering mongrels crouching and snarling in his memory. What did she want to know? Why did he fight so hard to keep it from her? He didn't like her questions, but it was his refusal to answer even himself that made him stand and pace a few steps away.

"You've had serious relationships, though. Haven't you?" she asked.

He forced a shrug. "I've known women."

"I wasn't implying otherwise," she said, coloring to the tips of her small ears.

He wanted to kiss them. He wanted to kiss every inch of her.

She pressed, "I just wondered if you'd had relationships. Commitment."

"Sure and what woman wouldn't want such a thing from me? I've barely a pot to piss in."

"Some women care more about the man than they do his money."

"Well, I've yet to meet one."

She shifted, and he took a perverse pleasure in knowing that he'd made her uncomfortable. It didn't matter that he'd delved into her personal life. He didn't like her returning the favor.

"So that's why?" she said, dispersing any hope that she'd given up on the questions. "You don't think you have enough to offer?"

He turned his back to her, running a hand over his face. "Not entirely. I seem to have a knack for meeting women in their time of need."

"That's a bad thing?"

"Only in that our union tends to be a bridge to something else." He glanced at her over his shoulder, suddenly wondering if he'd just described his time with Danni. Surprised by the tight knot in his gut at the idea of it. He didn't want to be the bridge with Danni MacGrath. He wanted to cross over it. He wanted to stand on the other side with her in his arms. And that bothered him. It worried him because women were creatures he'd never quite understood, and if he managed to foray that gap between them, he could not predict what she would do.

"Have you ever been in love?" Danni persisted, but she sounded ill at ease as she asked. Despite the wisdom of keeping his back to her, of keeping his thoughts shielded in that way, Sean turned to watch another wave of the delicate pink spread over her cheeks.

"I suppose the closest I came to love was with Molly Clark. Her husband had died, and she was alone in the world with five children to feed. I came to help her with the chores. Cut peat for her fire and brought her food when I could."

"How did you meet her?"

Another question he didn't like. It was too hard, reaching back in his memory, and the anger nipped his heels again. "Jesus, I don't even remember."

"Did you sleep with her?"

"Now why would you want to know that?"

She tried to smile, tried to pretend the question had been light-hearted, teasing. But the pink flush darkened, crept from brow to throat, and there was real pain in her eyes. Why would she feel pained by the question? The woman mystified him.

He said, "She had five children and only the wee hours of the night to spend with a man."

"And did you? Spend those wee hours with her?"

"Aye," he said, thinking of those stolen minutes in the dark of her room when the moon began to fade and the sun pondered its rise. She'd welcomed him into her arms, turned her soft touch to his skin. He remembered the warmth of her, the need in her kisses, the slumberous weight of her body shifting under him.

"Like a dream lover," Danni said softly, somehow plucking the memory from his head.

Sean scowled at that. What did she mean, "dream lover" ? But a part of him knew, a part that went scurrying into the dark when her bright beam sought it out. It was real enough, what he'd shared with Molly, even if he couldn't recall her face now. Perhaps not as vivid, not as fiery as what he and Danni had shared that morning. He stopped the thought there. He didn't know for a fact if they'd shared *anything*, did he now?

He chewed on his lip for a silent moment, wondering what went on behind her lovely gray eyes. She sat unmoving, arms still wrapped around her knees, and her stillness struck him as unnatural, as if she'd suddenly been set in plaster and hardened to a point where moving would shatter her into a million powdery fragments.

"Sean, there's something I need to . . ."

She paused and he waited, a tightness clenching his chest. What did she need? What was she going to say? The words seemed to drag her down, clog in her throat. And some instinct told him not to pressure her. Not to force those words out. He didn't want to hear them.

As if sensing his thoughts, she licked her lips and looked away, and a confounding wash of gratitude went through him. Whatever she'd been about to say, she'd changed her mind.

"I—I was just going to ask, when did your mother . . . when did you lose her?"

His relief vanished as quickly as it came. She couldn't know the barbs attached to her question, but they bit at his skin and tore his flesh.

"I told you, five years ago—from now—from this time. I was nine."

"Were you really there?"

He nodded. "And my brother."

"I didn't know you had a brother," she said.

He didn't respond to that. Even now, it was too painful to talk about.

He looked up and saw Danni's eyes fill with distress. She didn't know the details, but she'd guessed they were tragic. She asked, "How ... I mean, why—why didn't Niall go to prison?"

He took a deep breath, seeing that she'd want details, knowing he couldn't evade them. "My mother had a foul temper, and when she drank, there was no calming her," he said softly. "She'd rant at the butcher with the same ire as she would her husband—everyone had seen her in a fit of it. On that day—the day she died—she was especially drunk and especially angry. She pulled a knife on my father and they fought over it. It was so fast, I didn't even know what had happened until I saw her on the floor, with a knife in her chest."

Danni started to say something, but stopped.

"Go ahead—whatever it is, go ahead and say it."

"Well, if they were fighting over the knife she pulled, it does sound like an accident, Sean. Is there a reason you'd think he did it on purpose?"

Don't ask, Sean wanted to shout. *Don't ask me that.* Ignorance was the only way out of the dark labyrinth surrounding them. What she didn't know couldn't hurt her. Couldn't shred her hopes like tissue paper.

"Other than the fact that he was twice her size, you mean?"

She nodded, scrutinizing his face with those gray eyes, peering into his very thoughts. Searching for what he couldn't quite hide. Suddenly, she looked away and Sean knew she'd found it.

"Was it because of *my* mother?" she whispered.

The question hovered between them, an invisible line he didn't want to cross. "I think so," he answered truthfully, because he couldn't lie. Not to Danni.

"I saw them today. Together."

"Where?" But even as he asked, he knew. In the shower. Or rather, beyond the shower.

"You believe he killed her, don't you?"

"Fia?" he asked. "Or my mother?"

"Either. Both."

"I don't want to believe it."

"I don't either."

Which wasn't, for either of them, the same as not believing it. He swallowed, trying to force that lump in his chest away.

"When are you going to tell me the truth, Danni?" he murmured.

She frowned, looking guilty. "I am. I have."

He moved closer, put his hands on the arms of her chair, and looked straight into those beautiful eyes. "Where were you, when you saw them?" She swallowed, squirmed, tried to look away, but he took her chin in his hand and forced her to answer. "Where, Danni?"

"Beneath the ruins," she said so softly he had to strain to hear her.

The answer shocked him. He knew where she was talking about. He'd grown up here, explored the island like a Viking on a quest.

"It's not safe at the ruins," he said.

She almost smiled at that. "I was careful."

"Were you? Or was it another dream? Like the banshee?"

She didn't answer. He could see the fear of it in her eyes. This wasn't something she talked about, something she trusted others with. Knowing that made him all the more desperate for her to tell *him*. To trust *him* with her dark secrets.

"What are they like, your dreams?" he asked.

She looked hurt as she stared into his eyes, wounded by the realization that he'd somehow circumvented all of her carefully constructed barriers and now stood on the brink of discovery. He wanted to reassure her that he'd never use her secrets against her, but he didn't know for certain that it was true. Nothing in this cracked place and time could be taken as certainty.

"What's it like when you see things?" he pressed.

She hesitated another moment before saying in a voice thick with resignation, "Like I'm there, only I know I'm not. I feel things—the air, the cold. But I can't change anything. I can only watch."

"How do you know? Have you ever tried changing what you see?"

She frowned. "I can't. I'm not really there. The people I see, they don't see me back."

"Ever?"

She faltered, her brows pulling together, puckering the skin between them. For the second time that night, he wanted to lean over and press his lips to that silky point, smooth it out.

"Once," she began and he had to lean close to hear her. "Once I thought—I felt like—my mother saw me. Just for a moment. And today, earlier, I thought she heard me."

The air seemed to still then, change into something solid and unyielding. Afraid his next question would turn it to stone, he asked, "Is it what's happening now? This. Us. Are we really here? Or is this all an illusion that I've stumbled into?"

Her startled look became every thought that flashed through her mind. Surprise, denial, fear, and question. Possibility. "No," she breathed.

"Are you sure?"

"I can't—I've never been able to talk or be seen. No, it can't be that."

He held his relief at bay because even in denial, she wasn't certain. "Just before we . . . before we fell through. In your kitchen, I felt like the walls were fading on us." Sean struggled to find the words that could describe the experience. "Like they were turning to glass and when they were done, I wouldn't recognize what was outside."

Her nod seemed reflexive. A jerky agreement she didn't realize she'd made.

"Can you call them?" he asked.

"The visions? You mean, can I make one happen?"

"Can you?"

"I don't know. I've never tried. It's always been someone coming to me. Someone wanting something."

"And why is that?"

"How would I know? I don't understand it. I don't even know why it happens. Before you, it had been years—so long I'd forgotten what it felt like."

He froze, staring at her with narrowed eyes. "What does that mean? Before me?"

"I saw you. Before you came to my house that morning."

"You saw me?" he repeated stupidly. His mouth was dry and his tongue felt thick. He remembered the look in her eyes as he'd stood on her porch. As if she'd recognized him. As if she'd been *expecting* him.

"You said it was someone coming to you. Someone wanting something. What did I want?"

Me. She didn't say it, but it was there in her face. In the luminous window of her eyes. Well, it was true. He wanted her more than he'd ever wanted anything in his life.

"Why have you never tried to make one happen?" he asked.

"Why would I?"

He regarded her steadily, letting Danni find her own answer to the question. In honesty, he didn't know it himself. But something inside was driving him. A question in his subconscious he couldn't bring into focus. It forced words from his lips.

"It's a mystery, how we are here. I can't grasp the way of it. But I can't deny that it's happened either. Not when I'm sitting at this table. Not when I've stared into my own face. It's impossible, but I'm thinking that somewhere there is an explanation."

She pushed out of her chair, forcing him to move back. Her momentum took her a few steps away before she stopped, arms crossed protectively over her middle.

"All I'm asking, Danni, is for you to consider that nothing is what it seems. We are twenty years out of synch as you pointed out to me just this afternoon, and no amount of rationalization can make it sane. But it seems to make more sense that the answer lies within you and not with the Book of Fennore."

"What if it's you?" she demanded. "Why does it have to be me? Nothing like this ever happened to me before you came knocking on my door."

"It couldn't be me," he said, with a grim laugh. "There's nothing special about me."

"Isn't there, Sean? Are you so sure about that?"

She stared at him, willing him to see something that was beyond his ability. What did she mean? What did she want of him? How could she possibly think it—*this*—could have anything to do with *him*?

"Haven't you felt out of synch for a long time?" she demanded.

And he nodded, without even realizing he meant to do it. Yes,

yes, *yes*. He *had* felt unconnected, unaligned with the ticking of the clock, with the passage of the days. Adrift, lost, unaware of either. And then suddenly, here—now—when it made no sense at all, he felt eminently united with the spin of time. How could that be?

Something she saw on his face made Danni step back. Recant. "Never mind. This conversation is pointless," she said. "Neither of us is special enough to change history. Whatever—however we've come to this place, it had nothing to do with you or me."

And yet, like a door that once opened could never be closed, the idea remained there, solid between them.

"I'm tired," she said. And she looked it. Her gaze skittered toward the bed and then away. There was no couch, no extra bedding. Just the one narrow mattress on a spindly frame, crouched in the corner.

Sean stared at it, too, and then asked the question that had consumed most of the day. Somehow it was more pressing than how they'd come to be here. More urgent than who was or was not the instrument of their journey. He moved until he was standing right behind her. The top of her head reached his chin, the scent of her hair and her skin filled his senses.

Gently, insistently, he turned her. He felt the resistance in her body, in the gaze that climbed to meet his own.

In a voice he barely recognized as his own, he asked, "Did we make love this morning or was that just a different kind of dream?"

Chapter Twenty-two

I T seemed Sean waited an eternity for her to answer. An eternity with nothing in it but her eyes, as mysterious as the evening fog, thick with silvery mist and wrought with the unknown. He saw his own confusion mirrored in their depths, and he knew that if making love to her had been only a dream, it was one they'd shared.

"It was a dream," she insisted.

"Then how is it we dreamed it together?"

She frowned and shook her head. "We couldn't. We didn't."

"Aye, we could," he said, moving closer. "Aye, we did."

The vulnerability was back in her eyes, but this time he knew—he *knew*—it came from a different place. She was comparing the passion of that dream to the image she held of herself. Because of the stupid men she'd known, she thought she was lacking. Somewhere along the way, she'd made up her mind that they were right and she was incapable of passion. Sean saw this, saw it as clearly as if it were spelled out in the air between them.

Even now she was withdrawing, battening down hatches, locking passageways. She couldn't see what he knew instinctively. There was nothing cold or reserved about Danni MacGrath. He wanted to prove it to her. But in a moment when he should have been reaching out, he found himself hesitating.

Her hair lay in a swirling mess around her head, her skin glowing like pearl, her face bare and sweet. There was innocence in Danni, but there was also fire and passion. Dream or no, he'd felt it this morning and he wanted to feel it again—wanted desperately to feel it *more*.

He dropped his gaze to the pulse that beat at her throat. The man's T-shirt clung to her breasts, peaking at hardened nipples. The stretchy pants fit her lean, shapely legs, molding curves and muscle all the way down to the thick white socks, and even those were somehow sexy, somehow intimate. He skimmed back up, imagined catching the hem of her shirt and pulling it over her head, baring those soft shoulders, the curve of her throat, the slope of her breasts.

A train wreck, that's what this was. But the course was set and the outcome inevitable.

She didn't say a word as she watched him, letting her own eyes move from his face to his bare chest to his stomach. His muscles tightened in anticipation, as if her glancing look were a touch that would heat his skin. He wanted her to look lower, to see that just standing this close to her had him thinking of so much more.

Neither spoke, because words would be redundant.

He felt incapable of movement and so he waited for her instead. Waited for the questions in her eyes to become answers, decisions. She swayed closer and the soft scent of her filled him with aching need. He wanted to bury his face in her hair, inhale, taste that scent. Taste every inch of her.

Her hands settled against his chest, light as petals, hot and silky and moving over the taut muscles. Searching, finding. They paused just over his heart, feeling the erratic beat, the labored pounding. He thought she could feel the blood rushing through his veins, urging him to move, to take. He felt hot, hotter than humanly possible. Like he might suddenly combust and melt into something only she could ply with her feather touch.

She stilled, those small hands holding his heart. Then she tipped her head back and he was staring into eyes of winter smoke and midnight slate. They were wide and round and hurt and bewildered. Why didn't he touch her back?

"I'm afraid," he said without meaning to.

Afraid that he'd fall into those eyes and never find his way out again. Afraid that this, which felt so real, could somehow be snatched away if he grasped too tightly. Afraid of returning to that land of numbness that had become his life. Afraid now to chance an escape.

The answer—a self-fulfilling prophecy—made him exhale with twisted humor. Danni bit her lip and then smiled back, slowly, sweetly, sexily.

"Don't be," she said, and it was his undoing.

With a muffled groan, he reached for her, pressed his hands to her hips, swallowing the small curve with his grasp and splaying his fingers across the soft flesh of her behind.

She moved in the wake of his capitulation—with tentative boldness, then with growing confidence that made his head light, his heart thump even faster. Her arms were around his neck now, her hips brushing the unmistakable erection trapped painfully in his jeans. It was the pain, glorious and real, that broke the last tie of his reserve.

He hauled her up hard against him, and the sound she made in her throat was like scented oil on wildfire. It filled every sense and ignited every receptive nerve in his body. Like he'd imagined, he caught the hem of her shirt and tugged it up in one smooth stroke. She lifted her arms in mute acceptance, standing before him like moonlight harnessed in shimmering flesh. Her skin glowed like a rare white opal, pale and alive, soft and warm. Her breasts were small and high, perfect as only God could create. He touched one and then the other, still fearing that she might vanish if he went too far, went too fast. Grasped too greedily.

"It must have been a dream . . ." she murmured against his throat.

She didn't finish the thought. She didn't need to. It was in his head, the remainder of it. It must have been a dream because it couldn't compare to the reality of this moment.

He scooped her off her feet and carried her to the narrow bed, slowly, because now that he'd committed, he wanted every moment, every second of it to last. She pressed soft, wet kisses to his chest and throat as he followed her down to the mattress and braced himself over her. He framed her face with his hands, trembling with the feel of her skin against his, her body beneath him. Slowly he settled his mouth over hers.

Her lips met his with acceptance and demand. She let him touch and tease, sharing the air between them before opening and inviting him in. Her breath was sweet and his tongue brushed against hers, velvet on velvet, sensitive and sensual. The feel of her, the taste of her, it was like a drug shooting through his bloodstream, enhancing every second until his world consisted only of Danni and the sweetness of her surrender, the completeness of his own.

He pulled back, stood so he could slide her pants and panties down her long legs and fling them somewhere behind them, white socks knotted in the mix. His boxers and jeans joined the tangle, leaving them both stripped and vulnerable. Sean breathed deeply, trying to slow his heart, slow the urge that wanted to bury itself deep within her. He saw something flash in her eyes, determination, resolve. For a moment he feared she'd changed her mind, and he wanted to shout, to grab her, to force her. But it wasn't rejection he'd seen.

Naked, she came up on her knees and took him in her hands, paralyzing him with a thousand sensations. The muscles in his stomach clenched and his legs felt wobbly, but she kept him standing as she leaned in, letting her fingers explore his sensitive skin as her other hand stroked up with a firmness just shy of the most exquisite agony.

More roughly than he'd intended, Sean took her face in his hands and kissed her again, using tongue and teeth, and the power of his desire to make her feel him, as he felt her. He pulled her off balance and she fell against him, but her hands continued their wondrous torture even as she kissed him back, tasting him, electrifying him with the feel of her hot response. How long had he been thinking of this? Wanting this? It seemed a lifetime.

He wouldn't last if he didn't stop her. He pulled her tight against him and lowered them both until he spread over her, hip to hip, mouth to mouth. She released him with a tug of reluctance that nearly drove him to release.

She was saying his name, speaking it reverently against his lips, against his throat, the bunched chords of his biceps. She was seducing him, making him feel inexperienced, like it was his first time. Not like this morning when she'd been pliant and obedient, answering his commands with eager acquiescence.

"Do you remember the dream?" she breathed against his ear.

Yes, he remembered it, but it was nothing to this bursting tension and need.

"You said things, you told me to do things. . . ."

"I remember," he said, pulling her higher so he could kiss her breasts, tongue the hard points of her nipples.

She arched against him, her wet heat sprawled low on his belly, just out of reach, just out of touch. He ached to grab her hips and force her down, drive himself deep inside her and watch her beautiful face as he did it. What fool could ever have called her cold?

She was kissing him again, everywhere, humbling and empowering him with her passion. She teased him with the soft wetness of her mouth until he couldn't take it anymore. Then she paused once again.

"Sean?" she said, burying her face in his neck. He felt a flood of heat follow his name and shifted so he could look at her. Her face had turned red and she wouldn't meet his eyes.

"What is it?" he asked as the flush spread to her neck and chest. "Danni, what is it?"

"I want . . ." she began, and then she looked away again in embarrassment.

"Yes," he said with a surprised laugh that was as tight and strained as every other inch of him. "God yes, whatever you want, tell me and I'll do it. Yes."

She peeped up at him with a look that was at once pleased and aghast, as if she couldn't believe she'd had the bollocks to ask. He wanted her to tell him what it was that she wanted, he wanted to give it to her, now. Immediately.

"I want to do . . . what we did in the dream," she whispered.

What they'd done? What *hadn't* they done in the dream? It had been the mother of all fantasies. Until this.

"I want that, too," he said, because of course he did.

She took a deep breath and then held it. A small sigh seemed to signal something inside her that she was ready. She shifted again so that she straddled him, breasts pressed to his chest in a torment he would happily endure forever. His legs dangled over the edge of the bed, and he pressed the balls of his feet to the floor as her touch charged through every inch of him. Her mouth found his, and she kissed him deeply, her tongue soft and exotic against his own.

And then she began to slide down his body, her touch growing bolder as she moved lower. She nipped at his hip, pressed her lips to the point just below his belly button. Then her hands were around him and her mouth. Holy mother of God, her mouth.

He made a sound of sheer agony and she froze. "I'm sorry. Did I hurt you?" she asked in a horrified voice.

Sean's disbelief was only outweighed by his need. "God no, Danni, you're perfect. You're making me—"

But she'd heard all she needed to hear, and she went back to the task at hand with a renewed fervor. Sean propped himself on his elbows, watching her as she kissed and stroked and licked and, heaven save him, she sucked. He was trembling with the effort to hold back when she seemed determined to break him down.

"Danni, honey," he said, out of breath, out of time. "If you don't—" She raced her tongue over the head in a hot, wet circle. "If you don't—"

"What?" she cried suddenly, her voice filled with frustration. "What am I doing wrong? Why haven't you . . . why aren't you—"

She met his eyes and saw his absolute shock. Saw that he'd been holding back, wanting to please her before he exploded.

"Oh," she said.

He didn't give her a chance to say more. He hauled her up, rolling her onto her back as he slid between her legs, stomach to stomach, heaving chest to heaving chest, mouth to mouth. Every part of him seemed to fit with her body. He trembled as he held her, as he slid into the heat and wetness of her and began to move in slow, torturous strokes. Everything became an isolated sensation, the feel of her fingers in his hair, her mouth against his, her breasts soft and flattened by the hard wall of his chest. He shifted, moved his hand down the flat of her belly to touch her there, where every soft and feminine mystery seemed to exist.

She moaned his name and arched her back, dragging him deeper into the depths of her secrets. He rubbed in tight circles and he moved inside her, focusing on the rhythm of her body, the harsh rush of her breathing, the soft murmur of her voice as he brought her to the same dizzying edge he was poised upon. She came with a cry that took him with her. They held onto one another, as sensations tore through him in unbearable pleasure. It felt like something cracked deep inside him and light spilled out, chasing away shadow and fear, leaving only this moment with Danni seared in his mind.

His heart felt like it might burst from his chest as he braced himself above her and looked into her beautiful face. In just a few days, she'd come to be the centering point of his world. She'd come to mean more to him than life itself. How it had happened, he didn't know. But he couldn't pretend it wasn't true, not even to himself.

And with the acknowledgement, came the fear again. Dark, insidious, solid. If he lost her, he would die. Literally, figuratively. The realization drove him to an edge that he couldn't look over. Wouldn't look down.

He did the only thing he could. He held her tighter, finding sanctuary in her feel, in her scent. He kissed her like his life depended on it, sensing that somehow it did.

Chapter Twenty-three

THEY lay in silence late into the night, face-to-face, fingers touching, skin pressed to skin. Danni learned of his childhood, listening to the deep flux of his voice as he spoke of growing up in Ballyfionúir, where he'd known most everyone. He talked of his mother and how she'd scrub Sean and his brother within an inch of their lives before marching them to mass each Sunday. She'd carried a flask in her purse and had partaken of more than communion wine during the service. The ebb and flow of his voice was another caress in the darkness and one she fell into, like a dark pool of warm water.

As she watched his mouth forming words, watched memories move through his eyes, she thought him achingly beautiful. At almost the same instance, she was struck by the truth of their situation. It twisted what they'd shared into a few heartrending moments before reality would rip them apart. For whatever reason, Sean was alive in this time, but in her time—the time she knew and wanted to live in again—he was a ghost. The tragedy of it nearly drove her from the bed. A random image came to her then—one of a movie she'd seen in the group home, before Yvonne had taken her in. It was an eighties movie, about a man who'd never known love until a strange woman had suddenly appeared in his life.

She remembered Tom Hanks as the hero, goofy and charming, besotted by the beautiful woman with the long blonde hair and strange ways. He'd brought her home with him, intent on marrying her and living happily ever after—until he'd discovered she was a mermaid. Drunk and disillusioned, Tom Hanks had turned to his brother in hurt bewilderment and told him that all his life he'd been searching for someone to love and now that he'd finally found her, the woman of his dreams was a fish. A fish.

The delivery of the line had been classic and never failed to bring laughter. It didn't make her smile thinking of it now though, because the twisted pain behind the flippant statement was far too real for her. Danni had been looking for someone to love her whole life, too. And Sean was *more* than everything she'd wished for.

Only in her case, the man of her dreams wasn't a fish. He was dead, or would be by tomorrow's end.

She'd almost told him earlier, should have told him when the opportunity was there, so close. It was almost as if he'd been waiting for her to speak those words. But she couldn't do it. She was afraid of more than being left alone. She was afraid of losing him. Afraid of what the truth would do to this fragile bubble they now lived in.

Sean went on talking, unaware of the turmoil in her heart. Listening to him, she noted the confusion that clouded his eyes as he moved past the years of adolescence into manhood. The vivid details of his recollections dimmed as he struggled to remember life after he'd become an unwitting specter. Overlooked, or noticed only by a few—those sensitive to his energy, those who feared the shadowy image that never quite came into focus.

He'd taken their reactions as aversion. Why would they like and accept him? He was the son of the man who'd killed his own wife and then wiped out another man's young and happy family. He didn't blame them their censure.

Colleen had been the only constant in his life after Fia and the children disappeared, after Niall took his own life in remorse. . . .

After Sean had been killed. Danni pieced together what he didn't say.

Occasionally it seemed he would meet someone with a sixth sense, someone who could really see him, and the details would suddenly appear again. He didn't know how relief filled his eyes then, how these pockets of awareness became confirmation of his existence.

But Danni understood it. She thought of what he'd told her earlier, about the widow he'd gone to in the middle of the night. *Dream lover*, she'd called him, imagining the lonely woman visited by Sean—solid, muscular, *warm* Sean. Had she seen him, like Danni did? Or had he been a fantasy she imagined as a dream, like the one they'd shared yesterday morning?

"Hey," he said, tracing a finger over her jaw. "I've put you into a coma with my boring stories, haven't I?"

The very idea of it made her smile. Sean was a lot of things she hadn't expected, but *boring* wasn't one of them. She could listen to that deep and sexy voice day in and day out and never get tired of it. She leaned closer and kissed him. The feel of his mouth was addicting, like the taste of him, the scent of him. They'd made love for hours—*hours*—until her muscles felt tired and sated, but she still wanted more. A stockpile to last her when he was gone.

The thought sobered her. *No.* She would find a way to make sure that didn't happen.

* * *

IT was several hours before dawn when Danni slipped from bed and dressed. She'd slept a little, but each time she dozed off, the warmth of the man sleeping beside her would wake her again to dwell on the quandary of how and where and *who* they were. Her thoughts had finally driven her from the bed, from the man who'd aroused feelings in her that couldn't be allowed to take root. At any minute the air could turn again and spit the two of them out of this time and place and back to a future that was pointless.

She couldn't love a dead man.

Restless, she paced the kitchen until she began to feel caged. The sense of being trapped finally coerced her outside, where sounds of the sea pounding relentlessly against the rocks, thundering and receding with steadfast determination, eased her tension. Beneath the black tapestry of sky, she could see lights out on the water. Fishing boats already pushing off, fighting the tide.

Danni breathed in the damp and salty scented air, turning her face to the sliver of moon hovering low on the horizon. Dawn was not far away.

She nearly screamed when a shadow moved to her right and Colleen materialized from a flat boulder where she'd been sitting. As if it was the most natural thing in the world for Danni to take a stroll in the darkest hours and for Colleen to happen upon her.

"You've been waiting for me," Danni said, and it wasn't a question.

"For longer than ye know, child," Colleen answered, taking up her seat again on the boulder. "Sit down, ask me your questions. You'll be having some by now."

"And you'll tell me the truth if I ask them?"

"And why wouldn't I?"

Danni sat down, trying to mask her frustration at Colleen's noncommittal response. Danni wanted to ask about Sean, but she was afraid—afraid that giving her questions a voice might somehow strip away this tentative happiness she'd found. But she knew that was a fool's way of thinking. By tonight they'd both be dead. Still she couldn't start there. Not with Sean.

"What happened to my mother?" she asked instead.

"She went to America," Colleen responded coolly.

"Try something I don't already know. Why did she leave my father? Was it because of Niall?

"Of that I know less than you. I only know she took you and your brother and went to find her sister."

"Her sister? In California?"

"I believe it's true, but I'll not swear to it."

"She took us both? Me *and* Rory? But what happened to him? And why was I left in Arizona?"

Colleen looked down at her feet and shook her head. "I can only guess from what I know of you and what I know of her and what I hope is the way of it. I think she must have found her sister and left Rory with her. Then she took you to Arizona—don't ask me why because I cannot tell you."

"Then what?"

She gave Danni a bleak look and disheartened shrug. "It could only be bad, whatever it was. Nothing else would have kept her from her children."

"Unless she decided to go back for Rory and just left me behind." The words burned in her throat.

"You don't believe that, do you now? And neither do I."

Danni looked away. She didn't know what she believed anymore. But this could be her only chance to find the truth, and she couldn't avoid asking what she needed most to know just because she was afraid.

"And what about Sean?" she whispered. "How does he die?"

"You haven't seen it for yourself?" Colleen demanded.

Danni crossed her arms, looking beyond Colleen to the sea. "What I saw was very confusing. I couldn't tell exactly what was happening. I think Sean—young Sean—was already dead. He was on the ground and Niall was holding him. They were in the cavern, beneath the ruins."

She glanced over in time to see Colleen's eyes narrow. There was a spark of something burning deep inside them. Maybe hope, maybe despair. Danni couldn't tell.

"My mom is there with me and Rory."

"What about me?" Colleen asked.

Danni shook her head. "There's another man, but I couldn't see him. I don't know who he is, but he's angry and he's arguing with my mother—or Niall. I don't see my father at all. He must come later. Too late to help them."

"And I'm not there?" Colleen repeated, her voice sharp.

"No. Should you be?"

"Since Michael was a lad, I've seen it," she said softly. "And though I've no idea how, I know I've lived it."

"Lived it? What does that mean?"

Colleen shook her head. "Tell me more."

Danni wanted to press her, but the intensity of Colleen's expression made her go on. "The argument between the man I can't see and Niall or my mother seems to escalate, and I hear a gun and there's pain. I feel pain. Like I've been shot. And then I'm outside again, with Sean. Grown-up Sean. We're standing beside a grave and when I look in, I see myself—as I am now. A woman. I'm in a grave with Michael—Sean. The boy."

"And the ruins are to your back, the dolmen in the distance."

"How do you know that?"

"I've seen it myself, many times."

"All of it? Or just the grave?" Colleen didn't answer. Frustrated, Danni asked another. "Why did you say you've lived it?"

Colleen shifted uncomfortably. "You'll think me a lunatic," she murmured.

"I already think that," Danni countered, and the old woman looked up with surprise.

"Fair enough, I suppose. I'll tell you then, though I doubt you'll believe me. It begins each time at a different point. The first, it was just the Book I saw."

"The Book of Fennore?"

"And what other Book would I be talking about?" she snapped. "Other times, I've seen the grave or the cavern."

"For the love of God, Colleen. For once could you be less cryptic?" Danni asked.

"I've no liking for that vinegar tone, child."

"I'm sorry. But I feel like I'm running out of time."

"Aye, and right you are about that. But you see, what comes to pass has happened over and over again. It's not just seeing, I have. It's living it as well."

"I don't understand what you mean by that."

"Sure and you rushed me. What is it you expect?"

Danni let out a breath of exasperation and wry amusement. Her grandmother might look like a sweet old woman, but any fool who took it for more than a deceiving appearance would soon find out that beneath her façade was steel will.

Colleen gave a heavy sigh and went on. "What's at work here, on Ballyfionúir, it's out of order. Out of *all* sense of order. 'Tis always been this way. The old ones will talk about it, if you're buying the pints and the music has mellowed their tongues. They'll tell you tales of people appearing like a bolt of lightning only without the thunder to warn you. Or others who have just gone missing, suddenly there and then not. Erased by God and drawn into another place."

Legends, myths, built and spread over the ages. That was what a sane person would call it. But Danni had given up on sanity—and so it seemed sanity had given up on Danni. Were the *old ones* Colleen spoke of other time travelers? People who appeared and disappeared . . . like Danni and Sean had? Danni would have scoffed if she wasn't proof herself that it could happen, had happened.

"Is it only here that the stories are told? In Ballyfionúir?"

"Oh no, the whole island is filled with magic from the shores to the clouds. Can you not feel it?"

Danni nodded. Yes, she felt it. "Is it because of the Book of Fennore?"

"I cannot tell you the answer to that. I do not know it myself. What I do know is that this isn't the first time I've lived the days leading up to that awful night when everything I love is lost. I've lived them many times."

Her skin puckered with goose bumps as Danni asked, "Why don't you try to stop it, then, if you know what's going to happen?"

"Are you thinking that I haven't? That I just stand by and watch?"

"I don't know what to think, Colleen."

"Twice I've tried, but fate will have its way. The devil couldn't change it unless he was drunk."

"But what happened when you tried?"

"The end was the same and yet it wasn't. I will not talk of it," she said, and there was a dark pain in her voice that cut through Danni like slivers of metal peeled from a blade. "I can only say I made it worse, both times. I cannot try it again."

Danni watched her, waiting for her to continue, but she fell into agitated silence.

"You're there when it happens?" Danni repeated softly. "But I didn't see you."

"This last time, I couldn't watch it again. I couldn't face it and do nothing. Yet I knew anything I tried would only end with it worse than before. So I removed myself, hoping . . . always hoping . . ."

She trailed off and something in her eyes made Danni feel like she'd missed a vital clue.

"So you're saying you keep reliving your life?"

"Not all of it."

Not all of it? What did that mean?

"I suppose I could say it's your life I live."

Danni frowned. "My life . . . ?"

And then suddenly understanding broke over her like the foamy white surf violating the soft sands and fragmented shells of the beach. Tonight grown-up Danni would die, but her child-self lived on to be abandoned in Arizona, always searching for what she couldn't find, what she couldn't have. And tonight, young Sean would die, only his spirit would live on, forever seeking justice. The two would exist on opposites sides of the world until one day Colleen would send that spirit to find Danni and bring her back to this point in time, when it would all happen again.

"You knew we were coming—Sean and I—because we've been here before," she whispered.

Colleen nodded.

"But we don't make a difference. We just come back to die. Is that what you're saying?"

Colleen's bottom lip trembled, and her eyes glimmered with unshed tears.

"But something has changed this time, hasn't it? You think something's different. Why? What is it?"

"I cannot tell you," she whispered, her voice cracking. "Fate, destiny. It can't be bent by one person's will, can it now? Not by looking back and doing it differently. The Lord knows I have tried to alter the course time and again."

"Don't talk in circles, Colleen. Tell me what to do. Tell me how to save him."

"And make it worse? Perhaps exchange one life for another? Take away the one chance to change it again? Can you not hear what I'm telling you, child? I have tried and I have failed. Whatever is to come, it must come from you."

She'd tried and she'd failed, yet Colleen had managed to do something right—or wrong. Something that culminated in *this* moment, this moment of truth. Unless this too was just another piece of the repeating ritual.

"What has the Book of Fennore to do with me, Colleen? Am I supposed to use it? Is that what you're talking around?"

The moonlight gave Colleen a waxy sheen. She looked unreal, perched in the greedy black of night, bathed by the glow of harsh unyielding brightness. The lines on her face mapped the deep valleys of her sorrow, the jagged edges of her joys, the fanning rivers of her hope. The breeze teased the ends of her cloak and tugged at the stray wisps of her hair. She looked lost and alone, but resilient and determined.

"Trust yourself, granddaughter," Colleen said softly. "If it's the Book you think you must use, then that is what you should do. Only you know the answer to this riddle."

"Why only me?"

"It is you who wrote it," she said.

Danni clenched her eyes shut against the wave of anger rising inside. Why couldn't Colleen give her a straight answer? Yes or no, go or stay. Use it or run from it.

"Just tell me the truth," she said, unable to keep her resentment at bay.

"Aye, we all are wanting that. The truth. But who is to say what truth there is? Not myself, for I've guessed it wrong too many times before."

Danni opened her eyes again, hearing the whispered words repeating in her head. *Fate, destiny. It can't be bent by one person's will, can it now?* Was she asking or telling?

"It can be changed," Danni said suddenly, fiercely.

"Really? And who would be doing the changing? You?" Though her words came with a sharp bite of doubt, Colleen couldn't hide the eagerness in her tone.

"Maybe," Danni said.

"Sure and don't you sound convinced? Maybe. *Phhssht.* Was *maybe* what God had in his mind when he created the world?"

Danni raised her brows. "Maybe. Maybe that's why it's such a mess."

Colleen grinned at that. "A tongue you have in your head, darlin'. It does a grandmother good to hear it." Colleen patted Danni's hand. "Ask me another," she said. "For I know if there's an answer, you'll find a way to ferret it out."

"Tell me about the Book," Danni said softly. "Did my mother bring it here?"

"I only know what I've heard, and hasn't that come to me by way of the wind and every window it's blown through before mine? All legend. It is what it is."

"Sean says the Book can't be used," Danni said.

The old woman paused, considering. Danni wondered what thoughts went through that sharp mind. She waited, tense and unsure.

"The Ballaghs have always been known to be healers and mystics," Colleen said, seeming to ignore the implied question. "*Marked man*—'tis roughly what the name means. And isn't it true, for marked we've been through the ages. Powerful and feared were the Ballaghs."

She gave Danni a meaningful look.

"Is that why I see things?" Danni asked. "Because there's Ballagh blood in my veins?"

"Aye, you get it first from me and then from your mum."

"My mother is a Ballagh?" Danni murmured, thinking of Cathán asking Fia if Danni was related to her. Now it made sense.

"Oh yes, a direct descendent of a MacGrath and Ballagh union. The same is true of your father."

In her mind, Danni pictured the twist and turn, the weave and grain of the bloodline. Ballaghs and MacGraths as entwined and knotted as hemp.

"Does my mom see things, too?"

"Now how would I be knowing that? She'd think me a crazy woman if I asked her. But she bears the birthmark, same as you. Same as me." Colleen pushed up her sleeve and showed Danni the small rose shape in the crook of her arm.

"What about Sean?"

"Indeed, what about him?"

"Who were his parents?"

"*What* is the question you're meaning, I think. My husband was a Ballagh as was his wife who died bringing Sean's father into the world. And when Niall chose a wife, wouldn't you know, another Ballagh."

"So Sean has no MacGrath in him?"

"Well sure, somewhere in his family tree there'd be a MacGrath. But Sean is perhaps the purest of blooded Ballaghs in centuries."

"And does he, I mean, has he had visions?"

"He's never shared them with me if he has. But visions aren't the only thing the Ballaghs are known for. Oh, the list is long of the powers a Ballagh might possess. They say once upon a time there was a Ballagh who could stop the curse of death from stealing the dying."

Danni's mouth went dry. "Stop it how?"

"Well now, if I knew that I'd be a millionaire, wouldn't I? But that's not what you mean, is it? What is it you're wanting to know, girl?"

"Does Sean have . . . powers?" She felt ridiculous even asking the question, but it was even more absurd to ignore what was happening all around her. Ballyfionúir was a place of magic, of the unbelievable.

"Oh aye. He's a great sorcerer. Do you not see how he's enthralled you?"

Danni looked up at that and saw humor in Colleen's eyes. But behind it there was something else. Something more. The look sent a shudder through Danni's body.

"I watched the Gardai dig up that grave and pull Michael's body out of it. And yours, I saw that, too. But wasn't it the very next morning Michael was at my table waiting for his breakfast?"

Michael's spirit, anyway, but Colleen didn't have to spell it out for Danni. Did his appearing to them both qualify as a *power*? Danni thought of how he'd seemed to her the night he'd shown up on her doorstep. She hadn't thought him a ghost. Even after she knew, when he'd touched her, kissed her . . . it had felt real. Not as real as last night, but real enough that she'd believed it.

"He's not the only ghost on this island, though, is he?" Danni said. "What about the white ghost?"

"What do you know of the white ghost?" Colleen asked sharply.

"I've seen her."

"And what business was she about? Did she offer you a thing? Anything?"

"Her comb."

Colleen sucked her breath in through her teeth.

"I didn't take it. Sean told me to never take it."

"Aye, he's a good boy. So he knows of your sight?" she asked, curious.

"I told him it was a dream, but he guessed the truth."

"Lies are never the answer, child. If you're to save one another, there can be no secrets."

"And is that what I'm here for? To save Sean?"

"And he, you."

"With the Book? Is that it? I'm supposed to use it?"

Colleen shook her head. "And how would you be doing that? To use it you must have it. To have it, you must know where to find it."

"You've looked for it, haven't you?" Danni asked suddenly. "You've seen it, too, and you tried to take it."

"I've only seen it once," Colleen told her. "In the hands of my son, just before he destroyed all that I loved."

"You saw it in real time? Not a vision?"

Colleen nodded, her eyes on Danni's face. "And you?"

"Only visions. Twice, now."

The smile that curved Colleen's lips held too much satisfaction for Danni not to know she'd been led to this point. Inexplicably, but inerrantly led.

"And what have you seen?"

"Enough to wipe that satisfied smile off your face."

"'Tis not satisfaction," she said.

"What, then?" Danni demanded. "The Book of Fennore is evil. I could feel that, and I wasn't even there. Not really."

"True enough. It can give you everything you wish for, but what it takes . . . It steals the part of you that makes you a person, that makes you human."

"But you would have me try to use it anyway?" Danni asked, hurt, wounded to her soul by having to ask the question.

"I cannot tell you what you should or shouldn't do. Can you not hear my words?"

"I hear just fine." And Danni's tone said that she did. Colleen was willing to sacrifice Danni if it meant saving everyone else. Suddenly she was tired, tired to the core of her being. She stood and took a step toward the cottage.

"I'm just the messenger here, Danni," Colleen said softly.

"Funny, Sean told me the same thing. But you know what? That doesn't make it any better. I hear the Grim Reaper is just a messenger, too."

Colleen's eyes narrowed. "Do not use that tone with me, Dáirinn. I am still your grandmother, and I will have the respect I am due."

"My grandmother?" Danni repeated incredulously. "That's a technicality, Colleen. The reality is you are a stranger. Nothing more, nothing less."

"And whose fault would that be?"

Speechless, Danni stared at her. *Whose fault?* Was she nuts?

But Colleen's eyes were blazing now, and she stepped up to Danni and pointed a finger at her. "I'll tell you since you seem to have lost your tongue so suddenly. The fault is yours, Dáirinn MacGrath. And yours alone."

The breath came out of her lungs with a whoosh. "How can you say that? Do you know what life has been like for me? Do—"

"Ach, spare me the sad tale. What has life been for Sean? For Niall? Your mother? What of them?"

Danni was shaking her head, trying to grasp how Colleen could lay fault at Danni's feet. "I was a child when all this happened."

"And even then you could have stopped it. But instead you put it all behind you and never thought of it again. You *forgot*," she spat.

"You think I did that on purpose? My God, Colleen, you think I *chose* to live that way?"

"What I think is not important."

"But you're accusing me—"

"By the end of the day, everything I love will be taken from me. I've not the time to woo you round to the truth. Ye can stop it."

"You can't be serious?" Danni said, feeling helpless under the weight of Colleen's censure. "Look at me. I'm not some omnipotent being who can just snap her fingers and change the world. I can't even get my own dog to follow me home."

"And yet here you stand."

"Because of you. *You* brought us here."

"No, child. It wasn't me and it wasn't Sean. Look inside to see how you came to be here." She turned then and walked away.

"Wait," Danni said. "What else . . . How am I supposed to . . . What do I do?"

"And what answer would you have me give? You can do whatever it is you set your mind to. Isn't that how the saying goes?"

"But I don't even know where to start."

"Then I'd be setting my mind to find out, wouldn't I now?"

And with a curt nod of her chin, she started down the path without looking back. The fog rolling off the sea gobbled her up and left Danni alone in a white and black world with no place to hide.

Chapter Twenty-four

As Danni went back inside the one-room cottage, she could still hear the waves beating against the rocks, demanding submission, eroding the shore and pummeling it into silken sand. That's how Danni felt inside, like something that had been rendered into particles that no longer resembled their origin.

She sat on the couch and curled her legs beneath her. The house was silent but for the soft and steady sound of Sean breathing just a few feet away in the makeshift bedroom. She'd left the curtain open and she could see the shadowy shape of him in the bed. She listened, feeling out of place even in her own skin as her conversation with Colleen repeated in her head.

Even then you could have stopped it.

Her entire life she'd been trying to pretend that she was just like everyone else. But she'd never fooled anyone, had she? No matter how good she became at hiding who and what she was, others had always sensed there was something about her. Something not quite right, not quite normal. From foster families to the men she'd known, they'd sent her back.

Now, here she was. Living an impossibility. Having conversations in the middle of the night with a stranger claiming to be her grandmother. Someone who thought she had the power to change her world.

She closed her eyes, hearing Colleen's words in her head, repeating like a mantra. Was it Danni who had brought them here? Or was it the Book?

She'd accepted that it wasn't a dream or a vision that had thrown her twenty years into the past. She even remembered thinking in those moments before the air had turned and she'd felt herself falling—thinking how unfair it was that Sean had come into her life this way. How she wished she could make it different.

This was real, however impossible, and maybe she *was* responsible for it. So what did it matter if she took another giant leap into the dark side. What could it hurt to push out, to see if there was more that she could do?

She pulled her legs up to her chest and wrapped her arms around them. Closing her eyes, she focused on Niall, trying to follow him with her mind. She could see him clearly in her head—the way he'd stood inside the cavern, watching her mother swim like she was a mystical sea creature spewed into his world by powers of enchantment. He'd looked like a dying man, faced suddenly with the chance of life. She honed in on that, on his desperation. Concentrated on the push-pull of his conflicted emotions.

She felt the familiar gathering, the tension in the air. It pressed in, swirling around her as she reached for it. Close, so close. She could see it all, but she couldn't wrap her mind around it, couldn't find a way to reel in the lines that held the turning at bay. And then it ebbed and began to fade.

No.

She clenched her eyes tight, throwing her mind out and into the fray, but the turning was too thin to catch, too elusive to grasp. She couldn't force it.

It had been stupid to think she could.

She let out a breath of defeat, frustration, remorse. Colleen was wrong. Danni was different, but she wasn't special. Things happened to her, not the other way around, not because she caused them to happen. Resting her chin on her knees, she stared at the outline of Sean on the bed. The vibration of air hovered just above, just out of reach. Teasing her. Taunting her.

"What are you doing?" Sean's voice rumbled across the room and startled her.

"I thought you were asleep," she said, hand over her heart.

He sat up, and she felt his gaze moving over her, though she couldn't see his face or make out his features.

"I woke up and you were gone. Where were you?" he asked.

"Outside. I needed some fresh air."

"Alone?"

No, I was just chatting about the impossible with your grandmother— wait, actually it was my grandmother.

"Yes."

He seemed to be waiting for her to say something else. To do something more. But she could only stare at him, drinking in the sight of the pale moonlight against his muscled chest, gleaming over the strong arms. Remembering the things they'd done last night made her face feel hot and her stomach jittery. But what she'd learned this morning knotted her insides and made it hard to catch her breath. She felt inadequate. Stupid. Numb.

He climbed out of the bed and pulled his jeans on, carelessly buttoning the fly as he crossed to where she stood. His eyes were searching as they traveled over her stiff posture. The air above her suddenly surged down, and she knew, suddenly, that it was within her reach. Like a door flung open, she could see the way in.

"Are you okay?" he asked, stopping beside the couch. When she didn't answer, he tilted her chin up and looked into her eyes. "Talk to me, Danni?" he said.

The feel of his warm fingers against her skin, the caring in his deep, smoky voice seemed to ignite other things around them. She felt the hiss and hum of the air as it rushed at her like a burning wind, and she faced it. In her mind, she opened her eyes to the vision and she called it.

She felt herself falling, falling into the depths of it and then the air, the room, Sean, all of it began spinning even as the air gathered tight like a blanket. Then it spread out, thinning, pulling and reaching like a net with an open weave and sticky threads. Instinct had her fighting before reason could make her embrace it.

Sean felt it, too. She saw it in his face, saw the surprise, the shock of it. His hand moved from her chin but only so he could grasp her fingers, hold on as the world twisted sickeningly. She thought of how he'd described the walls like glass, changing what was on the other side into something unrecognizable and watched as it happened again.

And then, with a grinding wail the walls vanished completely.

Chapter Twenty-five

DANNI was standing in the familiar valley, drenched in the shadow of the ruins. At her feet was the place where the grave had been before, but now the telltale hump of dirt was flat and covered with grass and flowers. The ocean roared and crashed, fishy and heavy with brine and numbing cold. The sheep in the distance grazed mindlessly, moving as one in a slow, methodical dance.

She looked down to the hand clasped with her own. Sean—barefoot, shirtless, clad only in his blue jeans—stood at her side. He'd been with her before—the first time when he'd guided her. But this was different. She frowned as she stared at their clasped hands. His palm felt warm against her own. He was solid. Real. Like Danni, he was *in* it, not merely a part of it. A small distinction with an enormous implication.

He tightened his grip, drawing her gaze to his face. He was pale, his eyes wide and troubled.

"What is this?" he asked her.

She fought the layers of disbelief pressing down on her like thick, binding ropes. "A vision," she said.

And she had called it, willed it to happen. Sitting on the couch with arms around her knees, she'd reached into the depths of herself and summoned it.

No. Impossible.

But it wasn't impossible, only unprecedented. She had called it, followed it like a kite on a string as it hovered around her and then reeled it in.

Again, a voice inside her taunted. The first time she'd brought him with her hadn't been a vision, it had been through time. She didn't understand how she'd done it, but something inside was urging her to take responsibility.

"Where are we?" Sean was asking, but she wasn't sure if his lips actually moved or if the question simply unfurled in her head. The idea of him talking directly in her mind made her queasy, frightened.

"Danni, where are we?"

She stared into his eyes, knowing he wasn't asking *where* in the sense of location, but in the sense of time and purpose. She'd brought them here, and he wanted to know why. It was reasonable. She wished she knew the answer. But she didn't. She had no idea.

He nodded as she formed the thought and tugged her hand, pulling her closer. It was unnerving feeling him there, beside her. Knowing she wasn't alone in this. Always before she'd been alone, hadn't she? Even as a child when she'd thought of it as flying, had there ever been anyone with her? A memory moved in the dark recesses of her mind and was gone before she could bring it into focus.

They faced the winding path that led from the ruins down to Colleen's house. From here, they could see how it snaked around rocks and split off like tree branches to different destinations. As they watched, a boy appeared on it where the path bent over the crest of a hill. He was running, laughing while two more boys chased him down the other side. They were suddenly closer, and Danni stared into the face that had become so familiar to her, saw the gray green eyes, the thick fringe of lashes, the dark hair glinting in the sun. She'd seen him as a man, as an adolescent, and now as a young boy, carefree and happy. It was Sean. Of course it was Sean.

Beside her, the grown man stiffened and took in a deep, hissing breath. He tugged at her hand, trying to pull her back, away from the boys. She sensed his anxiety escalating at her resistance, but she didn't yield. She was supposed to follow the children. She knew it suddenly and completely.

"We have to go with them," she said. "Hurry."

Ignoring his protests, she began to walk, covering the distance with exaggerated speed, towing Sean despite his reluctance. She was afraid to let go of his hand, afraid if she did he would be lost in this place where nothing was real, lost in her mind if that was, indeed, where they were.

The three boys stopped in front of Colleen's house and chattered for a while, then one broke off and continued down the road. Sean—Michael as he'd still been called at this age—and the younger boy stayed behind. The boy with Michael had dark hair and a smattering of freckles across his nose. His eyes were a clear blue, his face elfin in shape with a pointed chin and ears that stuck out a little too much.

"Who is he?" she asked, though some part of her knew the answer already.

Stone-faced, Sean confirmed it. "My little brother."

The boys waved good-bye to their friend, calling childish insults to each other and snorting with laughter as they parted ways. Young Michael was still grinning as he and his brother reached the front door, unaware of Danni and Sean following them. Oblivious to the battle of wills as Danni tried to pull Sean along.

From inside the house, the sound of raised voices rang out, sharp and angry. A woman screamed a filthy oath and a moment later glass shattered in a brittle explosion. Beside her, Sean tried to back up, twisting to pull his hand free. Danni could feel his horror, his struggle to contain it, and in that moment she realized what was about to happen. This was the day Sean's mother would die.

Dread sank deep in her gut, but she kept her grip on Sean's fingers, hiding her fear from him as she moved closer. She reached up to touch his face with her other hand. She forced him to look at her.

There was pain in his eyes, a vulnerability so at odds with his bulk and strength that it might have seemed feigned but for the very real anguish she saw in him. She couldn't release him though. She knew that.

"We're here for a reason," she said, laying her palm against the hard line of his jaw. "Remember, I told you? Someone here wants something from me." She paused. "Sean, I think it's you."

She'd confused him with that. She could see it in his face. But no amount of explaining would ever make sense of what she meant. Instead she tried another way. "We're not really here, Sean—not like before. We haven't gone back in time and we won't stay here, but we need to see it—whatever *it* is—before we can leave." She stared into his eyes, trying to convince him what she spoke was the truth. "Trust me."

The words seemed to penetrate, and slowly the tension eased from his face, his neck, his shoulders. He nodded and allowed her to lead him inside the house.

The front room was dim, the air layered with wisps of cigarette smoke that swirled in an airless dance, sullying walls and clouding the mirror that hung just inside the door. There were brown curtains on the windows, all of them pulled tight except for one that gaped at the top. Michael and his brother stood in the middle of the room, frozen as the angry voices grew louder, more vindictive. The boys crept forward, moving like the dust and smoke floating in the solitary shaft of light breaking through the curtains. At the kitchen door, Michael paused, pushing his brother behind him as he peered inside. Danni could feel his angst. It gripped her, made her move faster.

"A fool it is you think I am," a woman said, her voice shrill and harsh.

Danni rounded the corner and stepped into the tiny kitchen. The woman who'd spoken was short and painfully thin, with red hair too bright to be natural and dark brown brows. Her face was angular, her cheeks sunken, but Danni could see Sean's brother in the fine bones, pointed chin, and clear blue eyes. She held a teacup and a cigarette with an alarmingly long ash in one hand and jabbed a finger at the man standing in front of her with the other. Her movements were clunky, encumbered. Obviously it wasn't tea she was drinking.

"You think I'm a fecking fool don't you, you bloody bastard?" she shouted, red lips pulled back in a grimace.

"You've got the half of it right. I think you're a fool, and it's a drunken one you are, Brigid," the man answered, turning with a resigned sigh. A giant man, with broad shoulders and long legs, Danni knew who he was before she saw his face. Niall Ballagh, the man she'd focused on when she tried to call this vision. Still, a part of Danni was convinced it was Sean who'd forced the time and place.

The boys stood unnoticed in the shadows of the doorway, watching with wide eyes and pale faces as Niall snatched a bottle from the counter and poured some in a glass. He gulped it down and filled it again.

"Do you think I like coming home to this?" he demanded. "I break my fucking back all day while you get pissfaced and meaner by the bottle? What of the boys? They'll be home soon."

"Home?" she sneered. "This isn't a fucking home. *This* is a hovel. A hovel, you hear me?"

"The whole of Ballyfionúir hears your shrieking, woman."

"Jaysus, why I married you I'll never know. 'Sure, he's a handsome one,' me mum said. 'But he'll come to nothing if he hasn't come to it by now. He's the reek of fish on him already,' they said. 'He'll reek of it until he dies.'"

"The life of a fisherman is an honorable one, woman. There are worse things a man can do to put food on the table."

Lost in her own drunken need to emasculate her husband, vandalize and destroy his pride, his life, his world with her slovenly disillusionment and resentment, Brigid slurred on. "I wouldn't listen though. I'll never know why I didn't listen."

"No and I will be as in the dark as always," Niall countered. "I didn't force you. I hadn't a gun to your head."

"And sure I wish you had. I wish you'd blown my brains to kingdom come, is what I wish."

Brigid emptied her teacup in one long swallow and then tried to grab the bottle away from Niall. He fought her for it, pushing her back as she screamed with fury. Her cup hit the floor and broke into a thousand pieces as she jerked around, making her hand into a claw. She raked it down Niall's face with a howl of satisfaction, and then snatched the bottle and held it up triumphantly.

Beside Danni, Sean's breathing came faster. Cautiously she looked down at the boys, watching as their chests heaved with the same short, rapid breaths.

Brigid tipped the bottle and drank straight from the neck while Niall blotted at the blood oozing from the scratches on his face.

"Christ in fucking heaven, you're a crazy bitch."

"And you are nothing but a failure dressed like a man. *She* thinks it, too."

Brigid stumbled and staggered against the counter, dropping her cigarette as she fought to save the bottle from slipping. She'd stepped in the broken glass and cut her bare feet, but she didn't seem to notice the pain or the bloody footprints she left in her wake. "A failure," she spat. "Always ogling another man's wife. You think I don't see? I have eyes, and it's fine that they see."

"Brigid," Niall said, his voice pitched low, pleading.

In his eyes lurked hurt, confusion, and just a little bit of guilt. After what she'd seen earlier, Danni couldn't help wondering . . . couldn't help believing that Brigid spoke of Danni's mother, Fia.

"Brigid," Niall repeated. "You've got it wrong, love. You're the only woman for me. Wife, my heart is true to you."

He stared at her, eyes beseeching, and even though Danni had seen him with Fia herself, she believed him. At this point in time, his words rang true.

Brigid swayed in place, scanning his face, seeking the lie she seemed sure she'd find. "I see you watching her like she's a fecking fairy princess. Deny it. Go on with you, tell me it's not the way of things."

Niall swallowed hard, giving his head one brief shake. "Never have I been unfaithful to you, Brigid. Never will I be," he said simply.

Again, there was truth in the words—Danni could see it as clearly as Brigid claimed to see his longing for another. But he hadn't answered her question and the both of them knew it.

"Faithful," she spat. "Not in your heart."

"In every way I can be."

She wavered then, and Danni caught her breath, wanting to rush forward, to beg her to believe him. Because Danni knew what they'd come to see, and like the rigid man at her side, she wasn't sure she could bear it. She clasped Sean's hand with both of hers, holding on as he watched his parents with silent horror.

"Well, I can't say the same, Niall Ballagh. I'll not be faithful to a man whose heart is black like yours."

"Mind your tongue, wife."

"Oh, I mind it," she said, squaring her shoulders, thrusting out her breasts. She circled her lips with her tongue in a drunken gesture that fell far short of seductive. But she made her point. "Trevor isn't even your son. You know that? He's not even yours."

Niall grew very still, staring at her with black eyes and a hard jaw. "You'll take that back," Niall warned.

"Or what?"

"Or I'll ring your fucking neck, that's what."

Brigid laughed hysterically and took another swig from the bottle.

"It's the truth. I don't even know who his father is there were so many. Could be Patrick Walsh, maybe. Or Harold O'Conner it could have been, or—"

Niall moved with a speed that belied his size. One moment he was standing by the table, holding a towel to his raw face, and the next he was across the kitchen, yanking the bottle from Brigid's grasp and slapping her hard with the back of his hand.

Her head snapped back and a trickle of blood trailed from the corner of her mouth. The look in her eyes when she leveled them at Niall made Danni's blood run cold. With the insulation of rage, Niall blithely turned away and started across the room. Brigid pulled herself up, looking at the bright blood smeared on her fingers with sparking outrage. Calmly she opened a drawer and withdrew a knife with a long, wicked blade.

"Oh my God," Danni breathed. Tremors began to shake the solid man beside her. Still holding his hand, she turned to him, pulling him against her, wishing she could shelter him, knowing it was futile to try. The two little boys went unnoticed as they cowered in the doorway. She wanted to hold them, too, but there was no way to do it.

Unaware of anything but his anger, Niall splashed four fingers of whiskey into his cup and drained it. His hands shook. In his eyes, Danni saw wretched grief, the kind that ate away at the soul until it had consumed everything in its wake.

Brigid moved silently now, holding the knife in a strong fist as she closed the distance between them.

"No," Trevor shouted suddenly, startling them all. The boy took a step forward just as Niall spun around and Brigid lunged. But Michael was there first, grabbing his brother around the waist. He carried the kicking and screaming boy back to the door and set him down.

"You stay there," Michael said, his face pulled in a mask of fury and determination.

Wishing he'd taken his own advice, Danni watched Michael rush back into the brawl. Beside her, Sean made a sound of disbelief and a shudder went through him.

Everything seemed to slow then. Danni was aware of Sean trying to shake her loose, trying to step between his parents even as his younger self did the same. He dragged Danni with him as he fought to separate the two, but he couldn't stop what was happening. Not now. Not then. Only when the knife passed through him did he realize how insubstantial he was in this world. The eyes he turned to Danni were both tormented and enraged.

Brigid sidestepped and came at Niall with dogged determination, and instinctively Danni pulled Sean away, though the logical part of her knew it was unnecessary. Like cursed spectators, they watched Niall struggle to disarm her, but her rage and her drunkenness gave her the strength of a man.

Michael tried to force Niall and Brigid apart—just as the grown-up version had tried to do—but only managed to become tangled in their legs while his little brother screamed from the doorway.

Brigid stumbled over her son, but didn't stop, didn't slow, didn't care that her actions would traumatize him for life. The knife was over her head now and she brought it down hard, burying it in the soft flesh of Niall's shoulder. Niall shouted with pain, trying helplessly to lift his son and move him to safety, telling him, "It will be all right, son. Go on now," even as Brigid was on him again, throwing her weight behind the blow as she took aim at his heart.

Niall managed to get Michael to his feet, turning to push him toward his brother as Brigid plunged the knife into his back. It seemed to hit bone and stop, but his howl of agony echoed in the small kitchen. Undeterred, Brigid yanked the blade free and went for Niall again. With his son out of the way, Niall spun to stop her, catching her arm this time before she could bring the knife down. There was blood pouring from his shoulder and from his back, pooling on the floor. Niall teetered weakly, looking as if he might pass out.

He kept his senses enough to wrestle with his wife, trying to pry her fingers from the blade with all his might. But Brigid was uninjured and intent on killing him. He managed to slam her back against the counter, tried to bring her wrist down hard on the edge of the sink. She held on with the strength of a woman scorned. Fading, Niall wrapped his one free hand around her throat, and began to squeeze as he fought to control the knife with his other.

The boys were screaming, watching as their mother's face drained of color, as she gasped for breath, her feet dancing in macabre rhythm against the bloody floor. But still she gripped the knife. Still she tried to wield it.

"You're killing her," Michael screamed.

But what choice did Niall have? If he let her go, she'd do the same to him.

Even as tears filled her eyes and clogged her throat, Danni couldn't tear her gaze from the terrible scene in front of her. The blade inched closer, Niall squeezed harder and then finally, at last, Brigid dropped to her knees, letting the knife clatter to the floor. Spent, Niall slumped down beside her, still holding her throat, only now the fingers were loose, the touch almost apologetic. Blood streamed from his wounds, turning his shirt a sticky dark red. It seemed there was blood, everywhere. On the floor. Splattered against the faded cupboards. All over Michael.

"Why do you make me hurt you?" Niall asked, and tears streamed down his face. "Why do you—"

With a face like a mask of rage, Brigid snapped her head up, grabbed the knife, and lunged again. Niall's eyes widened with fear as he watched the glinting blade arc toward him. For a moment, there was resignation, acceptance in his eyes, and Danni thought he'd welcome it, the release that death would bring. And then the look was gone and he moved, throwing his shoulder into her side with a slam that knocked her into the cupboards.

For a long moment, no one moved. No one spoke. The boys seemed to have stopped breathing as they huddled together. Michael held Trevor's face against his chest to shield him from the sight. Brigid sat propped against the cabinets, staring with shock at the knife protruding from her chest. Niall made a sound like his soul had been ripped out and shredded. He half crawled, half dragged himself to her side, crying as he looked into her eyes. Her lips moved but no sound came out.

"What? What did you say, Brigid?" Niall asked, brushing her hair away from her face. He leaned closer, putting his ear to her lips. She spoke again, still so softly Danni couldn't make out her words. But whatever she'd said, Niall understood. He held her, weeping as he rocked her body. Then her face froze, her eyes became fixed and sightless, and the last breath wheezed from her lungs.

With a shout of pain and rage, Niall stared at her. He'd lost a lot of blood and his face was as pale as his dead wife's, but he fought to stay conscious until at last his eyes rolled back and he fell, his head bouncing upon impact with the floor, his arms splayed like Jesus'.

Chapter Twenty-six

THE air turned with a shriek, violently wrenching Sean and Danni from the bloody kitchen back into the cottage. It left her feeling sick, like she'd been on the spinning top ride for hours on end. She glanced at Sean's face, wondering how he'd fared. But he looked back with an expression so blank it frightened her. Was he breathing? Was he alive?

"Sean?"

His eyes shifted to her face. They were dark and stormy gray, deep and desolate green. There was rage in them. There was bewilderment and fear and agony all churning behind the shock of what had happened.

"Sean, I'm so sorry. I didn't know I could take you—it's never happened before. I didn't know that was what we'd see. Your parents . . . I'm sorry. I wouldn't have made you see that—"

He made a sound deep in his throat and turned away. For a moment it seemed he might say something, but then he didn't. Without a word, he took clean clothes from the dresser. The click of the bathroom door as it closed behind him echoed through the silent rooms. Numb, Danni listened to the old pipes groan as he turned on the shower. She could picture him, all strength and hard sinew, layered muscles rippling as he stripped away his clothes and tried to cleanse himself of the horror he'd survived . . . again.

But she knew it would stay with him, like a permanent dye that couldn't be dissipated with soap and hot water. By the need to forget.

Even as she hurt, she understood—he'd just relived something so horrifying even Danni couldn't bring herself to think of it. Those were his parents who'd fought so bitterly, who'd spilled each other's blood. It was his mother who lay dead on the cold kitchen floor while he, just a little boy, tried to shield his brother from the terrible truth of it. Of course he wanted to forget.

She glanced back at the closed bathroom door, trying not to make the barrier between them about her—about the two of them.

In the kitchen, she found eggs and a hunk of something that looked suspiciously like uncut bacon. She scrambled the eggs and sliced the meat into a skillet, moving methodically, like the sheep on the hillside. There were potatoes in a hanging basket. No meal was complete without potatoes, she'd heard the women she'd worked with yesterday say. Dutifully she scrubbed and sliced them, adding another chunk of sizzling bacon to the pan. Health conscious Danni winced at the thought of all the grease and fat and carbs in this meal. But what did it matter, really? One way or another, it would all be over soon, wouldn't it? She would either find herself in a shallow grave or back in her own time, abandoned again. What did it matter which? Neither option seemed to include Sean, did it?

Danni sagged against the counter, letting that roll over her. She knew it instinctively. Whatever happened here, she and Sean would not walk away together.

By the time Sean emerged from the shower, breakfast was ready. His eyes were red, and she knew his grief hovered just beneath the surface. He avoided looking at her as he stood beside the table, waiting for her to sit down before he joined her. If she'd touched him, if she'd asked him to talk to her, he would have cracked in two. She could see it in the stiff way he held himself, in the pleading look that begged her not to break him. Not now. Not until he had the chance to regain some sense of control.

Though she wanted to ignore his silent request, Danni forced herself to honor it. He needed to deal with his emotions before he shared them. She didn't like it, but she understood.

They ate in silence, both of them hungry enough to clear their plates, neither seeming to notice what they chewed and swallowed. It might have been dog food for all the enjoyment it brought.

Finished, Sean carried his dish to the sink and began to rinse it. "Leave it," Danni said gently.

He let it clatter to the bottom and then looked up, bracing his hands on the side of the sink as he faced the window. He was a portrait of tension, the muscles of his arms and shoulders bunched tight, his jaw clenched, eyes narrowed. He was holding something inside, something huge and painful, heavy and unwieldy. She could see it in every line, every edged inch of him. She paused at the table, watching. Wanting to reach out to him, but fearing what she might touch. She didn't know what she could offer. Didn't know what he would reject.

He left without saying good-bye, and she let him.

Chapter Twenty-seven

AFTER she'd finished washing the breakfast dishes, Danni showered and got ready for the day. Colleen had added to her wardrobe, and now there was a soft pair of jeans and a cream cable knit sweater among her choices. She pulled them out. As she did, she saw a pair of leggings and an oversized T-shirt at the bottom of the drawer. She paused, stumbling over their familiarity while at the same time wondering how she could possibly recognize them when the clothes weren't even hers. And then she remembered . . . she'd been wearing them in that first vision. It was the outfit she would die in . . . the one she'd be buried in with Sean—young Sean.

"Not if I don't have it on," she whispered defiantly.

But along with the defiance came the reality that she was running out of time and was no closer to knowing how destiny conspired to put her in that grave with a fourteen-year-old version of the man she'd fallen in love with.

Brooding, frustrated with her inability to connect the dots, she watched as the first ray of sun crested the horizon, heralding the dawn of another day. It turned the sky dusky and pink then gilded red, golden, and finally blue. Blue like Brigid's eyes. Blue, like Danni's heart.

She'd been told to report to the MacGrath house by seven. It was just six thirty as she left the cottage, but she didn't want to be late again and risk Bronagh's wrath. Besides, what else did she have to do?

She replayed the morning as she went. First Colleen, telling her she could do whatever she set her mind to doing. Then the vision . . . the vision she'd *called* . . . but hadn't changed. Sean's mother was still dead, his father still, in a tragic way, responsible. She hadn't prevented it, no matter how much she wished she could have. What good did it do to dredge up something so painful if it could only be relived? It wasn't a gift she had. It was a curse.

She entered the kitchen through the back door as she'd been instructed the day before. Heavenly smells wafted in the moist, hot air of the enormous kitchen. She was early, but Bronagh was already bustling in from the dining room with an empty pan and a harried expression. "Ah, there you are now. Early as well. And good it is. I've pies in the oven and a potato casserole yet to make."

"It smells wonderful in here," Danni said, smiling.

Bronagh beamed at the compliment. "'Tis the twins' birthday, you know, and wouldn't they love to have all their favorites today?"

Of course they would, Danni thought, her heart aching at the love she saw in Bronagh's face, in the care she took to make their birthday special.

Clearing her throat, Danni asked, "What do you want me to do today?"

"Can you follow a recipe on your own? And don't be telling me you can if you can't."

"Yes, I can."

"Good," Bronagh said with a nod. "Here are the steps. Pay attention to the order, for it matters. You'll need to halve the ingredients as well." Bronagh's brows descended in a scowl. "You know how to do that, too?"

Danni nodded and took the handwritten recipe card from Bronagh's hand, trying to look more confident than she felt.

"Fine. I've shopping and errands to run with Mrs. MacGrath.

The pie will need to come out of the oven when the timer goes off. You'll do that for me?"

Danni nodded. "Of course. It smells wonderful."

Bronagh smiled and the expression crinkled her eyes and changed her face completely. "It's a peach cobbler, one of Betty Crocker's own," she said proudly. "The children love it. And wait until they see the cake I've ordered from the bakery. 'Tis a wonder Mary Elizabeth O'Malley is with batter and frosting."

Bronagh gave her pie one last look, checked the timer, and left Danni to her task. There were no less than thirty ingredients listed on the card and nearly as many steps in the preparation. She propped it up where she could see it and began gathering what she'd need. As she worked, the kitchen door opened and the twins came in.

"Good morning to you, Mrs. Ballagh," they both said politely as they leaned against the counter to watch her.

"What's that you're making?" Dáirinn asked.

"Well, I hope it's not a mess."

"Looks like it could be," Rory told her, eyeing the items she'd set out. "Though it does smell good in here."

"Bronagh's got a pie in the oven."

"Oh," they said in unison with sage nods.

Danni stared at the two, wondering how she'd ever forgotten she had a brother. Wondering where he would be after tonight. When she returned to her own time, would he be lost to her again? A fierce clenching inside her cried out against the idea of it.

You can do whatever it is you set your mind to . . . .

"You two are up early," Danni said.

"Mummy brought us breakfast in bed," Rory told her. "She made us pancakes with Mickey Mouse ears."

"One day we'll go to Disneyland," Dáirinn added. "Have you ever been to Disneyland, Mrs. Ballagh?"

Danni had gone with Yvonne and her children many years ago. It had been at once the most amazing and disappointing day of her life—a glaring showcase of all she'd missed contrasting with all Yvonne offered. She'd been sixteen, almost seventeen, but she'd ridden every ride, eaten every candy, ice cream, and chocolate-covered banana offered. And cried herself to sleep that night, her stomach aching and her heart hollow and hopeful.

"As a matter of fact, I have been to Disneyland. You'll have an awesome time."

Pleased, they both smiled. "Mummy has something fun planned for later. A surprise, but we must stay out of the way until then," Rory said. "It's very hard when everywhere is in the way."

"Are we in your way now?" Dáirinn asked.

"No. I'd like the company."

Dáirinn smiled, and Danni's heart beat painfully in her chest. It was like being split wide, staring at her own face but seeing an expression that had never been there before. Contentment. Security. Self-assurance. All of these things she'd had at five, but lost along the way to the woman she was now. She'd been loved once. Cherished. And she'd had a companion, a brother. A twin.

She looked up and caught Dáirinn staring at her with a peculiar glitter in her eyes. It was wariness and something else, something that made Danni still as she returned the look. The child shifted, glancing over her shoulder at the open door. Silently she slipped from her stool and shut it.

"Why'd you do that?" Rory asked.

Dáirinn slid back on her stool without answering. Still watching Danni, she took her brother's hand and held it. The gesture was not random, nor was it insignificant. If she hadn't known it instinctively, Danni would have guessed it by the solemn expression the twins wore now.

She felt suddenly diminished in the shadow of their union. She was shrinking as the world around her enlarged until she was only a speck about to be blown away. Expressions flitted over Rory's face, and she realized with a plunging awareness that the twins were communicating. Somehow, in some complex and unfathomable manner, Dáirinn was downloading whatever it was she knew. In a moment, it was over, and now both sets of eyes watched her with that peculiar *knowing*.

Disturbed, Danni cleared her throat and scooped flour from a canister, trying to hide her uneasiness. But she was chilled by what she'd seen. Shaken by the calm composure with which the children watched her. She wondered how Sean had felt when he'd looked at her this morning—had he experienced the same hair-raising disquiet?

Taking deep breaths, she stirred the ingredients in her bowl.

"Is it the Book you're here for?" Rory asked softly.

Danni's head snapped up. "What?"

"I told you, she doesn't know why she's here," Dáirinn scolded.

"Is that true?" Rory said.

Numb, Danni nodded and shrugged at the same time. At this point, she didn't trust anything she might think she knew.

"Did Dáirinn bring you here, then?" Rory turned in his seat and faced his sister. "Did you?"

Danni was holding her breath, waiting for the answer. But Dáirinn only stared calmly back.

"How would Dáirinn bring me?" Danni asked, though she was afraid of the answer. The idea was too complicated, too bizarre to contemplate.

"You've seen the Book, haven't you?" Dáirinn said. "I can tell that you have. It's frightening, isn't it?"

"You've seen it, too?"

Dáirinn nodded. "I don't understand why you want it, though. It's not good."

"Do you know where it is?"

The siblings exchanged another silent conversation before answering. Danni watched them, holding the measuring cup filled with flour in her hand. What she felt went beyond shock. Beyond fear. Deep inside an ancient instinct to flee rose up. She had to get out of here.

Finally, Rory spoke. "The Book moves," he said.

Moves? Danni cleared her throat and set down the measuring cup. Trying to appear relaxed but failing—dismally failing—she said, "What does that mean, it moves? You *are* talking about the Book of Fennore?"

"It was here," Rory said. "But then it went away, and we don't know where it went to."

"Was it stolen?"

They both shook their heads.

"How can you be sure?" Danni asked.

"I feel it," Rory said simply. "It talks to me sometimes."

Dáirinn made a small, jerking motion at his words. She didn't like that he'd said it aloud.

"I won't tell," Danni said.

"I know it," Dáirinn snapped. "Why else would we be telling you anything? But I know what the Book can do, and it isna right to talk of it."

Danni's chest was tight and her throat burned. "You know what it can do?"

"She means what it does to people," Rory said softly.

"It drives them mad," she finished.

"But . . ." Danni chose her words carefully, not sure what it was she wanted to say. "I thought it brought power."

"Aye. It can. It does. But that's not all that comes through when the door is opened."

Danni swallowed hard. What else? What else came through?

"Are you hoping to see its magic?" Rory asked.

"I've seen magic," Dáirinn said importantly. "Many times. One night I flew from my bedroom to the docks, and I saw my cousin get tangled in the nets. He was pulled under and no one knew. I told me Mum and she told Uncle Patrick and he set to watching my cousin. And do you know when my uncle was below deck who should get tangled in the nets and go under but my cousin? My uncle wouldn't have known if Mum had not told him, but he did know and so he pulled up the net, and there was my cousin nearly drowned."

"So you saved his life?" Danni said, searching herself for the memory. But if it was there, it eluded her.

"Aye. And one Sunday at church I heard Father Lawlor tell of how he'd been robbed the night before by a poor soul who thought Jesus had forsaken him. Father said he would have helped the man because sure enough Jesus had brought him to the church to be the worker they needed. If the man had only come with open hands and heart, he would have been fed and loved. So I flew to the night before and I told the poor man not to steal, because Jesus loved him. And to come in the morning and Father Lawlor would give him a job where Jesus could watch over all he did."

Danni stared at the child, stared into her own face, hearing the sweet voice, the sincerity in her tone. And feeling the echo of memory deep, deep inside. She could picture that night at the church, walking through the doors without opening them first. Finding the beggar ransacking the sacred altar. He'd been terrified to see her, a child in a white gown with silky curls and gray eyes. He'd thought her an angel with a heavenly message.

It had been a vision, and yet he'd seen her. Spoken with her. She had turned back time and changed the outcome. She'd *changed the outcome* . . .

"She can't really fly," Rory confided. "She just thinks she can."

"And you can't really talk to the horses," Dáirinn snapped back.

"You're jealous," he quipped. To Danni, he said, "It's not just horses I understand."

"No?" she said, thinking she needed to sit down. She needed to sit down quickly.

"Mum told you not to tell," Dáirinn said.

"She told you not to tell either," Rory shot back. "And you blathered your story, didn't you?"

Dáirinn scowled and crossed her arms. Danni stared at Rory, watching him make his decision about whether he would say more. But she'd already remembered what Rory could do. He understood. He understood not just people, but animals, too. All kinds, from birds to beasts. Not like a language, but a comprehension. As if their wants and needs became pictures in his head. And it didn't stop there.

"Once there was a man who came to our door," Dáirinn began.

"It's my story, I'll tell it," Rory interrupted.

Dáirinn clamped her mouth shut and sat back with a huff.

"He was a tourist," Rory picked up where Dáirinn had stopped. "And he didn't speak English or Gaelic or any other language I'd heard."

"But Rory knew what he was saying. Sure and he could tell Daddy what it was *and*—"

"I said I would tell," Rory said crossly.

"G'wan, then."

"And I could speak what my Daddy said back to the man. It was Russian, I learned later. I could speak Russian."

"He can't do it now, though," Dáirinn said, a little smugly. "Only then."

Rory shrugged, shooting a dirty look at his sister.

"Tell us what you are going to do?" Dáirinn asked next.

"What I am going to do?" Danni said.

"Well, you're not here to make pasties are you?"

Danni looked down at her hands. "Casserole," she said.

The twins snickered, watching her with expectant eyes. Danni knew what they wanted, but how could she answer their question? Did she really know why she was here? Was there an actual reason? Or was it an accident that had tumbled her through time? Colleen had seen it coming. Dáirinn looked as if she'd anticipated her arrival. What did that mean?

You can do whatever it is you put your mind to . . . .

She thought of Sean and her heart ached. Here, now, he was so real. Solid, achingly beautiful.

"I'm here to save someone," she said softly.

"You've the right of it," Dáirinn said, as if she'd already known the answer. "But the Book is gone, if using it was your hope. 'Tis a blessing, though. Do you understand?"

"No."

Rory said, "If it is a life you want saved, the Book can make it so. If it's a treasure you're wanting, it can give that, too. Whatever dream you may have, the Book brings the power to grant it."

"But it cannot be used in such a way," Dáirinn said. "It does not give without taking, and the greater the gift, the higher the price."

"It will take a piece of your soul," Rory said softly. "Take it like a coin from your purse. You might not even notice that it's gone until one day you need that coin and you no longer have it."

A piece of her soul. Would it be a worthy trade for Sean's life? For those of her mother, her brother . . . herself? Would the piece she gave today—from her grown self—affect the young one sitting in front of her now?

"Aye, it's a puzzle, isn't it?" Rory said. "You may not miss the piece you've given up, but someone else might."

"What do you mean by that?" Danni said.

"Well, a heart you've lost cannot break," Dáirinn answered. "But what would your one true love feel if the part he most loved of you was gone?"

"She read that," Rory said.

"I didn't."

"In a fairy tale."

Dáirinn opened her mouth in hot denial but Danni interrupted. "How did you get so smart? You seem much older than five."

Both pairs of eyes swiveled to her face. "Do you think the world is made up of only what you see?" Dáirinn asked instead of answering.

Danni shook her head.

"Neither do we."

The statement felt heavy in the air between them, and Danni didn't know how to respond to it. She sensed the simple declaration should answer her query, but it only left her with more questions, more confusion. Since she'd awakened yesterday morning, she'd been trying to find out why they'd been brought here. Now she sensed she was close to the truth. These two children knew—not only why she was here, but what would happen next.

Colleen's harsh, pained voice whispered in her head. *Even then you could have stopped it.*

Danni stared into Dáirinn's eyes, believing it now. Dáirinn might be able to change the course of fate, but she was afraid—afraid of the cost. Afraid of the Book. Danni was afraid, too, but she would risk it. If it meant holding back the tide bent on washing her life away, she would risk everything.

She needed help though, and perhaps she could find it here, with the two of them.

"There's something . . ." Danni began, but she stopped, trying to decide how or even what to say.

Suddenly Dáirinn leaned forward and held out her hand. Danni looked at it, so small and innocent there in front of her, but she hesitated, knowing that touching Dáirinn—touching *herself*—could open a door she didn't know how to close. Dáirinn raised her eyes in mute challenge.

Before she could change her mind, Danni clasped Dáirinn's hand in her own and then Rory put his over both of theirs. For a moment, nothing happened, and then Danni felt a humming, a low vibration that trembled through her fingers, up her arm to the heart of her. She wanted to shy away from it, to pull her arm back and break the connection, but she didn't. She was done with running away and denying what she didn't want to face.

In her mind an image formed. Frowning, she realized it was Sean's brother and she was seeing him on the floor of the kitchen, lying in a pool of blood beside his mother. Dead. She frowned, not able to comprehend why she would be seeing this. Sean's brother hadn't been on the floor, hadn't died. Why . . .

Before she could ask why she'd seen something that hadn't happened, the kitchen door swung open. And Cathán MacGrath walked in.

Chapter Twenty-eight

SEAN slowly made his way to the bay where the *Guillemot* was docked. The fog was thick as the sun shot its first ray over the horizon, making him feel as if he walked through a damp web. It obscured the harbor and the ocean beyond. Only the road and the thundering crash of waves let him know he was going in the right direction.

The heavy gray mist fit his mood. He'd grown up around strange and unexplainable things. He was Irish, and who among them didn't believe in another way, another reality? He didn't expect fairies to emerge from the hills and start with their mischief, but he knew the world was much more than rich earth, roiling seas, and the heavens above.

He looked around him. Here he was, a man out of time. Misplaced, out of step with his own rhythm. Yesterday, when he'd tried to put an explanation to how he'd come to be here, he'd blamed—or credited—his grandmother. But now . . . after this morning, he thought it was Danni. . . . Could she have brought them here in the same way she'd brought him to the worst of his childhood horrors in those dark hours before dawn?

He remembered how she'd looked yesterday when she'd awakened in his arms. She'd been as baffled by what was happening as he. She couldn't have faked her shock when they'd both realized that somehow, impossible though it was, they'd awakened twenty years earlier. If she'd done it, it hadn't been intentional.

So where did that leave him? Them?

He rubbed his hands over his face, feeling the rasp of stubble. He'd forgotten to shave this morning. He forgot a lot, but he couldn't recall ever feeling the whiskers on his cheeks and chin being so rough, so crisp and abrasive before. The feeling brought another sense of disquiet into his head. How many times in the past twenty-four hours had some ordinary sensation caught him like this? Made him think that it had been an eternity since he'd felt the things he was feeling now?

"For fuck's sake," he mumbled, increasing his stride, now desperate to reach the *Guillemot* and busy his hands so he had no time for this pensive idiocy.

But the train of his thoughts chugged on, taking him up a winding track, past harrowing canyons, clanging over defunct switchbacks. Last night, with Danni . . . He closed his eyes and everything inside him tightened at the memory of her body wrapped around his. Her soft mouth touching him, kissing him, making him feel like nothing else in the world mattered—had ever mattered. Jesus, it had been like a sensory explosion—every second of it. So real, so tangible, so opposite anything he'd known. Again, he saw his existence before her through the insulation of a cocoon, shielded from the experience, the taste, the scent of life itself.

So why was it now that he could suddenly *feel*? Pain . . . joy . . . the ache of needing . . . the agony of wanting . . . the sweet reward of giving.

His grandmother had told of the remarkable things she'd seen since his earliest memories—things she had no way of seeing, no way of knowing. And he'd suspected all along that Danni had the same gift, though she'd never said as much. But what Danni had done this morning was beyond his ability to comprehend.

He could still hear his mother shrieking, insane with her drunkenness and rage. He'd never forgotten that day, how he stood in the shadowed entrance of the kitchen, too frightened to even try to shield his brother from the erupting violence. He'd never forgotten the blood, the death hanging with the stench of old cabbage and cigarettes in the sudden quiet.

But what had happened this morning and what had happened that day so long ago . . . they weren't the same thing. He understood now that his terror and imagination had added an element of malice to the memory. A possessed rage in his father that had been notably missing.

But what about the other? What about Trevor?

It started in the same way, he and his brother coming home from school, laughing with their friend Connor. They'd heard the raised voices when they entered and had gone to the kitchen where they'd watched in horror as their parents' argument escalated from his mother's usual litany of drunken discontent to unalterable brutality. But then . . .

All those years ago, Trevor had jumped into the violence and tried to stop it. Trevor, not Sean. Sean had stood petrified in the shadowed doorway, watching his world slashed to pieces by the same butcher knife his mother used to cut the potatoes for their dinner. He hadn't prevented Trevor from racing into the middle of the fight. He hadn't protected him. And in the end, his mother's frenzied thrusts of the knife had found Trevor with unerring accuracy. She hadn't meant to do it—hadn't even realized she'd stabbed her own son.

Only after Trevor had fallen to the floor did the paralysis that gripped Sean relent. He'd rushed forward, lifted his brother and carried him away from his warring mother and father, back to the doorway. Sean remembered holding his hands over the raw and lethal hole in Trevor's chest. Watching helplessly as the blood, as the life poured out of him.

Only after his mother lay dead did his father notice his two sons and realize he'd lost more than his wife.

But today, Sean had stopped Trevor. And his father . . . his father had protected his oldest son, risked his own life to keep Sean safe.

In the end, his mother was still dead, but by her own actions. He knew in his heart that part of it *hadn't* changed. His hurt and rage had warped the memory until it placed his father vengefully over her corpse, knife in his hand. But Niall had only acted out of self-defense—both times. He'd never wanted to hurt Sean's mother.

Christ. Sean didn't know what to think now. What did it mean that Trevor had survived the surreal reenactment that morning? Had Danni only shown him what he'd always wished he would have done? Protect and save his little brother? The guilt over not doing that very thing had eaten away at him all his life. How many years had he spent hating himself for it? Perhaps he'd twisted Danni's dream—her *vision*—into what he so desperately wanted.

Lost in his own confusion, he came upon the dock suddenly. He smelled it first, the reek of gutted fish, waterlogged nets, and tar. Next came the sounds of the waves slapping against the moored boats, the creaks and groans of sodden wood, the hollow thud of the hull brushing the dock pad. The thump of footsteps on the deck. Then he was through the fog and stepping on the blackened creosote-treated pier that jutted out to the bay. Half a dozen ships were anchored here. A half dozen more slips already empty. The *Guillemot* was still tied off and rocking.

"You're late," Niall said, giving Sean a hard look.

Michael glanced away from the spool to watch, and before Sean could respond, another boy came up from the cabin and smiled at him. He had a round and open face, still soft with youth and innocence. A thousand freckles dusted his nose and cheeks and bright blue eyes sparkled at him. He gave Sean a quick, shy smile that showed a missing front tooth. The sweetness of it clenched around Sean's heart. *Jesus, it was Trevor....*

"I said you're late," Niall repeated, this time with irritation.

"Sorry," Sean said, still distracted by the image of Trevor. It couldn't be real, could it? Trevor was here, *alive.*

Sean moved quickly aboard and went to work pulling in the lines and raising the anchor, moving with the quick efficiency that came from a childhood spent on this very deck.

But he couldn't help stealing glances over his shoulder at the boy—a stranger and yet so achingly familiar—who stood next to Michael, whispering in shared camaraderie.

Underway, heading into the rising sun, Sean stared at the glittering sea, thinking it looked like the end of the world, where the sun flamed over the rippling waters. He couldn't get his mind around what was happening, what had happened. As he struggled with his thoughts, Niall came to stand beside him, glancing occasionally over his shoulder to Trevor at the wheel. Michael sat beside him, teasing his brother and laughing at something Trevor said back.

Christ in heaven, Danni had changed the past.

She'd saved his brother.

He drank in the sight of the two boys, bonded by blood and life. Reunited by the will of a woman Sean would never understand. But he was grateful—so grateful he wanted to drop to his knees and weep—no matter that it was unnatural, however Danni had done it. He glanced away, fighting to keep the tears stinging his eyes in check.

Not only had Danni changed the outcome, but she'd changed Sean's perspective on what had happened that day. This morning, he'd seen the look on his father's face as his mother plunged her knife into him. There'd been so much grief and sorrow in his expression that it defied words. It went deeper than the slashing blade, deeper than the sea itself. And he'd seen his father take the blade of her knife to save Sean from the same fate.

There wasn't time to dwell on it now, but the realization lifted a weight Sean had borne for nearly as long as he could remember. And relieved of the burden, he felt lighter. Stronger.

Soon they were baiting the leaders and dropping them into the sea. It was steady, strenuous work, but somehow it soothed Sean, allowing him to deal with the pressure of his thoughts without having to openly acknowledge them.

Michael and Trevor worked side by side through the morning. Gone was the bristling hostility Michael had worn the day before, and in its place were camaraderie and laughter. While he worked, Niall glanced at his sons with pride. Today they both smiled back.

The day progressed, moving with the sun and tide. They filled the hold completely and were calling it a day early. Sean was glad. He needed to see Danni, to explain why he'd been so distant with her this morning. Hope she understood that it was shock that had driven him to silence and then solitude. Not her.

As they pulled the lines and headed back, Sean came to stand beside his father. It was peaceful and somehow soothing to be there with the man he'd loved and hated with such warring intensity. They were the same height now, both layered with muscle and sinew over long heavy bones. Brawny men with large hands and broad shoulders. Built for physical labor.

"It's a grand vessel," Sean said, leaning back against the dash.

Niall made a sound of humor. "The *Titanic* she's not, but she's Irish made and seaworthy."

"Well, the last of it's more than the *Titanic* could boast."

"I suppose."

They rode in silence for a moment and then Niall asked suddenly, "What are you doing here, son?"

The question surprised him nearly as much as the casual "son," at the end. The leap through time had brought Sean's age very close to Niall's, and yet his father seemed many years older. It was there in his eyes, in the sag of his shoulders.

"I've come to work," Sean answered.

"Aye, that's what Mum says." The look Niall turned on him was piercing. "It's not the way of it, though, is it?"

"You tell me. You seem to know."

Niall gave a bitter snort of laughter. "That's God's truth. I seem to know."

The cryptic response settled around them and Sean tried to decipher the meaning. "You're talking of Nana's gift?" he said at last.

Niall gave him another sideways glance. "Am I? And what gift would that be?"

"She sees things."

"Aye."

"She knows things she shouldn't."

"True again. But no, it's not her. I was thinking of my Brigid, God rest her soul. She had the gift herself, though it was more a curse than anything. I used to pray Christ to save me from her." He looked past Sean to his oldest son. "He told you about his mum?"

Sean gave a hesitant nod. "It was an accident, they say."

"Do they?" Niall asked, brows raised with disbelief. "It's good of you to lie, but no, they don't say it was an accident at all. They say I killed her."

"Did you?"

"We killed each other. Her with her fecking knowing. Me with my refusal to believe. Sure didn't she tell me you'd come."

"She told you *what*?" Sean exclaimed, feeling yet another tremor of shock rock him.

"Brigid said I'd feel as if I knew you when you did. But she couldn't tell me why, could she now? She could only ever tell me what she saw. Not when it would happen, not how or why. It would drive a saint to sin."

"And you're not a saint."

"No."

Niall reached for a thermos and poured tea into a plastic cup. He took a drink and then handed it to Sean.

"So perhaps you'd be so kind as to tell me what she could not? Why are you here? Why do I feel like I know you?"

Sean stared at him, wishing there was an answer he could give. How could he possibly explain what he didn't understand himself?

"I had to come," he said finally. "I'd no choice in the matter and that's God's truth. But I've no why to give you."

Niall nodded. "Fair enough. You mean me no harm, that much I can tell."

Sean raised his brows at this, not in denial but in curiosity. How did he know that Sean was not a threat?

"Oh, I've got my own little bit of it. Not like Brigid. She was Ballagh through and through. A little too much, if you get my meaning. I suspect somewhere in her family tree more than one branch was sired by the same root."

Incest. Inbreeding. *Grand*, Sean thought. Even his genes were a fucking mess.

"Her gift drove her mad. She'd no control over what she saw and no way to reference it. What came to her could have happened ten years ago or forty into the future. All she knew was that she saw it. She thought me unfaithful, though I swear on her grave I never was. She saw me with another and that's all she knew."

He stared at Sean with a penetrating intensity. As if he was trying to convince both of them.

Niall sighed. "We'd been married just a short time before I realized how our lives would be for years to come—a windstorm of possibilities, caught at random by a faulty net. She soon lost the ability to distinguish what was real, happening in this world, from what she saw. She was beautiful and sweet and full of life when I met her, when I made her my bride. But in the end, that girl had been trampled by the sickness in her head. Do you know what she said to me, as she lay dying in my arms?"

Dry mouthed, Sean shook his head. He hadn't been able to hear her final words.

"She said, 'thank you, my love.' I sat there, bleeding myself, for she went like a lioness and took a pound of flesh with her, and she thanked me. There was blood everywhere, mixing with tears, turning my sight into a red haze. My heart broken in two. When behind me, I hear my sons and there they are, watching me like I was a wild beast that need be feared. But then they both came to me and cried in my arms. If I'd died right then, I think I would have been all right, knowing they didn't hate me."

Niall's expression was a soft echo of the one Sean had seen that morning. Resignation, pain, and twisted hope all rolled into one.

"It's that one I worry about," Niall said, looking at his oldest son. "He's like her in some ways. A good heart, a sturdy soul. He'd give you his last meal without you ever having to ask. But he's a Ballagh—as much as Brigid was. For all he fights it, he has the gift, the curse."

Sean stiffened, feeling as if he'd been submerged in ice. It wasn't true, what Niall said. He didn't have a gift. He'd never seen anything before it happened. Certainly nothing like what he saw that morning.

"You're saying he knows things, too?" Sean asked.

Niall gave a shake of his head. "In a way. Was a time when Michael would point me out to sea, and I would go wherever he told me for he always knew where the lines should be dropped. He'd tell me what storms were about before they'd even gather. And his mother—oh, he was good with her. 'Da,' he'd say. 'Mum is up in her ways. Have a care with her.'"

The words crashed over Sean, battering him like stones against a glass wall. A part of himself fractured and he remembered. Once upon a time, he'd been able to predict the weather, the seas, the moods of those he loved. He could see inside a person, see what was beneath the skin like a canvas of color. A black heart couldn't hide from him anymore than a pure one could.

"When did it stop?" Sean asked, knowing Niall was staring at him with shrewd eyes, but unable to mask his churning confusion.

"I couldn't say," Niall murmured. "When he lost his mum, he sealed himself up. He may still have the knowing. He doesn't share it anymore though. Not with me. Not with anyone."

Sean nodded, though it was more a reflex than an acknowledgment of anything.

"What about Trevor?" he asked.

"No, God bless him. He seems to have escaped the curse."

Sean heard his mother's voice in his head, filled with venom. *Trevor isn't even your son* . . .

"Ah, here we are," Niall said, steering into place by the dock. "It's a good day's work you put in today. I'm glad to have you aboard."

And with that the conversation ended. But for Sean, the questions only multiplied until he couldn't think anymore.

Chapter Twenty-nine

CATHÁN looked startled and a little annoyed to see his children perched on the stools in front of Danni. He tried to mask it with feigned indifference, but the result was a twisted smile and hard eyes. To cover her own apprehension, Danni scooped flour into her measuring cup and spread it over the potatoes. She'd already added too much flour, she was sure of it, and Bronagh's dire warning to mind the ingredients came rushing back. But there was nothing she could do about it now. She ran her finger down the list to the next item, watching Cathán from the corner of her eye as she did.

The children remained silent when their father shifted his attention from their faces to Danni's and back. No doubt he'd heard the furious whispers when he opened the door—seen their hands clasped together across the counter—and the sudden cessation of conversation didn't sit well with him. Danni couldn't fault his instincts. She was a stranger having secretive discussions with his young twins. He should be suspicious.

"What's going on?" he asked, almost managing to sound unconcerned. "Are you two bothering lovely Danni?"

The two heads shook in unison. "She said we could keep her company," Rory told him.

"I did," Danni offered, smiling. "They are great company. You must be very proud of them."

"Of course I am. They are quite remarkable children. However, I must pry them away from your captivating presence. Birthday or no, it's time for their riding lessons." He gave the twins a mild look. "Unless you want me to cancel?"

"No," they both exclaimed in unison.

Riding lessons. Danni didn't remember those either, but apparently she'd enjoyed them. The twins seemed happy as they scooted from their stools and started for the door.

"Wait a minute," Cathán said, stopping them. "Where is your mother? I was looking for her as well."

"She had errands," Dáirinn said.

Cathán nodded and made a "go on" motion with his hands. The twins left quickly, but Danni caught their curious glance back as the door swung shut behind them.

"Hard at work again, Mrs. Danni Ballagh?"

The name caused her heart to miss a beat. "Yes. I'm afraid I'm not doing Bronagh's potato casserole justice, though."

"I never liked it anyway," he said.

The timer on the oven chose that moment to go off. Danni pulled Bronagh's golden cobbler out and set it to cool. All the while, her father moved around the kitchen, looking over her shoulder. It made her nervous having her back to him, but she didn't know why. Perhaps it was her own sense of guilt for trying to pry information out of his kids. This was her father, a man who'd obviously loved her as a child, a man devoted to his wife, even though Fia didn't return the sentiment. There was no reason for Danni to be uptight around him.

She returned to the counter and finished slicing a stalk of celery to add to the casserole.

"Where is your husband this morning?" Cathán asked, and she realized he'd moved to stand behind her.

"He's working on the boat with Niall," she said, wishing he wouldn't get into her space. He seemed blithely unaware of personal boundaries, though, and she tried not to be weird about it.

"Industrious people, you Ballaghs."

"I suppose."

He shifted and she could feel the heat of him on her back. Something brushed against the skin at her nape where her hair was pulled up, and she jumped, bumping into him as she spun around. He didn't step away, and she found herself boxed in between the *L*-shape of the counter and his body.

"Why don't I think you're really married to him?" Cathán asked darkly.

"I beg your pardon?"

"You don't wear a ring."

"I had to sell it," she said, amazed at how quickly the lie came to her lips. "For food and rent. We've been through hard times."

He shook his head. "It doesn't seem right that such a beautiful woman should be married to a man who can't even keep a ring on her finger."

That damned nervous titter escaped Danni's lips.

"What were you doing with my children, Danni?" he said, watching her with a narrowed gaze.

"I—nothing. We were just talking."

"Whispering," he said.

She shook her head, but the anger she saw sparkling in his eyes made her pause. Her father wanted to protect his children—of course he did. And lying to him would only increase his distrust of her. But she couldn't tell him the truth, could she?

She considered that. If he knew what was going to happen tonight, he would move heaven and earth to stop it. Danni could certainly use an ally in all this and maybe, just maybe, her overprotective father might be the answer. She couldn't tell everything—certainly not about her and Sean—but if she could hint that there might be danger awaiting his family tonight . . .

Mentally she rolled her eyes. Was she nuts? If she told him that, he'd assume *she* was the danger. And who would blame him for thinking it?

So what could she do?

She hadn't seen her father in that first vision, but the article she'd read on the Internet said he'd been there, in the cavern. That he'd witnessed Niall's attack—apparently arriving too late to prevent it. But if she could just get him there sooner, maybe it would tip the balance and enable him to make a difference,

She wasn't naïve enough to think it would save his marriage, but it could save Sean's life. Fia would probably still run off with Niall, but Sean would be alive. He'd have a chance.

Still, there was the matter of the Book of Fennore and the visions she'd seen of it. Her mother had been in both. Danni couldn't guess what had happened between the time she'd seen Edel use the Book and now, but it stood to reason that once Edel disappeared, Fia's mother had forced Fia to take her place. Did that mean that Fia had it now? Was she using it? Or was there another possibility?

What if Fia was trying to get rid of it? She had a thing with Niall, was having his baby, and she wanted to go to America. That much Danni knew. If she sold the Book of Fennore, Fia would take care of two critical issues. First, she'd have the means to leave and live elsewhere, and second, she'd no longer carry the burden of owning such a terrible thing.

The idea took root in Danni's mind and grew. Perhaps she'd tried to set it up for tonight, but the buyer would double-cross Fia. Maybe he was the unseen man from the vision. If he'd threatened to kill Fia and her children, if he'd already killed Sean . . . That would be reason for Fia to run away and hide. It would explain why she'd never returned to Ballyfionúir. Why she'd changed her name . . .

"You're thinking very hard, Danni. Is it such a difficult question? Why were you whispering with my children?"

Cathán's voice snapped her back to the kitchen. He was still watching her with that cold suspicion. There was no way she could tell her father any of this. It was all supposition—theories based on little more than a hunch. He'd have no reason to believe her and every reason to doubt her.

His gaze glittered over her face to her throat, to the necklace that lay against the agitated rise and fall of her chest.

"Who are you?" he demanded. "And don't tell me you're Ballagh's wife because I don't believe it. You're lying about it. I've known it from the first moment. You pretend to befriend my wife and children, but you want something. What is it you're after?"

"Nothing, Mr. MacGrath. I'm just doing my job. If you'd prefer I didn't speak to your children again, I won't. But we were only talking."

"That's not true. You were holding hands. I saw it. Is it a fool you take me for? You think I haven't seen how they read each other? You think I don't know what they can do with just a touch?"

She swallowed hard, hearing the undeniable threat in his tone. He took a step closer, intimidating her with both his size and the cutting gleam in his eyes.

"What did they tell you? About the Book of Fennore perhaps?"

Danni couldn't stop the sharp breath she sucked in. "Do you know where it is?" she blurted before she could stop herself.

He moved quickly then, grabbing her by her arms and jerking her up to his face. "Why do you want it?"

"I don't," she lied, but he was beyond listening anyway.

"You were going to use them, weren't you?" he said, his voice deceptively low. "You know how to use them."

"Use them? No, I wasn't—"

He shook her hard, making her bite her tongue as her head slammed back. "How?" he demanded. "Are they strong enough to control it? Is that it?"

Danni wasn't answering any more questions. She tried to wrench herself free of his grasp, but he had her pinned between the corner of the counter and his body. Then he took her chin between his fingers, forcing her to meet the cold ice of his eyes. Yesterday there'd been humor mixed with the hard sparkle, and earlier she'd thought anger brought the glitter to them. But now, looking into those frosty depths, she realized it wasn't right, wasn't natural how the light bounced off them. Like diamonds. Hard and faceted. She'd seen eyes like that before. In the vision, when Fia's sister, Edel, had touched the Book. Edel's eyes had gleamed and glittered just like Cathán's did now.

"*You're* using it," she breathed, her voice filled with horror. Renewed panic hit her, and she struggled anew to free herself. "Let me go," she shouted, bringing her knee up. But he was too close, had her pinned too tightly, and she couldn't get leverage. She was trapped.

The idea of it—the reality of it—sparked its own fire within her. She began twisting wildly, but he was bigger, stronger. He grabbed her wrists and wrenched them behind her back until she arched with pain. Then he captured both her hands with one of his and held her that way while he brought his free hand to her throat.

"Tell me what you know of the Book," he said, fingers tightening around her neck, just enough to let her know he would hurt her.

Danni slammed her head forward, hoping to connect with his nose. But he was too tall, and she only managed to crack her forehead against his mouth. Pain shot through her skull, making her woozy. But her attack had caught him by surprise, and he loosened his hold enough for her to squirm free. She ran for the door, but he reached, managed to get a fistful of her hair and yanked her back, almost pulling her off her feet. She staggered into him, and he caught her from behind, holding her arms crossed over her chest like a straitjacket. His mouth at her ear.

"It's mine, Danni Ballagh. I'll kill you before I let you have it."

A part of her mind rebelled, refused to grasp the threat that still shivered over her skin. This was her father. This was her *father*.

"Please let me go," she said in a rush, hating the pleading note. "I don't want the Book. I'm afraid of it." Sensing he believed that much, she pressed. "I'm too weak to use it."

"The lust for power has a way of destroying weakness," he said, giving her hands a vicious jerk.

What he planned next Danni would never know. For just then, Bronagh's sharp voice came from the kitchen doorway. "Mr. MacGrath! What are you doing to the poor girl?"

Cathán released Danni so suddenly she sagged against the counter. Then she moved quickly, circling to the other side before he could grab her again. Her chest heaved, but she couldn't seem to catch her breath. Her arms hurt; her head ached. Unshed tears of fury and fear burned her eyes as she stared at Bronagh's fierce expression.

"I caught her stealing," Cathán said in a cool tone.

Before Danni could sputter out a denial, Fia walked in just behind Bronagh. For a moment, no one spoke as they each looked from one to another. Danni saw Fia's eyes linger on Cathán's split lip.

"Mrs. Ballagh," Bronagh said to Danni with stilted formality. "Is this true? Are you stealing?"

Cathán's sound of outrage stifled Danni's response. "You'll do well not to question my word, Bronagh. Is it more than a servant you think you are? If I said she is, she is."

Bronagh paled. "Yes, sir." She glanced guiltily at Danni before asking him, "Do you want me to call the authorities?"

Cathán wet a towel and dabbed at his face. His mouth was bleeding and it would swell. "No. Just get her out of here. I don't want her in my house again."

"Yes, sir." She couldn't look Danni in the eye as she said, "Mrs. Ballagh, please take yourself elsewhere. I will send your wages by way of Colleen."

"No wages," Cathán said. "Christ knows what she's stolen already."

Fia said nothing as she stared from her husband to Danni. But Danni sensed she had some glimmer of understanding that what they'd interrupted was not a thief being caught red-handed. She wouldn't go against Cathán, though, that much was clear. Danni thought of the bruises she'd seen on her mother's body and now the cause of them seemed brutally clear. Her father . . .

Stiffly, Danni untied her apron and left it on the counter. Without a word she fled.

Outside, the air felt cool against her skin, and she took deep breaths, trying to banish the nightmare of the last few minutes. She wanted to run. She wanted to hide. Her shame felt like a scarlet shroud. The sound of tires crunching gravel moved her forward. She couldn't face anyone, not now. With her emotions clashing, she raced across the paddock, down the path she'd seen yesterday to the rocky shore. There she picked her way carefully to the cove and the shadowed entrance to the cavern beneath the ruins.

Inside it was cool and quiet, and she drew a strange, inexplicable comfort from the endless spiral patterns on the walls surrounding her, from the rhythmic lap of the tide against the stones. Finally, Danni let her tears fall. She cried for the child inside her, so disillusioned that she wanted to scream her anguish, feel it echo against the rough stone walls and dark pool. All her life she'd dreamed of finding her family, of learning they'd loved her, searched for her, wanted to embrace her now. She'd pictured them impoverished but devoted to one another. Or wealthy, though grief-stricken from the loss of their child. She'd dreamed every scenario imaginable, but nothing had ever come close to the reality.

Her father had the Book of Fennore—had used it. He'd said he'd kill for it.

She shuddered, thinking of those moments when she'd considered him as an ally, thought of telling him as much as she could. What would he have done with the knowledge? Used it to hurt her?

What kind of hellish life did her mother have? How much did the twins know of it? And what had Cathán meant when he'd asked Danni if she'd figured out how to use his children? Use them to what end?

She huddled in the cold damp of the cave, shielded by the dark shadows. She'd had little sleep the night before and she was exhausted, but her thoughts buzzed in her head.

Cathán had the Book of Fennore.

And he would kill to keep it.

Chapter Thirty

DANNI couldn't say how much time passed before a sound pulled her from sleep. She opened her eyes, wincing as her muscles protested. Gingerly she turned her head and looked around. There were footsteps coming from the narrow stairway leading up into the castle ruins. Shifting so she could watch the doorway, Danni listened.

The shuffling went on for some time, and she had the sense of someone moving back and forth from one landing to another. The steps down were slow and labored, then they'd stop, turn, and go up again with a lighter gait. Then the process would repeat. Danni scooted from her hiding place to investigate further when a flashlight beam bounced from the doorway, making her crouch down again. A moment later, Fia MacGrath appeared, hauling a duffle bag. She set it on the ledge near the pool and then went back up the stairs. A few minutes passed and she returned with another. When she'd finished, two duffle bags and one suitcase were stacked beside the water. Fia stared at them for a long moment.

She looked small, defenseless, and utterly spent. Danni thought of the look on her face when she'd come into the kitchen. There'd been curiosity and fear. Anger and hurt and resignation, but there'd been something else—confirmation. Then conviction. Resolution. Whatever Fia had seen, whatever she'd assumed, it had pushed her to a decision.

Danni closed her eyes at the ultimate irony. Wasn't it a cruel twist of fate that in trying to save her family, Danni had inadvertently become the catalyst to make Fia run.

Colleen's words came to her then. *I can only say I made it worse.* Is that what Danni was doing now? Making it worse? Yet Colleen was convinced that Danni could put it all right . . . that she could do whatever she put her mind to.

"Jaysus fecking Christ," she muttered.

What no one was telling her was *how*—how did she make her mind do what her heart so wanted? She certainly hadn't been successful at that when she'd tried this morning. No matter how desperately she'd wished she could stop the horrible events from unfurling, the result had been the same. It would take something more than just Danni wanting to make a difference. Obviously she couldn't do it alone. She needed the Book of Fennore.

It will take a piece of your soul, the twins had told her.

But wasn't her soul a small price to pay if it meant saving Sean? Because what would life be without him? In a few short days, he'd come to mean that much to her. She loved him, as stupid, as *inconvenient* as it was, she loved Sean Ballagh and she would do whatever it took to save him.

Even if it takes that part that makes you human? a voice in her head taunted, and Danni immediately pictured her father's eyes . . . that faceted glitter . . . the cold promise, *I'll kill you before I let you have it.*

And she believed him.

Unaware of Danni's presence, Fia scooted the bags to the wall where the deep shadows concealed them. With a nervous glance around, she hurried back up the stairs. Danni waited until the footsteps faded before following.

The winding staircase was worn and crumbling. In some places the steps had disintegrated altogether, forcing her to test each foothold and circumvent gaps. The walls around her were moldering and slick and the passageway was so dark she could barely make out her feet. The higher she climbed, the more complete the surrounding blackness.

She began to feel panicky, frightened by the feeling of being swaddled, wrapped so tightly in the blanket of darkness that she couldn't breathe. The sensation built until she feared she could go no further, and then it gradually eased until she could see her hands moving in the pitch-black like small white birds fluttering beside her. Then, finally, light up ahead. She breathed a deep sigh of relief.

She emerged on a walkway high up on the keep's ruined wall. A parapet once lined the walk, but most of it had succumbed to time and elements and tumbled down to the sea, leaving it exposed to the harsh wind. Forty feet away, the walk connected to another tower—Fia's obvious destination.

Steeling herself, she began to cross the walkway, keeping center and moving forward as the wind buffeted her body. The view was magnificent, and she couldn't help her glance at the never-ending paddocks, the tiny village tucked in the haven between the hills, and the sea beyond. Moving white caps and crashing power gave a sense of forever endlessly rolling on.

She reached the tower out of breath and passed into the dubious shelter of its walls, nearly screaming when Fia stepped in her path and demanded, "And why are you following me?"

"I'm not," Danni sputtered, but she obviously was. "I just wanted to see where the stairs led."

"Now you have. What else were you wanting to see?"

"Nothing."

Fia crossed her arms over her ribs, her eyes narrowed with suspicion. She was frightened, Danni realized. Frightened of Danni.

"I won't tell anyone that you're leaving," Danni said softly. "That's not why I'm here."

"Isn't it? Enlighten me then on your true reasons for being in my house. For following me. I know it's not my husband you're after. I'd be sorry he troubled you, but it was good to see you bloody his fecking mouth." Fia snorted with derisive amusement. "You've more courage than I. But there's a reason you're here. What would that be?"

Another long minute of silence followed as Danni tried to answer that. *I'm here to change my past*, probably wouldn't inspire Fia's confidence.

As if hearing the thought, Fia made another scornful sound and turned away. Panicked, Danni realized she intended to leave.

"Wait—I . . . there's something I need to tell you."

Fia paused, but she didn't turn around. "About my husband? Don't trouble yourself about that. Sure it is that I know him already."

"No, it's about tonight," Danni said.

"What do you think you know about tonight?" Fia asked.

"He'll catch you," Danni said. "And when he does, he will hurt you and the people you love."

Fia watched her with steady eyes. She didn't ask how Danni knew. But she didn't walk away either. "He already hurts us."

"But by the time tonight is over, Niall and Michael will both be dead and your family will be scattered."

"Perhaps that's one way of it," she said calmly. "Perhaps not."

Danni took a deep breath and reminded herself that Fia didn't know who Danni really was. Why should Fia believe anything she said? "Just listen to me, whatever you have planned for tonight, don't do it. Don't go."

"Don't go?" Fia repeated incredulously. "Is it certain you are that not going will change anything? You seem to know what will happen if I do go, but what if I do not? What then, Mrs. Ballagh? What would happen then?"

"I don't know."

"Aye, you don't. Let me tell you what *I* know. Forever it's been like this—two paths ahead of me. I've seen them clear enough without having to be told. On one side I risk everything I want, everything I've hoped for my entire life. And on the other, I risk the only thing that matters to me—my children. I hoped I was wrong, but I know now I'm not. He's found the Book and he uses it, even now. If I don't get away, he will use the children against me. He'll take them from me and he will use them for his own purposes. In whatever way he must—do you understand me? As for me, I will disappear and never be found. Either way. Same fate, different place."

The weight of her words, the finality in her tone, slumped Danni's shoulders forward. *Same fate, different place.*

"As for Niall, he knows the risks—I've not sugarcoated what will happen to him, for his fate is tied to my own. Should he have the power to do it, my husband will wipe Niall and his children from the earth. He knows this as well."

"So you've convinced yourself there are only the two choices? Run away or do nothing? What about standing your ground and fighting him?"

"Fight him? Have you looked into his eyes? Have you seen what lives inside him? A fight with Cathán would be a fight to death. Who is it you think will survive that battle? Me? My children? Are you really such a fool?"

"But there has to be something you can do."

"No one would be happier than myself if that were true." Fia frowned as she studied Danni's face, considering. "I feel as if I should know you," she said. "And yet I know we've not met before. Why is it you're familiar?"

Because I'm your daughter . . . .

As if she'd heard the words, Fia's eyes widened and her face blanched to a deathly white. "Jaysus," she breathed, staring at Danni.

A small spark of hope flared inside Danni. Her mother had finally realized who Danni was. But just as quickly, the hope died. It wasn't recognition Danni saw in Fia's expression. It was horror.

"It was you that night, wasn't it?" Fia breathed. "It was you I saw in the corner of my mother's house. . . . But how? It was so long ago. . . ."

She was talking about that night when she'd watched Fia's sister use the Book of Fennore. Danni knew it without question.

"That night, in the shadows," Fia went on. "You came for the Book. It was you who took it."

Frowning, Danni shook her head. She hadn't taken the Book. She'd never even touched it. "The Book of Fennore?"

Fia stumbled back, head shaking as she spoke. "How did you do it?" she said. "Why would you take it? You know not what it is. What it can do. You're a fool if you think to use it."

"I don't know what you're talking about. I didn't take . . ."

But Fia was already turning, hurrying through the open passageway and racing down a different flight of stairs to the ground below. Danni looked out of the tall narrow window and saw her exit the ruins with a furtive glance and quicken to the house, moving like the devil was on her heels.

Danni covered her face with her hands. What had she meant? She'd seen Danni when the vision had taken her to Fia's house the night her sister had used the Book of Fennore and disappeared, but why would she think Danni had taken it? She hadn't even touched it.

Yet.

The word was in her head before she'd even thought it. And what did that mean? That sometime before tonight Danni would go to the house again, only this time she'd bring the Book back with her?

The very idea made her blood run cold and her legs tremble. Slowly she leaned back against the wall and slid to the floor. She hadn't been able to change the outcome in the vision of Sean's parents, but she had been able to take Sean with her. And if Colleen was to be believed, it was Danni who'd brought them both to the Ballyfionúir of their past. But Danni still didn't know *how* she'd done it.

Whatever it is you put your mind to, Colleen had said.

She'd also told Danni to use the Book if that's what she thought she should do.

Dammit, was it? Was using the Book of Fennore the answer?

And assuming she could go to where she'd last seen it, was she even capable of bringing the Book out of the vision? She'd taken Sean with her, but could she do the same with an object? Something like the Book of Fennore?

Apparently so, for why else would Fia have said it?

Danni licked her dry lips and drew in a breath. The sun was at the height of noon. It would be hours until it set and brought the dark of night, but Danni was out of time. She couldn't dwell on the questions any longer. She had to seek the answers and she had to do it now.

Because the only time she had left was the time to try.

Chapter Thirty-one

DANNI closed her eyes and forced herself to relax, willed the tension from her limbs. It wasn't easy sitting on a stone floor against a stone wall, but by degrees she was able to banish the stress and strain from her muscles and clear the clatter of confusion from her head. She reached for the Celtic pendant on the gold chain and held it in her hand, concentrating on that night she'd seen Fia's house, focusing on the storm, the window, the cold.

She felt the damp wind against her face, and she pushed into it, embracing the fear that raised the hairs on her body. The sound of rain pounding rooftops, sluicing down drains, and overflowing into puddles came next. And then the cold. Cold that went as deep as her bones.

Slowly, Danni opened her eyes. She was there, in front of the window, peering at the bright room crowded with elegant furniture. The room was deserted now, the fireplace empty. No one noticed Danni moving to the door, testing the knob. It was locked.

For a moment, frustration gripped her. *Now what?* She'd managed to get back here, but there was no way in. She could feel panic and futility fighting to control her and she calmed herself. She remembered—she wasn't really here, was she? Doors had no meaning in this twilight existence. She pressed a hand against it, expecting resistance and finding it. Then she stepped back, pulled a deep breath into her lungs and let it out.

There is no door. It can't stop me.

Eyes shut, Danni walked straight at it. Only when she no longer felt the rain on her face did she open her eyes. She'd done it. She was inside. Quickly she moved to the chest where she'd seen Fia's mother store the Book of Fennore. Another lock offered a barrier, but this time Danni didn't hesitate. She reached her hands through the heavy wood, found the old-fashioned locking gears on the other side . . . focused on giving them the same substance she'd managed to strip from the doors. Her fingers closed around the levers and pulled them in opposite directions. The lock released and the lid popped open with a click.

And there it was. The Book of Fennore.

It was wrapped in canvas as she'd seen before, but still she had to brace herself to touch it. Carefully she hefted the thick Book from the chest, concentrating on its mass, making it real in both worlds. She didn't let herself think beyond the moment, the task, but she couldn't ignore the tremor that traveled from the Book through her body. As if it was excited to see her. As if it had been waiting.

She set the Book on the floor, closed the coffer, and relocked it. As she lifted it again, she heard voices outside and a moment later a key turning and the front door opening. She turned, hurrying now though a rational part of her insisted they wouldn't see her. But they might see the Book. That was real, regardless of the fact that she held it. It might call to them in the same way it called to Danni now.

She raced to the corner where she'd hid that first time just as the three women came into the room.

"I won't do it," Edel was saying. "And don't try to send Fia. It will kill her."

"You will do it, if I wish it so," Edel's mother snapped.

"Be careful what you wish for, mother," Edel said softly.

Danni held her breath when they walked right past where she huddled in the shadowed corner. The threesome wore different clothes than when she'd seen them the first time. A different night, then. Had Danni managed to come before Edel used the Book, before the Book devoured the last of her sanity and took her away?

The mother looked like she might argue with her eldest daughter, but instead ordered Edel to start the fire while she made tea. Fia hovered in the room, looking like she didn't know what her purpose in this, or anything, might be.

"You won't let her send me, will you, Edel?" Fia asked when their mother had gone into the kitchen.

Edel looked up, her eyes sparkling strangely but not with that maniacal sheen they'd had before. Edel shook her head, expression sad and resigned.

"I will do all I can, Fia. But my time is coming to an end. Can you not see that?"

Fia's eyes became luminous with unshed tears. "You haven't used it so much, have you?"

"It doesna matter. Each time I put my hand in the blackness, it takes from me. I've not much left."

Fia went to her knees beside her sister and held her. But it was Edel who gave comfort.

"Shhh, my darling Fia. I will protect you if . . ." She trailed off and suddenly lifted her head to scan the room. "Did you hear that?"

"What?" Fia asked, looking around as well.

Edel rose and circled the room with Fia following like a puppy. Her eyes flitted to the corner where Danni stood, lingered for a long, frightening moment and then moved on.

"What do you hear?" Fia asked.

Suddenly Edel gasped. Danni followed her widened eyes to the window where a man stood just on the other side of the glass, looking in at them. He was there for just a moment before he jumped back, but Danni saw him and so did Edel.

The man's eyes had been hard and gleaming, malevolent and aggressive. There'd been a man at the window the first time Danni had been there, too. He hadn't seen Danni then, but this time . . .

This time they hadn't just seen each other. This time there'd been recognition for both of them.

The man at the window was Danni's father, Cathán MacGrath.

"What is it? What did you see?" Fia asked, moving forward to peer out at the falling rain. As before, he moved away so quickly he might have vanished into thin air.

Another jolt of fear shot through Danni. She hadn't been imagining him in Arizona, she realized. It hadn't been a man who *looked* like her father she'd seen. It *was* her father.

But how was he doing it? The same way Danni did? And why was he there—now and then?

Why else, a voice in her head responded. *He's looking for the Book.*

Something else hit Danni at that moment. She remembered the psychic who'd been waiting for her that day when she'd seen her dad . . . The girl had spoken of a spirit—one all the psychics could see hovering around Danni. Danni had assumed it was Sean, but the girl had said that it . . . Danni frowned, trying to recall the psychic's exact words. She'd said that Danni was running away, and in running, she would destroy herself. And then she'd said the spirit wanted that. It made him happy.

"What did you see?" Fia asked again, panic in her voice now.

"There's nothing there, Edel."

"You're right. It's nothing but my imagination playing tricks tonight. Would you get the fire going for me?"

Nodding uncertainly, Fia knelt at the hearth and continued where Edel had left off.

Edel stayed by the window a moment more, and then she slowly turned and met Danni's eyes. They stared at one another for a long, long time, leaving Danni with no doubt that Edel could see her.

"I will stand with you if Mum tries to make you go again," Fia was saying as she added what looked like mud bricks to the fire.

"Do not worry yourself about the Book, sister," Edel said, still looking at Danni. "I think it will not be a problem, for either of us."

Danni's skin felt clammy as she clutched the heavy Book to her chest. Her heart banged so hard against her ribs, she feared it might seize up and stop altogether.

Smiling with confusion and relief, Fia looked over her shoulder at her sister, but her gaze snagged at the corner and she froze. In slow motion, Danni saw Fia's hands cover her mouth, her eyes widen with fear and surprise as a scream filled her lungs.

Turn, Danni shouted silently in her head, willing the air to turn and get her out of there. *Turn!*

And it did. It turned with a hiss that blurred Fia's features, the room, the darkness. It whisked Danni out on the other side with a force that slammed her head back against the stone wall of the castle cornice.

Danni was panting, covered in a cold and clammy sweat. Her heart still hammered away and she was trembling—just like the Book she clutched in her hands. She stared at it, hating it even as she rejoiced in its presence. She'd done it. She'd brought back the Book of Fennore.

Chapter Thirty-two

LONG afternoon shadows had gathered in the little house while Sean waited for Danni to come home. They'd had a good morning on the *Guillemot* and had docked before noon with a full hold and high spirits. Sean had hurried back to the cottage to find Danni. He needed to talk to her, to make up for his cold abandonment this morning. He wanted nothing more than to hold her and tell her he was sorry.

But she wasn't there. She wasn't at the MacGrath house either. When he'd gone looking for her, Bronagh told him in no uncertain terms that Danni had left already. Bronagh was vague about when and abrupt about where Danni had gone. Something had happened, but he hadn't a clue what it was.

He'd checked with Nána after that, but she had no information to give except to tell him to go home. Wait if necessary. So he had. He'd gone back to the little cottage where they'd slept last night, hoping she'd returned. But all that waited for him were four walls, the bed they'd made love in, and the resounding certainty that all was not right.

He'd been sitting in the kitchen for hours, drinking tea then whiskey while the minutes crept by. About an hour ago, he heard scratching at the front door and opened it to find Danni's little dog on the other side. Bean looked at him with hopeful eyes and then disappointment. The way the day had begun, Sean fully expected the dog to bite him, but she only followed him inside. Apparently willing to let bygones be bygones in this foreign land, Bean now lay balanced on the arm of his chair, and Sean absently stroked her silky head. He was sure the dog felt his anxiety—shared it most likely.

He knew he'd hurt Danni this morning when he'd shut her out. But he'd been stunned by what had happened, too shocked by it to talk. He'd needed the time alone to process. Surely she understood that.

But as the minutes stretched into an hour, then another, Sean began to doubt. To worry. When he finally heard footsteps on the porch, he wanted to jump to his feet and yank open the door.

Bean lifted her head when Danni walked in, but obeyed the pressure of Sean's hand and remained silent and still. Sean didn't move either. Instead he sat quietly, sipping his whiskey and tea. Watching.

She moved slowly—stiff limbed and quiet as she shut the door behind her. She held her jacket in a bundle clutched to her chest and moved like it held great weight. Without looking around, she headed for the curtained-off bedroom and opened the top drawer in the battered dresser. She stuffed the jacket inside it as she pulled out some clean clothes and headed for the bathroom.

"Where have you been?" he asked, his voice deceptively soft. Only the slightest tremor hinted at a fury that had gathered inside him as he watched. It surprised him but it felt good, too. Now that she was here, the overwhelming tide of fear, of worry, that something had happened to her, crashed over him. It was anger born of desperation—he recognized that even as it consumed him.

He'd been afraid she'd gone on one of her visions and left him behind. Alone. Terrified that she wouldn't come back.

He wanted to grab her, hold her, and never let her go. He wanted to tell her he loved her. That life without her wouldn't be worth living. He wanted to marry her, grow old with her, take his last breath in her arms. But his frustration, his undeniable sense that everything he wanted was about to be lost, twisted inside him. And what came out was anger—inexplicable and unrelenting. Anger at himself, at the conspiracy of fate that had brought him to this point.

Danni spun around at the sound of his voice. She looked small and frail, as delicate as the petals of white bramble blooming on the hillsides. The shadows cast dark circles around her eyes and turned her into a shaft of pale light in the gloom. Her gaze settled on Bean and a whisper of a smile curved her mouth. The dog she was glad to see.

"Where have you been?" he demanded again.

"I went to the house—"

He cut her off before she could finish. "*I* went to the house. They told me you'd left. That was hours ago."

"Oh. I went for a walk."

He stood so suddenly his chair rocked backward. Bean jumped down and scurried to her mistress. Danni knelt and stroked the little dog with gentle fingers.

Sean's simmering emotions came to a boil, thickening the stew of his conflicted anger. "And was it to the moon you walked, Danni? Is that what kept you for hours without being seen?"

"No," she said softly, straightening. "I was down at the cavern. At the ruins."

The ruins? He stared at her open-mouthed. "Do you know how old the castle is? Do you have any fucking idea how dangerous it is beneath it?"

Mute, she nodded. *Grand. She'd known and gone anyway.*

He could see the gleam of those huge gray eyes, but not the expression in them. Not what she was thinking. What were those luminous eyes hiding?

"What were you doing down there?" he asked, striving for calm, knowing this rage wasn't reasonable, wasn't rational. Feeling as if something were goading him but not understanding what it could be. In his whole life he'd never been tempted to use force on a woman, but Danni drove him always to the edge of the unknown.

"I was thinking," she said softly, then turned her back on him and resumed her course to the tiny bathroom in much the way he'd done that morning. But he couldn't let her go as calmly as she had him.

"Thinking?" he repeated, his voice rising despite his intentions. He tried to control it, tried to trap it like the wild beast it was. But he couldn't. "For fucking hours? Did it not occur to you that I might be a bit concerned about your whereabouts?"

"I'm sorry," she said, but she was at the bathroom door now and he could see she meant to close it. To close him out.

"You'll answer me, by God," he shouted. "I want to know what the bloody hell you were doing. Who were you with?"

And there it was, what he'd been too frightened of to even admit. Last night she'd come inside and told him she couldn't sleep. Told him she'd been alone. But he'd been sure he'd heard voices, certain she was lying. . . . And here it was again, the same lie. And just like his mother had before him, he feared she'd been with another. The very idea of Danni—*his* Danni—being with another man, cut Sean to the bone. He didn't believe it, and yet he couldn't control the torch of anguish burning inside him.

Danni stared at him, her back suddenly ramrod straight, her shoulders stiff. Her rigid posture somehow an answer to his question. She hadn't been alone but she wouldn't tell him who she was with. It was there in the defiant tilt of her chin, the hard line of her mouth. Every nerve in his body shrieked with confusion and jealousy and fury, egging him on when confusion insisted he stop.

"You are not to go *anywhere*," he said between clenched teeth, "with *anyone* without my knowing. Do you hear me Danni?"

She took jerky steps forward, moving like a zombie in the old horror films he remembered from his childhood. "I will go where and with whomever I please, Sean. Don't *you* presume this farce of a marriage gives you any right to tell me what I can and cannot do."

It felt as if she'd struck him, and he could only stand there, speechless, as she spun back around and stalked to the bathroom. The door slammed and he heard the lock turn.

She might as well have doused him in petrol and struck a match. His vision clouded for a moment then snapped with clarity. The water came on and he heard her moving about, stripping her clothes. Why had she gone directly to the shower? What did she mean to wash from her skin?

Nothing, sanity urged. *You're behaving like a lunatic*, it insisted.

And it was right. He knew it was right. But a voice seemed to be whispering in his head, assuring him that his rage was justified. *She's lying to you*, it said.

He was at the door before he realized he'd moved. From the other side, the metal hooks holding the shower curtain squealed as she pulled it back then rattled as she closed it again. He stared at the door—the door that was locked to him—hearing again her taunting words. No *right*, she'd said. *Farce of a marriage*, she'd called it, as if last night had merely been foreplay.

His shoulder was to the door, and he hit hard, low, and centered. It was made of thin wood with a cheap lock that gave with a splintering pop. The door slammed back on its hinges, startling a small yelp from Danni. She peered around the curtain, water streaming over her face, eyes as big and round as all the world. Even now, even dripping wet and exhausted, she was the most beautiful women he'd ever beheld.

Mine.

The thought filled him, consumed him, exploding from within, pressing down from all around. One step had him standing right in front of her. He saw fear on her face, and it filled him with twisted satisfaction. She should be afraid. She belonged to him in the same way his hands, his feet, his heart belonged to him. In the same way he belonged to her. To say otherwise was to rouse a monster that couldn't be contained.

He ripped the curtain from her grasp, sending the hooks sliding down the pole in a hiss. She stood before him nude, her skin slippery and glistening in the weak light cast from the dangling bulb above. Her hair hung in wet ropes over her shoulders, against the ivory of her chest. Her throat was slender, delicately arched, her collarbone a fragile ring at its base with the necklace he'd given her lying against the pearl of her skin. Her breasts were full, heavy, tipped with hard nipples of dusky rose. He followed the valley between them like the river of water streaming down to her belly, over the curls at the juncture of her thighs, down the long silky legs to small dainty ankles and feet.

She was a wonder, a beauty that defied description. And she was his.

She flinched when he reached for her, and his waning anger flared again. Uncaring of the water that soaked his shirt and pants and pooled on the linoleum floor, he cupped her face in his hands and kissed her. He'd meant it to be hard, demanding, *dominating*. He'd meant it to show her that she belonged to him. He wanted acknowledgment, acceptance—he wanted submission. But the minute his mouth touched hers the warmth, the sweetness of it melted the icy rage inside him and at last tamed the monster of fear.

Remorse and shame flooded him, and he wanted to pull back, to drop to his knees and beg her forgiveness. It felt as if he'd been suddenly freed from the raging demon inside. But he couldn't part from the sweetness of her taste long enough to speak. Couldn't take his hands from the silk of her skin.

He shifted, gentled his kiss until his lips begged for what his heart needed. He kissed her like she was the air in his lungs, the blood in his veins, the beat of his heart. Softly, respectfully, he let his fingers explore the contours of her cheeks, the silk of her jaw, the curve of her throat, and the fragile shell of her ear.

He expected rejection. He expected dismissal, for what could this lovely creature see in him but flaws and failure? He wanted her with every fiber in his body, but he could only have what she would give.

Then unbelievably, her mouth softened and then her arms were around his neck, pulling him against the slick heat of her skin, demanding he oblige the need of her kiss. Her mouth was hungry, desperate, and he didn't understand it even as he crushed her to him, still standing on the other side of the tub, half drowning in the spray of the shower. He took her breath, made it a part of himself and then sent it back to fill her lungs, to race with her heart.

His hands roamed over her shoulders, the fine bones of her spine to the tantalizing curves below. He gripped the soft flesh there in his two hands, bringing all the softness of her hard against him. She made a deep seductive noise that filled his head and his senses. She tugged his shirt from his pants, working the buttons free then pulling it open so she could press against him. Skin to skin, heat to heat. It was like dying, her touch. It was like heaven, redemption, and damnation all rolled into one living, breathing fantasy.

Mine. It came again, the pulsing and possessive need to make her his and only his.

But then that insidious voice in his head whispered, *She lies.* He tried to block it out, but it was crafty, coming at him again. *Who was she with?*

"Sean . . ." She spoke his name on a breath, the plea inherent and urgent.

But the taunting voice chanted, *Who was she with? Why does she lie? Who was she with? Why does she lie?*

The fiery blaze of his fervor cooled and brought him back to his hurt and anger and fear.

How could she think this—what happened between them—was a *farce?* How could she even think of living without him? For God as his witness, he could not think of living without her.

And who had she been with in the cavern?

He hesitated when everything inside him demanded he take her, fill her with himself, and never let her doubt who she belonged to. And he could do it, he knew. She was vulnerable and she cared for him—he knew she cared. But that wasn't enough. He wanted her to love him, as he loved her. He wanted the decision to come from within her heart, not because he'd roused her to the point of no return.

She's a liar, the voice in his head crooned.

Sean held Danni between his hands, unable to stop touching her even as he pulled away. She looked at him, her eyes heavy with passion, her features soft with desire. Slowly she focused, realizing he'd withdrawn. Her gray gaze settled on his face. A part of him burned out of control, became ash whipped by the wind as he stared into those beautiful eyes and watched them widen with surprise.

"Is it farce that makes you say my name like it's a prayer?" he said softly. "Farce that makes you beg for my touch?"

Her brows drew together, and a flush crept from her slender throat to her cheeks.

"You are more mine than any wife by name or deed. You'll not forget it in the future."

And then he turned and walked away, leaving the damaged door, like his heart, open behind him.

Chapter Thirty-three

A T first, it was only surprise that hit Danni. Gripped by a cold
numbness, she stared at the door, uncaring that the shower still
spat its warm stream, that she stood naked and exposed in the draft.
Then a voice that seemed at once inside and out began to whisper,
*Who does he think he is? How dare he talk to you that way? Hurt him.
Hurt him.*

The voice lit a wick of anger, and it hissed with a life of its own. It
burned its way from her head to her feet, moving her before her brain
had a chance to register the enormity of its blaze.

She twisted the knob on the shower, grabbed a towel, and stalked
dripping wet out of the bathroom. Bean scurried to get out of her
way, but Sean stood in the kitchen, unaware of the storm that approached. Danni was shaking, her entire body trembling with the
waves of indignation. She tried to speak. Tried to spit out the vehe-
mence locked in her throat. But her rage was too great. *How dare he
treat you that way? How dare he make demands that he had no right—no*
ability *to back up?* The voice fanned the flames. *He's* dead *for God's
sake. Not the kind of man you'd want for a husband anyway.*

There was a heavy glass ashtray on the coffee table. She scooped
it up and threw it at him.

The weighted glass slammed against the cupboard beside him and clattered to the floor without shattering. He spun around, but his look of shock only incensed her more. The voice applauded her efforts and provoked her to try again.

"What? You expected me to just take it? Sweet little Danni, too nice to fight back after she's manhandled in the shower? Do you think because of last night you can touch me whenever you want? I am *not* yours. Not now. Not *ever*."

The shouted words felt like balm against her injured pride and battered emotions. If she said it loud enough, repeated it enough times, maybe it would be true. With an angry tightening of her towel, she stomped to the curtained bedroom. But Sean had recovered from his surprise and was there, blocking her way.

"What?" she demanded. "You want to see if you can get a leash on me? Chain me to the bed?"

The idea of it obviously appealed to him, and the ghost of a smile pulled his mouth before he had the good sense to stop it. But it was enough. The nagging voice in her head demanded she slap that smug look away. Danni had been through too much in the past few days. Her emotions had been pushed and pulled, tattered and torn. Refashioned into something she didn't recognize, someone whose reactions she could no longer control. She raised her hand to strike, but he caught it before the satisfying connection could be made.

Her other hand swung and he caught that, too, stepping her back against the wall, restraining her wrists and pinning her body. Her towel fell away in a damp puddle at her feet, leaving her naked and exposed yet again.

Hurt him, hurt him, HURT HIM, the voice shouted, and suddenly she recognized it. That voice wasn't coming from inside her head. It was the Book. Christ, it was the Book.

She was breathing hard—deep, ragged breaths that burned her throat and rushed in her ears. Sean was, too. She realized the Book must be taunting him as well, driving them both into a frenzy of emotions that neither of them understood.

She felt his chest heave up to meet her own. The contact burned, soothed, threw her already chaotic feelings into a dizzying plunge. He stared into her eyes, holding her captive with the stormy sea she saw within him. She wanted to look away, but there was so much more beneath his stare than anger. There was hurt. Desperation. Agony. She saw that he was as battered, as bereft and confused and tormented as her. That he understood even less of his own reactions than she did. But like herself, he'd turned all that churning emotion into anger, something that could be thrown. Something that could find a mark, find a purpose. His eyes narrowed, and she heard a whisper in the stifled air.

Who was she with, she's a liar, who was she with?

The words revolved around them, unheard but felt. Danni clenched her eyes tight, furious now with herself for bringing the cursed thing here. What was she thinking? That it would be safe in a drawer? She'd been warned repeatedly about it, but she hadn't heeded the danger. And here it was manipulating them both.

Hurt him, hurt him, hurt—

Enough. The word became action, a net she cast around the voice. She felt the rebellion, the resistance, and she tightened her thoughts, drawing in the corners, fighting its evil power like her life depended on it. In her mind, she stuffed that voice into a dark corner, sealed it up with a stone wall. Trapped it in a prison it couldn't escape. It shrieked in rage, but for now, its poisonous cries were contained, muffled and insignificant, behind her barrier.

It was a temporary fix, but it held. Her mind cleared and with it went the rage. The inexplicable need to hurt this man she loved.

And she hadn't even touched it yet . . .

As she watched, Sean's eyes cleared as well, leaving him bewildered. Shame colored the green and made them shimmer.

It seemed he would speak, a quick intake of breath, his tongue moistening his lips. She was afraid of what he would say, afraid of what he wouldn't. There wasn't time for explanations. There was only here, now, the moments before she had to remove the indescribable darkness and evil of the Book from the drawer she'd foolishly placed it in and take it back to the cavern. Touch it.

Sean continued to stare into her eyes, deeply, beseechingly, hungrily. And she understood that the fire that was melting her heart and soul burned within him as well. There was no way out of this inferno.

She leaned forward, fighting the hands that still held her wrists and pressed her mouth to his in a hard, hungry kiss. It staggered him, amazed him, and the power of it flooded her veins. He didn't know whether to respond or rebuke, and that pleased her, too. She took his choice away, using teeth and tongue to tease and provoke. The sound he made was fuel to her ecstatic blaze. He groaned deep in his throat, and then his hands were cupping her face, long fingers digging into her scalp. Making her feel him.

She responded in like, tugging at his wet shirt, tearing it from his shoulders. He released her just long enough to cooperate. Then her fingers were digging into the hard muscles of his chest and arms, pulling him into the scorching furnace of emotion and desire.

He fumbled with his pants, trying to hold onto her and work them free at the same time. She ground her hips against him, hindering and encouraging with equal measures. At last he had them open and she shoved them down as he grabbed her hips and jerked her up to meet him.

He was hard and engorged, and he plunged himself into her without tenderness or finesse. There was nothing gentle, nothing loving about it, and it might have hurt had she not been ready and waiting. Had it not been what she'd waited for, what she wanted. She needed to feel with every sense she possessed, needed to embrace the pain and the glory of these moments which could be their last. She arched her back, wrapping her legs around his waist as her head thumped the wall.

She pressed her mouth to his, stealing his breath, taking from him everything she could. She left him defenseless, slave to his own driving need and her demanding mouth. He held her in place as he pumped relentlessly, brutally. Each time he buried himself in her then withdrew to do it again, she felt the rising inside her, the violent building and clenching. The suicidal height and intensity that increased with each fierce thrust.

And then it came, that dizzying moment just before everything inside her turned liquid and molten in an explosion of heat and hurt and pleasure. She felt like a torch, bright in the blackest night, hissing and burning and illuminated. An instant later he came with her, shouting her name as he drove himself deep, deep inside her, letting loose the rage and fear, letting it meet and tangle with her own. Letting their combined heat incinerate the crazy violence that impelled them both to this dangerous edge.

She felt the tension in him leave, her own following willingly. He turned his face to the hollow of her throat and tenderly kissed her neck.

"I'm sorry," he said.

"Don't be. I wanted it."

He looked up, seeing the truth in her eyes, understanding that she'd felt the same consuming passion, the same driving need to seize tight and to ward off. To hold on and to let go. Then he was moving away from the wall, still holding her, still connected. She wrapped her arms and legs more tightly around him and held on as he lowered her to the bed.

Chapter Thirty-four

Danni had only hours to decide what she was going to do. One part of her wanted to pull the covers over her head and pretend that nothing would change, pretend that tomorrow she'd awaken in Sean's arms just as she had that morning and the morning before. But Danni had spent most of her life denying what she didn't want to face. She refused to do it any longer.

In the drawer of the dresser, she sensed the Book waiting, watching. She'd managed to contain it before, but she was growing weak with the effort. She could feel it draining her strength.

Sighing, she wiggled out of bed, took a pair of panties from the dresser, and shrugged into Sean's discarded button-down shirt which she found on the floor. A flush covered her face as she thought of how she'd ripped it from his body. Bean looked up from the rug at the foot of the bed and wagged her stubby tail.

"Where are you going?" Sean asked, his voice thick and sleepy, rumbling deep in his chest.

"Water," she answered. "I'll bring you some, too."

When she returned, he was sitting up, propped by pillows, his hands linked behind his head. She stared at him, admiring the flat ridges of his stomach, the hard broadness of his chest, the slope and gleam of muscles rising from shoulder to bunched bicep. The perfect weave of sinew and bone. He was beautiful in shape, in face, in mind. She climbed on the bed beside him, legs together and tucked beneath her.

He thanked her for the water and drank it down. After the wild sex they both seemed suddenly shy, neither meeting the other's eyes. There was still much unsaid between them, and it turned the intimate aftermath into tense waiting.

Finally, he sat forward, putting a large warm hand on her bent knee. "What happened today?" he asked softly.

"My father threatened me. In the kitchen," she said.

Sudden tears burned her eyes, and she covered her face with her hands to hide them. Sean cursed beneath his breath, and then he was kneeling beside her, pulling her into an embrace that was gentle and solid.

"I was going to ask for his help but . . . he's been using the Book of Fennore, and it's made him crazy. Bronagh and my mother both walked in, and he told them he'd caught me stealing . . ." she trailed off, stuttering over the horror of it.

Sean rubbed her back in slow gentle circles. "What did they say?" he asked.

"Bronagh told me to leave. I don't know what else was said after."

"Is that why you went to the cavern?"

She nodded. "I had to hide. I was so upset. He said he'd kill me before he let me have the Book. My father is a monster. I was so happy to meet him but he's . . ." She took a deep breath, unable to speak it.

"Look at me," he said, squeezing her shoulders. "Danni, look at me." He waited until she complied and then, staring deeply into her eyes, he said, "Who or what he is—it doesn't matter. It doesn't define who *you* are."

She wanted to believe it, but his words were such hypocrisy that she couldn't. "Doesn't it? Haven't you been measuring yourself by your father's failures and crimes all these years?"

Sean's mouth tightened, and she knew he wanted to argue. But at his core, Sean was an honest man. He couldn't deny the truth, even to himself.

"Well, I guess that makes me a fool," he said softly. "I'm sure you already knew that."

She stared into his face, into the turbulent sea of his green eyes. She almost wished for the insulating anger she'd felt in the shower when he'd left her shaking and needing. But there was too much pain here now, in this moment of truth. Too much heartbreak and finality, for she knew what needed to be said next and there was no room for petty anger. No room for vengeance.

She pulled away, and he let his arms fall as he watched her. His gaze was intense, focused and probing. She felt like he was seeing through her, to the pain inside.

"There's something I need to tell you," she said.

"There's something I need to tell you, too," he answered.

That caught her off balance and made her ask, "What is it?"

He smiled, though he still managed to look serious and intent and somehow vulnerable. Unsure of himself. Unsure of her.

"I'm sorry, about earlier, in the shower. I meant what I said, though. What's between us, what I feel when I'm with you, it's real."

His hand moved to her throat, slipping back to tunnel through her hair and pull her closer for his kiss. She closed her eyes and gave herself up to the warmth and surrender of it.

"I'm in love with you, Danni. I want to be with you. Always. Forever."

There were tears in her eyes again, only these were not the hot and bitter tears of her anger and humiliation. These were huge, glistening drops that slid down her cheeks. He loved her. And God knew she loved him, too. But he didn't know the whole truth about what had happened to them on her fifth birthday. And when he realized she'd known all along and kept it from him. . . .

He pressed his lips to her face, to the salty tears. "Don't cry," he said, and his deep voice was low with pain.

"Sean . . ."

He heard the note of doom in her voice and stiffened, lips still pressed to her cheek. Slowly he pulled back, staring into her face with guarded eyes.

Danni stood, needing to put some distance between them before she spoke. She didn't know where to begin explaining to this man that he'd been dead for the past two decades. And what scared her the most, what had kept her from speaking of it before, was one looming question: What would happen when he knew? What was his existence made of? Was it his belief that he was alive that made him seem so real? If she shattered that, would he become the ghost she knew him to be?

"Do you remember when you came to my house?" she asked.

"It was just a few days ago."

"I know. But do you remember how you got there?"

He frowned. "What do you mean?"

"How you got there, Sean. Did you take a cab?"

He shook his head, brows pulled together in consternation. "No."

"You didn't have a car. I would have seen it."

"I don't know where you're going with this. What's your point, Danni?"

"And how did you get back to your hotel?" she asked.

He shrugged. "I guess I walked."

"Maybe you did. But you should remember it, shouldn't you?"

He shook his head, noncommittal. But now he looked angry. Feeling as if something were breaking inside her, she went on. "What about the flight over from Ireland? Do you remember that?"

"Of course," he said, but the frown had become a scowl and she knew he was trying to recall it even as he spoke.

"Where did you layover?" she asked.

"What?"

"A flight that long had to have a layover. Which city?"

Mutely, he shook his head again.

"Think about it, Sean. You can't remember because you weren't on a flight."

"So you're saying, what? You think I came to Arizona the same way we came here?"

"Not exactly."

"Quit skirting whatever it is you're trying to say, Danni. What's your point?"

She took a deep breath and let it out slowly. "After you came to see me, in Arizona, I looked up Ballyfionúir on the Internet. I found an article about you, about what happened here the night my mother disappeared."

"About me? Why? What did it say?"

"It had a picture of your father. It was taken . . ." She swallowed, her throat burning with hurt and dread. "It was taken before he killed himself. There was a picture of you, too, Sean. From when you were young. The age Michael is now."

"Why was there a picture of me?"

She paused. Now that she was at the edge, at that moment, she didn't think she could go on.

"Why was there a picture of me?" he repeated.

"Because . . . because it said you'd been killed that night. It said your body was later found in an unmarked grave. In the valley, by the ruins."

He stood suddenly, naked and beautiful, tormented and silent. He was remembering. She saw it, felt it in the emotions flashing across his face.

"You weren't alone, though," Danni went on, her voice cracking. "There was an unidentified woman with you. She was dead, too."

He stared at her, the fury of his confusion rolling like waves over them both.

"That woman . . . It was me."

Chapter Thirty-five

SEAN prayed Danni would smile, laugh. Tell him she was joking. But of course she didn't. She stood there looking miserable and hurt, staring at him with those big gray eyes. He concentrated on the faceted silver and pewter, rainy day slate that swirled together around the black of her pupils. Anything to keep his thoughts from following where she led.

It said you'd been killed that night. . . .

"Whatever you read was wrong," Sean said. "Obviously."

Danni continued to stare at him as he struggled to sound sure. To convince her.

You weren't alone, though . . .

When she spoke, her voice was gentle, soothing. But her words— they came like tiny darts, puncturing his skin without drawing blood. "I don't think it was wrong, Sean. It said yours and the unidentified woman's bodies were the only ones ever found."

"Are you hearing yourself? If I'd been killed at fourteen, explain how I'm here now, a grown man?"

"I can't."

"Exactly."

"But I can't explain how either one of us is here, now. Our being in Ballyfionúir twenty years in the past isn't even a possibility."

"Not for me, maybe," he said, still trying to keep it light. If he didn't take it seriously, then how could she? "But you do this kind of thing all the time."

"No, I don't. Until you barged into my life, I hadn't had a vision in years. Not since I was little."

"My life has been ordinary up until now."

"Has it really?"

There was demand in the question, and it cut him to the bone. He'd told her he loved her, and she'd spun the conversation into this miasma of accusation and plea. This inquisition intended to make him doubt his own fucking existence.

"Do you remember when you came to the antique shop to see me?" she asked.

He stared at her, trying to follow the jump in topic. He couldn't. What did that have to do with the death and bodies?

"In Arizona," she went on in a patient voice. As if she was talking to an imbecile. "We talked about going to dinner, and then those women with their kids, they were staring and we thought it was weird. But it wasn't. They were staring because I was alone, talking to myself—at least that's how it looked to them, like you weren't there."

"Can you hear yourself? A couple of women give you strange looks and you've twisted it into—"

"It's more than that and you know it. They didn't *hear* you, Sean. They didn't *see* you."

"Now I'm invisible?"

"No, dammit. Not invisible. Dead. You're dead, Sean."

The words rang out like a clap of thunder. They sucked the air from his lungs and made him gasp, cough, stagger back a step. He should be laughing at that. Clearly she was unwell. Did he look dead for fuck's sake? But the feeling of being suctioned away from inside out wouldn't permit laughter.

"Not all your ducks are quacking, are they, sweetheart?" he said, trying to hide his malaise, his fear. Because that's what it had become, this hollowed-out feeling.

"Don't make jokes."

"Well, I'm having a hard time thinking what else to do, seeing how I'm dead."

"Not now, you're not," she said.

"And you're not making a bit of sense."

"Think about it," she said grimly. "In a few hours, something is going to happen. My mother is going to try to leave with the twins. I think you and your father are going with them. But something goes wrong. A boy and a woman are murdered and their bodies are left behind."

"But that makes you dead, too."

She looked frustrated, wild-eyed, and serious all at the same time. "Listen to me. We are both here and alive *now* because we've come back in time. We are here *before* the murders. And if history repeats itself, then tonight Michael—you as a boy—will be killed."

"And then what happens to me as a man? Let me guess. I sprout fucking angel wings and fly away?"

She swallowed and looked down. "I'm only guessing," she began, and her voice shook. The sound of that tremor running through her words eliminated the last of his insulating disbelief. As crazy as it sounded, she meant what she said, and it hurt her. "But I would say that when the boy is killed, the man will cease to exist."

His laugh was thin and forced. It brought the little dog's head up from her paws to watch them warily.

"You will never have the chance to grow up, Sean. Not really. You'll spend your days wandering this town, never acknowledged. Never seen. Isn't that how it was?"

He stared at her, remembering the emptiness of his life, the vacuous and nomadic days. The purposelessness. But still a desperate man inside him tried to pretend that it wasn't true. "Then who came to your house in Arizona? Tell me that? And if you get killed, too, then why don't you 'cease to exist' as well?"

"Because I'm still alive as a child. Don't you see? In my case, the woman who will die isn't real yet . . . Dáirinn will still grow up and become her. Me. But for you, the child dies before he can become a man. . . ."

Sean stared at her and to his horror, he did see. It was insanity, and yet didn't it answer so many questions? How many times since he'd come here with Danni had he been overwhelmed by the tangibility, the clarity and delight of every experience? How many moments had he passed just drinking in the feel of the damp Irish air against his skin, the lilt of his words rolling off his tongue, or the scent of this woman filling him with pleasure?

"How did you get to Arizona, Sean?" Danni asked again.

He tried to avoid answering. Tried to deflect it, ignore it as he'd done the first time. But there it was—a giant black question mark against the white of his memory.

"I don't know."

His response brought a shimmer to the gray of her eyes, turning them into gloam and gale. A distorted reflection of himself glistened in their depths. He didn't want to look there. He wanted to hold his illusions close and tight. But it was too late.

All those years, all that time when he'd felt like he was going through the motions but not really connected to the cause and effect around him. How many days had he felt ignored, snubbed, rejected? He'd been invisible, seen only by his grandmother. And perhaps worst of all, he hadn't even known it.

His legs felt weak and he staggered back, sitting down heavily on the bed. Danni reached out, but he recoiled from her touch as comprehension filled his mind.

A memory rushed to the surface and rolled over him. He watched it play in his head as if he were a bystander to a horror he'd somehow managed to bury for all these years. He'd been fourteen and angry, furious and guilt ridden by the deaths of his mother and young brother. The weight of responsibility sickened him like a disease.

Five years after their tragic deaths Niall had fallen in love with Fia. Sean had suspected it even before he'd had it confirmed when he'd seen them together. And all he could think of was the accusation his mother had hurled across the kitchen that day. She'd accused Niall of loving Fia MacGrath, and Niall had denied it.

Sean had followed his father the night Fia MacGrath had disappeared. He'd come upon them in the cavern, thinking it was time to confront his father. To tell Niall how much he hated him. But then Cathán MacGrath had shown up with his gun and something had snapped inside of Sean. Sean had stood by and done nothing to help his brother or his mother that day so long ago, but he couldn't do the same when Cathán threatened his father. He'd thrown himself in front of Niall, a man he thought he hated, and taken the bullet meant for him.

He could see it now, his father's face as he held Sean, crying and begging Jesus to tell him why, why. . . .

Christ in heaven, if what Danni said was true, then whatever had sent him into this tailspin of fate would repeat. The beautiful sensation of living, of really *living*, would evaporate like the fog, and he'd never be the wiser until once more she brought him to this moment—here and now—where everything would be stolen away again.

He glanced at Danni, caught her staring back with an expression that made him pause. She looked . . . guilty. Why? What did she have to feel guilty about? She turned her face away and the answer rolled over him.

She'd known. She'd known from the start, and yet she'd said nothing. She'd touched him and made love with him, knowing it would all end tonight—not just that her mother would disappear with Danni and her brother, but that Sean would die. Was it just a game to her? A foray into the imagination, a fantasy that could be lived without risk to herself? Because she would go on. But for Sean it was the end of the road.

"Never trust a MacGrath," he said softly, repeating the words that his kinsfolk had said a hundred times before.

"Sean, don't," she whispered, looking at him like she cared what he thought and what he felt. But he didn't believe it. He didn't believe her. He'd been so enthralled by the idea that she saw him, that she *got* him, that he'd never even realized he wasn't getting her. Not anymore.

Angrily he pulled on his clothes and turned to the door. "Have a nice life, Danni," he said. "Maybe I'll see you on the other side. Then again, maybe not."

Chapter Thirty-six

THE door slammed behind Sean, leaving Danni standing alone in the tiny cottage. *Alone again*, she thought. Her destiny.

She wanted to go after him, to beg him to understand, to come back and spend the last hours they had together. But she knew that wasn't the right thing to do. Because she didn't want these to be their last hours. And she wasn't going to stand by while fate stole her hopes and dreams once more.

She didn't know what had catapulted her to this time and place. Perhaps it was the Book of Fennore. Perhaps it *was* Danni. Whatever the reason, she refused to waste the chance to make a difference. To make *everything* different. If Colleen could be trusted, she'd made this journey before, but hadn't managed to change the course of history on her previous attempts. She refused to fail again.

The twins said the Book was gone. That it moved, and a part of her suspected that the motion they sensed was actually Danni whisking it through time.

There was no doubt in Danni's mind her father had been using it before then. His sudden wealth . . . the strange look in his eyes . . . the tension she sensed when he was near . . . the fear she'd seen in her mother. How many times had he put his hands on that sinister black cover and wielded its power? How many pieces of his soul had he surrendered to it? A handful? Or all of it? Was there anything left of the man Cathán had been before the Book of Fennore had called him? Before it began whispering in his ear as it had with Danni and Sean tonight?

Danni was certain it had been Cathán she'd seen in Arizona, Cathán she'd seen at Fia's house in the vision, when she'd watched Edel use the Book. And she'd seen him today, when she'd gone for the Book herself. Somehow he'd figured out how to travel through time. He'd done intentionally what Danni and Sean had done by accident. She shouldn't be so surprised—he shared the same blood that made her unique, didn't he?

She wished she understood how the Book worked or how history was impacted by it. She'd traveled back in time and stolen it, but returned to a world much as it had been when she'd left it. She and Sean were still here in Ballyfionúir, and her memories were unaltered. The change she'd made in the past by taking the Book of Fennore didn't appear to have rippled forward with any significance.

What did that mean where her father was concerned? It stood to reason that he "acquired" the Book of Fennore sometime after the night she'd seen Edel use it. But today she'd gone back to a point *before* that and stolen it. That meant it wouldn't be there later, when he went for it himself . . . didn't it? Would the impact of what she'd done only come into play from this point forward? She didn't know, couldn't wrap her head around it at all. Couldn't even conceive how she'd reached a place where she was thinking about the abstract concept of changing the past.

However it worked, Cathán had seen her at Edel's house, and for all his faults, Danni didn't think he was a stupid man. He would make the connection and know that Danni had the Book of Fennore. Perhaps the Book itself had told him.

She'd brought the Book here, not realizing what she'd invited into her home. Now that she knew, she understood that she couldn't use it near anyone she loved. She couldn't trust it, couldn't trust herself around it. What she needed to do now was get back to the cavern and use the Book there, before her father could stop her.

As frightening as the thought of it was, Danni was determined to go through with it. She would force herself to hold it and pray with all of her heart for salvation—for Sean, for her mother and brother, for herself. She would plead with that voice in her head, bargain her life if that's what it took.

Danni swallowed hard, remembering the vision, with the blood that had seeped out of the Book and how when Edel touched the cover, it had oozed like sludge, sucking Edel's hand deep into its midst.

Don't think about it.

But she couldn't stop the memory of the Book's dark and terrifying odor, the strange, jarring hum she'd felt to her bones, or the blood that seeped from its open pages.

None of it mattered, though. She would use it to change the events of this night, at any cost.

Chapter Thirty-seven

D ÁIRINN MacGrath knew that trouble was coming. She hadn't seen it, but she'd felt it building, like the pressure in a teakettle. Soon the steam would be hissing out in a shriek that would change the world. No one could stop it.

She was awake and waiting when Rory opened her door. "Mum's coming," he said.

"I know."

He climbed up on the bed beside her. "Have you seen anything else?" he asked.

"Only the same. Danni has the Book, but I don't know how she got it."

"We can't let her use it."

Dáirinn knew this already. She'd seen it enough times, in dreams. In visions. The Book of Fennore was greedy and it would take more than Danni could give. Danni didn't understand how different she was. How special. But the Book knew and it was hungry for her. It would devour her, and she would make it more powerful, more dreadful than anyone could imagine.

Danni could do what no else could even guess. She alone had the power to unlock the Book of Fennore. She could unravel the ancient

Celtic spiral of life. And once pulled apart, it would never go back together again. Not in the same way. Not as it should.

It would remain open and searching, preying on the defenseless, using the evil in the world for its own purpose.

Rory had told her this. Her brother understood the Book of Fennore, though he didn't know why he was connected to it. Dáirinn had no doubt it was the truth though. Rory never lied.

"You have to find, Sean, Rory. He's the only one who can stop her. But be careful. It wants you, too."

"I know it," Rory said solemnly.

Dáirinn gave her brother a hug, feeling again the plunging anxiety deep inside her. She didn't know the future, but she felt it dragging away her hopes like the tide eating away at the beach beneath the ruins.

Chapter Thirty-eight

Sean sat on the front porch of his grandmother's house as the sun went down. He hadn't knocked or let her know he was there, but he didn't think he needed to. Colleen had a sixth sense where he was concerned. He'd thought it was her love for him that brought it, but now he realized it was simply her way, her connection to the other-world. The world he belonged to.

"And what is it you're wanting out here in the dark?" she asked as she closed the front door behind her.

"It's where I belong, isn't it?"

She studied his face for a moment before taking the seat beside him. "Aye, some might see it that way. I'm not of that mind, though. I see you in the light plain enough."

At least she hadn't lied or pretended not to know what he was talking about. "Why did you bring me here?" he asked, and his voice betrayed the depth of his feelings.

"'Twas not I who brought you."

"You sent me to her, though. You sent me to find her and bring her home. You even bought me a plane ticket. Why go to all that trouble when you knew I was—"

She held up a hand, face blanched and eyes blazing. "Jesus, Joseph, and Mary, do not be saying it in my presence, Sean Michael Ballagh. You're no eejit. Why do you act one?"

No, not an idiot. Just dead.

He asked, "Why did you send me to bring her back?"

"Sure and there are things that we all must live with. If you're thinking I don't know that, then you're a fool yourself. The Lord paves my road, and I can do no more than follow it. He would not blame me for the choices I've made. Yes, I sent you to bring her back. And how can you even ask me why? She can change what happens tonight. I'd not be the woman I am if I didn't want her to try."

Sean didn't have a fucking clue what she meant and said as much.

"I'm saying there's a chance to change what will come. I'm saying, Danni is that chance."

"What about the Book of Fennore? Did you plant the idea of using it in her head?"

"What do you take me for? Sure and don't I know the Book of Fennore is not a toy to be played with. It's not a wishing well to toss a penny in. But it can be used, that's a certainty. And sure it can be used unwisely. 'Tis not a part of God's will, but it has power enough to be godlike. Whether or not our Danni uses it at all is up to her and her alone."

Sean turned in his seat and looked at the old woman who'd been his only companion for longer than he could remember. "She saved Trevor," he said.

Colleen nodded and her eyes glittered with tears. "When I saw him walk through me door, I thought my heart would shatter with happiness. It was like a dam breaking inside me."

It felt like a black void had suddenly filled with laughter and love. Trevor had been the heart of their family since the day he was born. His death had wrapped them in a dark shroud they'd never escaped.

"Does she know it?" Colleen asked.

Sean frowned. "Know what?"

"That she saved him?"

"How could she not? He was dead and now he's alive."

"But she wouldn't know that, would she now? Unless you'd told her?"

Sean slowly shook his head. He hadn't said a word about Trevor—not before and not this morning either. He'd assumed, of course, that she knew what she'd done. But he'd never mentioned Trevor to her, had not been able to say his name since the day he'd seen his little brother slain in the kitchen of their home.

At first he'd been too stunned to even speak. And when he'd returned from his father's boat, he'd found her gone. After that . . . he felt his face grow hot when he thought of what had come after that.

He frowned at his grandmother. "If you know what's going to happen tonight, why don't you stop it?"

"And what do you think I'm doing now? Twiddling my thumbs and dancing a jig?"

"You're putting a lot of responsibility on Danni's shoulders. A lot of faith in her . . . abilities. What if she can't make a difference?"

"Aye. But what if she can?"

"What if she makes it worse?"

"And how could it be worse, Sean?"

He didn't know the answer to that. But the question filled him with dread.

"She's trying to save you," Colleen said, placing a gnarled hand over his. "It would only be good manners if you did the same for her."

Before he could ask what she meant or how he could do it, they heard feet pounding the dirt, and suddenly, Rory MacGrath burst from the shadows. He was red-faced, out of breath, and could only manage to gasp a few unintelligible words while they stared at him in shock.

"Sit down, child," Colleen said. "What are you about?"

Rory pointed at Sean. "You have to come. It's Danni."

Chapter Thirty-nine

DARKNESS had never felt so thick and consuming as it did when Danni left the little cottage all alone. It waited just outside the small porch light's glow, impatient, hovering. Complete. She'd found a flashlight in one of the kitchen drawers, but the batteries were old and the beam was no contender against the blackness of the shrouded night. Shivering, Danni looked to the mottled sky, thick with clouds that blotted out the stars and cursed the thin sliver of moon.

A cold wind had picked up and it cut through her clothes and froze her to the bone. With the tide crashing in the distance, she felt numb and displaced. Unsure of her next step. Certain only that she must take one.

Carefully she clutched the Book, still wrapped in her jacket, as she traveled the uneven path leading down to the rocky beach. Her footsteps sounded unnaturally loud, but the frantic beating of her heart was louder still. Twice she stopped and turned, convinced someone was following. Against the hope that it might be Sean, came the fear that it wasn't. Hairs rose on the back of her neck, and she scanned the shadows, finding nothing more than her imagination stalking her in the dark. But the feeling of being watched persisted.

She stumbled on her way down the steep trail, but made it to the bottom without falling. A miracle, because halfway down, the Book of Fennore began to call her, pulsing frantically for her to hurry. Each step forward made it more demanding, more anxious. Made Danni more reluctant and more terrified. The sickening drone shook her resolve and filled her with dread. The thought of unwrapping the Book and gazing at the jewel-encrusted cover . . . of *touching* it . . . She wanted to run away and never look back.

But somehow she kept moving until the doorway cut from stone loomed in front of her. She forced her shaking legs to take her through.

"Just do it," she whispered to herself.

She'd held onto to her courage when she'd gone back to her mother's house to steal the Book. She could—she *would*—be fearless now. Just a few minutes more, and she could put all the wrongs of her life to right. She could save Sean. She could help her mother—make it so she wouldn't have to disappear. And Dáirinn and Rory wouldn't be torn apart and abandoned. She could have everything she'd ever wished for, if she could just keep it together now.

Danni took a deep, calming breath, refusing to let thoughts about the magnitude of what she intended to do crowd in. She was going to change the past. Not just her past, but that of many people. She'd seen enough sci-fi movies to fear the ripple that might wreak havoc on the world from doing so. But she had to believe that if she'd been given the power to do it, it was for a reason. Perhaps this was her purpose. She needed to be brave. To believe in herself.

She would have to send her father somewhere else to succeed. Somewhere far away. Another time, another place where he couldn't hurt them anymore. Without the Book, he would be just a man she would never have to fear again.

She repeated this in her head as she picked her way over the uneven stones to the cavern beneath the ruins. Her waning flashlight beam reflected on the rippling water inside, turning it black and white, transforming it into a living beast crouched at her feet. With another look over her shoulder, she propped the flashlight on the ground and removed her jacket from around Book of Fennore.

The canvas wrapping felt oily to her touch and the strange humming repulsed her as she lifted the massive Book. It throbbed in her hands, responding to her nearness by whining with more intensity and volume. The barriers she'd constructed in her mind wobbled and then crashed around her. Her fingers shook as she set the Book on top of a huge boulder beside her.

Carefully she pulled back the canvas, thinking of how her mother had done the same that first time when she'd shown Danni the Book of Fennore in the vision. Danni didn't want to touch it. With all her heart, she prayed she wouldn't have to touch it. But of course she would. How else could she do what had to be done?

She stared at the spirals that mated in the lock over the Book's cover and then at the embedded symbols on the cavern walls. The Book belonged to this place. She felt it. Feared it.

"It's beautiful, isn't it?" a man's voice spoke from behind her.

With a sharp cry, Danni spun to find her father leaning against the cavern wall a few feet away. Apparently not just her imagination had followed her. Why hadn't she trusted her instincts? Why did she always doubt what she knew?

"Stay back," she warned.

"Or what?"

"I'll use it."

The words felt clunky on her tongue. Ridiculous dialogue from an old gangster movie. She raised her chin, trying to look like she meant to follow through with her threat. The Book purred with satisfaction. It liked conflict. It liked the sparking tension in the air.

Cathán pushed away from the wall and moved closer. Taunting her. Daring her. In a moment, he would call her bluff. What would she do then? Let him take the Book away while she hesitated? He took another step, and she jerked her hand up, spreading her fingers wide and holding them over the cover.

"I mean it," she warned. Sweat beaded her brow and her legs felt rubbery. But he paused, considering her with his eerie glittering eyes. Would hers look like that when tomorrow came?

"Is it not what you plan to do anyway? Surely you did not steal it only to admire the thing?"

Danni didn't answer. Her throat was sealed by her suffocating fear.

"Do you want to know what happens when you touch it?" he murmured. There was a smile on his face, but the tremor in his voice gave him away. The Book scared him, too. But at the same time, it captivated him. His fingers curled and uncurled in anticipation of holding it again.

Cathán went on, his voice pitched low, harmonizing with the Book's ominous throbbing. "At first, it's like sinking into a bog. It's cold like you can't even fathom. It makes you feel so brittle that a strong wind might snap you in two. And then there's darkness. Like being buried alive, it is."

His eyes glittered wildly. They looked unnatural, hard and alien in his face.

Danni could sense his need, his desire for the Book and everything it represented. She was frightened of his answer, but at the same time, knew she needed to learn as much as she could about the Book of Fennore. With a deep breath, she asked, "So tell me, then, why you look like you can't wait to touch it again?"

He laughed and the sound bounced and fractured against the cavern walls and the rippling pool. "Crazy, isn't it? You're right—I can't wait. Watching you holding it, keeping it from me—it makes me feel nuts. Like I might rip your head off just to have it back."

The last came with a merry glance. *Isn't that the most unbelievable thing you've ever heard?* the look said. But there was promise in the words. There was threat and menace that Danni felt to the pit of her stomach.

He moved to her right, and Danni shifted to keep him in her sight. Using the thin barrier of canvas as protection, she gripped the Book tightly in her hands, but she was careful—oh so careful—not to let the canvas slip.

"My da could not tolerate me, did you know that?" he asked, confusing her with the random words. Frowning, she tracked him as he paced, circling the Book like a lion would his wounded prey. The pounce was coming. She had to be ready for it. If she faltered, she had no doubt he would devour her.

"I've no idea why he hated me," he continued, "for I tried very hard to please him. Still he looked at me like I was the devil's spawn. My own father."

She clutched the Book, thinking of Colleen, the baby she'd given up. The irony of Cathán's father thinking it was his wife who'd been unfaithful.

The glitter of Cathán's eyes darkened. "But I think you know why he couldn't stand the sight of me, don't you Danni? Is it the Book telling you, whispering in your ear? It does that, but you'll learn it for yourself in a few minutes, won't you? When you put your flesh against it. When you let it stroke your most cherished thoughts and fondle your darkest secrets. Like a lover, it is . . . a cruel and unpredictable lover that will shower you with gifts as it brands you with a burning iron."

He was playing mind games. She knew it, but she couldn't evade the picture he planted in her head.

"Oh yes, it's very intimate. Like making love, only without the affection, without the tenderness. I guess that makes it more like rape, doesn't it? But there is pleasure, once you submit."

"And do you?" she asked. Bravado raised her chin. She clung to it. "Submit? Roll over and give in? No wonder your father thought you weak."

"Brave words, but then you haven't touched it yet, have you now?"

She shrugged, leveling a steady gaze at his face, wondering if that was a crack she saw in his composure. Hoping it was, she pressed. "Maybe he thought you were someone else's son. Maybe he wished it."

Cathán's eyes narrowed. "Who told you that?"

"If he thought you were inadequate, of course he'd want to blame someone else for your lacking. It's what everyone thinks. They talk about it, about you. How you imagine yourself a king but you're nothing but a little man with an inflated opinion of his importance. They say marrying Fia was the only smart thing you've ever done."

Another fracture appeared in his composure, this one long and splintered. A smile curved her lips and satisfaction shot through her, warm and comforting, hot and thrilling. *It's the Book*, a voice whispered in her head. Pleasuring itself with pain.

"You're lying," he said softly. But he didn't quite hit that level of confidence with which he'd begun, and Danni pushed again.

"I'm just telling you what I've heard. They do find it funny, though, how you strut around like you're royalty. Your father commanded respect and loyalty, but you . . . they say it's a shame you're not more like him."

Danni felt a jolt of sheer delight coursing through her as she watched the effect of her words drain the blood from his face before suffusing it with the stain of humiliation. She hadn't even touched the Book yet, and it was already controlling her. Already dominating her thoughts and actions. Like a weed, it took root and grew wild inside. She felt it sprouting something dark and insidious deep within her soul. Something that would leave tendrils behind if she managed to dig it up.

It was Cathán's turn to smile. "Is it fucking your mind yet, Danni? Plunging in and out, looking for that weakness it can seed? And you haven't even touched it yet. You must have something it wants very badly for it to reach so far."

She swallowed hard, feeling those sharp tendrils, probing, twining . . .

"Is that how it found you?" she demanded. "It wanted something you have?"

His eyes gleamed. "A good question. One I couldn't answer until just now. It does want something I have. The question is, why would it think of you as mine?"

It took a moment for Danni to comprehend his words. She stood there, the Book of Fennore clenched in her hands, and the idea of it washed over her. Was he saying the Book had come to him in order to find Danni?

"That's right. It called me, sweet Danni. Called me like a supper bell. I could see it in my head, the way it gleams, the way it thrums. I wanted to touch it. To hold it."

He took a step closer and Danni shuffled back.

"It took years of digging through old documents, plotting my family line back to the ages before we wrote our history. I listened to every senile geriatric who claimed to know a thing about it. And then I found her, my lovely bride, just waiting for someone to save her from her greedy mother and failing sister. From the fate that waited just around the corner. Fia's mother would have made her use it once her sister . . . expired."

His voice had deepened and it wove a spell around her until it was all she heard. She watched him, fascinated and repelled by what he said. She knew what terrible fate her mother had been destined for, could still hear Edel's shriek and Fia's mother blandly planning to send Fia next.

"After her sister used the Book for the last time and never came back, Fia was more than happy to let me rescue her. She thought she'd seen the last of the Book of Fennore, especially once her mother passed, poor wretched thing. It was a terrible accident, her mother falling like she did. Like someone had pushed her down those stairs. I convinced her the Book was lost. That somehow Edel had taken it with her. Fia wanted to believe it, so she did."

He was closer. Danni hadn't seen him move, but he was definitely standing closer than he'd been before. She took another step back and felt the solid rock wall behind her.

"What will you use it for, Danni? What deep and dark secrets lurk in your heart?"

"It's not *my* heart that's dark. It's yours. I don't want to use it. But I have to."

"You must," he said his voice mellow and soothing. "Yes, I understand that. It was my reason as well. I couldn't lose my home, my castle. I *am* king here whether the idiots know it or not. I could wipe them out, just by wishing it. Sometimes I almost do—wish it. I think of them writhing on the ground, all those green paddocks stained red with their blood, slick with the carnage. Can you picture it?" he whispered. "I can."

She gulped, clenching her eyes against the vivid image that filled her mind. The Book responded to Cathán's grisly description.

Joyously it sang out, begging Danni to touch it, stroke it, embrace it . . .

"Making someone fear you doesn't make you powerful. It doesn't make you a king."

"Never underestimate the power of fear, Danni. It's a formidable weapon."

He took another step, and there was no place to turn, no room to evade. The Book shrieked with frustration, terrifying her beyond her ability to think. To react. A part of her mind simply shut down.

"Moment of truth, love," he said. "I want to help you. I do. Your eyes are like windows, and I see how frightened you are. Once you touch it, once you use it, you're never the same. You can never go back. Whatever it is that has made you desperate, tell me and I will make it go away. Let me spare you this horror. Let me shoulder your burden."

She felt strangely disoriented as she stared into his faceted, glittering eyes. He wanted to help her. Of course he did. He was her father and fathers helped their daughters.

Something shifted in his expression, and for a moment, he looked confused. He stared at Danni as if seeing her for the first time. "Who are you?" he asked softly. "Who are you really?"

She wanted to tell him. Some part of her still believed that once he knew, everything would be different. He'd open his arms with love and do what she'd always dreamed daddies do—make everything right. Even as she thought it, he changed again, and now he looked at her with sly calculation.

"I knew you weren't Danni Ballagh," he said. "You almost had me fooled, sweet Danni. But you're no innocent, are you? It's you that brings us back to this place again and again. Well, this will be the last time for it. I don't give a fecking shite if you're Herself in the flesh, I swear to you this will be the last of it."

Now the image in Danni's head was of the keening banshee. The white ghost. *Herself in the flesh.* Though his words were cold, she felt his fear.

"The Book is mine," he said. "It will always be mine."

He trapped her with his gaze as he reached for it. A voice in her head tried to shout, tried to warn her, but Danni couldn't move. The whining drone of the Book dulled her senses, feeding on the terror inside her. She felt drugged, powerless. Knowing it would be a fatal mistake to let him take it, Danni stood paralyzed as he reached for the Book of Fennore.

Chapter Forty

"No!"

The shout snapped Danni out of the trance Cathán had put her in. She felt light-headed, as if he'd somehow sucked the air from her lungs, the oxygen from her brain. At the opening that led to the stairs, Dáirinn and her mother stood like wax figures. Fia's expression was stretched in a mask of horror.

Cathán turned in a rage to face them, and Danni used the distraction to escape the corner where he'd pinned her.

"What are you doing?" Fia breathed, looking back and forth between Cathán and Danni. "Do you not know what it is? It's evil. Why would you bring it here?"

Before Danni could answer, she heard the sound of a motor, and a moment later, a dingy slid through the narrow oval at the mouth of the cavern. Niall Ballagh cut the engine and stared in shock at the cluster of people inside. The boat drifted for a moment before Niall regained some composure and barked an order at Michael to tie off the boat using the stake embedded in the cavern floor for that purpose.

"What's this?" Cathán asked, his voice as cold and dark as the waters lapping against the stones. "What in bloody hell is this?"

No one spoke as they stared at one another. Danni felt as if she'd been pulled out of her body to watch from above. She saw a shadow move at the doorway leading in from the rocky shore, and Rory appeared, towing Sean behind him. The two stopped and joined the suffocating silence.

Everyone was gathered now, just as they'd been in the vision. In a moment, Cathán would pull his gun, aiming for Niall, but mortally wounding Michael. Danni would be his next target—now she understood why. She still clutched the Book tightly in her arms. He would simply kill her and take it.

And then everything would begin again.

"No," she said. Her voice sounded strange in the cloying quiet, so she said it again. "No."

The time for questions—for doubt—had passed. Danni ripped away the canvas covering and held the Book of Fennore in her bare hands. It trembled, shivering with excitement as she prepared to go to that frozen, black land Cathán had described. As she braced herself for what would come. Closing her eyes, she said, "This will not happen again. . . ."

Before she could finish, Rory let out a scream that echoed like an explosion in the enclosed chamber of rock. Danni faltered and Cathán moved quickly, snatching at the Book. Danni fought for it, but he was too quick, too strong. Even as Sean rushed forward, Cathán wrenched it free with a triumphant shout. He didn't hesitate, not like Danni had. Using one of the boulders as a table to hold the heavy Book, Cathán planted his left hand on the cover and closed his eyes.

The vibration in the air took on substance until it seemed like they were all plunged into deep, frigid waters that pounded fiercely against a seawall. As they watched in horror, the vibration seemed to sink beneath Cathán's skin. He looked like a mirage, shimmering in the heat of a relentless sun. It seemed he wasn't really here anymore, yet they could see him fluctuating with the pulsing beat of the Book.

It was horrific and captivating and not one of them could look away. Cathán had a gun ready and pointing at them before anyone noticed that he'd fumbled it from his pocket with his free hand. It felt to Danni that everything happened at once, and yet, somehow it came painfully, dreadfully slow. Each instant registered before moving to the next.

"You'll never have my wife," Cathán said to Niall, the look of hatred burning in those terrifying eyes. Without warning, he pulled the trigger.

The bullet appeared to glide across the cavern, and Danni thought for one brief second that she might actually stop it. Perhaps it wasn't too late to change her destiny. Perhaps she hadn't failed.

But even as she moved to intercept it, she saw Michael rush at his father, push him out of the way just as the bullet slammed into the boy's chest and into his heart.

At the same time, the grown-up Sean bellowed with agony, and Dáirinn let loose a cry that echoed endlessly around them. Torn between going to the boy or the man, Danni hesitated, and Cathán's next shot caught her in the back. It felt like a fiery rod, jammed deep into her flesh. She fell to her knees then collapsed on the stone floor.

She was instantly numb and couldn't move her arms or legs. It took all her effort to turn her head. Sean was trying to make his way to her but he moved like a man underwater, and even as she watched, he began to fade.

"I love you," Danni tried to say. But her voice was just a hoarse whisper. Why hadn't she told him before? Why had she let him walk away without saying those simple words?

"Danni," he said as his image wavered. "You can stop it. You don't need the Book." Blackness crowded into her head, and his words became distorted. What did he mean?

"You can change it. Trevor is alive. You changed the past. You saved him."

It made no sense. What was he talking about? And then Danni remembered those moments when she'd clasped hands with Dáirinn and Rory, when the image that came to her had been of Sean's brother, dead on the kitchen floor.

Comprehension was there, hovering just above her ability to grasp it.

Still Sean struggled. "What happened when my mother died, it was different. The first time, Trevor died with her. But today . . . he's alive. You saved him."

She still didn't understand. But she couldn't ask because he was vanishing—*vanishing*. Tears streamed down her face as she saw the realization come over him.

"No," she whispered. He didn't know she loved him. He didn't know how much he meant to her. "Don't leave me."

He was gone in an instant.

A sob caught in her throat as hot tears streamed down her face. Danni turned her head and watched as a ghostly shadow stepped from Michael's inert form and faced her. Niall began to moan as he gripped his son's lifeless body against him.

It seemed like hours had passed since Cathán had fired his first shot, but only seconds had lapsed. Now it was Fia's voice she heard as her mother tried to keep Dáirinn from launching herself at Cathán—at the Book he held in his hands. Fia managed, but at the same time her other child raced forward. Fearlessly, Rory attacked, slamming his small body into his father's, catching him at the waist and knocking him off balance. Cathán stumbled back, pulling the Book with him while Rory grappled to take it away.

That wasn't supposed to happen, Danni thought as consciousness began to ebb with the waning thud of her heart.

Rory gave a mighty shout and yanked the Book free. For a moment, he stood petrified, his small hands sinking into the shining black cover. His eyes were wide with the horror of whatever he saw and then Cathán flung himself at the boy and they both disappeared into thin air.

Chapter Forty-one

Dáirinn stared at the place where her brother had been and fear like she'd never imagined closed on her. She could hear her mother crying, hear Michael's father sobbing, see the blood pooling beneath Danni's body. And in her head, she heard her brother shouting, begging her to help him.

Her arms and legs felt stiff as she jerked free of her mother's hands, crossing to where Danni lay. She knelt beside her, feeling the blood soak through the knees of her pants. It was already cool.

"What did he mean?" Dáirinn asked, looking into Danni's gray eyes, feeling as if she was looking into a reflection of her own. "He said you saved Trevor. What did he mean?"

Danni blinked her eyes and her lips moved, but she couldn't speak. She was dying.

"Come away," Fia said, trying to pull Dáirinn to her feet. "Come away from her." And then suddenly Fia stilled. She stared down into Danni's face, her own blanching as her fear became something else. Slowly she looked to her daughter, Dáirinn, and then back again. Danni saw comprehension, disbelief, and anguish war for control of Fia's emotions. And then something else gleamed in Fia's eyes. It was love; it was remorse. It was pride. In that split second, Danni thought Fia had realized the situation—somehow put together all the missing pieces and come away with the whole picture.

Whatever she might have said was lost, though, because Dáirinn used her mother's shock to dodge free of her grasping hands. Scooting closer to Danni, she demanded again, "What did he mean?"

Danni moistened her lips, looking to Michael, and suddenly Dáirinn saw the shadowy form standing over the boy's body. It was his spirit. She knew this even as his eyes lifted to meet hers. Her body went rigid. She felt like a tether bound them, pulling them tight into a circle that couldn't be broken. Dáirinn and Danni. Michael and his spirit.

She reached down and took Danni's hand in hers. Leaning over, Dáirinn stared into the eyes that looked so much like her own. In that moment, another deep understanding seemed to wash over her. They were connected, though she didn't know how.

Danni's husband had said, *You can change it.* He'd said Danni had saved his brother, Trevor.

Dáirinn's eyes widened as she snapped her gaze back to the spirit who'd materialized in almost the same way Mr. Ballagh had disappeared. An inkling of the truth hovered over her. Then she heard Rory's voice, weaker now as he shouted in her head. *Help me.*

Chapter Forty-two

DANNI focused on the intensity of Dáirinn's eyes and everything else fell away.

You can change it . . . .

It was Sean's voice and it was Dáirinn's and it was her own, speaking from some well of knowledge within her. *You can change it . . .* the voice insisted again. Louder this time.

She felt something stir in her heart. It shuddered and built until it was a pressure that threatened to explode. Danni stared into the eyes of her child-self and reached for that pressure, wrapped herself around it and let it expand and expound until it engulfed her completely. Surrounded by the shimmering spark of it, Danni focused on the center where explosions of energy snapped and popped and sizzled.

She forced any fear from her mind, because what did she have to lose now? Everything she'd ever wanted, everything she'd ever dreamed of was gone. But she could get it back, if she just believed.

She steeled herself for the pain that would surely come. In her mind, she stepped to the edge of that swirling nucleus lurking inside her. The searing jolt tore a gasp from her lips and brought her consciousness back to the cave. Back to the child holding her hand, feverishly begging her to do it—whatever *it* was. Danni pictured her thoughts like tendrils of smoke, seeping into quiet places, finding a way through the barriers that kept her separated from the child she'd once been. Dáirinn inhaled sharply, and Danni forced herself in with it, following the gasp into Dáirinn's lungs, through her blood to her heart, her mind. The child took another breath and suddenly they were one.

Danni's memories were streaming out like a film played in fast-forward for Dáirinn to see. She felt Dáirinn trying to slow them down so she could absorb them. Together they watched Fia hugging her sister in front of a bungalow on a sunny street by a beach, promising to be back soon. They left Rory behind in Edel's care as they climbed into their car. Then Danni and Fia were driving across the desert, her mother quizzing Danni about their new names, where they were from, who they were.

Fia had gone to Arizona because it seemed like the other side of the world. Cathán would never find her there. She'd separated her children for their safety, fearing together they might somehow send a signal that Cathán, through the Book, would receive.

She'd always intended to go back for Rory as soon as it was safe.

Finally Danni saw the answer to why her mother had abandoned her. Cathán had found Fia. Her mother had seen him first, though, and she did the only thing she had time for. She'd left Danni at Cactus Wren Preschool and ran, praying Cathán would follow her and not find the children.

As one, Danni and Dáirinn felt the memories, the years of not belonging. United, they experienced the years of isolation, of never feeling a part of the world. There was Yvonne with her smile and biting wit, offering sanctuary in the chaos. And then Sean was at Danni's front door and there was no slowing down anymore because it all came in a tide that washed over them both.

"We can change this," Danni said in her mind. "Help me."

Her free hand felt like lead as she tried to lift it. The effort pulled her shredded muscles and made her want to scream, but somehow she managed to get her fingers around the Celtic pendant at her throat. She felt it swell in her grasp, felt it burn against her palm. And then it moved—she felt the silver strands changing, unraveling, spinning into something new.

Dáirinn clutched Danni's other hand, and she knew the child felt it, too. They were scared—both of them—but they didn't turn back. They didn't push away. Dáirinn channeled Rory's pleas into Danni's thoughts until she felt a spark and then a flaring of life. The air around them began to tremble and quake, shaking loose stones that rattled down to the floor and plunged into the water. Her mother was screaming, but Danni and Dáirinn held on. Inside Danni's head, pictures flashed like lightning, then everything else seemed to warble and slow to a grinding halt, as if time had simply stopped.

Danni opened her eyes and looked around. Her mother stood with her mouth open, hands frozen in midgesture. Niall knelt beside his son, tears suspended on his face. Michael's spirit hovered motionless in the air.

Dáirinn looked down at Danni and found her staring back. She gave a small nod and then the air shifted slowly, screeching like a rusty wheel on an ancient axle. It whispered past them, gaining momentum, blowing faster and faster until it seemed to howl. The pool of blood beneath Danni began to shrink and Danni took a deep breath, her eyes clearer, her grip stronger.

Rewind, Danni thought, amazed. *We're rewinding time.*

The sounds came in stilted blasts. Suddenly her mother was holding another Dáirinn in her arms as the child tried desperately to break free. And then her father and Rory reappeared, fighting over the Book and then Rory was moving away. Sean seeped back into his flesh, standing just a few feet away from her. She met his eyes, bundled her thoughts tight and sent them into his mind.

One chance. One chance.

In reverse, Cathán fired his gun at Danni, only now the bullet made its way back *into* the gun. Cathán swung it away and aimed once more at Niall. The bullet jerked from Michael's body, seeming to yank him up from the ground and toss him back where he'd stood beside his father.

Danni squeezed Dáirinn's hand once and then she let go.

Like a rubber band stretched hard, time flew at them with a snap. Rewind was over and now the seconds rushed forward. Danni was on her feet, moving even before she'd caught her balance. Cathán raised the gun to Niall once more, but Danni knocked his hand just as he fired and the shot went wild.

He whipped the pistol against her face and pain exploded everywhere. Without wasting a second, he shot her point-blank in the stomach and then swung the gun at Niall and fired again. Danni watched in slow motion as the bullet streaked unerringly at Niall Ballagh. Once more, Michael lunged for his father, but this time, the grown-up Sean made it there first. The bullet caught him square in the chest and slammed him back against the wall. His heart stopped instantly and he sank to the ground, eyes sightless.

Danni's scream of agony came from the pit of her soul. Once again, she felt the life draining out of her. She was numb and death rushed at her like a blur and she welcomed it, for what was life without Sean? With her last gasping breath, she watched her fate unfold.

Rory was already fighting for the Book with her father, but Danni saw that Dáirinn wasn't going to let him go this time. Even as Dáirinn grabbed from behind, Rory disappeared as he had before, but Dáirinn held on. Danni felt the child throw her thoughts out like a rope and catch him. And then she pulled. Her brother came back with a *whir* that knocked them both to the ground.

But her father and the Book of Fennore were gone for good.

Everything became hazy then. The voices around her warbled and she realized she was fading, just as Sean was. She lifted her hand and it felt heavy, but she could see right through it. Fading, like a morning mist.

There was a moment of panic. What would happen now? They'd changed history. Changed their own lives . . . But the fear waned with her existence. She closed her eyes on the alarmed voices and she gave in to the tide of destiny.

Chapter Forty-three

I T *wasn't dream; it wasn't vision. It was some hybrid in between.*
She looked down at her own body, bloody and battered . . . defeated.
But she felt no pain. She felt no fear.

She stepped away, turning as a familiar voice called her name. She
smiled as she looked into his unusual eyes—not quite green, not quite
gray—and took the hand he held out to her. Without a word, she followed
him out of the cavern and into the bright light that waited.

Chapter Forty-four

O N her fifth birthday, Dáirinn MacGrath declared she would be called Danni and would answer to nothing else. When they thought of it, the people of Ballyfionúir attributed the demand to the child's queerness. It was the way of the Ballaghs and the MacGraths, and didn't they all know it? After Cathán MacGrath had disappeared without a trace—no doubt run off with some whore from Cork or even Limerick—the townsfolk tended to indulge the children. And who wouldn't in their shoes?

Sure and for years tongues wagged about Cathán's abandonment of his family. Some speculated he'd not gone off at all, but had been shot by an irate father for impregnating his daughter. Others wagered it more likely that a jealous husband had done in the wretched man. A small minority thought he might have pulled the trigger on himself and ended his sinful ways, the cheating gobshite.

And didn't some think a darker fate had taken Cathán Mac-Grath? Hadn't they all heard rumors about what he'd been up to? Didn't the old women talk about him when they were pissfaced on a Saturday night? They said he'd found the Book of Fennore. They said he would be cursed for all of eternity because of it.

Whatever his fate, he was missed like a famine—or not at all, as they say.

The MacGrath twins were raised by their mother and her second husband, Niall Ballagh, who brought to the union two sons from his first marriage. Lucky for the couple, Ballagh's mother was usually available to lend a hand. Fia had given birth to a lovely daughter six months after that momentous night when her husband disappeared. The baby girl was said to be a blessing of unimagined proportions.

It was widely agreed that Danni MacGrath was able to overcome the trauma of losing her birth father, but her twin brother Rory lacked the fortitude to do the same. A serious child, he became sullen and withdrawn. As the teen years approached, his pensive ways turned brooding and then destructive. At the age of twelve, the boy was sent away for a summer to live with his Aunt Edel and her American husband. A dentist, they say. The townspeople who had suffered his vandalism and petty thievery for years were much relieved—more so when the boy refused to return home. The gossip said young Rory sent word home and occasionally there was a picture, too. He had nice teeth, the boy did, and they all decided it was for the best that he'd gone.

Niall Ballagh's eldest son, Sean, attended school in London and became famous for his renovations of historical monuments. The youngest had not fared so well, but tragedy was nothing new to Ballyfionúir.

All in all, the townsfolk often remarked over a pint at Sulley's Pub, they'd come out on the right of things.

Epilogue

I T had been seven years since Dáirinn MacGrath—Danni to her friends and family—had left for New York and Columbia University. She'd graduated in the top of her class and worked freelance before becoming a staff writer for the *New York Times*. It was the culmination of a lifetime of goals and dreams, and she was a good reporter—a great one, she'd heard her editor say. She always seemed to know when a story was about to break or a witness about to spill his secrets. A gift, her editor called it. A gift.

But though she loved every minute of her life, as Danni approached her twenty-fifth birthday, she acknowledged that something was missing. She began to have dreams that tormented her and chased her through the nights. Dreams of losing something, something near and dear. Something irreplaceable.

Then she'd done the story on abandoned children and her life had changed completely. Her article sparked a reform in the child protection agency and in the adoption laws which prevented so many good couples from adopting children and placed so many hopeless children in abusive homes. The work she'd done had opened her heart to the plight of the lost and abandoned children of the world.

She decided then and there that she would make a difference to as many as she could. Her Nana Colleen had told her once that a person should look in their own backyard before they thought to clean up another's. And so Danni had come home to start here.

Ballyfionúir hadn't changed much in the passing years, and yet coming home for the first time in so long, it seemed to Danni that the differences were profound. There was a shine to the fishing village brought on in part by the increase in tourism. There were specialty shops and pubs, and dining establishments lining the cobbled road. The once faded buildings were now painted in stunning pastels with bright colored doors. There was still nothing in the way of hotels—the overriding opinion was that tourists should find their way home before the need for sleep came around.

Her mother had written and told her that her stepbrother Sean was back in town as well. He'd turned his eye on the MacGrath ruins and intended to restore it. A noble undertaking, though she'd much prefer it if they were simply destroyed. She didn't remember anything about the night her father had vanished, but it always seemed to her that something dire had taken place in the cavern beneath the ruins and she associated it with his desertion.

She let out a sigh, knowing Rory remembered much more, though he'd never talk about it. Rory had sworn he'd never return to Ballyfionúir and he meant it. She knew her mother missed him terribly and blamed herself, though Danni never understood why.

As she drove her rented car up to the house, she saw the workers and equipment everywhere. The grounds around the house and ruins looked to be in absolute chaos, and she frowned. She'd been dreaming of the peace and quiet of her home, not this bedlam of hammers and saws and huge cranes. It made her angry. Damn *Sean Michael Ballagh*, she thought even as her heart sped up at the idea that he might appear at any moment.

The last time she'd seen him, she'd been thirteen, he'd been twenty-two and gone to school in London for the past four years. Four years during which she'd changed from a schoolgirl to a teenager who dreamed of him coming home some day and seeing her as woman. He wasn't her real brother, after all, and she'd never thought of him as one.

But instead of sweeping her into his arms and declaring his intentions to wait for her to reach a marriageable age, he'd brought another woman home with him—a lovely thing with black hair and blue eyes and breasts that couldn't be real. He'd given Danni's ponytail a tweak and tossed her a soft stuffed animal he'd brought as a gift. It was a puppy, which she secretly loved. But at that moment, it made her feel like a child being placated and dismissed with a toy. She'd been so hurt and angry that she'd locked herself in her room and hadn't come out for the entire weekend, not even to say good-bye.

By the time he'd made it home again, she'd been off to college herself, and now twelve years had passed. Well, she was definitely a woman now.

She glanced down at her faded jeans and old sweater. She needed to shower and clean up before she said hello to him. No matter that her crush on Sean was long over, she was woman enough to want to look sophisticated and poised when she saw him—hell and gone from that gawky thirteen-year-old girl anyway.

She turned to go inside and see her parents when a small black and brown ball of fur raced at her from the direction of the construction. It was barking crazily and charging like Danni was a meaty stew bone in danger of being tossed out. *A dog?* Startled, Danni stepped back against the car as the animal came to an ungainly stop at her feet. It *was* a dog, she realized. A mongrel mixture of so many breeds that it barely resembled a canine. It had long thin legs and a stout body. No tail, but perky ears and brown eyes that now looked at her with adoration she didn't deserve.

"Hi there," she said, squatting down. The dog had fur like silk and wagged its entire body as she greeted it. "Is it a dog you're trying to be?" Danni laughed as she scratched behind its ear.

A stern voice called to the little beast, and Danni looked up to see a man following the same path the dog had from the midst of the construction.

He was tall with broad shoulders and the layered muscles of a warrior, though he moved with easy grace and long, purposeful strides. He wore a T-shirt that might have been white when he'd put it on but was now covered with dirt. A denim button-down hung open over it. Faded blue jeans hugged lean hips and long legs. Not just tall. Not just broad. A big man.

He stopped in front of where she knelt with the dog and hunkered down beside them. Danni's eyes followed the powerful line up from flat belly to muscular chest to his tanned throat, square jaw, coming to a stop at eyes not quite green, not quite gray. Eyes like the Irish Sea itself. She might not have recognized the man Sean had become if not for those unforgettable eyes.

For a moment she could only stare, and it seemed somewhere beyond her memory, beyond this moment in time, there was a history stretching out behind them both. An inexplicable past and future entwined and interwoven, binding them together. Images rushed at her . . . his arms around her, his body close and hot, his mouth on hers. But she'd never . . . *They'd* never . . .

And yet, like a song she couldn't forget, the thoughts played on and she knew she had . . . *they had*. And she'd been waiting her whole life to have what they'd shared again. It was crazy but it felt too real to doubt.

His eyes seemed to darken, and the look in that sea of green and gray somehow mirrored the complex and chaotic emotions churning inside her. He understood. He felt it, too. The knowledge rolled over her and stole her breath. *He felt it, too.*

He smiled then, a slow, knowing smile that spread across his face and showed the two dimples that Danni had fallen in love with so long ago. She felt herself smiling back, though her heart was pounding and her mouth was dry. The rest of the world seemed to fall away, and there was only Danni and Sean and endless possibilities. The future before them was bright and shining and waiting for whatever fate had in store for them next.

"Welcome back, Danni," he said, his voice a smoky baritone that brushed against her skin like velvet and made her lean closer. She reached out, needing to touch him, to believe in the overwhelming rush of what she felt. He took her hand, pulling her closer still, and a million thoughts filled her head, but not one of them was to resist. This was where she belonged, where she was meant to be.

He paused, his gaze moving over her face, as if to memorize every feature. And then he spoke again, his words as soft as the warm and fragrant breeze. "It's good to have you home. Isn't it forever I've been waiting to see you again?"

Dear Reader,

Thank you for selecting Haunting Beauty *from all of the many fabulous choices in your bookstores and libraries. I hope you enjoyed Danni and Sean's story. I know writing it changed my life.*

I love talking to readers and would love to hear from you. You can find me at www.erinquinn.info, where you can read first chapters of my upcoming releases and find my blog, where I probably talk too much but occasionally say something interesting. You can also e-mail me at write2erinquinn@aol.com. I promise you'll hear back.

All my best,
Erin Quinn

Turn the page for a preview of the next paranormal romance from Erin Quinn

Haunting Warrior

Coming soon from Berkley Sensation!

"HURRY, Ruairi. Hurry."

The whispered command tickled the inside of Rory MacGrath's ear, feather light and taunting. He brushed it away and rolled over, trying to block out what he instantly knew. He wasn't dreaming anymore. If he opened his eyes, he'd find the woman standing beside him.

He acknowledged this even as he accepted that seeing her wouldn't make her real, wouldn't make her more than a projection of his own mind. A fantasy he'd conjured and spewed into this semi-somnolence. He felt his heartbeat begin to race; his breath slowing and deepening—combatant symptoms to the paralyzing awareness.

He thought he opened his eyes, but couldn't be sure if he only imagined it. Either way, he saw her waiting impatiently beside the couch where he'd fallen asleep watching ESPN. The apartment was dark, lit only by the flickering screen of the TV behind her. It cast her in gray and white dreamscape shadows. And then the flashing screen went blank, and they were both bathed in darkness.

This—of all that was about to come—it was *this* that he hated the most. The black on black void held him captive for interminable moments.

Sound came before the light was restored. It was rumbling, indistinct, but a sensory input that his panicking mind grasped gratefully. There was something out there. Something more than his fear. More than his sleep-deadened body.

A flicker heralded the flame of a candle. An instant later others sparked to life until the boundaries of a room could be determined in the glow. He was no longer in his apartment.

He scanned his surroundings quickly before fixating on the woman again. It was impossible not to. She looked the same as she had last night and the night before and the night before that. She had dark hair—too burnished for black, too velvety rich for brown. It was full and silken and glossy as mink. It hung to her waist in a wave of body and bounce, gleaming with the flicker of the candlelight. Her eyes were brown, dark with flecks of gold that burned like the tiny flickering flames around her. Even his dream self couldn't believe their luminousness. Her lips were full and soft, one corner caught between her teeth. She looked exotic, her skin dusky and her features fine.

She wore a blue dress with white sleeves—something that laced in places where there should have been seams or zippers. It bloused and flowed over her round shoulders, past hips that made him think of sex in a deep, drowning way. The hem brushed a scattering of twigs and straw on the floor. Not even her feet peeped out.

She stood in the center of a room with three stone walls. Behind him hung a thick woven curtain that served as the fourth. He knew it without turning to look. There was a table with a pitcher on it in the corner beside a lumpy bed covered by a scarlet blanket. The room was damp and drafty, making the tapestries on the walls billow, but the woman seemed oblivious to the cold.

As he watched, she began to untie the dress, letting it fall, revealing a white shift beneath it. The thin material silhouetted her body for a moment before she began to remove that, too. Even as some part of him shouted again that she wasn't real, Rory succumbed to the seduction. She was every fantasy he'd ever had, ever wanted.

Her skin was so smooth it might have been carved from the

waxed light that made it gleam. Her breasts were full and heavy, and he felt the air leave his lungs as she bared them. She glanced up then—every time, every night, at just that moment. Almost as if she'd heard him. Her cheeks were flushed. Her eyes defiant. Anger, bordering rage, filled their depths. So much of the dream made no sense, but that part—that look of fury mixed but never diluted by acquiescence. It bewildered him the most.

When she was stripped bare, she stood in the flickering light and stared at something just over his shoulder.

And this was where the fantasy ended.

He turned—every time he turned—even though by now a part of him knew what he'd see. A tall man with overlong hair stood just behind him. A man dressed in a weird get-up that looked like it had come from a movie set. Archaic, like the dress the woman had stripped off.

The man wore a cloak made of some animal fur—not politically correct faux fur, but the real thing, with paws stretched flat at four points and the stub of tail nearly dragging the floor. It was flung back from his massive shoulders, revealing a heavy circle of gold round his throat. An obscure word floated to the top of Rory's thoughts. A torque. That's what it was called. It was as thick as Rory's fingers and engraved with Celtic spirals covering its surface. It looked heavy. The man's shirt had a wide slit for his head and boxy sleeves that fell to his forearms, and the front was embroidered with more spirals and symbols in purple and gold at the hem and seams. It hung to his thighs, like a dress. Beneath it were short pants that gathered below his knees and leather sandals wrapped midway up powerful calves, Roman style.

But even his bizarre attire was not the strangest part. What made Rory gasp was more tangible. It shook him no matter how many times he faced it.

The man looked exactly like Rory. He didn't resemble; he wasn't similar. Literally, he could have been Rory's reflection.

As Rory stared, he became aware of the ebb and flow of noises coming from beyond the curtained wall, a rumble that now distinguished itself into laughter and conversations he hadn't noticed while he'd watched the woman strip. He'd heard only the beat of his heart pounding in his ears then. Now sounds surged into the candlelit room, the drone of speaking men mingling with raucous hoots and jeers, an occasional giggle or shriek of mirth from the women. One man's words rose above the rest as the speaker threatened to come in and show Rory where everything went. The man used Rory's name, but pronounced it with the same Gaelic inflection that his dream woman had used when she'd urged him to hurry. Ruairi.

Rory frowned, realizing he recognized the voice. He knew he'd heard it before. From their expressions, it was familiar to the naked woman and his identical twin too.

A surge of lewd cheers followed the man's threat. Volunteers offered to help with the endeavor.

The taunts galvanized Rory's twin into action, and he began stripping away the strange costume with nimble, frantic fingers. He unfastened a gold chain holding the fur cloak at his throat and tossed the heavy garment onto the bed before bending to untie the sandals. Frowning, Rory went back to watching the woman as she watched his double. She stood straight and proud, neither hunching to cover her nudity or posing to flaunt it. She wore no expression, but her eyes sparked and flared with something Rory couldn't quite identify. It couldn't be longing. There was too much anger for that. Her fingers curled in on each other in a tight fist. Then they eased, then they contracted again.

But it was the way her gaze swept over his twin, the way her breasts lifted with a soft breath and her tongue moistened her lips that enthralled him.

He couldn't look away, though that distant awareness inside him was shouting again, warning him not to relax, not to be mesmerized by the rise and fall of those lovely breasts. But he couldn't stop himself as he stared at her, aching to touch her.

He knew the end of this fantasy dream was coming, as it always did just at this point when he felt he might explode with the want and need rising inside him. He braced himself for it, for what came after when he awoke alone and aching. She would torment him during the wakeful hours afterward. The sight of her, close enough to touch . . . to smell . . . to taste. . . . He would imagine she was everywhere, just out of reach.

But this time the dream took another turn, veering toward a new ending to a movie he knew by heart. It shocked him, the divergence.

Rory tensed, suddenly uncertain in unknown waters. What next? Would his body double do what the real Rory longed to? Would he take her in his arms and bury himself deep between the woman's warm thighs? Would watching them be better or worse than always wondering what came after that heated look in her eyes?

Her gaze flitted over his twin's body, lingering on the bunched muscles in his shoulders, the tight ridge of his abs, sliding lower to the hard-on that stood tight against his belly. She flushed and turned away, moving with jerky steps to the table where she filled a cup with wine and gulped it down. Rory found himself entranced by the play of candlelight on the slope of her spine, on the curve of her ass, the long length of leg. His body double watched with equal fascination.

She took another drink before facing his twin again, but whatever Dutch courage she'd gained vanished when she turned. She looked so vulnerable standing before the massive size and barely restrained power of his muscled twin. Rory wanted to intercede, not trusting his double with his dream woman. Even now, a part of him caught the irony in that. Rory was no more trustworthy than this stranger who looked like him.

He watched with growing frustration as the two met in the center of the room. As his twin reached out and touched her skin, slid his hands from shoulders to buttocks, pulled her tight against his body. It enraged him, watching. Confounded him, because he also felt some strange sense of participation. The old phrase, taking a shower in a raincoat came to him. It fit exactly. He experienced some of what his twin must be feeling, and yet only through the thick layer of distance.

His twin and woman backed up until they reached the crude bed and then fell on it. Rory's gut tightened as they came together in a tangle of limbs and passion. There was little love, that was apparent, but there was heat and need that perfumed the air and sizzled in the silence. The two seemed to clash in a battle for control, yet neither relinquished it and neither retained it. Rory could only ride the wave, dry and isolated while his mind and his body yearned to take his twin's place, be one with the complex and fervent confrontation.

When it was over, he was twisted tight and hard as a rock. He cursed under his breath, damning this dream world that had dominated him. Wishing to awaken but unable to bring his consciousness back to his sleeping body.

He heard a sound to his right. Confused, he looked at the stone wall and saw the woven banner with a crest at its center billow and then move. A man appeared—dressed like Rory's twin had been, only not so fine, not so resplendent. This man's clothing lacked the adornment and embellishment, but it had the same ancient look to it. He was armed with a bladed weapon—too short to be called sword, too long to be a knife. His manner said he knew how to use it.

What happened next came in a jerky blur—a film strip that jumped and dragged then sped forward without pause. His twin leaping off the bed, the woman sucking in a harsh breath that seemed to clog the scream she wanted to release. There was recognition on all of their faces, and Rory understood that this intruder was no stranger.

Unfettered by the vulnerability of his nudity, his twin crouched in a fighting stance as the new man circled him with that long and wicked blade clenched tight in his hand. Then they charged one another, one naked, one garbed. The fight was quick, silent, and violent. Rory's twin overpowered the other but not without a struggle. Then in a blur, he unarmed the attacker, slamming him against the unrelenting stone and crushing the intruder's throat with his bare hands.

Stunned, Rory looked from the dead man now sprawled on the floor to his naked twin to the woman who watched from between spread fingers. She rushed toward his twin with a look of horror on her face. Rory spun and saw that his double was on his knees now. His hands clutched his gut and something dark and viscous ran through his fingers. Blood.

Rory crouched beside the woman as she stared at a gaping wound across his twin's abdomen. Blood gushed from it, splashing her bare skin, seeping into the straw and twigs covering the floor. There was so much of it. Too much.

"Why?" she breathed the question, those eyes scanning his twin's face.

Yes, why? Rory wanted to know as well. Why had the intruder attacked them without provocation?

His twin was bent with agony and didn't answer. The woman tried to staunch the blood with the red blanket from the bed, but Rory could see it was pointless. The cut was too deep, too wide.

As his twin reached out a bloody hand to the woman, Rory knew the life was draining from him. It was like watching his own death, unbearable and inescapable. The look in his twin's eyes cut him as deeply as the gash in the other man's flesh. There was rage and there was pain. Desolation. Realization. And something deeper, more agonizing. A wound more painful than the one emptying his life onto the floor.

"It's the both of us he's betrayed, isn't it?" the woman said, her words so soft Rory thought they were imagined.

His twin closed his eyes and nodded once. Then he looked up and for a cold instant, it seemed he stared right at Rory. There was comprehension in the look—comprehension and shock. Then relief. Rory felt the *how* forming on his lips, but he had no voice here, in this nightmare that had morphed into something no longer symbolic but terrifyingly real.

His twin stumbled to his feet, and now he clutched an object in his hands. Rory gaped at it, reeling again from the shift this dream world took.

It was the Book of Fennore. Rory would recognize it anywhere, even here, in this warped fantasy he couldn't escape.

The Book had a black cover made of leather, beveled with concentric spirals, and crusted with jewels; gold and hammered silver twisted and twined around the edges and corners. Three cords of silver connected in a mystifying lock fixed over the jagged edges of thick, creamy paper. As old as the earth and sky, the Book was more than a bound text, it was an entity with its own consuming desires and twisted needs. Just touching it gave it access to the heart, mind, and very soul. Its call was irresistible. Its promises, unimaginable. Rory knew better than anyone.

A low humming had swelled around the three of them, a sickening buzz that lodged in the pit of his stomach and blocked out the sounds on the other side of the curtain. He felt hot and cold . . . and scared. The dream breached what little barrier remained between nightmare and terror.

The humming whine throbbed and pulsed—too low to be heard, too insistent to be ignored. With it came a blistering heat that burned like a coal in his head. A reasonable, alien part of him began to cite calming words—*It will be all right. It's just a dream. Just your imagination.* And once again, dream Rory recognized that the input was coming from his wakeful self. Dream Rory found that even more terrifying because that implied a plurality that went beyond the symbolic twin.

This can't be a fucking dream if I'm thinking all of that . . .

Everything began to shimmer, became the stuff dreams are supposed to be—translucent, then transparent, then transcendental. . . . Before he could wrap his thoughts around it, the woman turned her head to where he knelt beside her. The cold fear on her face struck an answering chord within him. She saw him.

She saw him.

She lifted a hand that shook and set it against his chest, as if to test his solidity. Her eyes widened; her mouth rounded into an "oh" of disbelief.

And the shock of her icy fingers against his hot skin jerked him awake.